by Shizuru Seino
Volume 4

TOKYOPOP®

Los Angeles • Tokyo • London • Hamburg

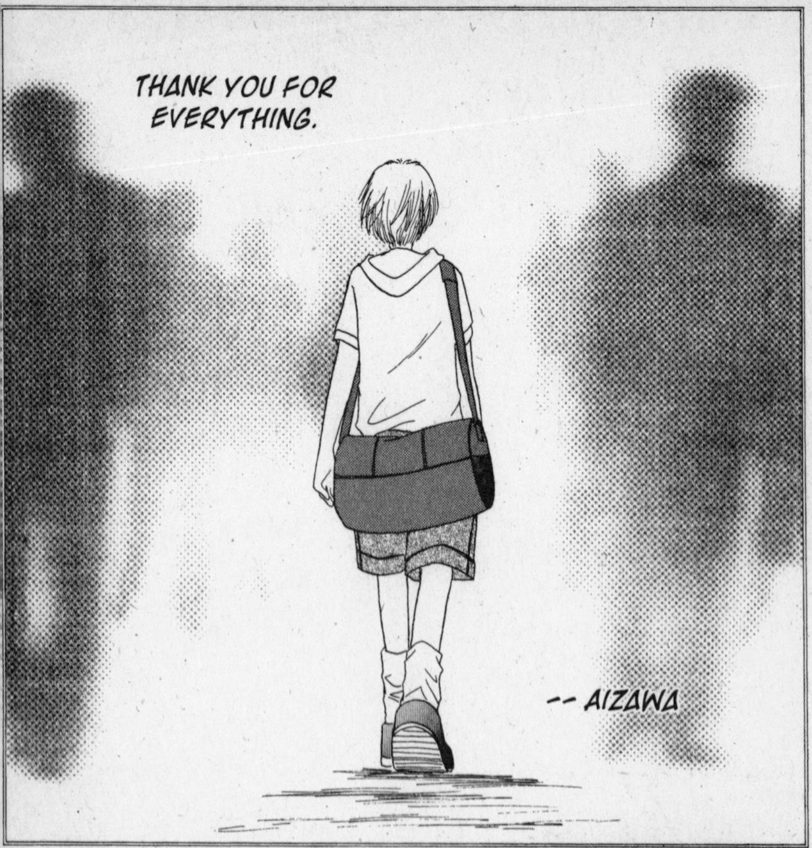
THANK YOU FOR EVERYTHING.
-- AIZAWA

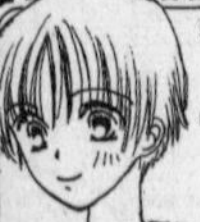

KYO AIZAWA

TO PLEASE HER FATHER, SHE DISGUISES HERSELF AS A GUY AND TRANSFERS TO A HIGH SCHOOL THAT IS FAMOUS FOR ITS BASKETBALL TEAM.

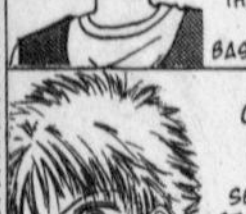

CHIHARU ENIWA

SEISHU HIGH'S STAR FRESHMAN PLAYER AND KYO'S OBNOXIOUS ROOMMATE.

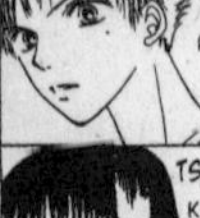

TSUYAKA SENPAI

KYO'S FRIEND FROM JUNIOR HIGH, SHE'S A YEAR OLDER THAN KYO, VERY BEAUTIFUL AND VERY FAST.

Previously, in Girl Got Game...

Girl Got Game

***KYO AIZAWA** TRANSFERRED TO SEISHU HIGH SCHOOL WHERE SHE PRETENDS TO BE A GUY IN ORDER TO PLEASE HER FATHER AND PLAY CHAMPIONSHIP BASKETBALL.

* AT HER NEW SCHOOL, AIZAWA ROOMS WITH **CHIHARU ENIWA**, WHO'S A BRILLIANT BASKETBALL PLAYER, BUT A BIT OF A JERK.

*HE TALKS TOUGH, BUT CHIHARU LOOKS OUT FOR KYO, AND SHE FINDS HERSELF DEVELOPING A CRUSH ON HIM AS A RESULT.

* ENTER **TSUYAKA SENPAI**, A FRIEND OF KYO'S FROM JUNIOR HIGH. TSUYKA TRANSFERRED TO SEISHU IN ORDER TO PLAY BASKETBALL WITH KYO. SHE CHALLENGES CHIHARU FOR KYO, AND WINS, FORCING KYO TO JOIN THE WOMEN'S BASKETBALL TEAM.

* CHIHARU EVENTUALLY WINS KYO BACK, BUT TSUYAKA TEARS OPEN KYO'S SHIRT AND REVEALS -- HER GENDER! KYO LEAVES THE DORM AS CHIHARU COMES TO TERMS WITH HER SECRET...

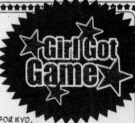

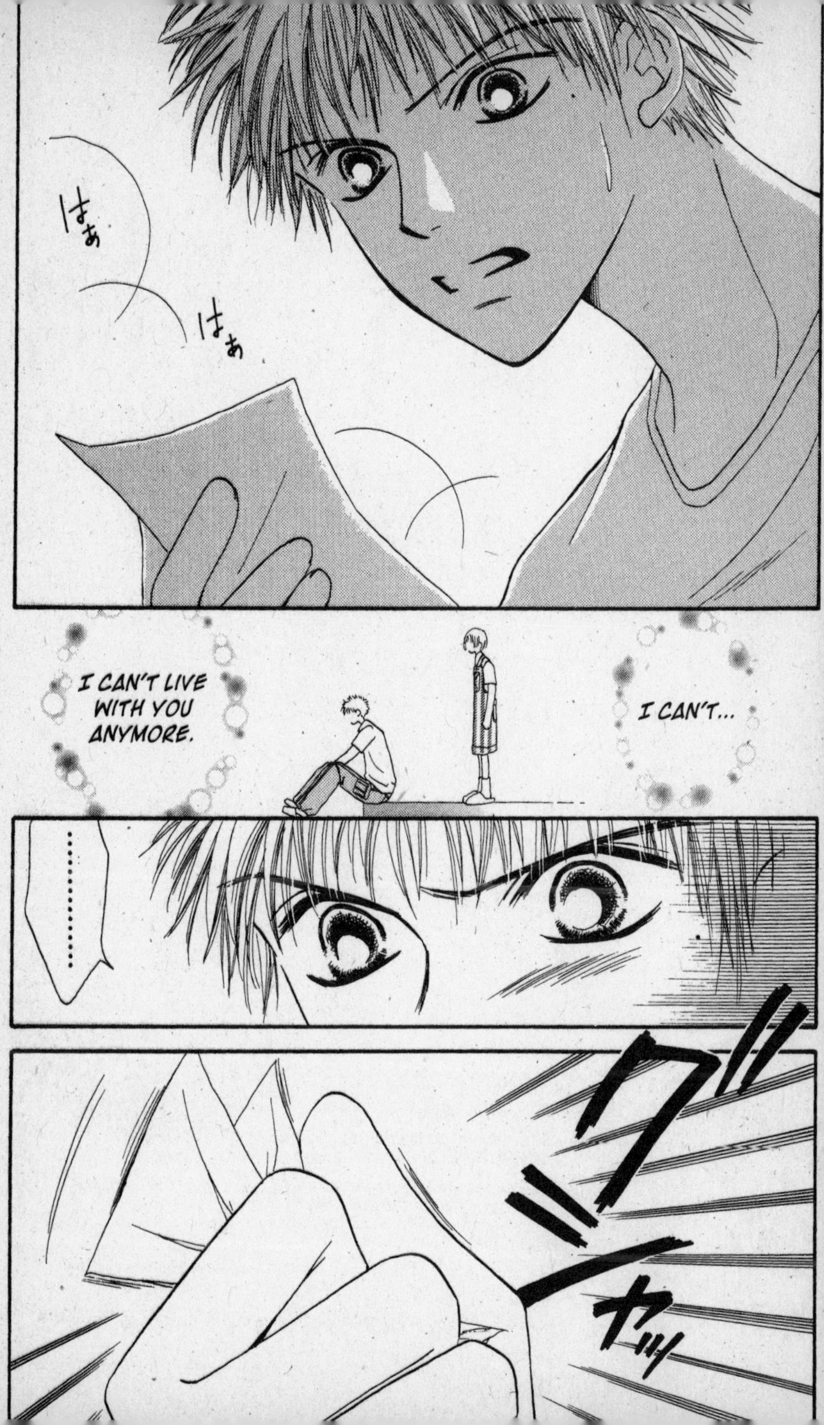
はぁ
はぁ
I CAN'T...
I CAN'T LIVE WITH YOU ANYMORE.
……
グシャッ

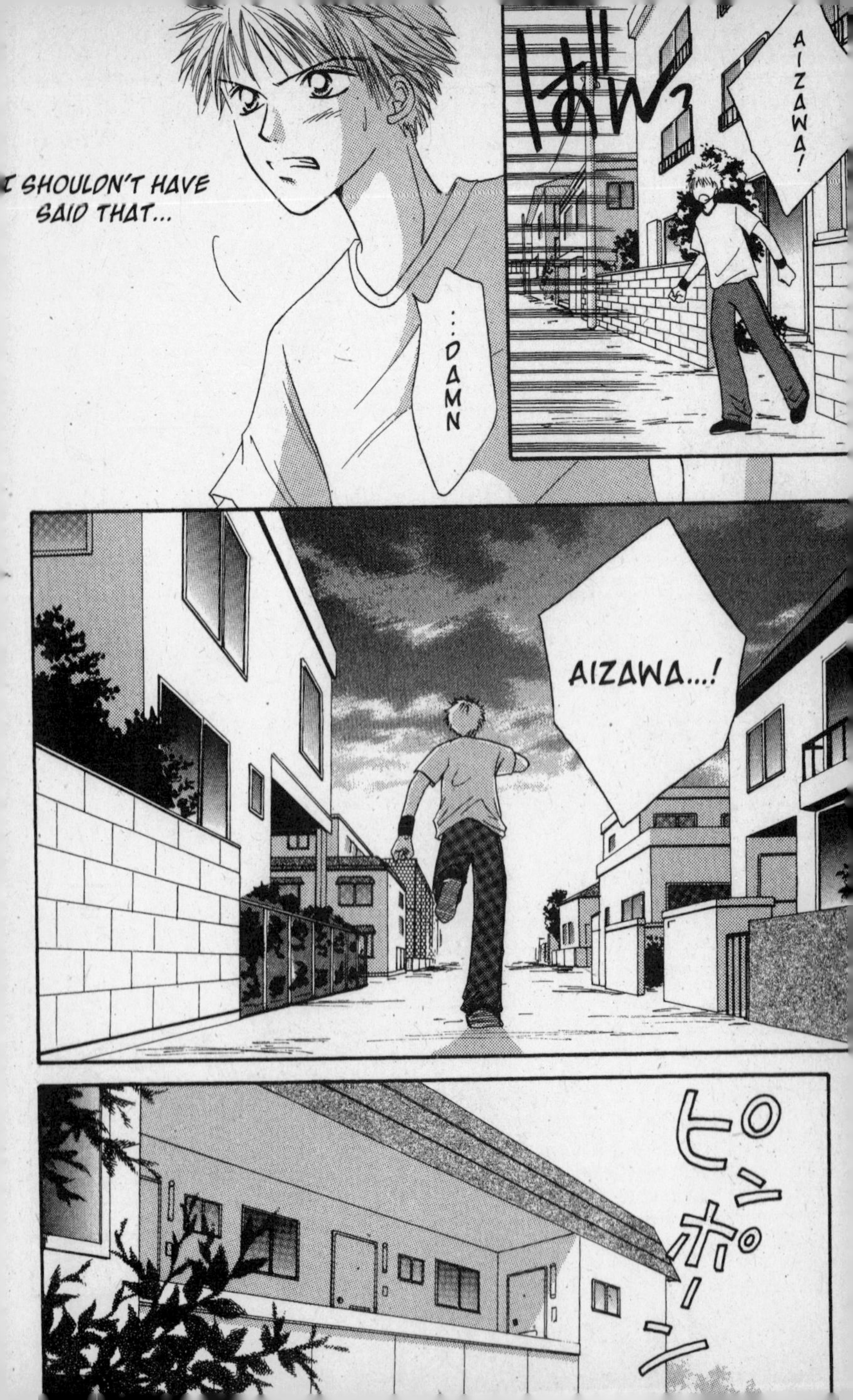
AIZAWA!
...DAMN
I SHOULDN'T HAVE SAID THAT...
AIZAWA...!
ピンポーン

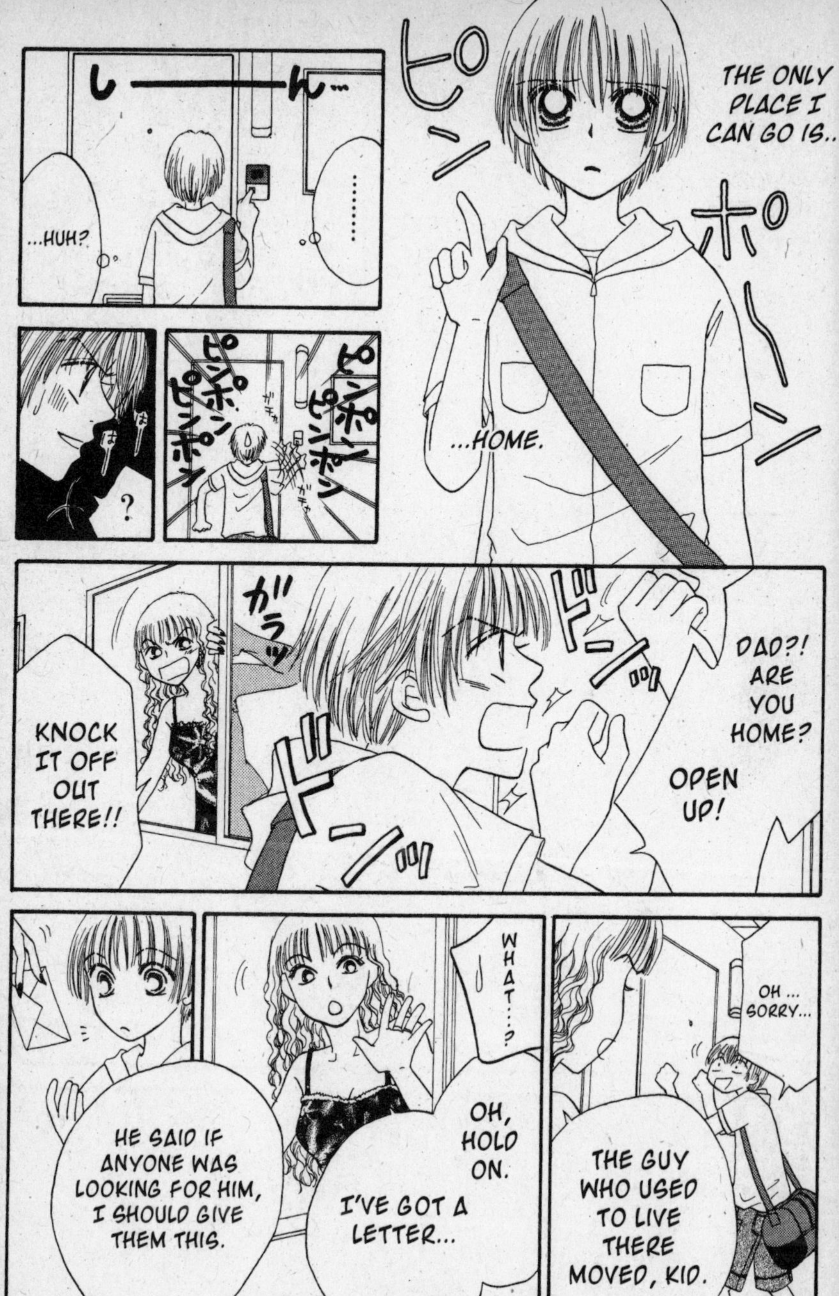
THE ONLY PLACE I CAN GO IS...
...HOME.
しーーん…
......
...HUH?
?
DAD?! ARE YOU HOME?
OPEN UP!
ガラッ
KNOCK IT OFF OUT THERE!!
OH ... SORRY...
THE GUY WHO USED TO LIVE THERE MOVED, KID.
WHAT...?
OH, HOLD ON.
I'VE GOT A LETTER...
HE SAID IF ANYONE WAS LOOKING FOR HIM, I SHOULD GIVE THEM THIS.

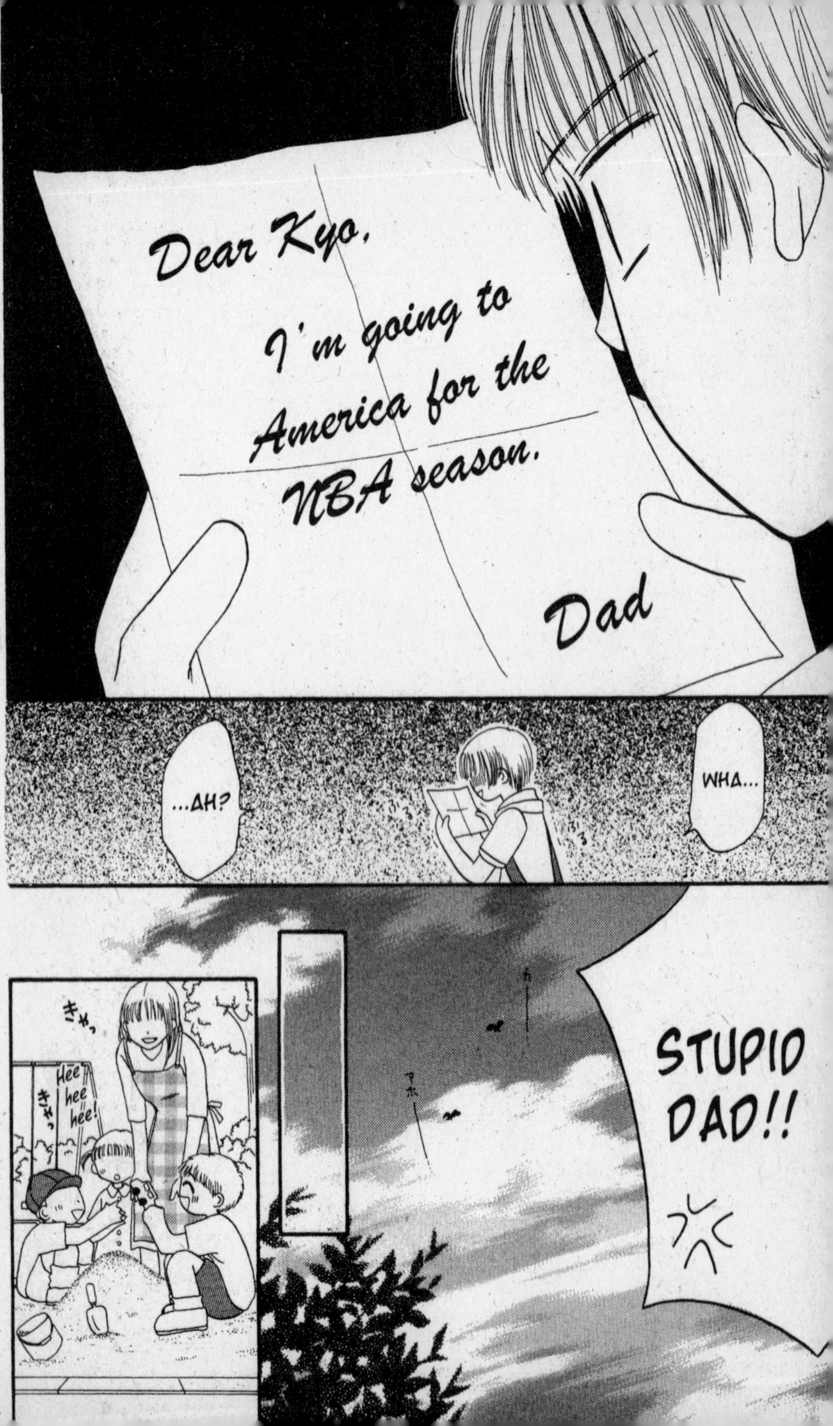
Dear Kyo,
I'm going to America for the NBA season.
Dad
WHA...
...AH?
STUPID DAD!!
きゃっ
Hee hee hee!
きゃっ

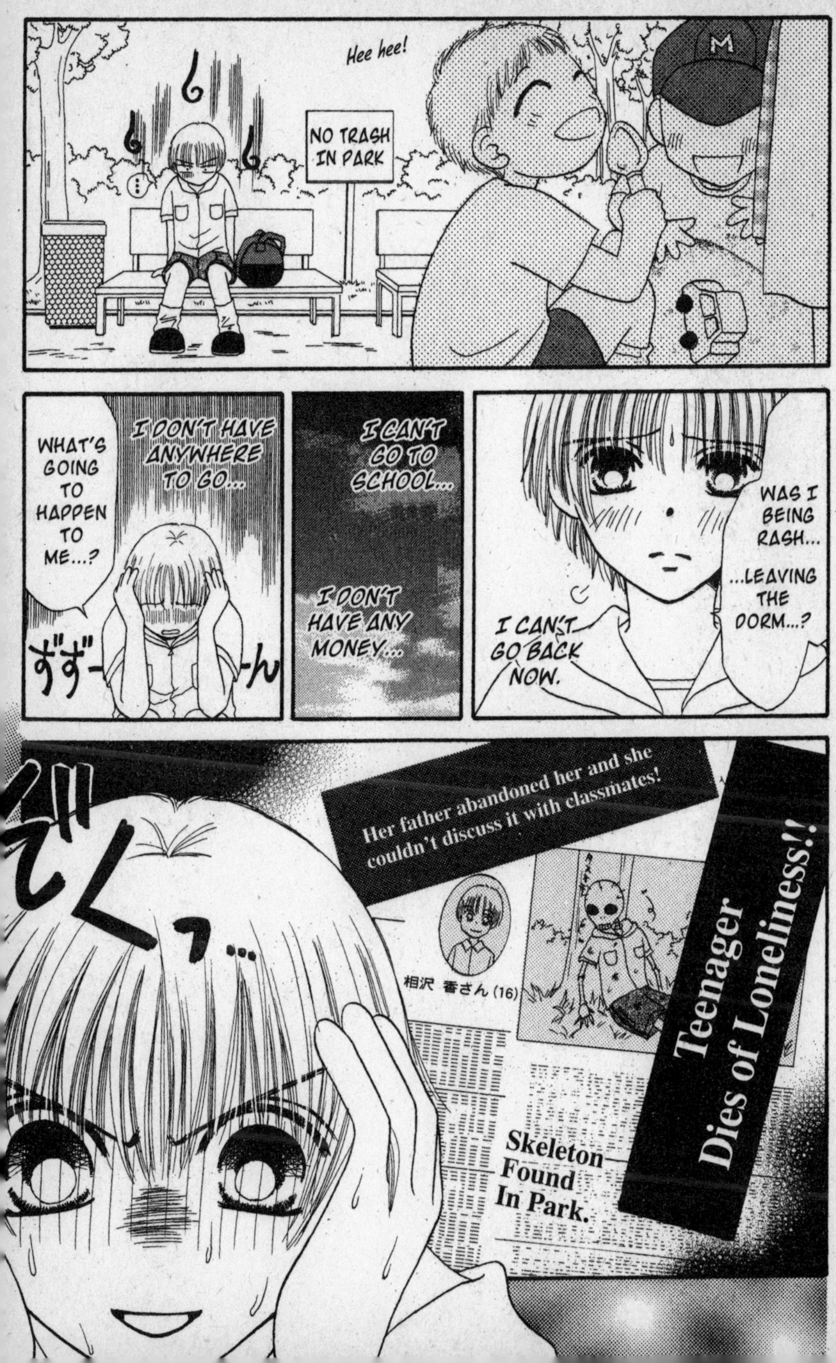
Hee hee!
NO TRASH IN PARK
...
WAS I BEING RASH...
...LEAVING THE DORM...?
I CAN'T GO BACK NOW.
I CAN'T GO TO SCHOOL...
I DON'T HAVE ANY MONEY...
I DON'T HAVE ANYWHERE TO GO...
WHAT'S GOING TO HAPPEN TO ME...?
ずずーん
Teenager Dies of Loneliness!!
Her father abandoned her and she couldn't discuss it with classmates!
相沢 香さん (16)
Skeleton Found In Park.
ぞくっ…

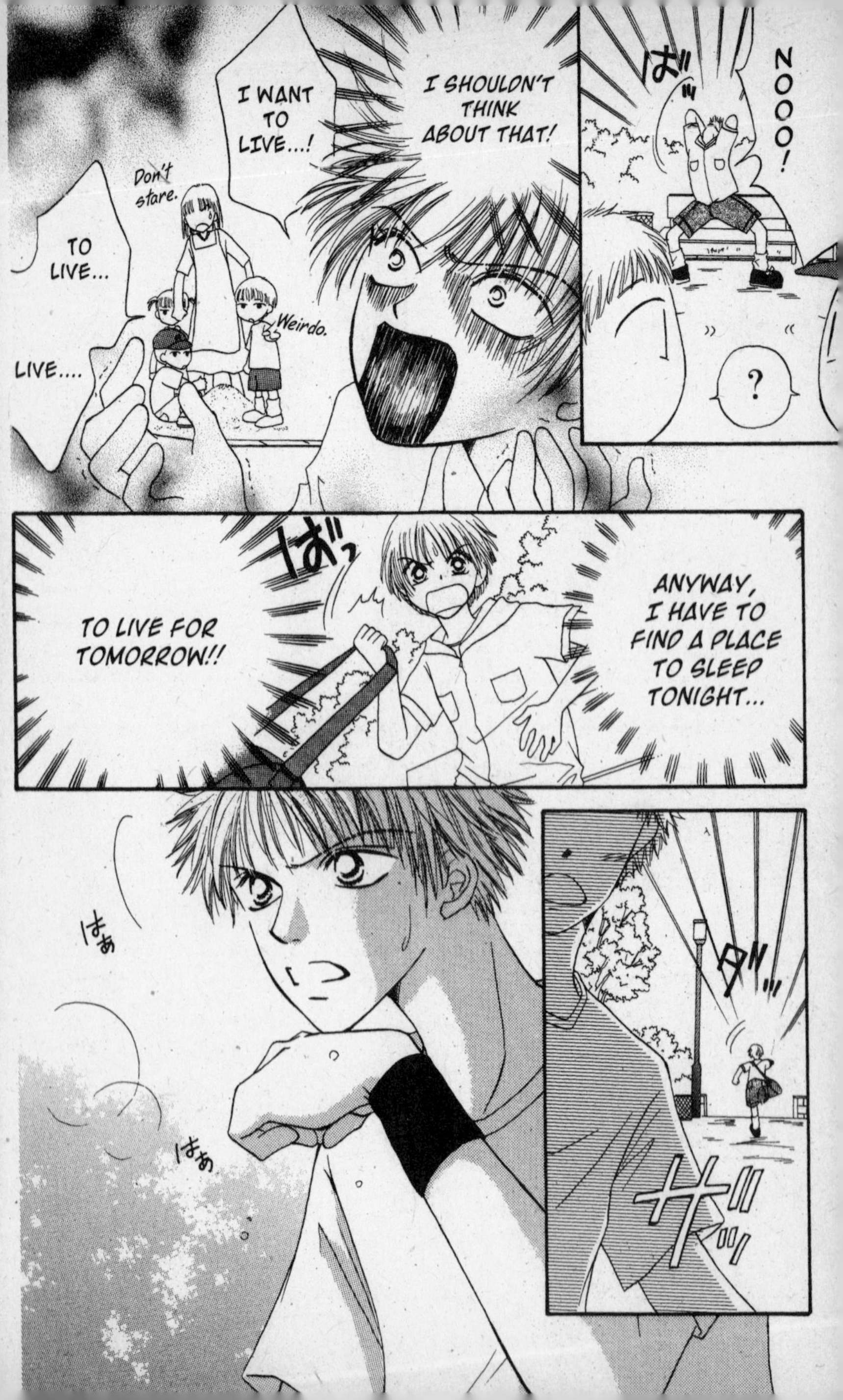
NOOOO!
?
I SHOULDN'T THINK ABOUT THAT!
I WANT TO LIVE...!
Don't stare.
TO LIVE...
Weirdo.
LIVE....
ANYWAY, I HAVE TO FIND A PLACE TO SLEEP TONIGHT...
ばっ
TO LIVE FOR TOMORROW!!
はぁ
はぁ

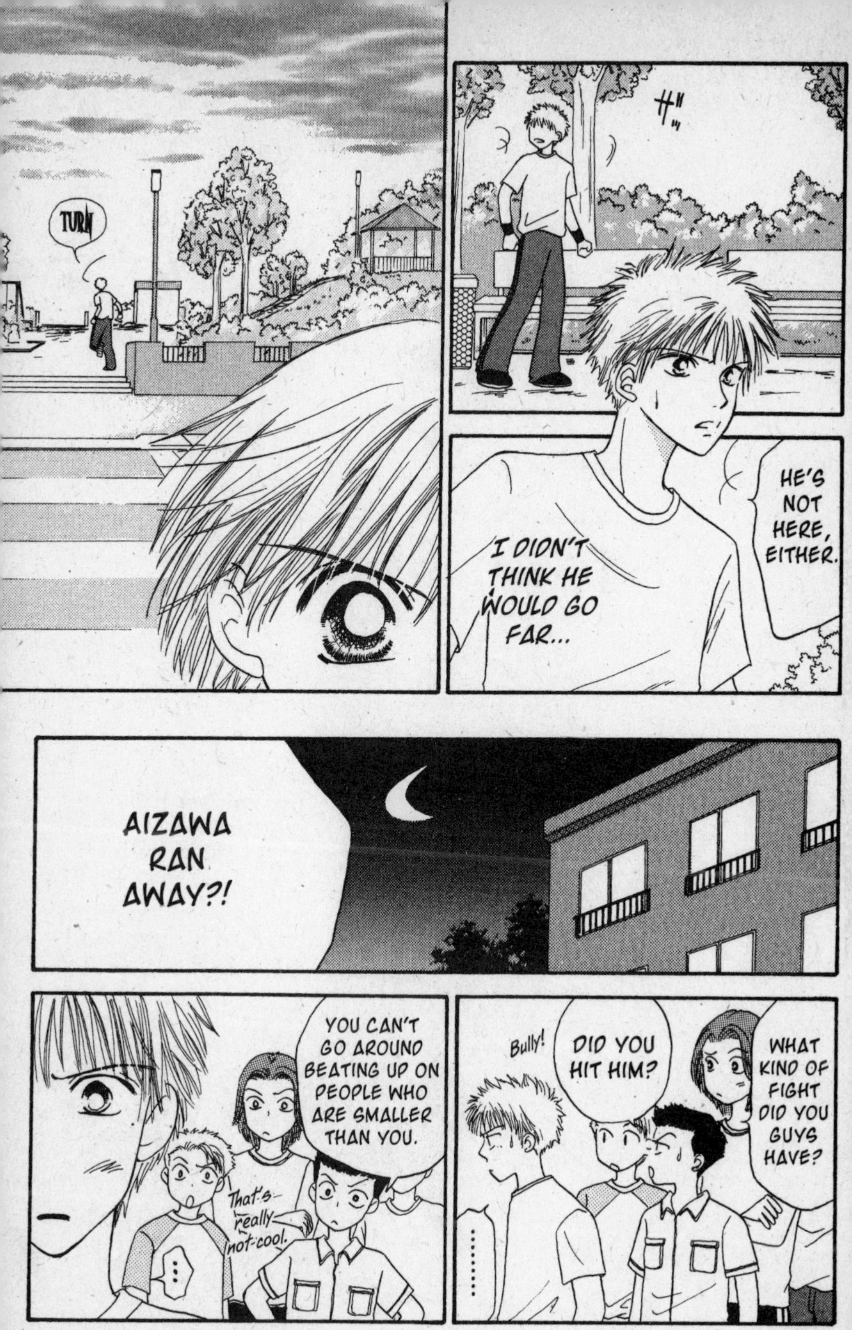
HE'S NOT HERE, EITHER.
I DIDN'T THINK HE WOULD GO FAR...
TURN
AIZAWA RAN AWAY?!
WHAT KIND OF FIGHT DID YOU GUYS HAVE?
DID YOU HIT HIM?
Bully!
......
YOU CAN'T GO AROUND BEATING UP ON PEOPLE WHO ARE SMALLER THAN YOU.
That's really not cool.
...

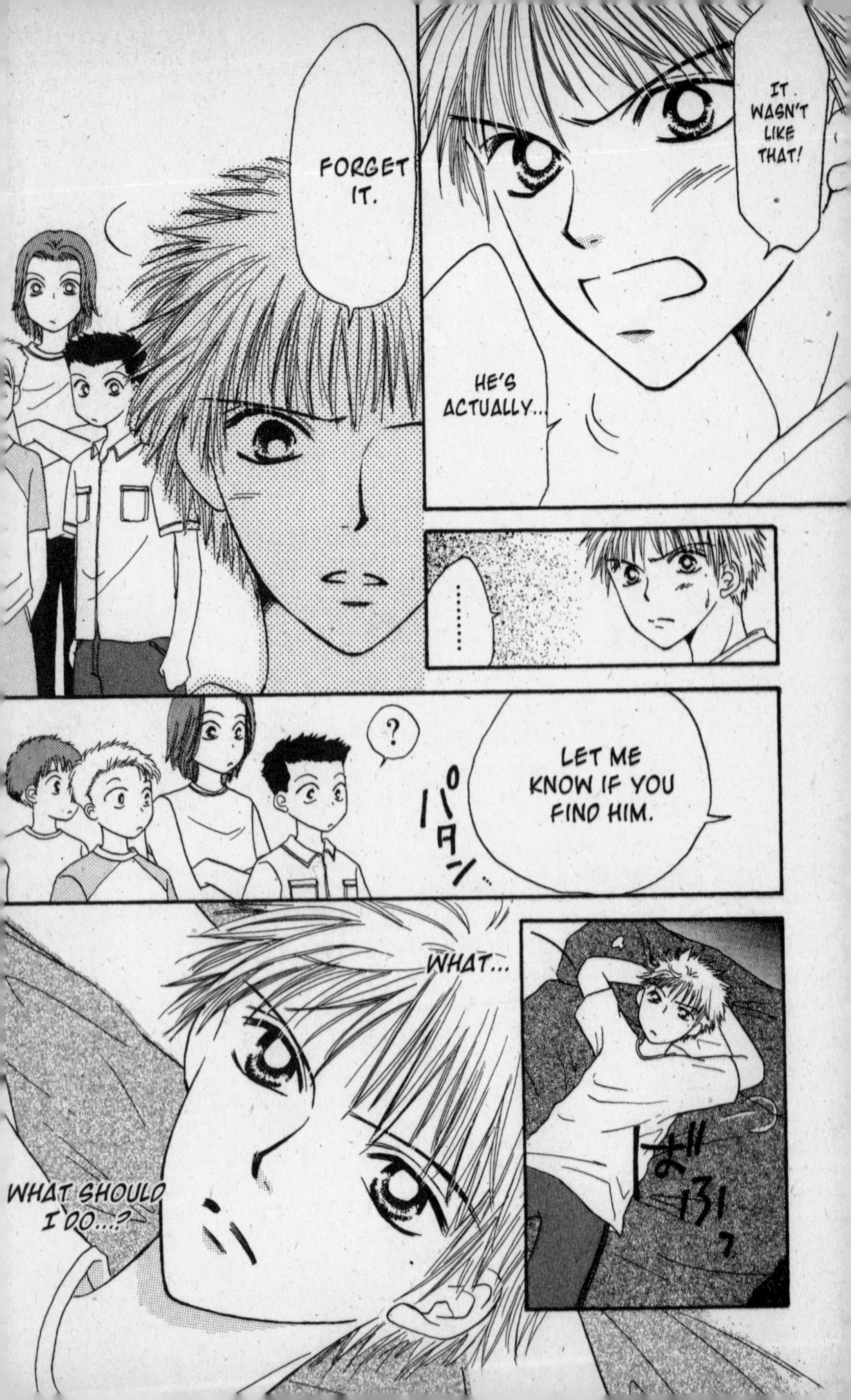
IT WASN'T LIKE THAT!
HE'S ACTUALLY...
......
FORGET IT.
LET ME KNOW IF YOU FIND HIM.
パタン
?
WHAT...
WHAT SHOULD I DO...?

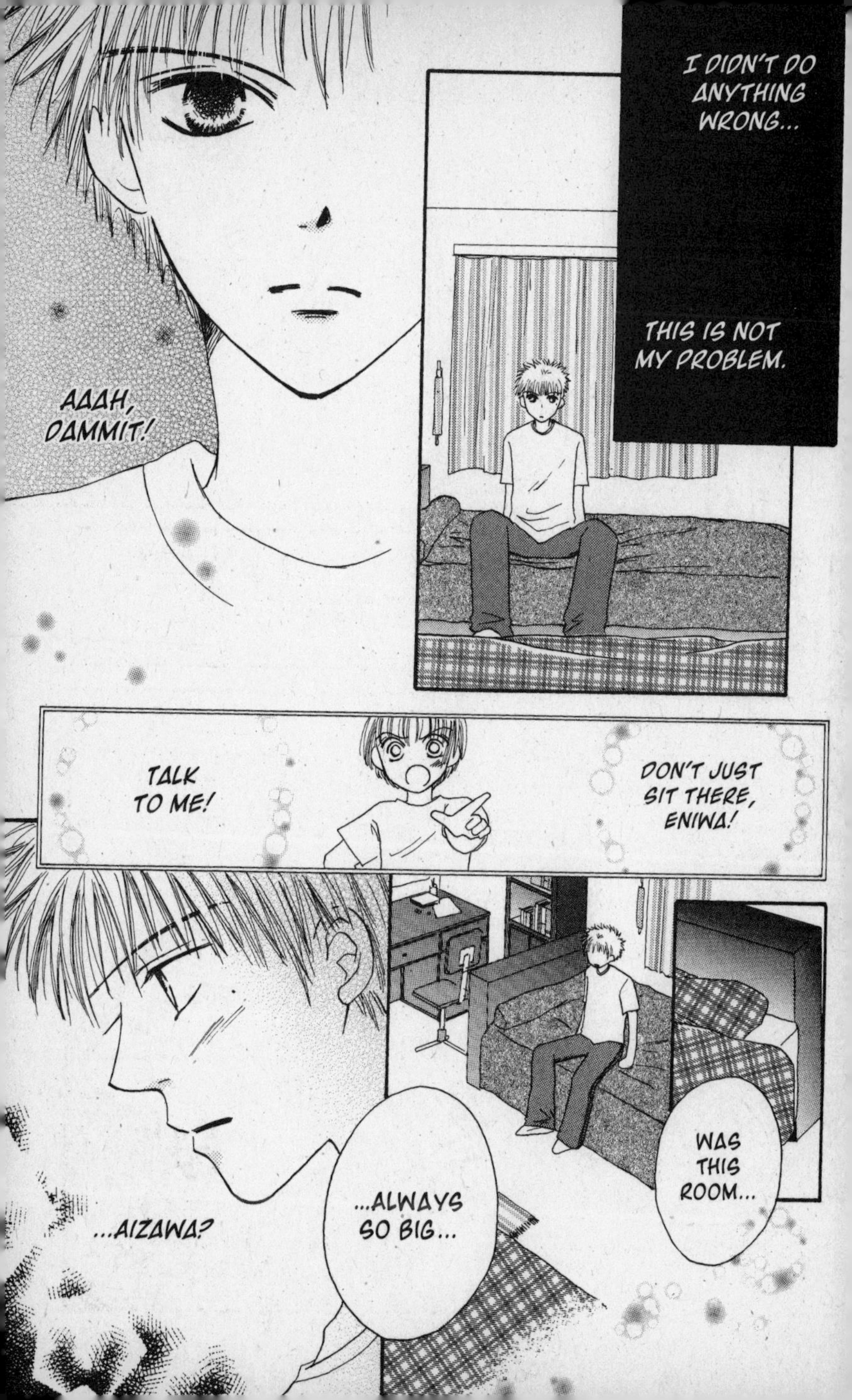
I DIDN'T DO ANYTHING WRONG...
THIS IS NOT MY PROBLEM.
AAAH, DAMMIT!
DON'T JUST SIT THERE, ENIWA!
TALK TO ME!
WAS THIS ROOM...
...ALWAYS SO BIG...
...AIZAWA?

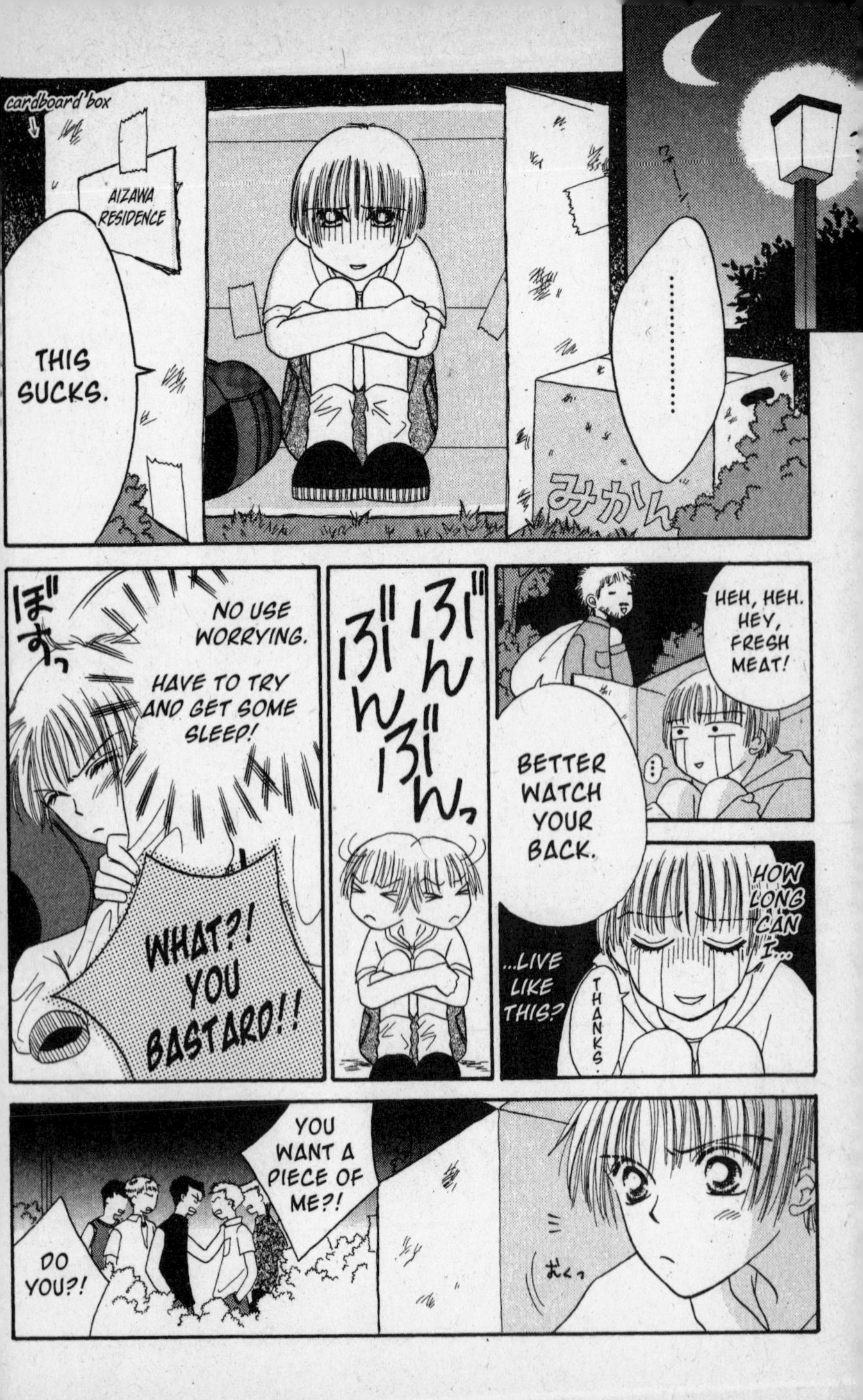
……
みかん
cardboard box
AIZAWA RESIDENCE
THIS SUCKS.
HEH, HEH. HEY, FRESH MEAT!
…
BETTER WATCH YOUR BACK.
HOW LONG CAN I...
...LIVE LIKE THIS?
THANKS.
ぶんぶんぶんぶんっ
ぼすっ
NO USE WORRYING.
HAVE TO TRY AND GET SOME SLEEP!
WHAT?! YOU BASTARD!!
YOU WANT A PIECE OF ME?!
DO YOU?!

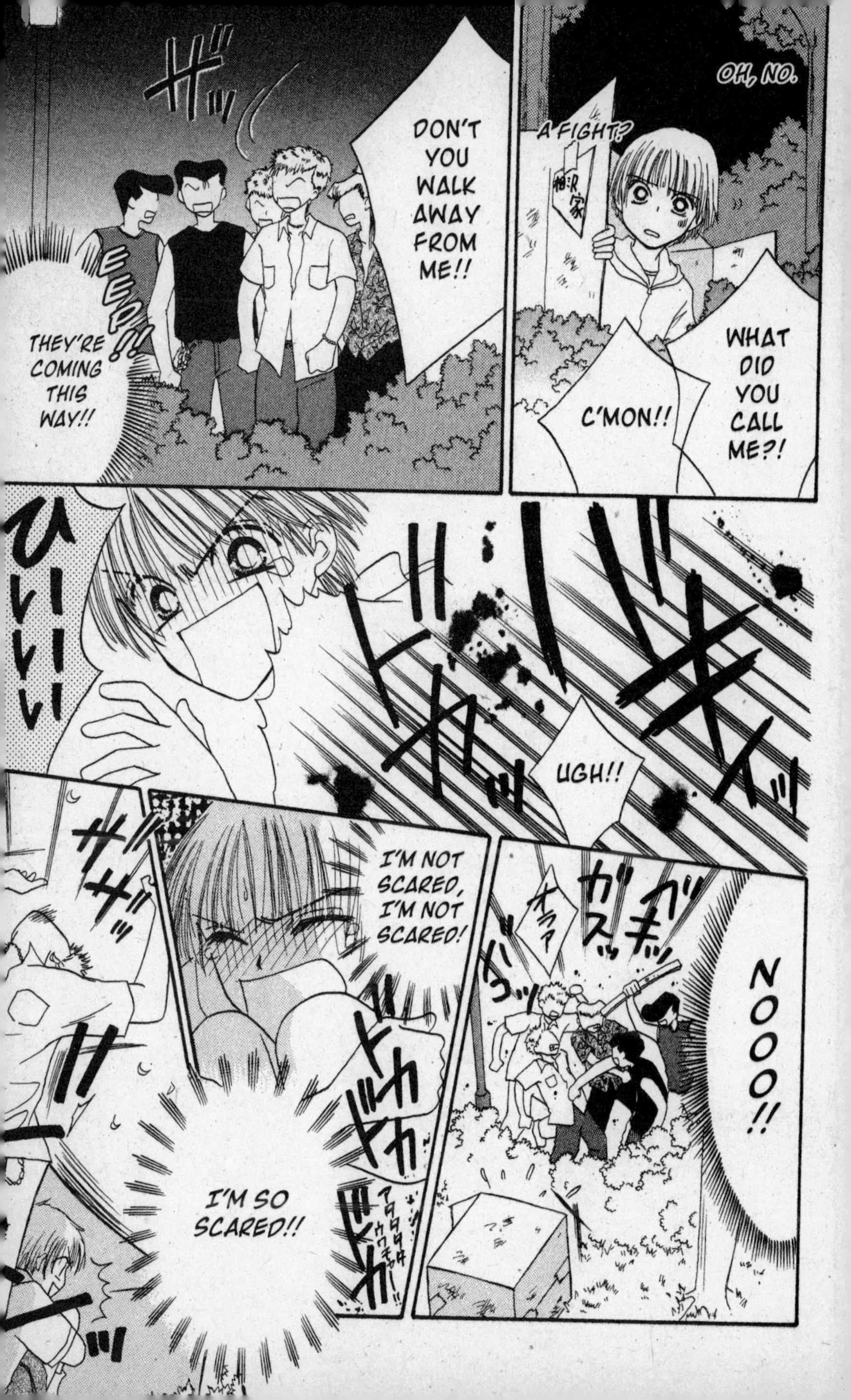
OH, NO.
A FIGHT?
WHAT DID YOU CALL ME?!
C'MON!!
DON'T YOU WALK AWAY FROM ME!!
EEP!!
THEY'RE COMING THIS WAY!!
UGH!!
NOOOO!!
I'M NOT SCARED, I'M NOT SCARED!
I'M SO SCARED!!

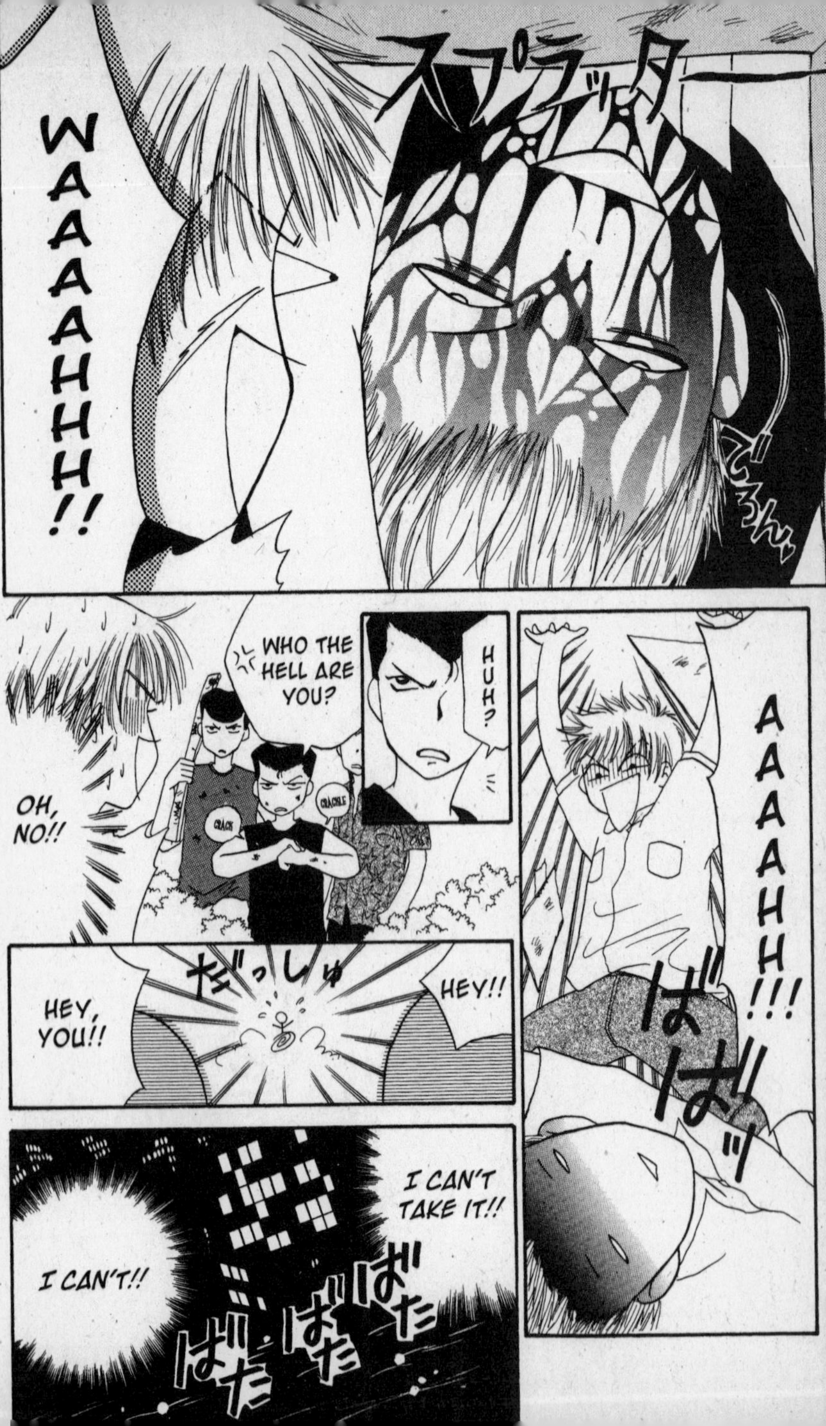
スプラッター
WAAAAAHHH!!
でろん
AAAAAHH!!!
ばばッ
HUH?
WHO THE HELL ARE YOU?
CRACKLE
CRACK
OH, NO!!
HEY!!
だっしゅ
HEY, YOU!!
I CAN'T TAKE IT!!
ばたばたばた
I CAN'T!!

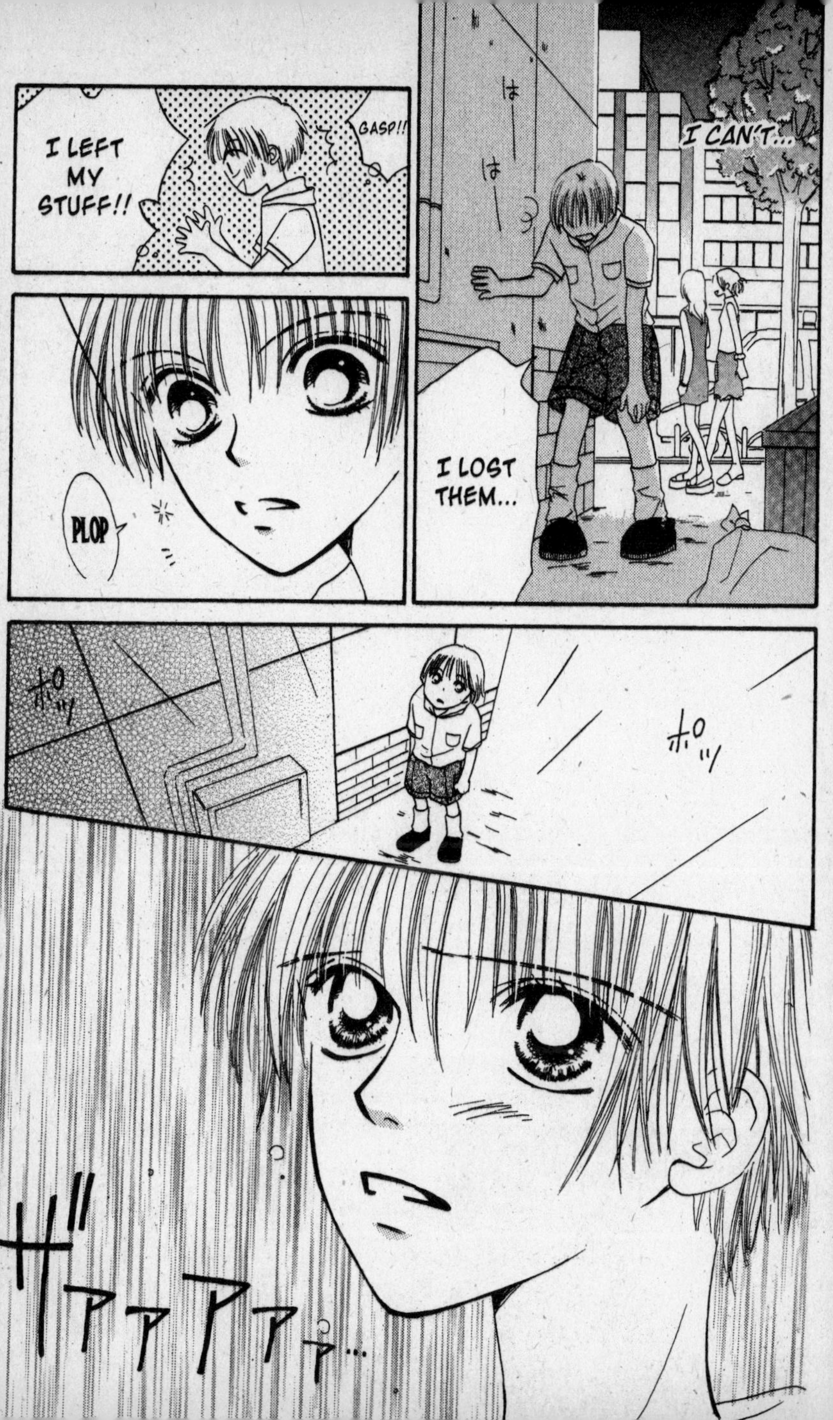
I CAN'T...
はーはー
I LOST THEM...
GASP!!
I LEFT MY STUFF!!
PLOP
ポッ
ポッ
ザァァァァァ...

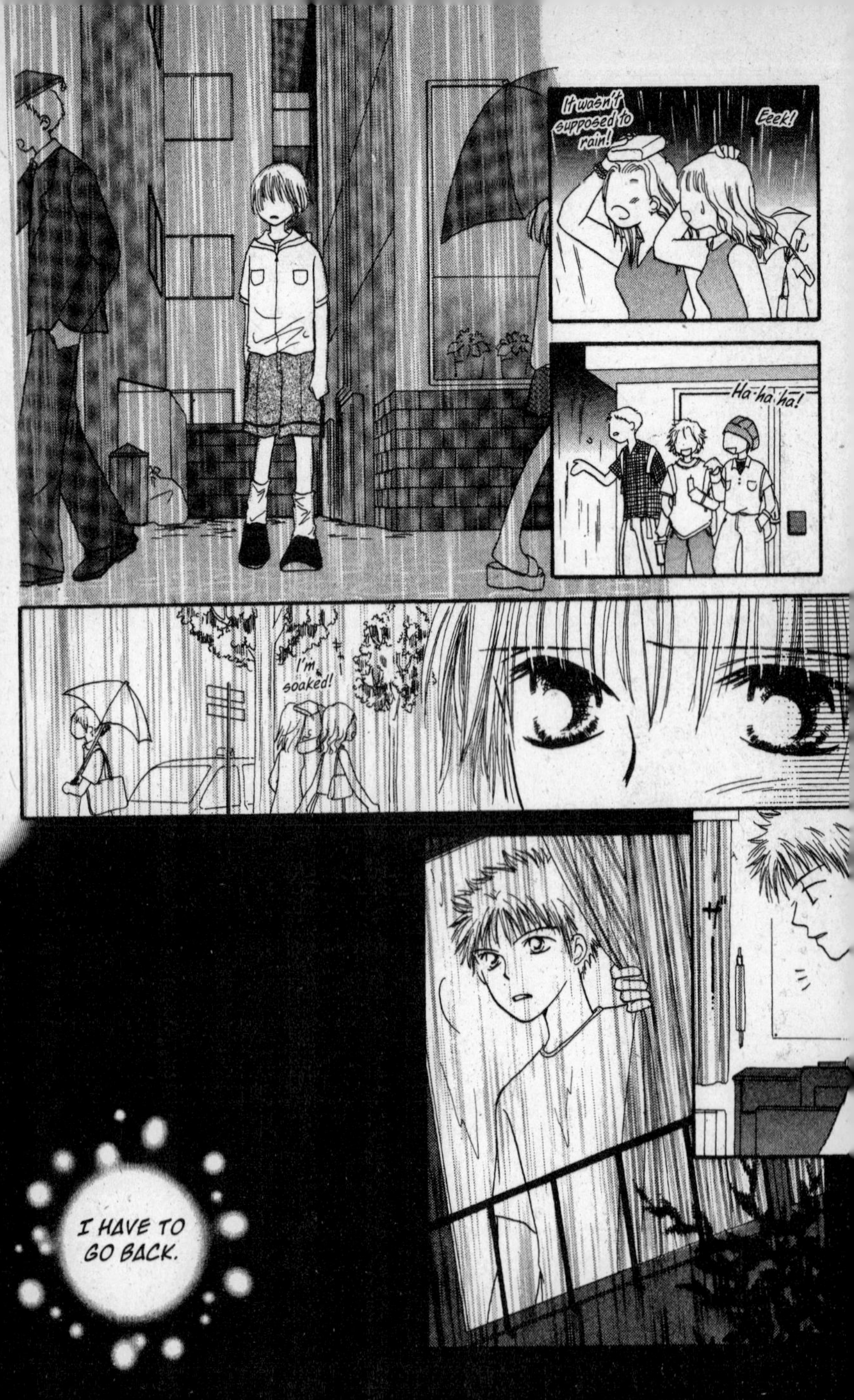
Eeek!
It wasn't supposed to rain!
Ha-ha-ha!
I'm soaked!
I HAVE TO GO BACK.

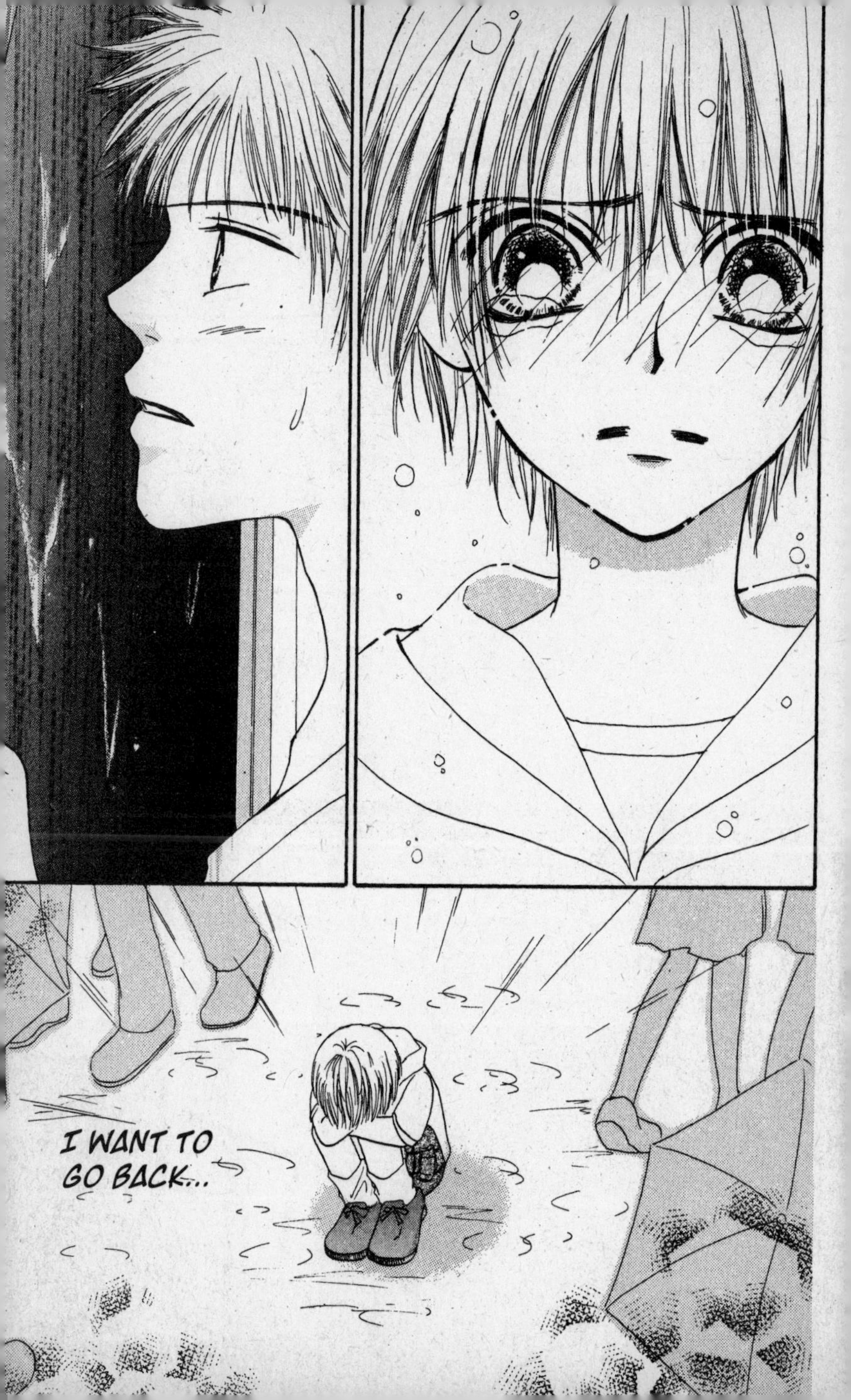
I WANT TO GO BACK...

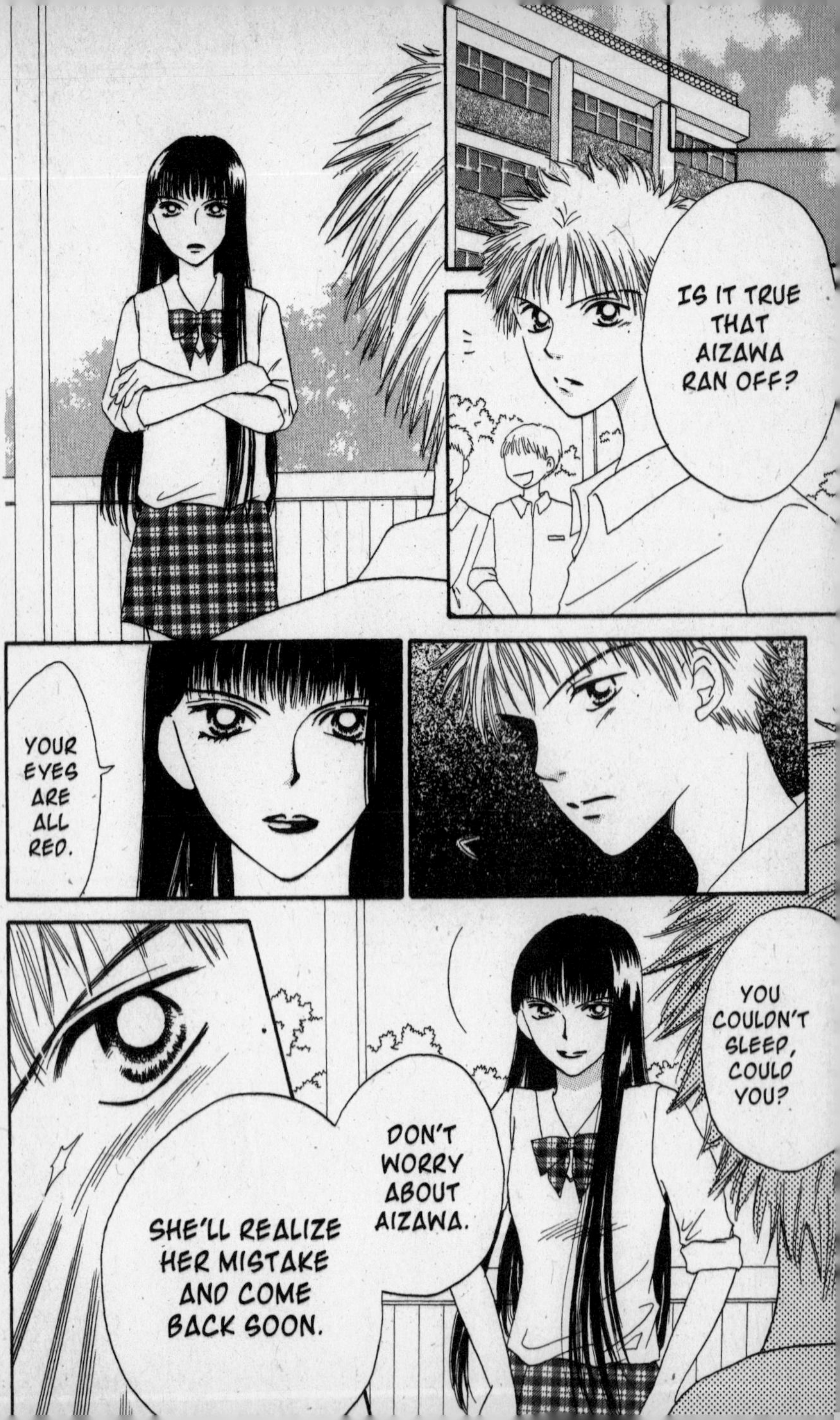
IS IT TRUE THAT AIZAWA RAN OFF?
YOUR EYES ARE ALL RED.
YOU COULDN'T SLEEP, COULD YOU?
DON'T WORRY ABOUT AIZAWA.
SHE'LL REALIZE HER MISTAKE AND COME BACK SOON.

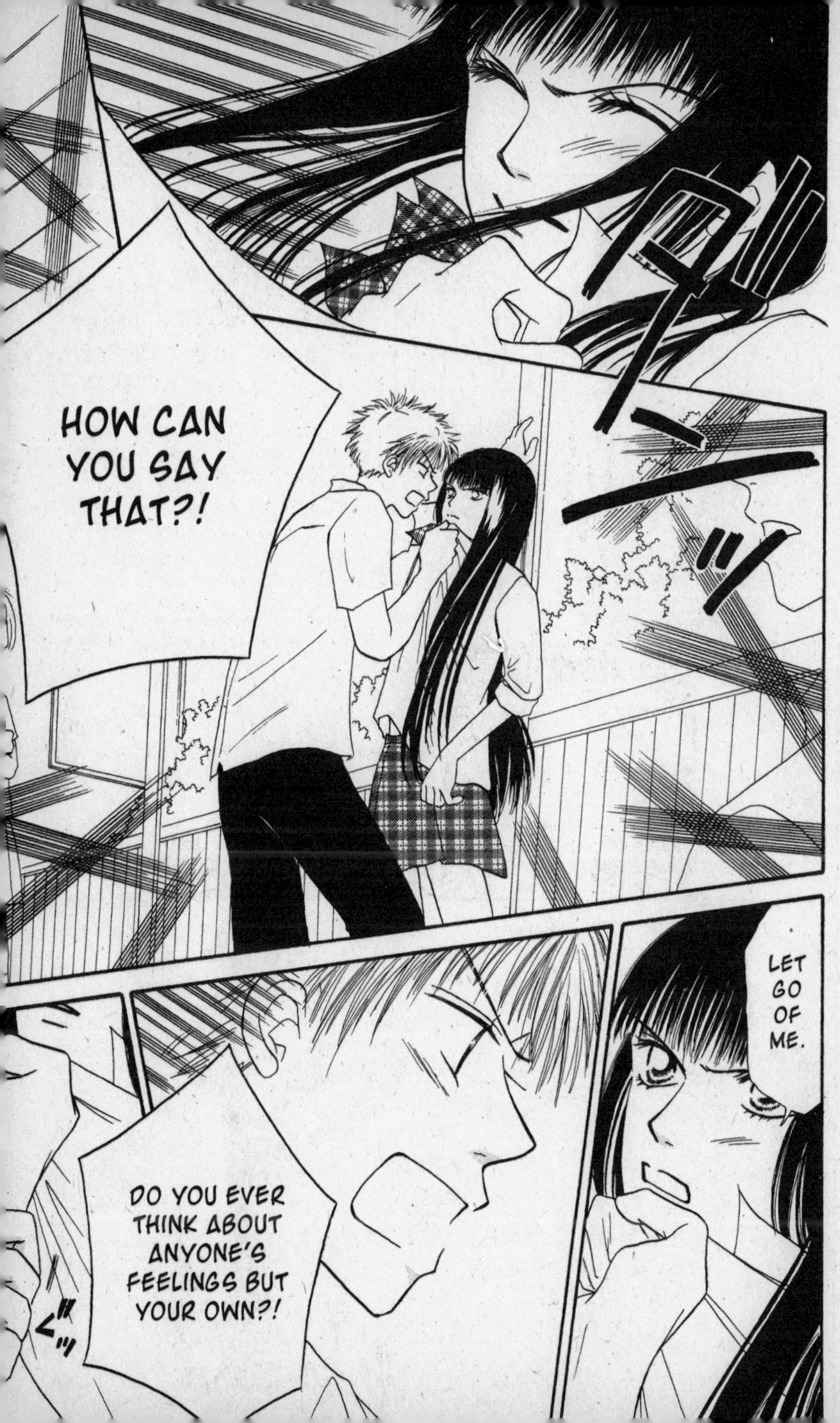
HOW CAN YOU SAY THAT?!
LET GO OF ME.
DO YOU EVER THINK ABOUT ANYONE'S FEELINGS BUT YOUR OWN?!

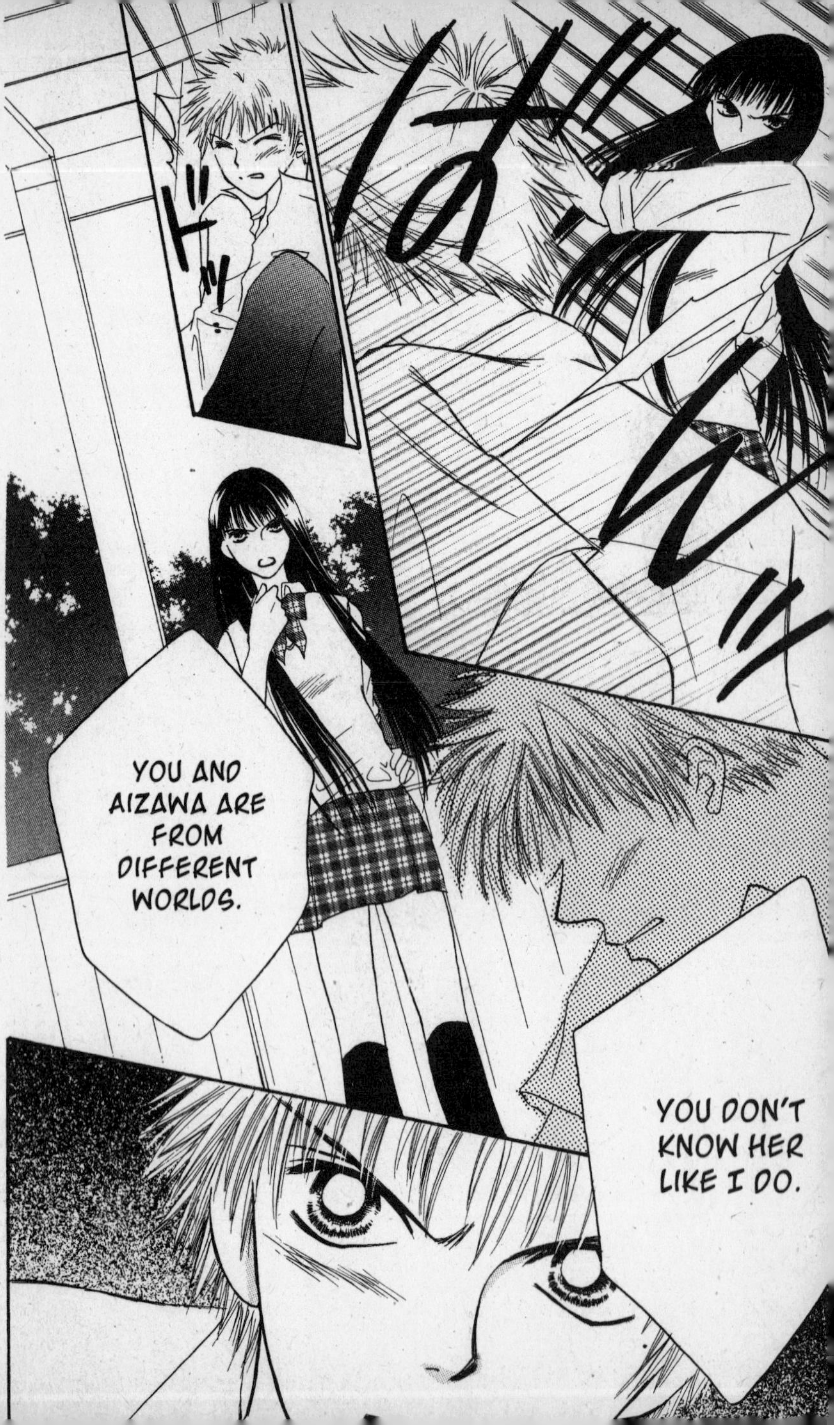
ばんッ
ドッ
YOU AND AIZAWA ARE FROM DIFFERENT WORLDS.
YOU DON'T KNOW HER LIKE I DO.

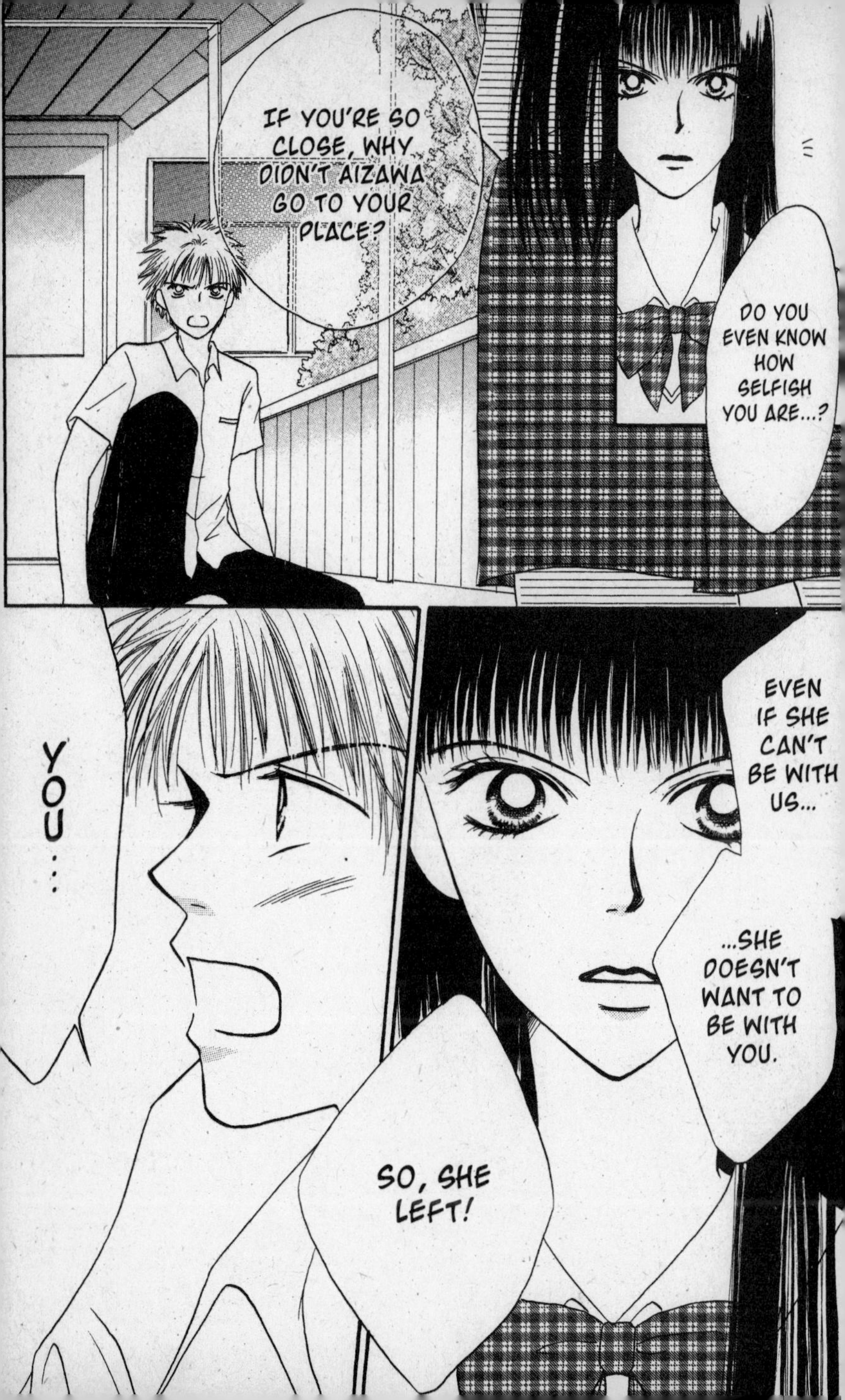
DO YOU EVEN KNOW HOW SELFISH YOU ARE...?
IF YOU'RE SO CLOSE, WHY DIDN'T AIZAWA GO TO YOUR PLACE?
EVEN IF SHE CAN'T BE WITH US...
...SHE DOESN'T WANT TO BE WITH YOU.
SO, SHE LEFT!
YOU...

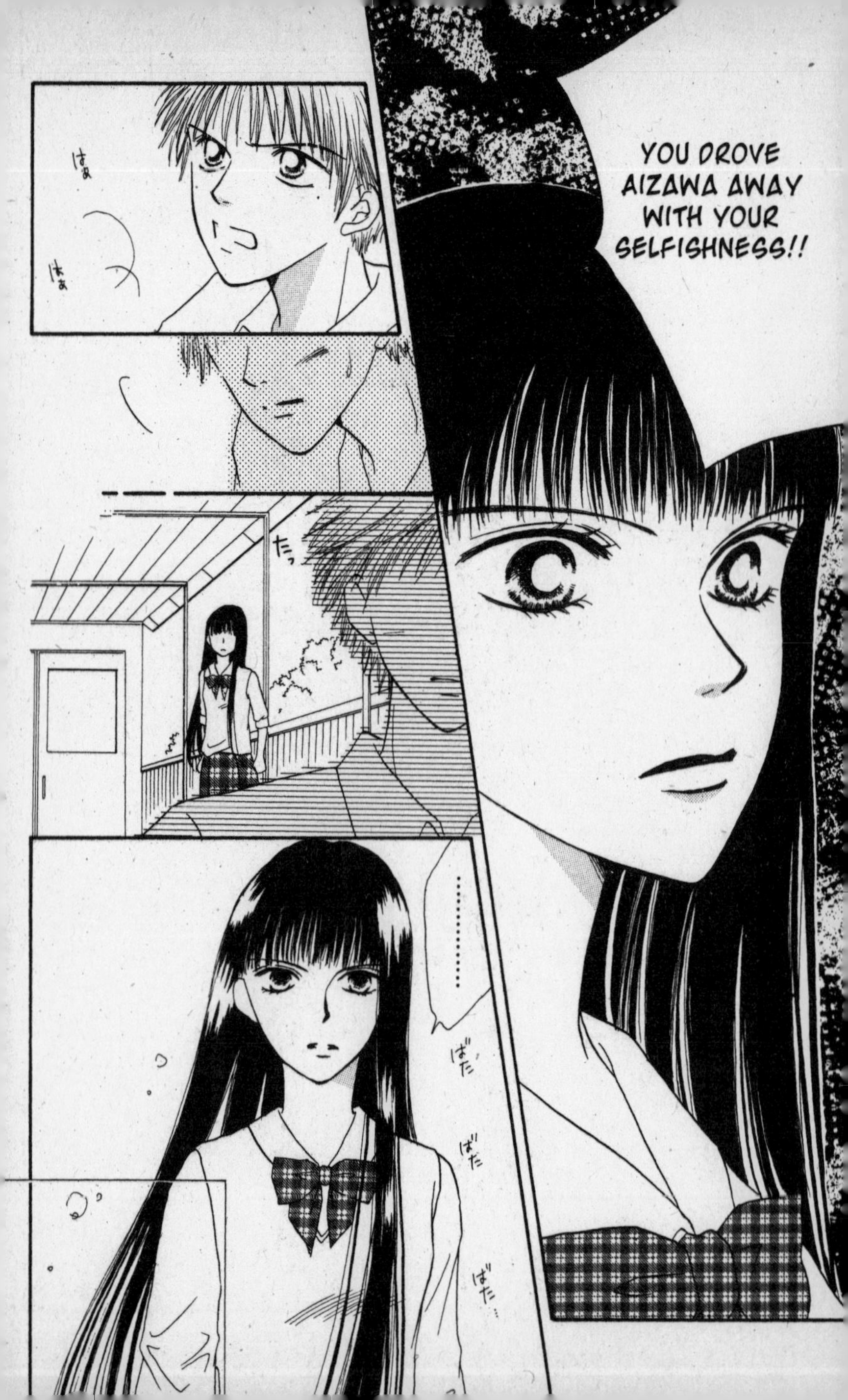
YOU DROVE AIZAWA AWAY WITH YOUR SELFISHNESS!!
はぁ
はぁ
たっ
......
ばた
ばた
ばた...

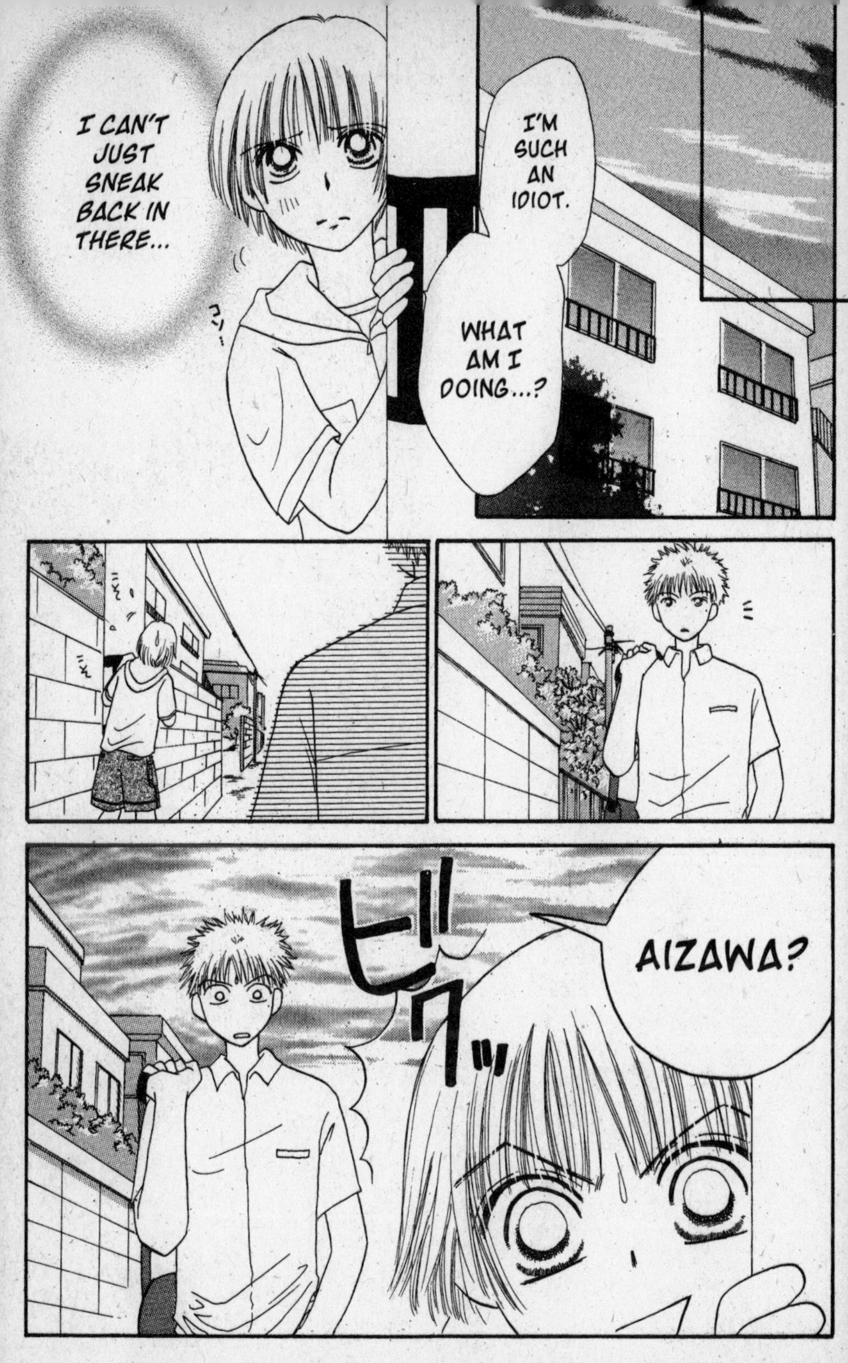
I'M SUCH AN IDIOT.
WHAT AM I DOING...?
I CAN'T JUST SNEAK BACK IN THERE...
AIZAWA?

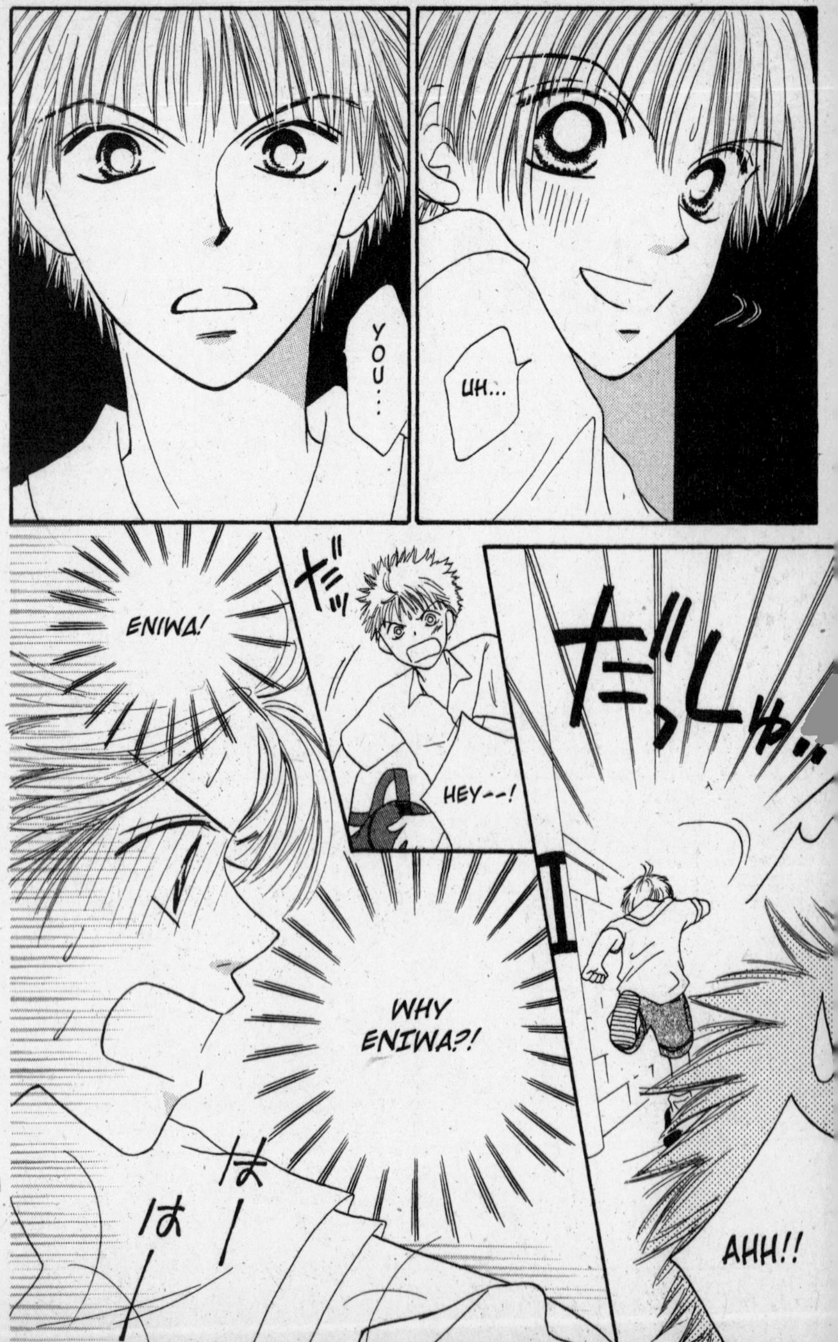

UH...
YOU...
だっしゅ...
AHH!!
ダッ
HEY--!
ENIWA!
WHY ENIWA?!
はーはー

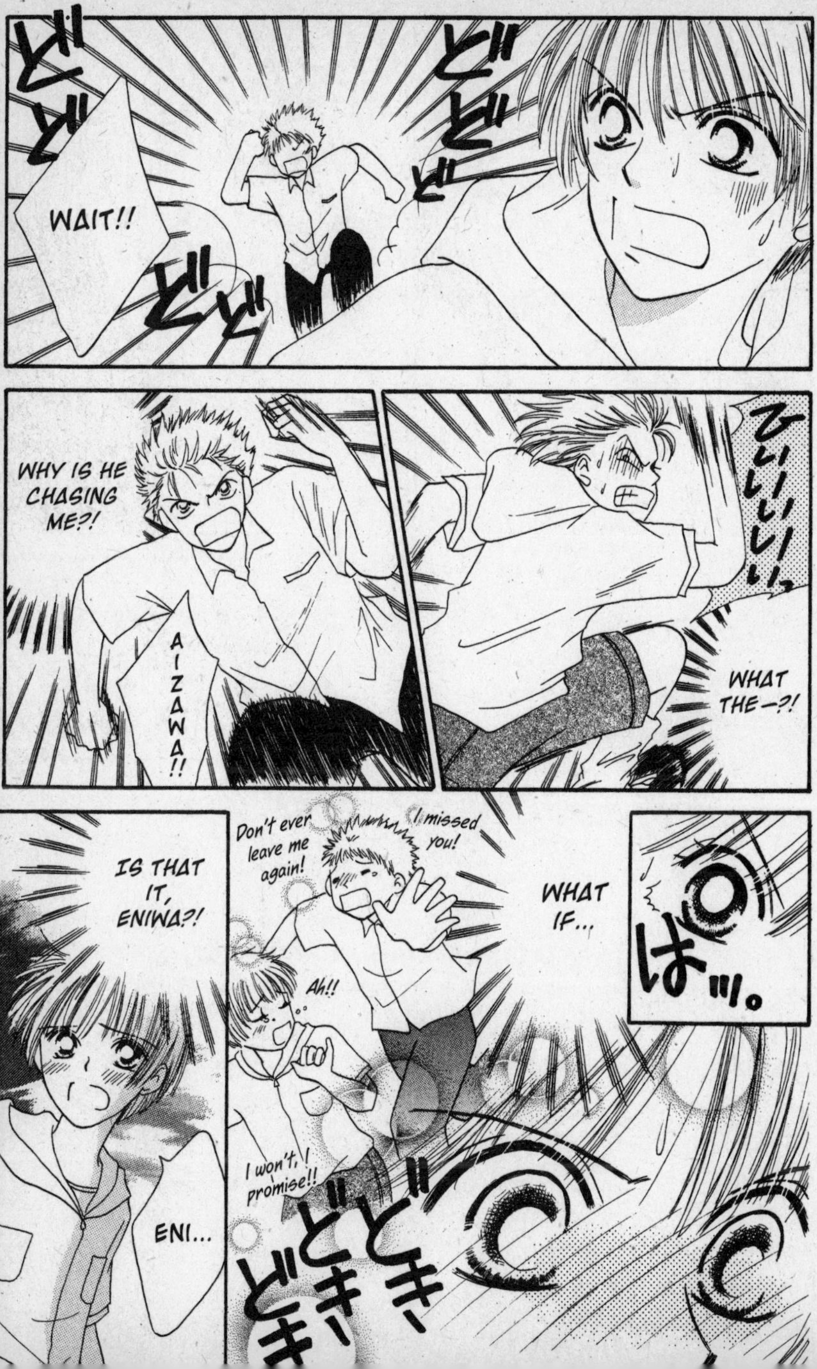
どどど
どど
WAIT!!
どど
ひぃぃぃぃぃっ
WHAT THE—?!
WHY IS HE CHASING ME?!
AIZAWA!!
はっ。
WHAT IF...
I missed you!
Don't ever leave me again!
Ah!!
I won't, I promise!!
どきどき
IS THAT IT, ENIWA?!
ENI...

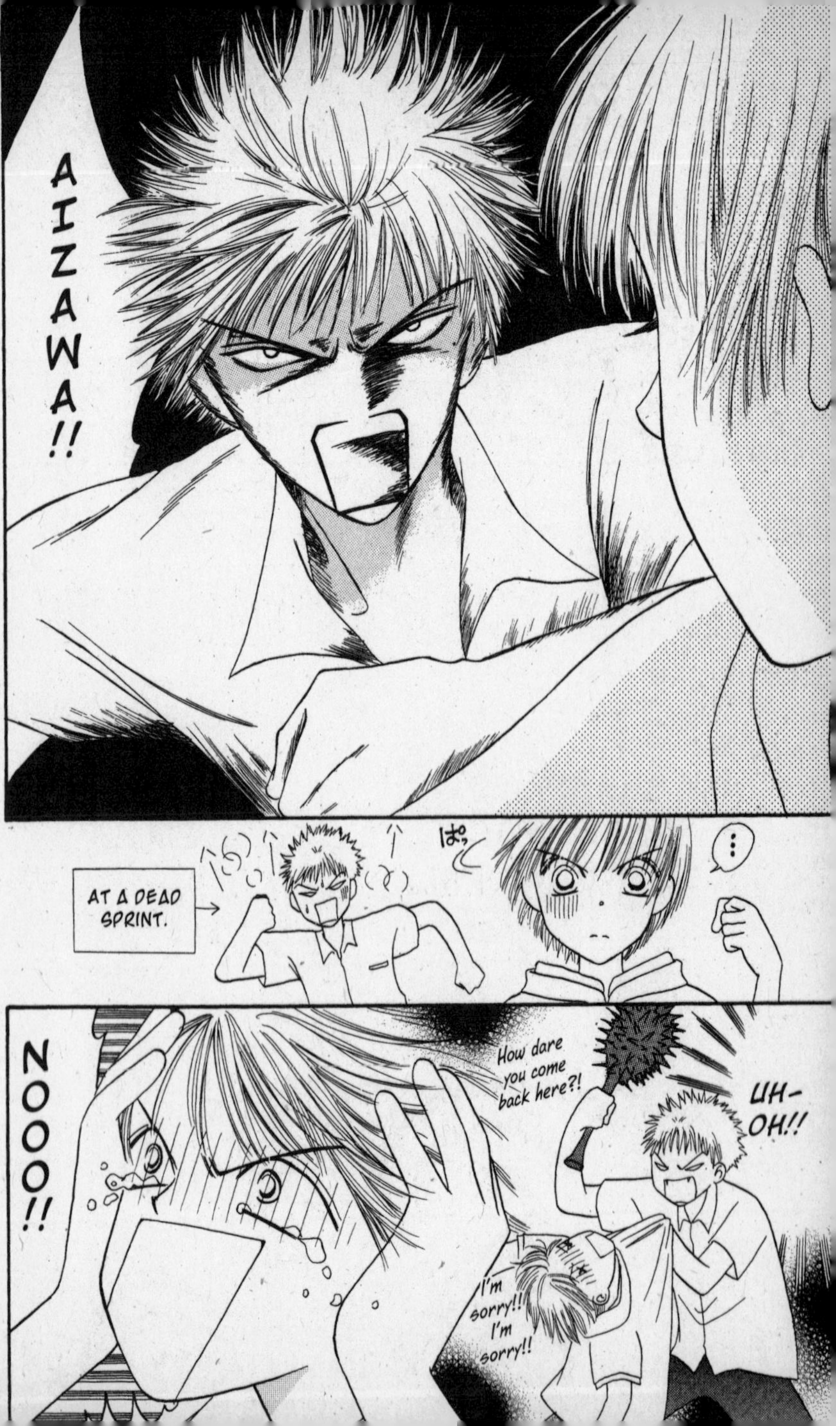
AIZAWA!!
...
ぱっ
AT A DEAD SPRINT.
UH-OH!!
How dare you come back here?!
I'm sorry!! I'm sorry!!
NOOOO!!

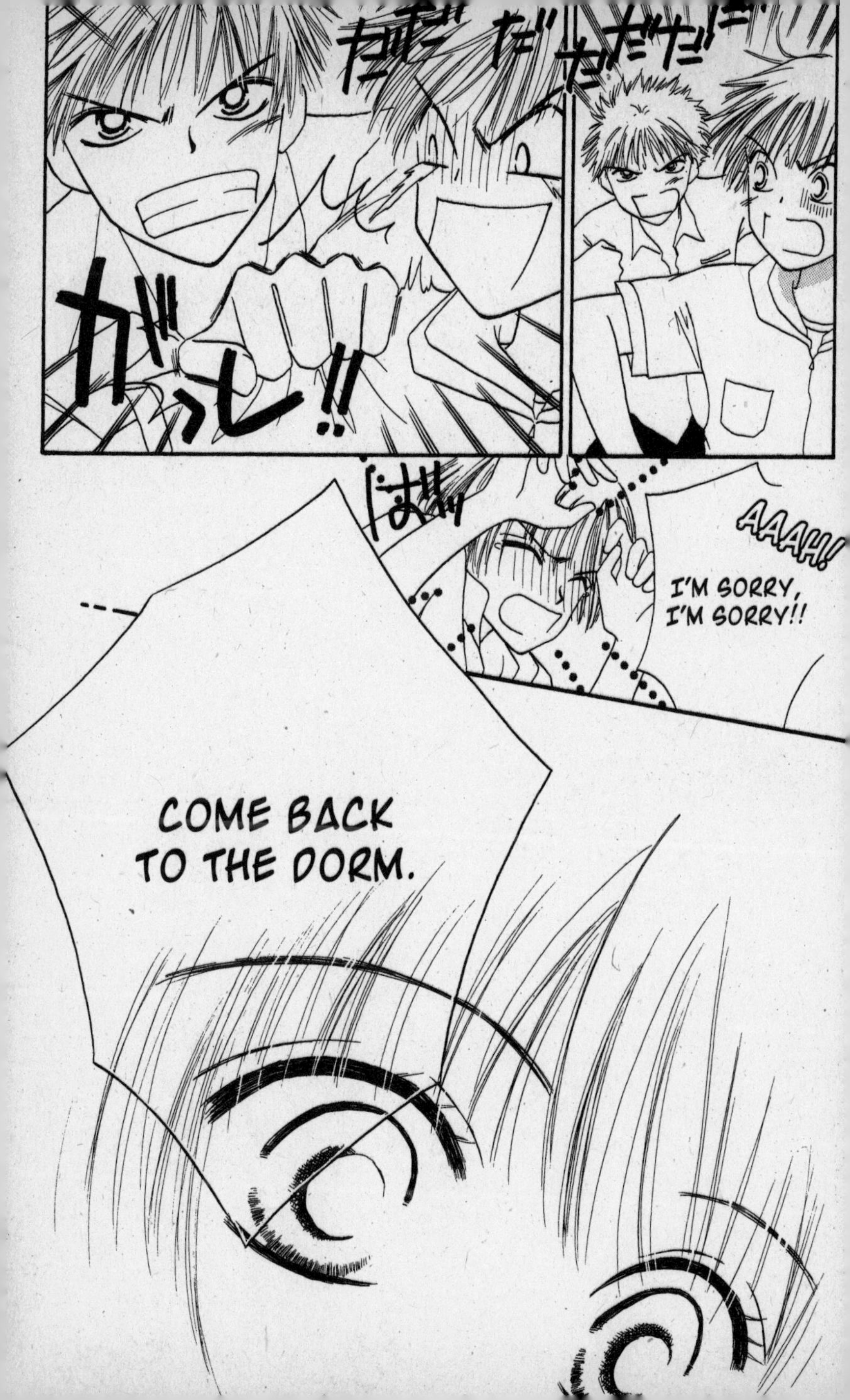
がっし!!
ばっ
AAAH!
I'M SORRY, I'M SORRY!!

COME BACK TO THE DORM.

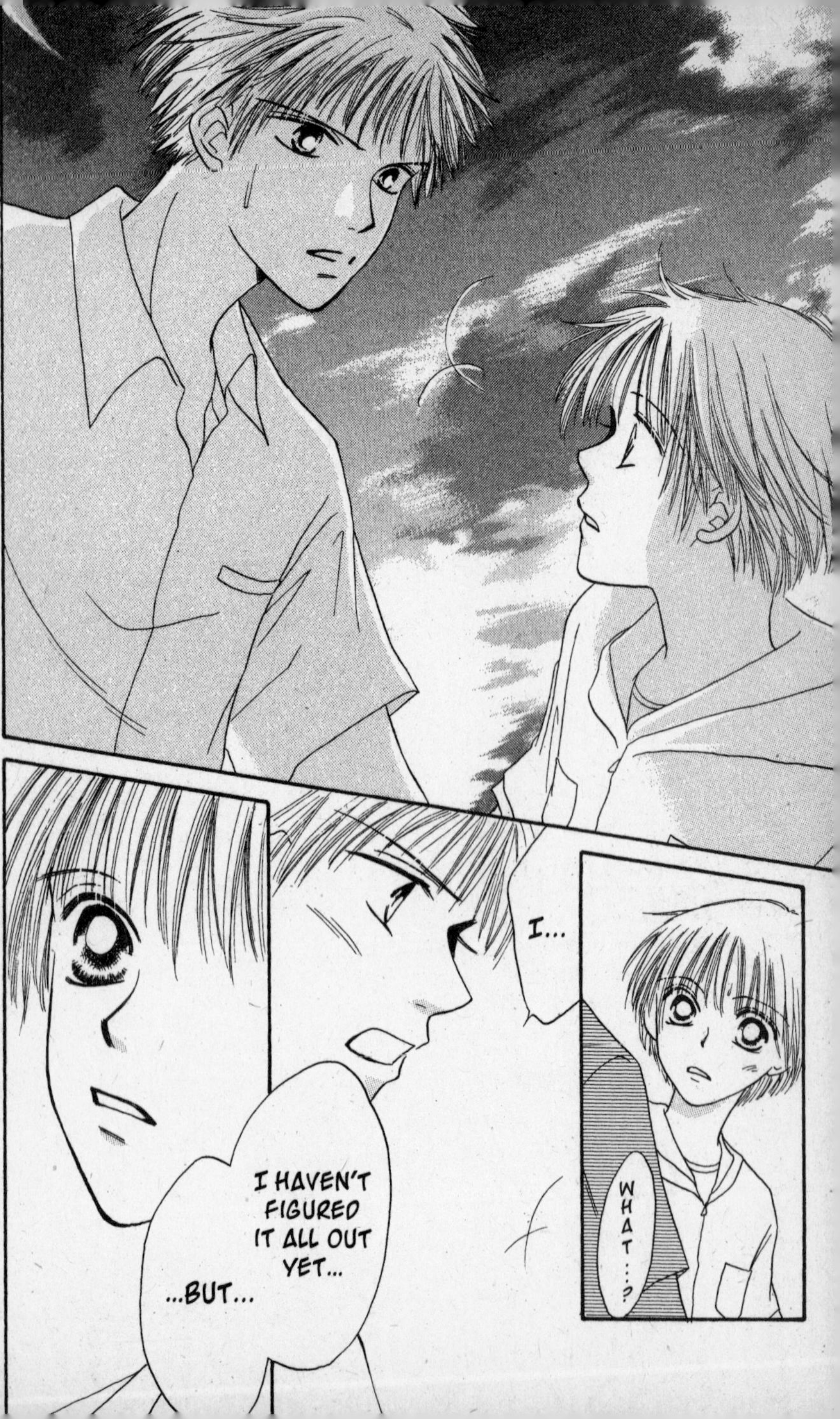
WHAT...?
I...
I HAVEN'T FIGURED IT ALL OUT YET...
...BUT...

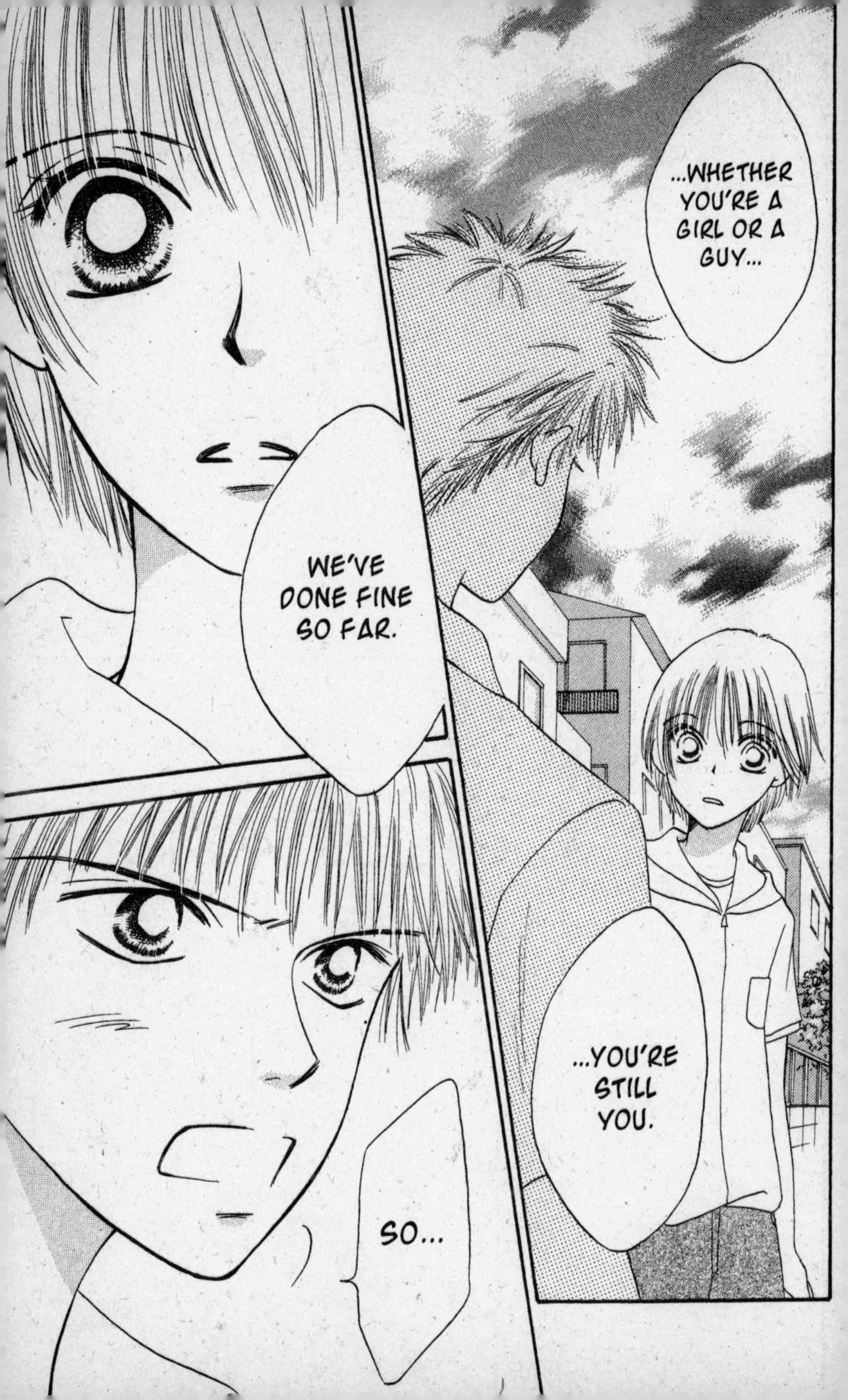
...WHETHER YOU'RE A GIRL OR A GUY...
...YOU'RE STILL YOU.
WE'VE DONE FINE SO FAR.
SO...

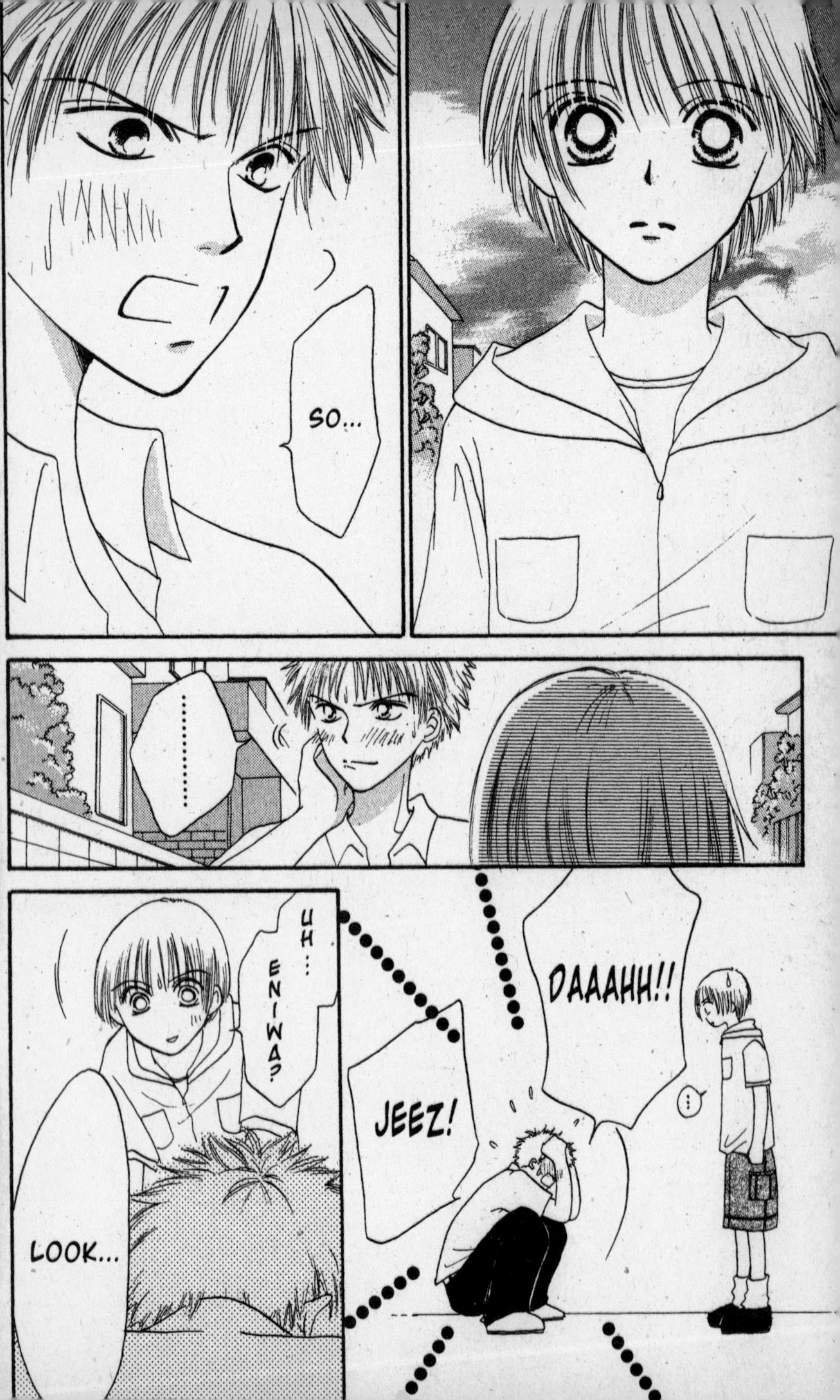
SO...
......
DAAAHH!!
...
JEEZ!
UH... ENIWA?
LOOK...

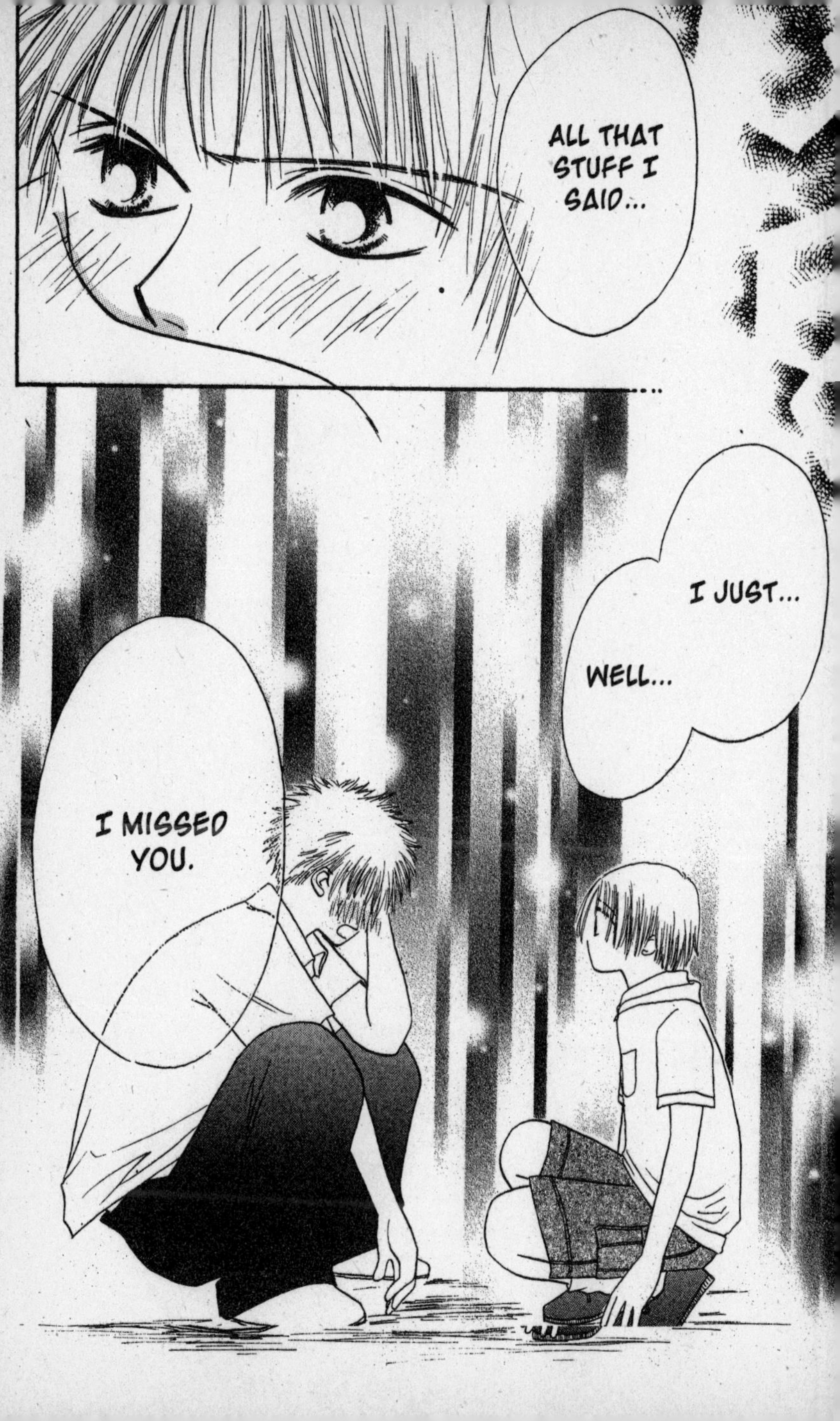
ALL THAT STUFF I SAID...
...
I JUST...
WELL...
I MISSED YOU.

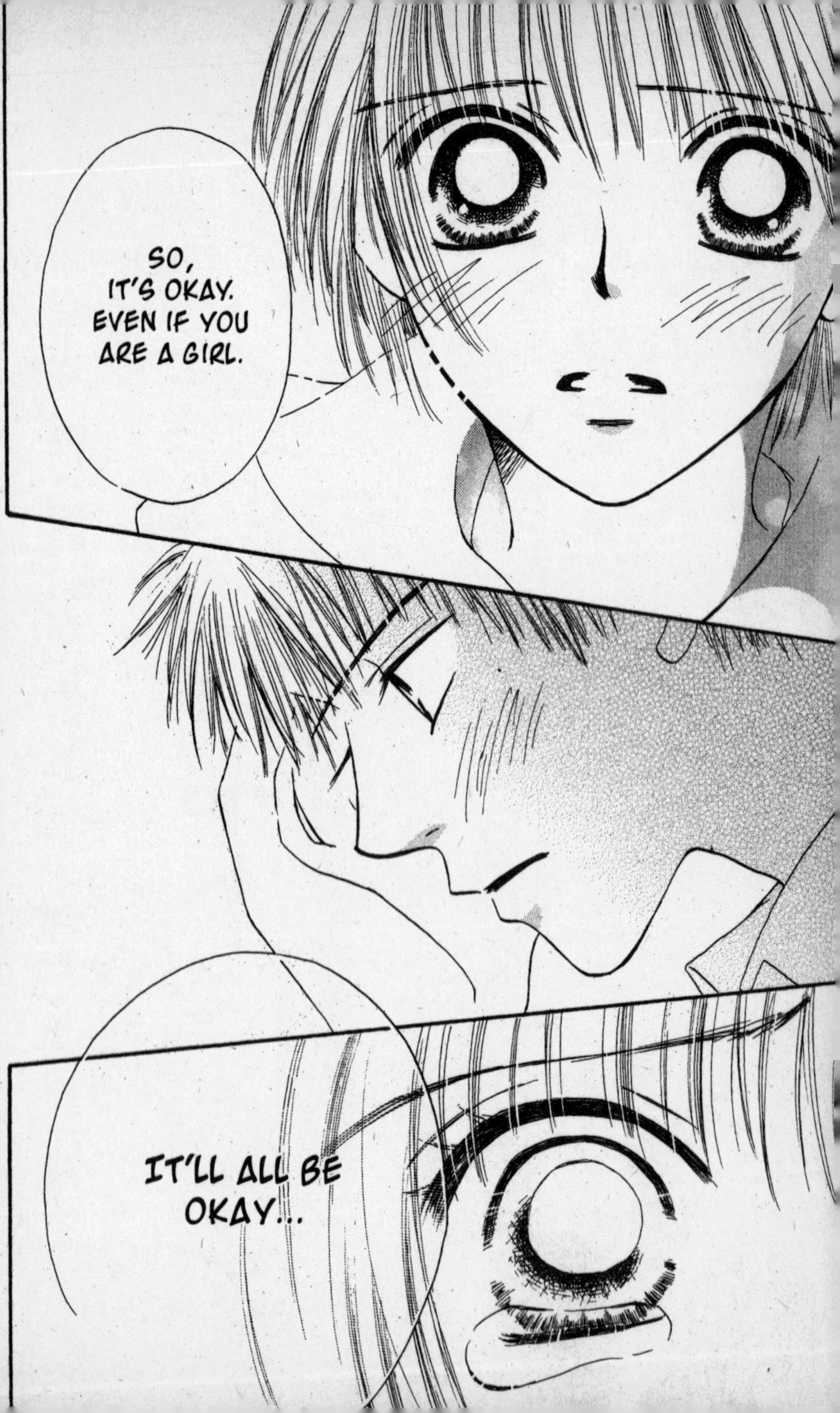
SO, IT'S OKAY. EVEN IF YOU ARE A GIRL.
IT'LL ALL BE OKAY...

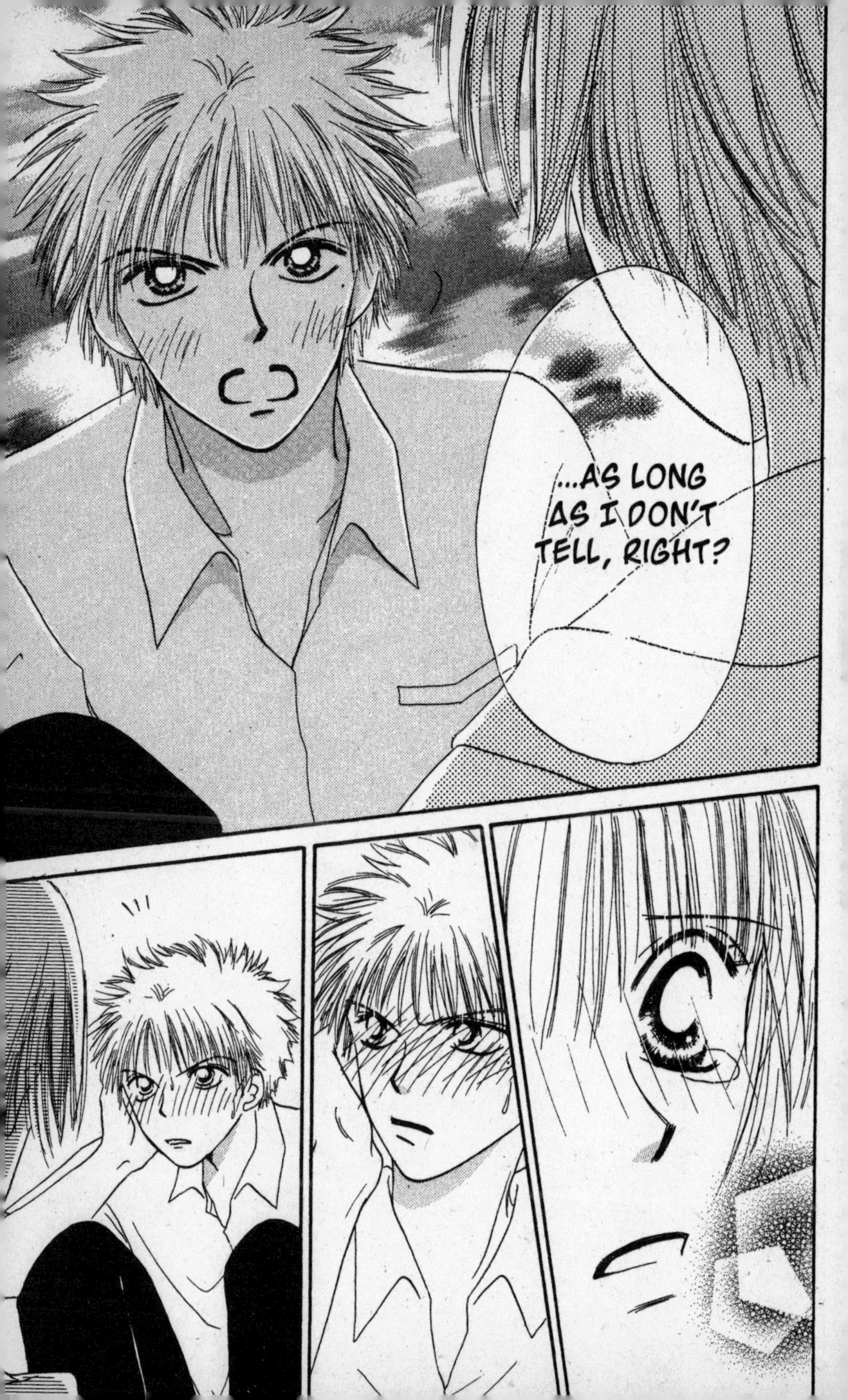
...AS LONG AS I DON'T TELL, RIGHT?

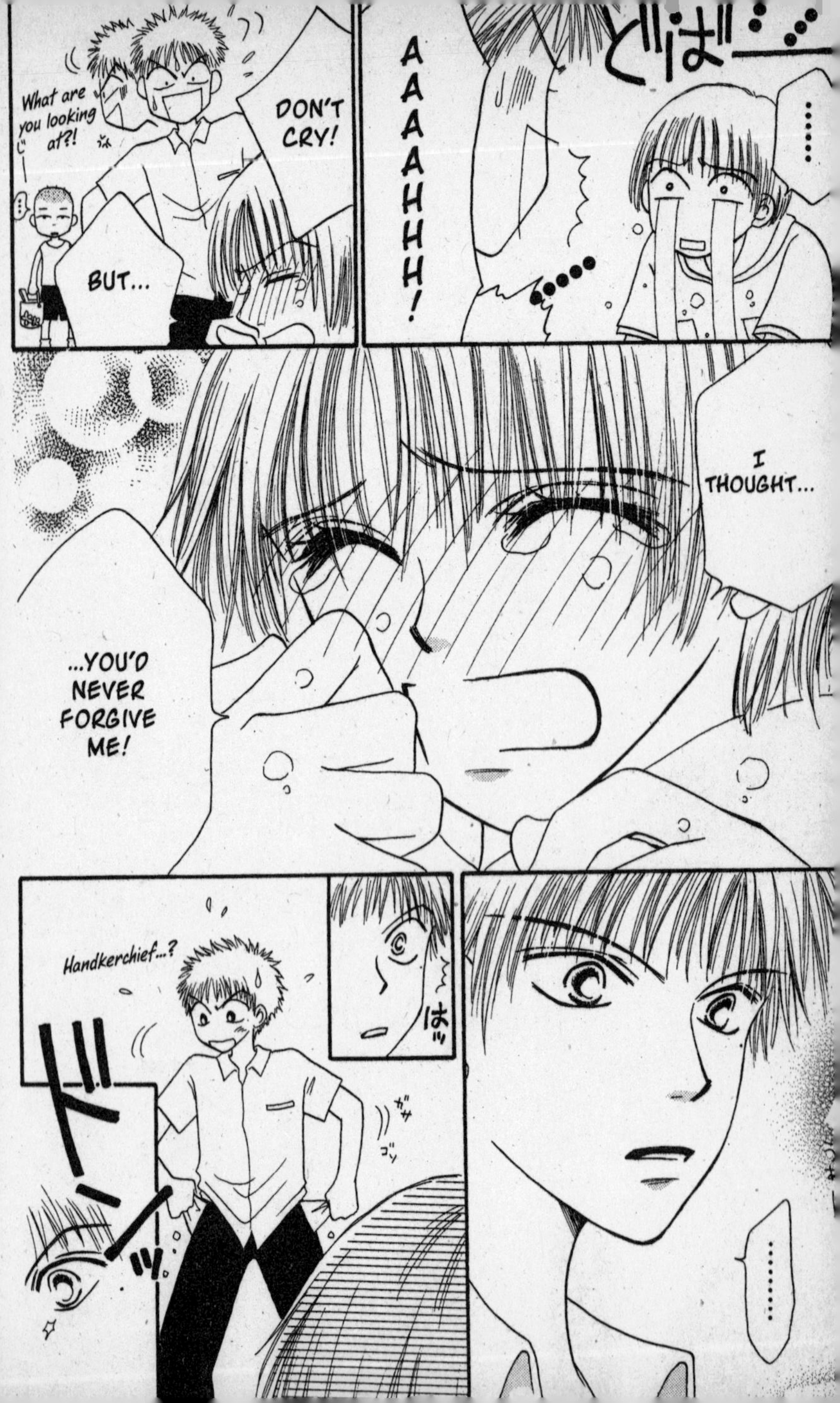

どばーっ
......
AAAAHHH!
DON'T CRY!
BUT...
What are you looking at?!
じー
...
I THOUGHT...
...YOU'D NEVER FORGIVE ME!
......
はッ
Handkerchief...?
ガサ
ゴソ
ドーッ

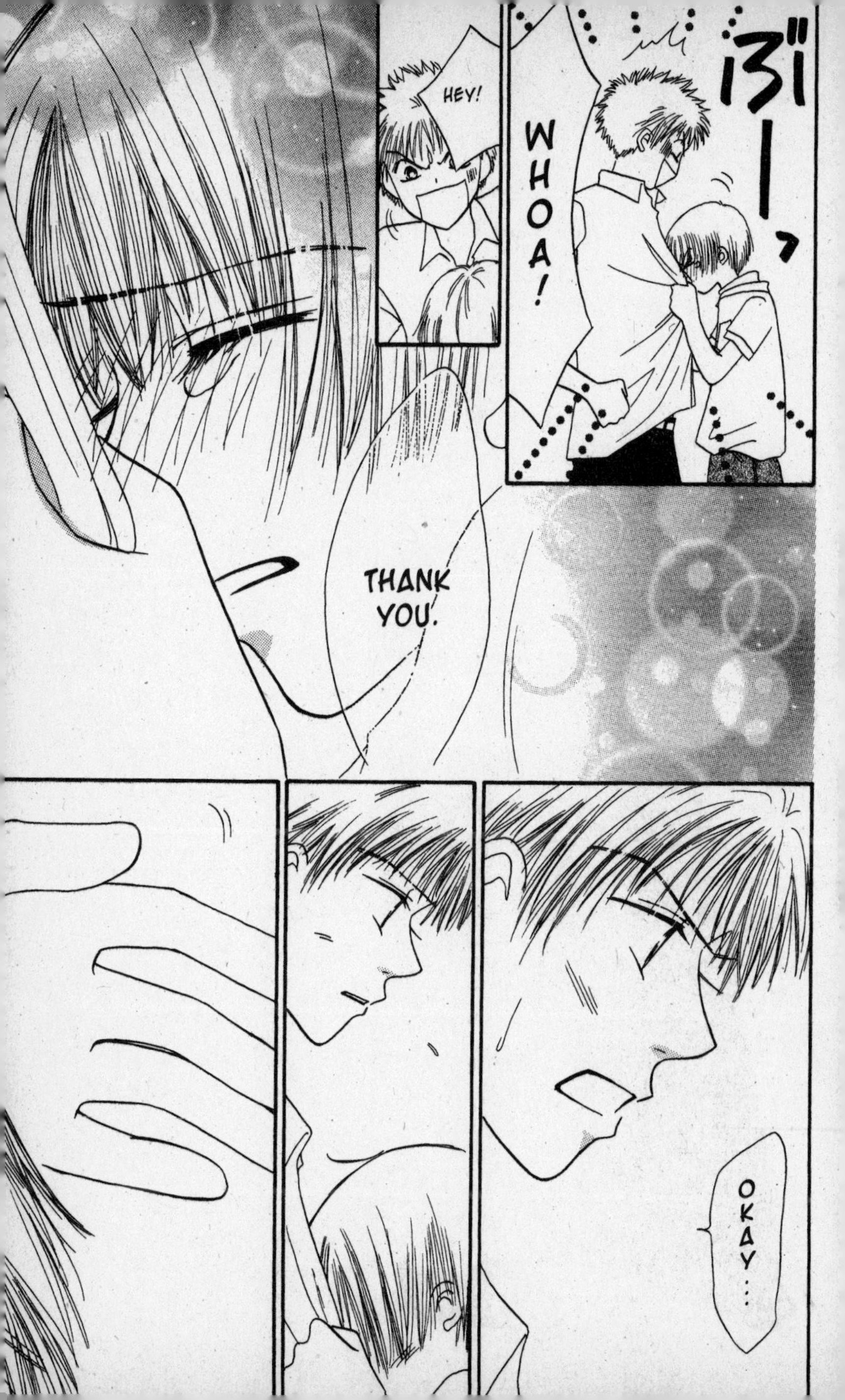
ぶーっ
WHOA!
HEY!
THANK YOU.
OKAY...

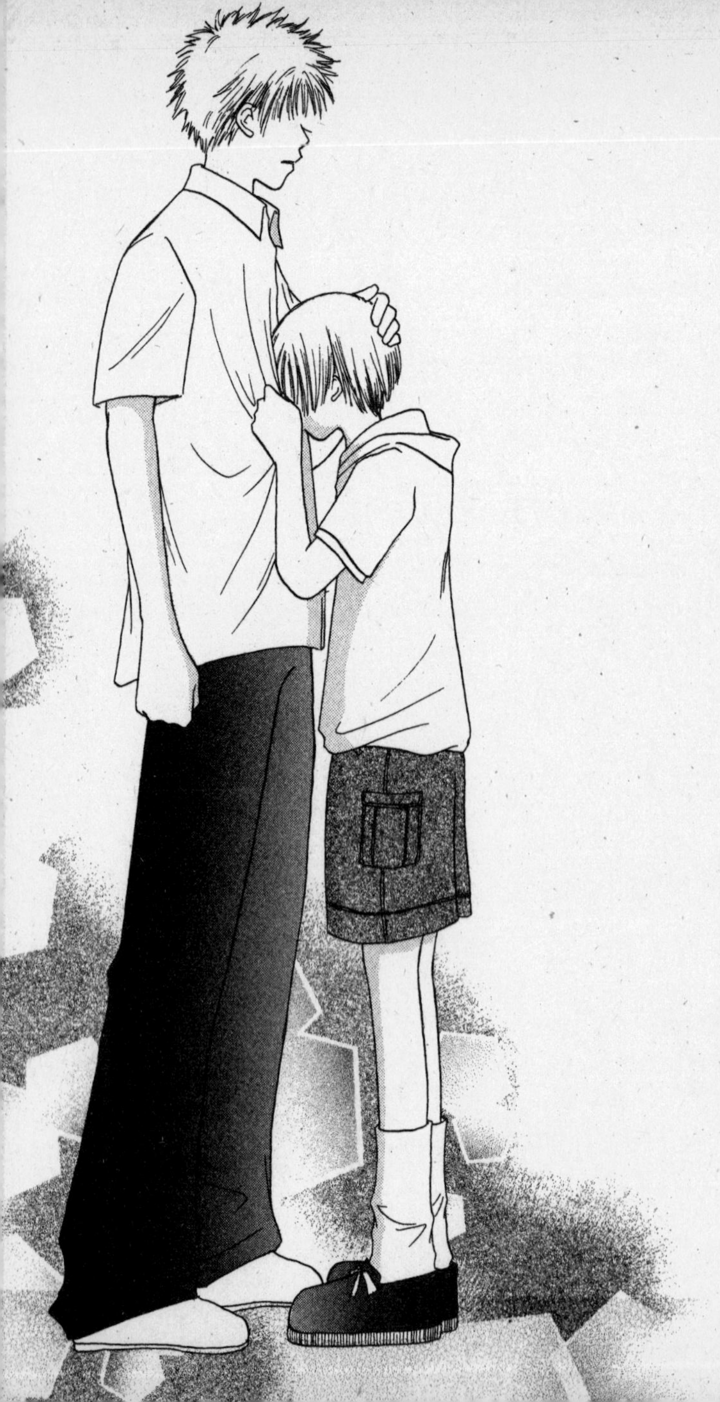

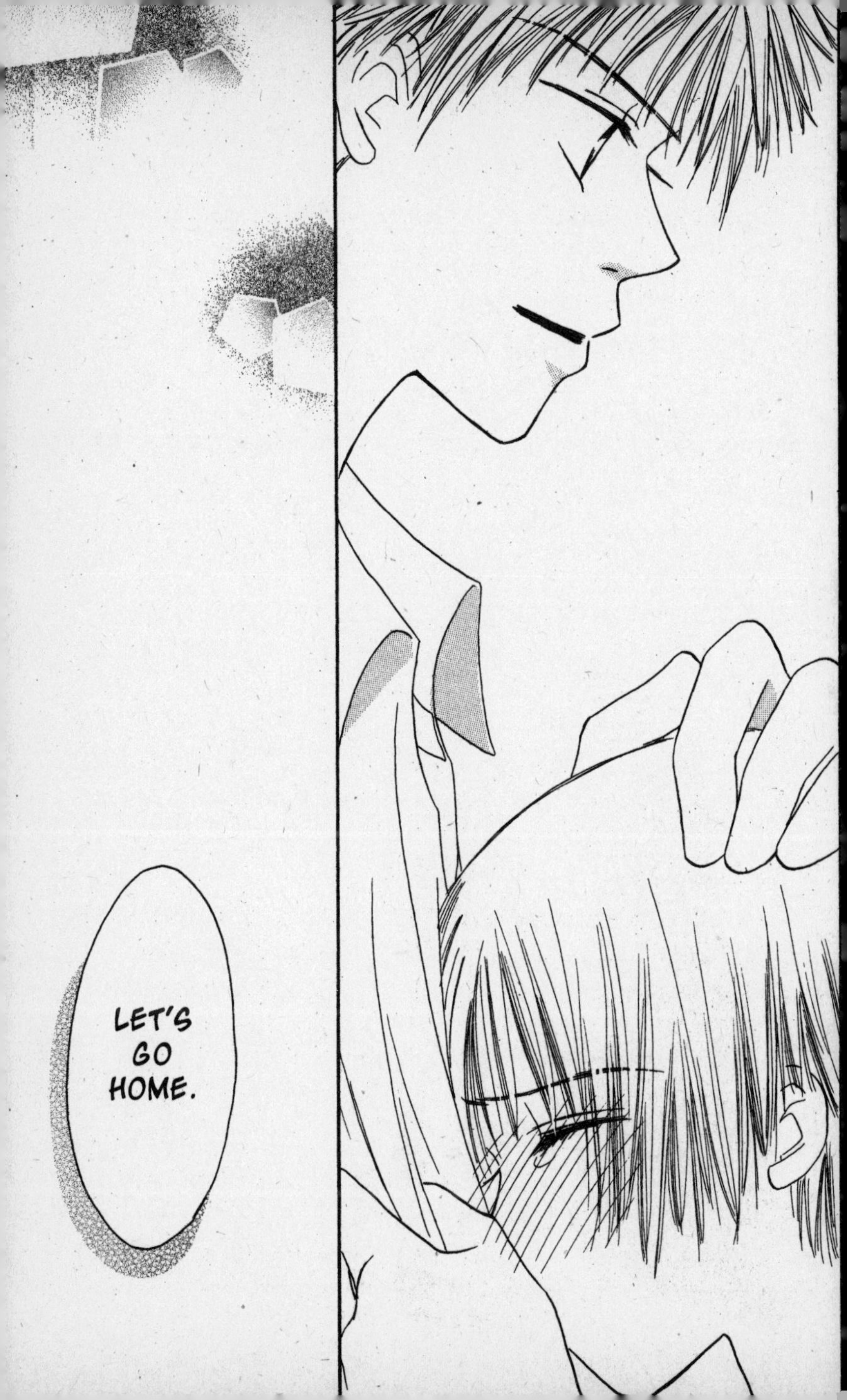
LET'S GO HOME.

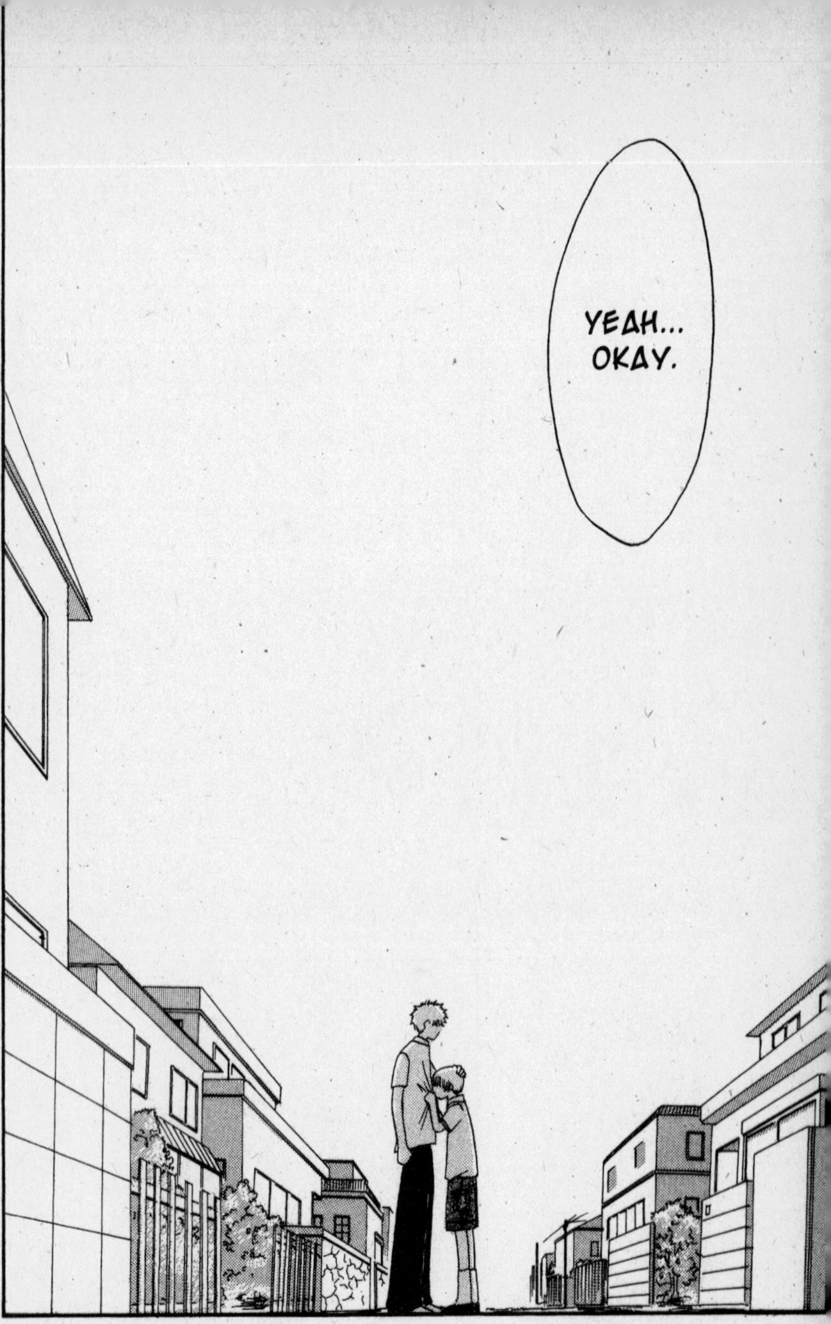
YEAH... OKAY.

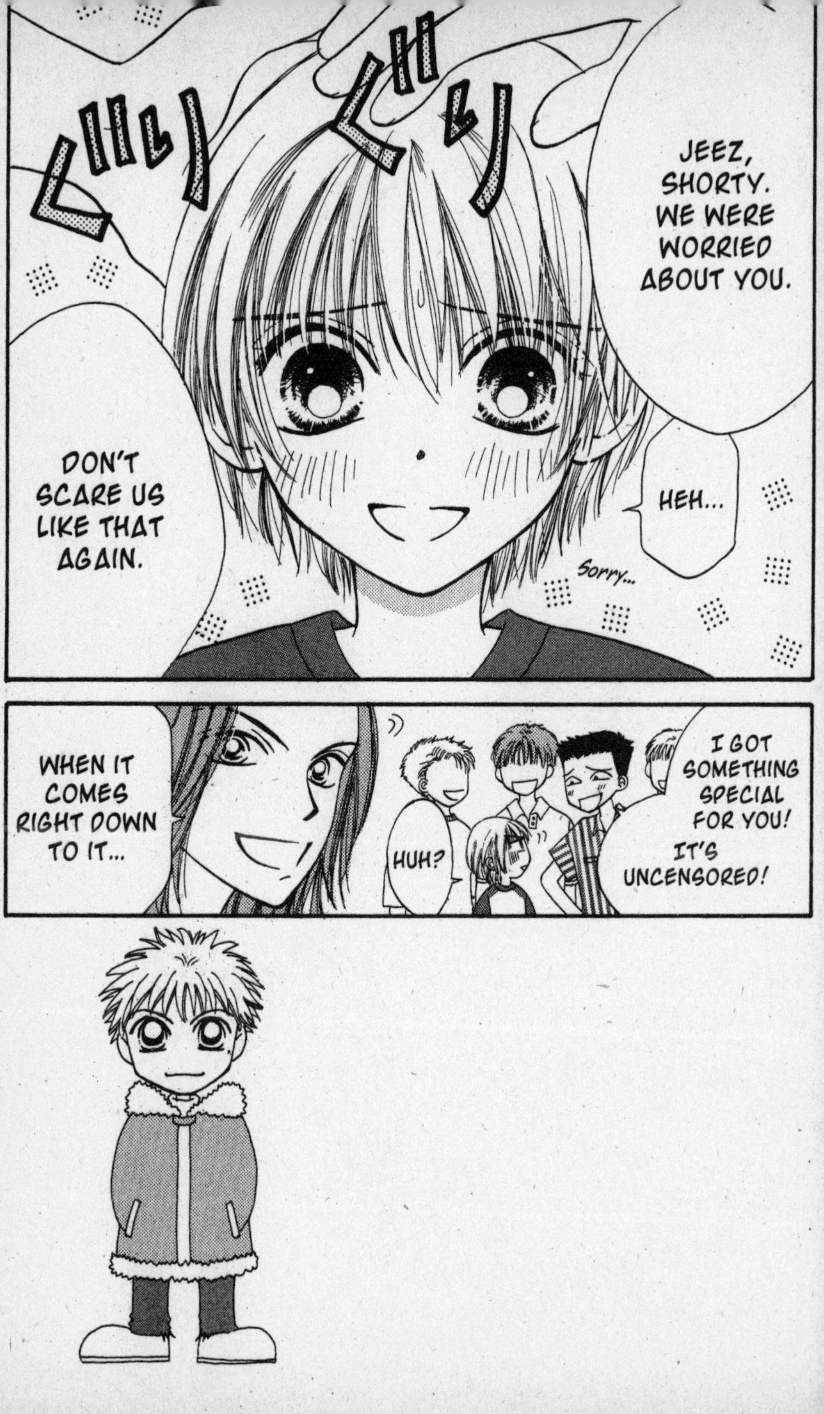
JEEZ, SHORTY. WE WERE WORRIED ABOUT YOU.
HEH...
DON'T SCARE US LIKE THAT AGAIN.
Sorry...
I GOT SOMETHING SPECIAL FOR YOU!
IT'S UNCENSORED!
HUH?
WHEN IT COMES RIGHT DOWN TO IT...

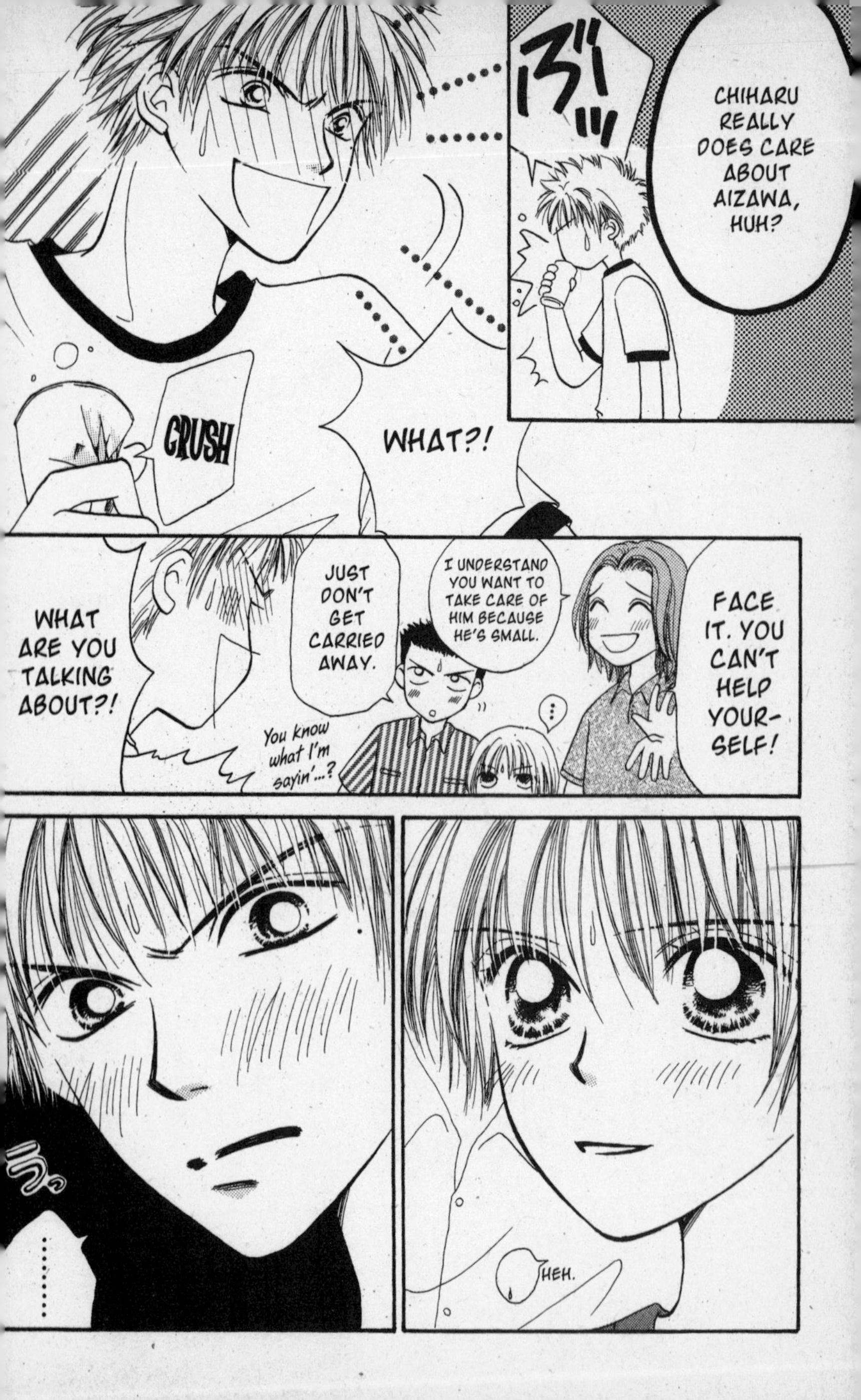
CHIHARU REALLY DOES CARE ABOUT AIZAWA, HUH?
WHAT?!
CRUSH
FACE IT. YOU CAN'T HELP YOURSELF!
I UNDERSTAND YOU WANT TO TAKE CARE OF HIM BECAUSE HE'S SMALL.
...
JUST DON'T GET CARRIED AWAY.
You know what I'm sayin'...?
WHAT ARE YOU TALKING ABOUT?!
HEH.
......

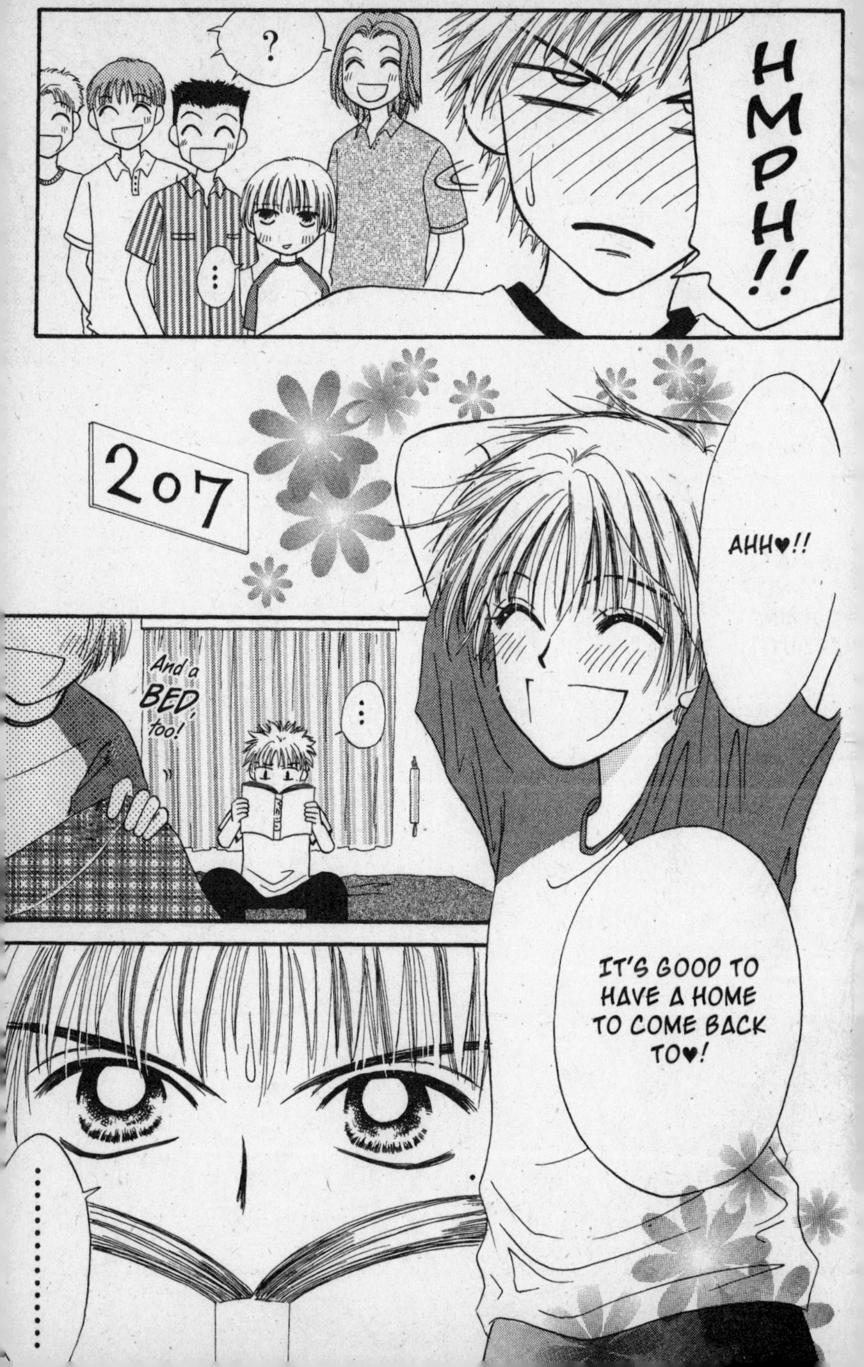
HMPH!!
?
...
AHH♥!!
IT'S GOOD TO HAVE A HOME TO COME BACK TO♥!
207
And a BED, too!
...
......

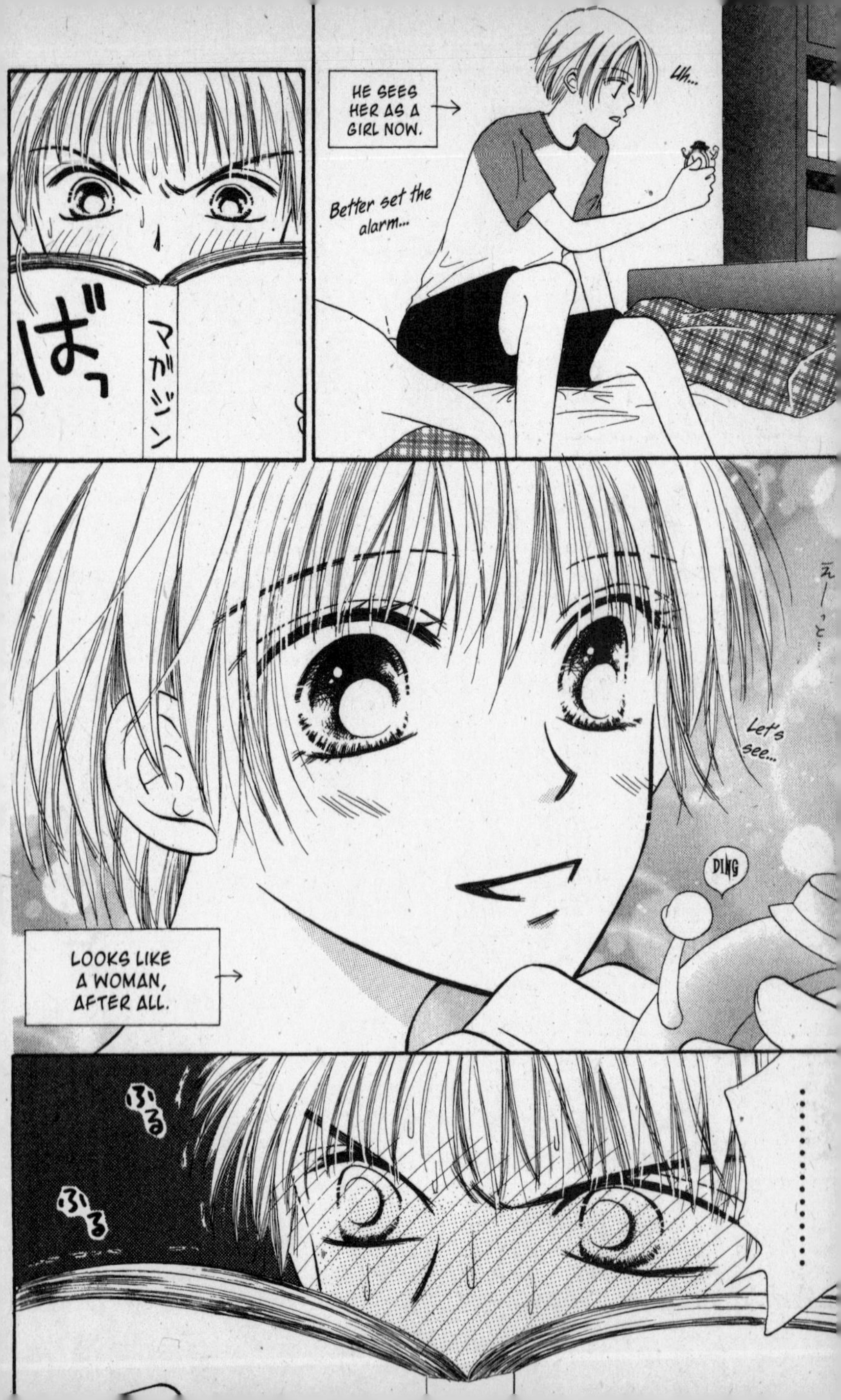
Uh...
HE SEES HER AS A GIRL NOW.
Better set the alarm...
マガジン
ばっ
えーっと…
Let's see...
DING
LOOKS LIKE A WOMAN, AFTER ALL.
……
ふる
ふる

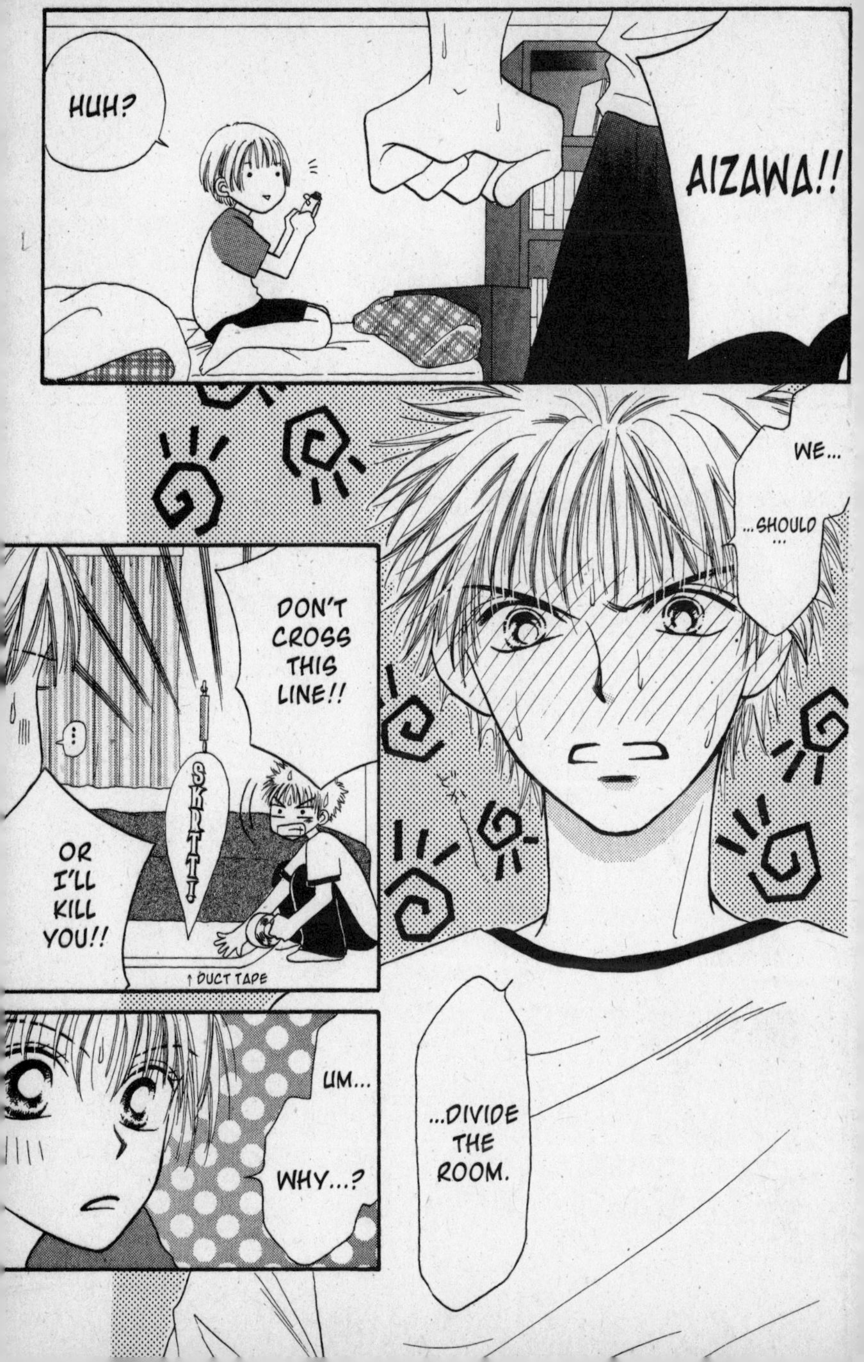

AIZAWA!!
HUH?
WE...
...SHOULD...
...DIVIDE THE ROOM.
DON'T CROSS THIS LINE!!
OR I'LL KILL YOU!!
SKRTTT!
↑ DUCT TAPE
...
UM...
WHY...?

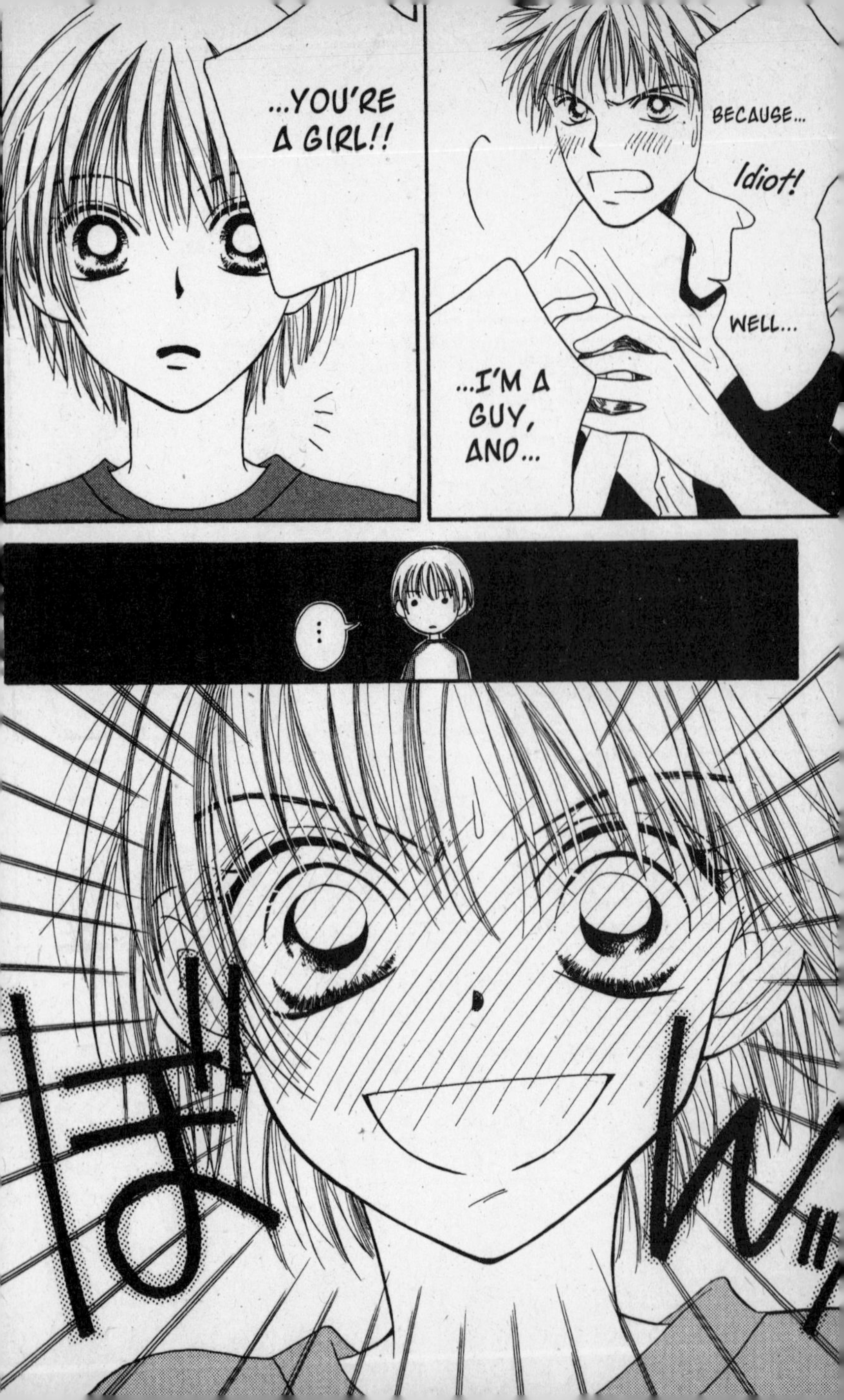
BECAUSE...
Idiot!
WELL...
...I'M A GUY, AND...
...YOU'RE A GIRL!!
...

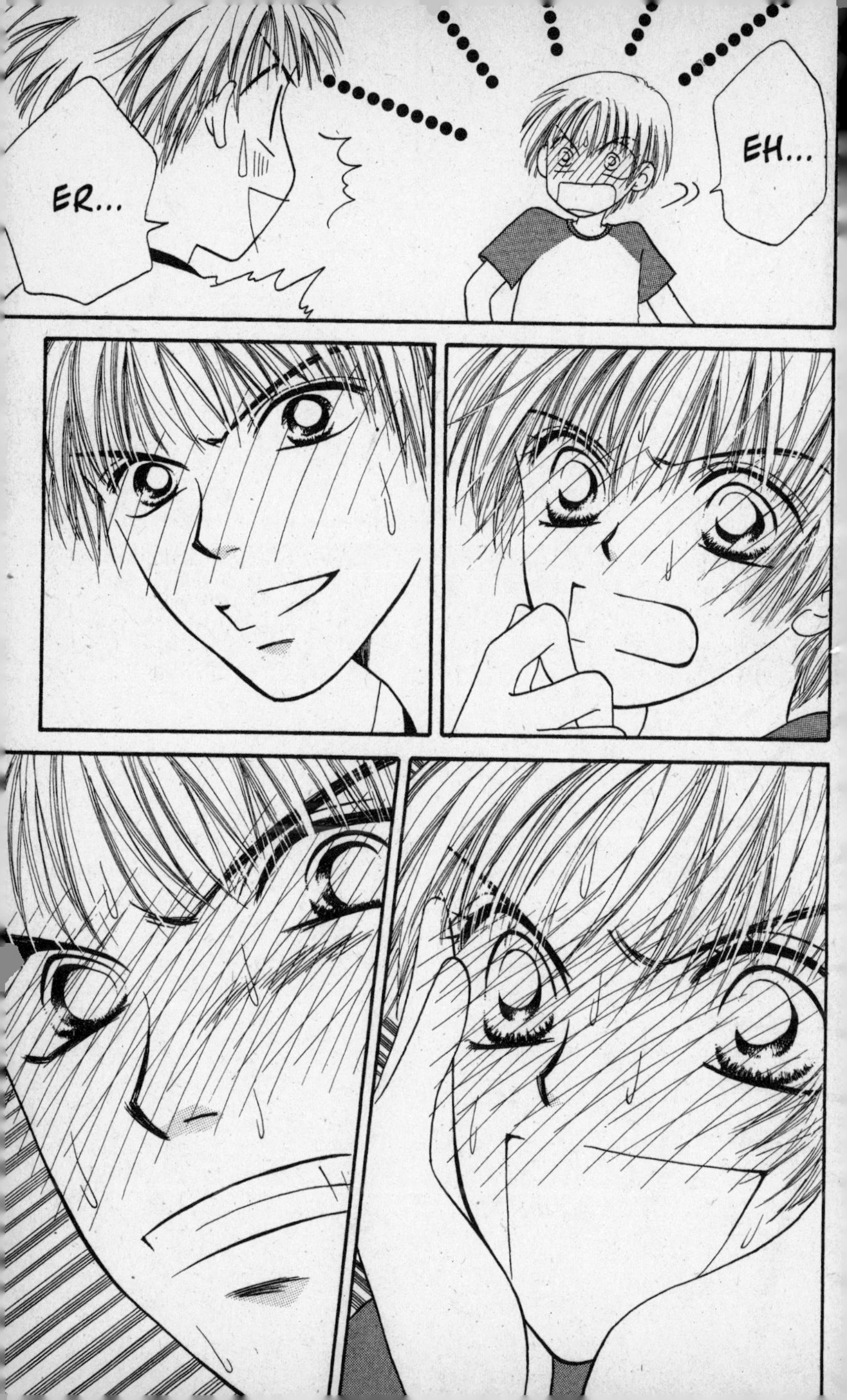
EH...
ER...

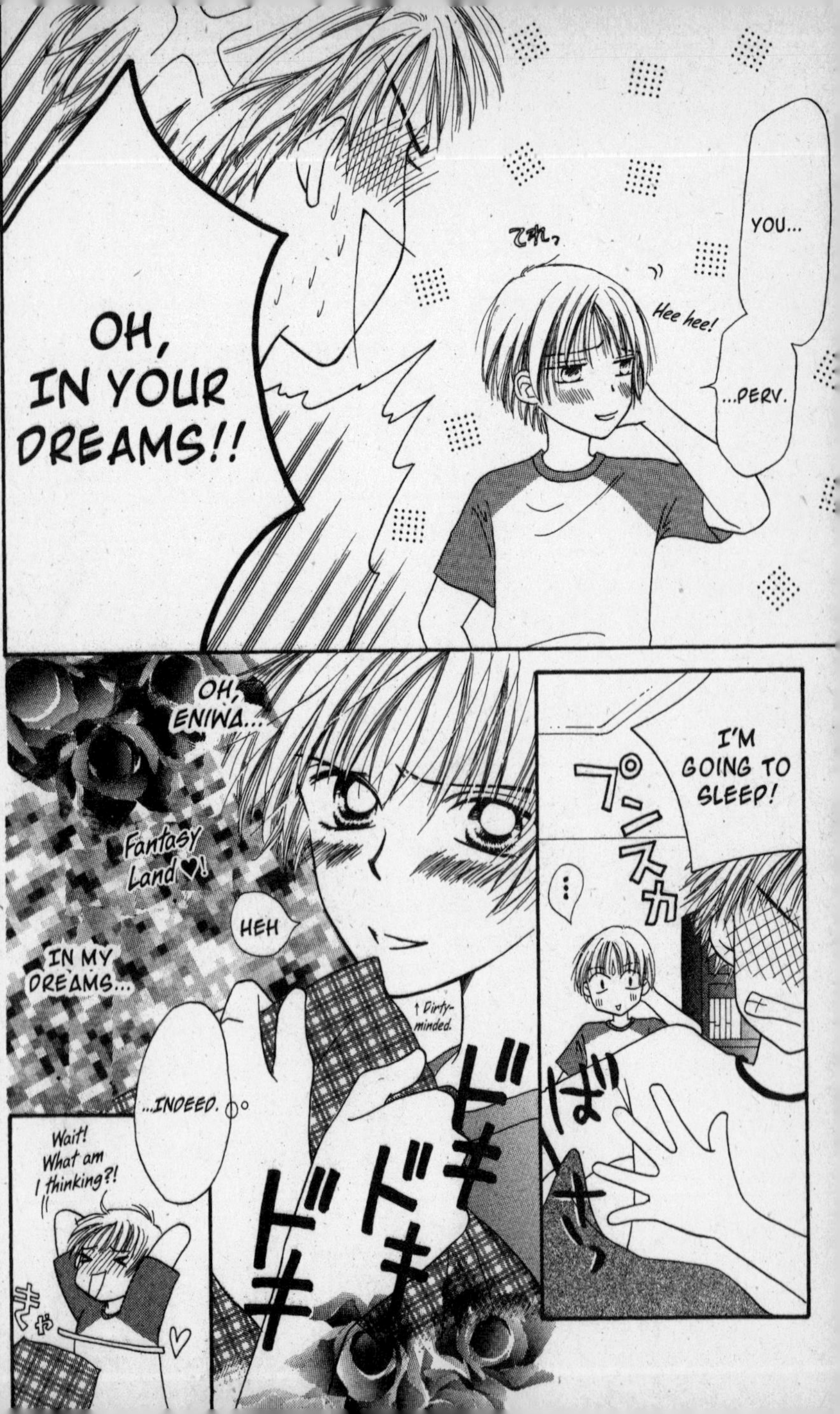
YOU...
...PERV.
Hee hee!
てれっ
OH, IN YOUR DREAMS!!
I'M GOING TO SLEEP!
プンスカ
...
ばさっ
OH, ENIWA...
Fantasy Land♥!
HEH
IN MY DREAMS...
↑ Dirty-minded.
...INDEED.
ドキドキドキ
Wait! What am I thinking?!
きゃ
♥

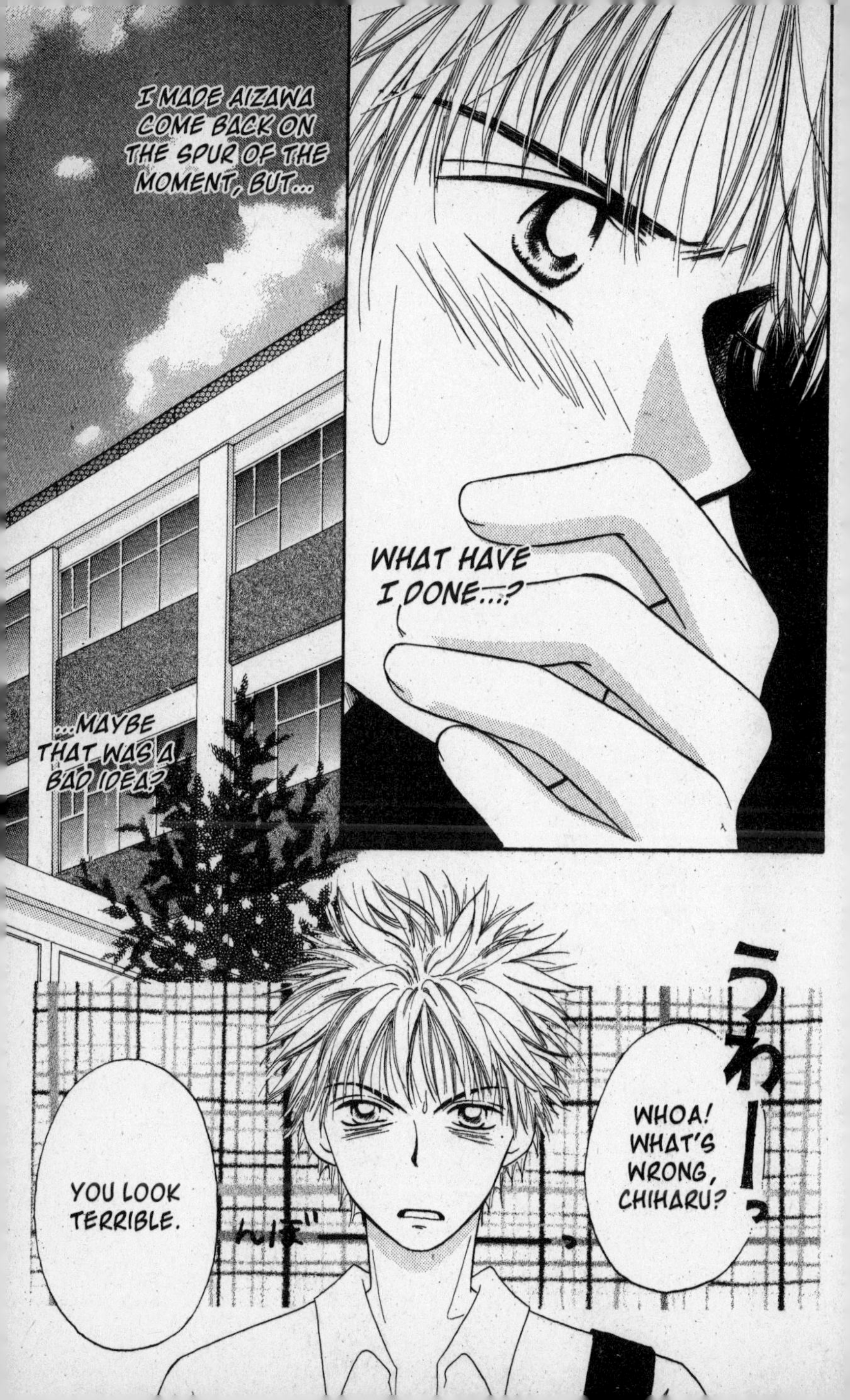
WHAT HAVE I DONE...?
I MADE AIZAWA COME BACK ON THE SPUR OF THE MOMENT, BUT...
...MAYBE THAT WAS A BAD IDEA?
うわーっ
WHOA! WHAT'S WRONG, CHIHARU?
んぼー
YOU LOOK TERRIBLE.

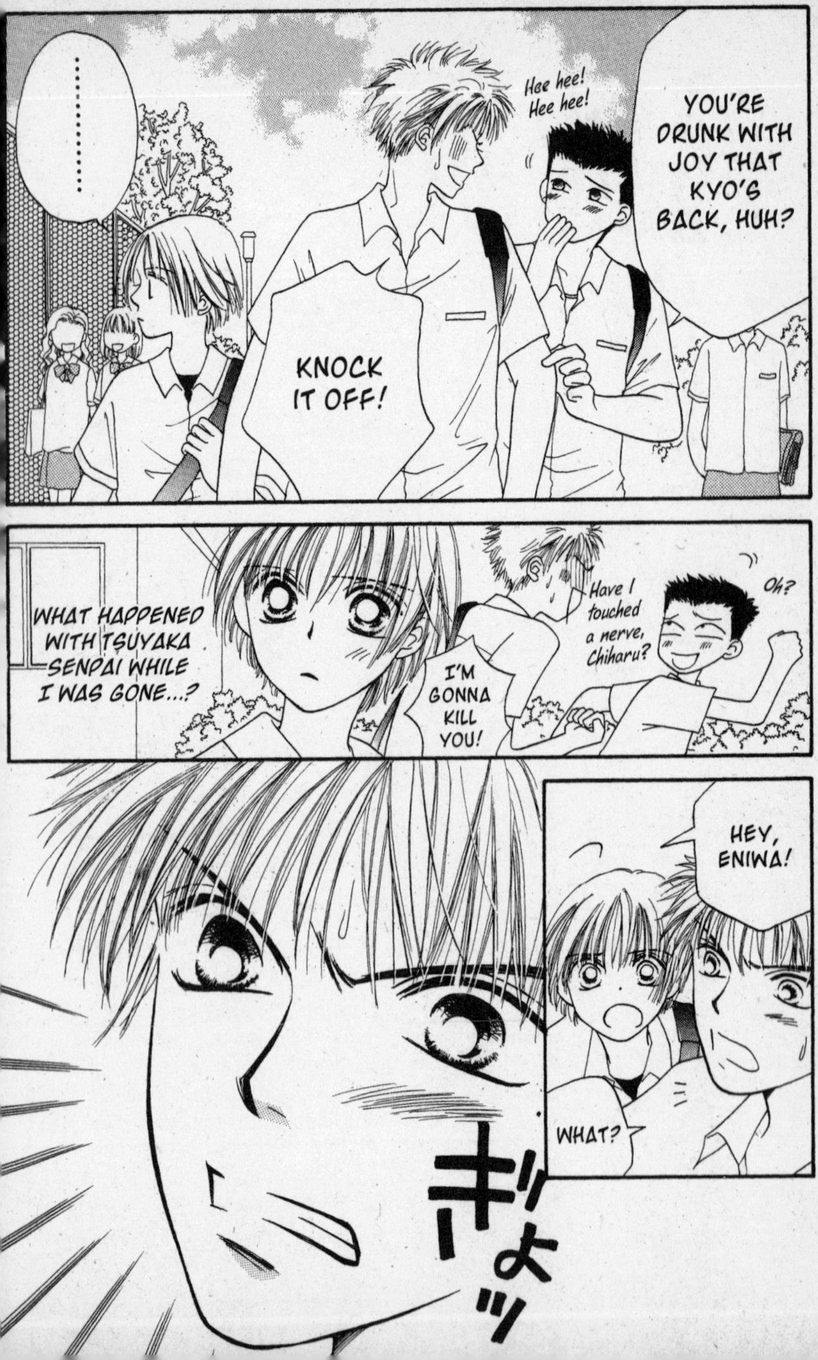
YOU'RE DRUNK WITH JOY THAT KYO'S BACK, HUH?
Hee hee! Hee hee!
KNOCK IT OFF!
……
Oh?
Have I touched a nerve, Chiharu?
I'M GONNA KILL YOU!
WHAT HAPPENED WITH TSUYAKA SENPAI WHILE I WAS GONE...?
HEY, ENIWA!
WHAT?
ギょッ

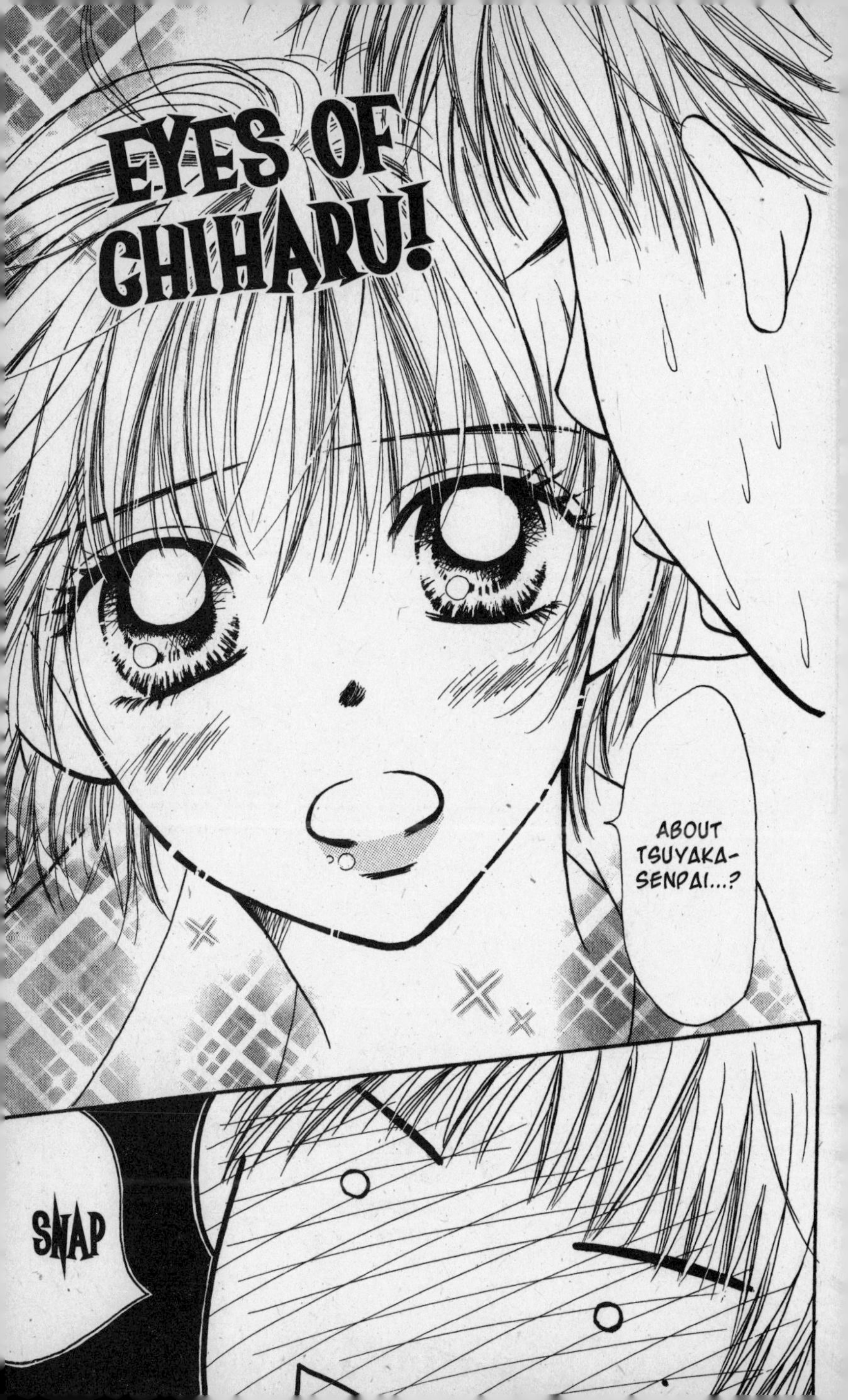
EYES OF CHIHARU!
ABOUT TSUYAKA-SENPAI...?
SNAP

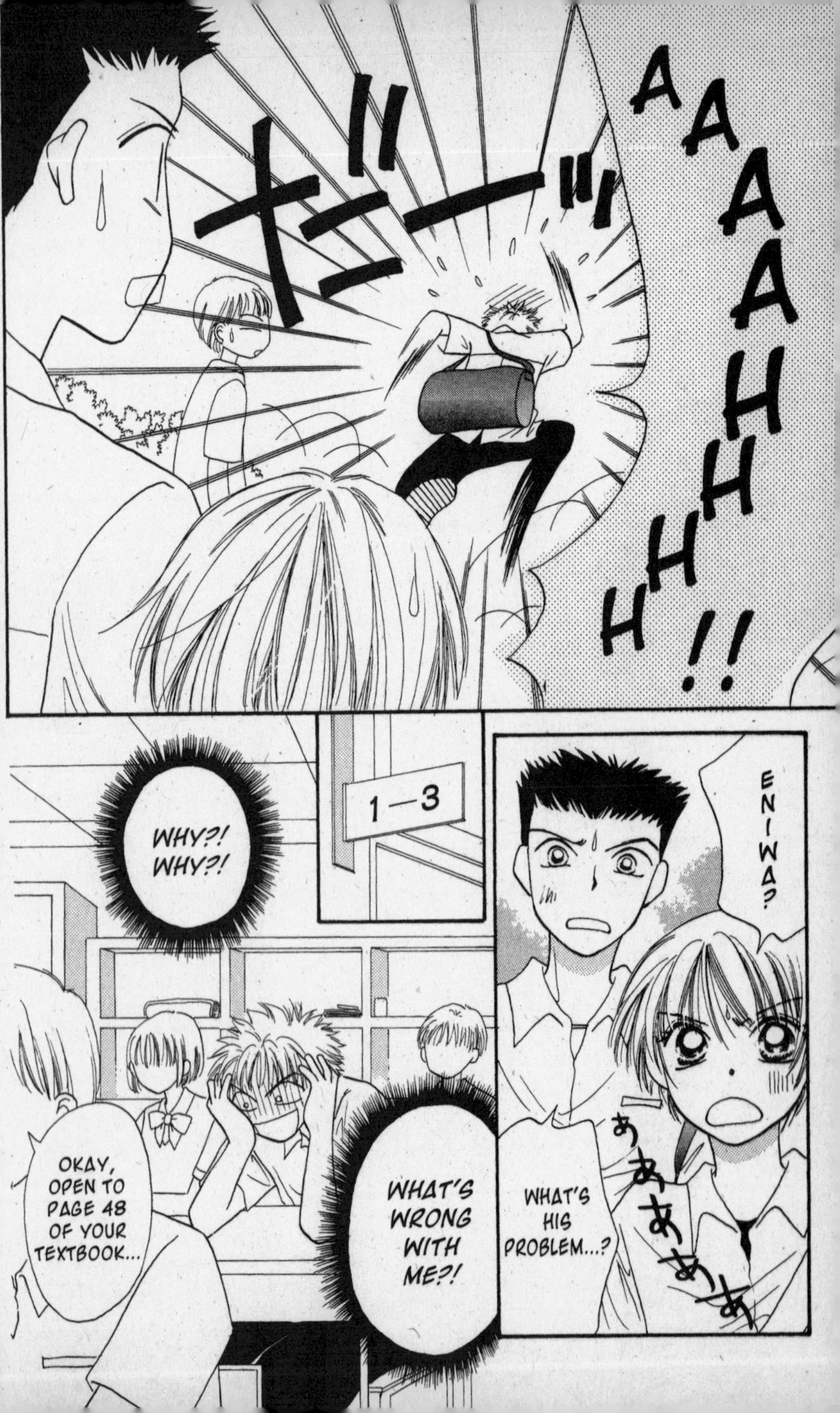
AAAAHHHHH!!
ENIWA?
WHAT'S HIS PROBLEM...?
ああああ
1—3
WHY?! WHY?!
WHAT'S WRONG WITH ME?!
OKAY, OPEN TO PAGE 48 OF YOUR TEXTBOOK...

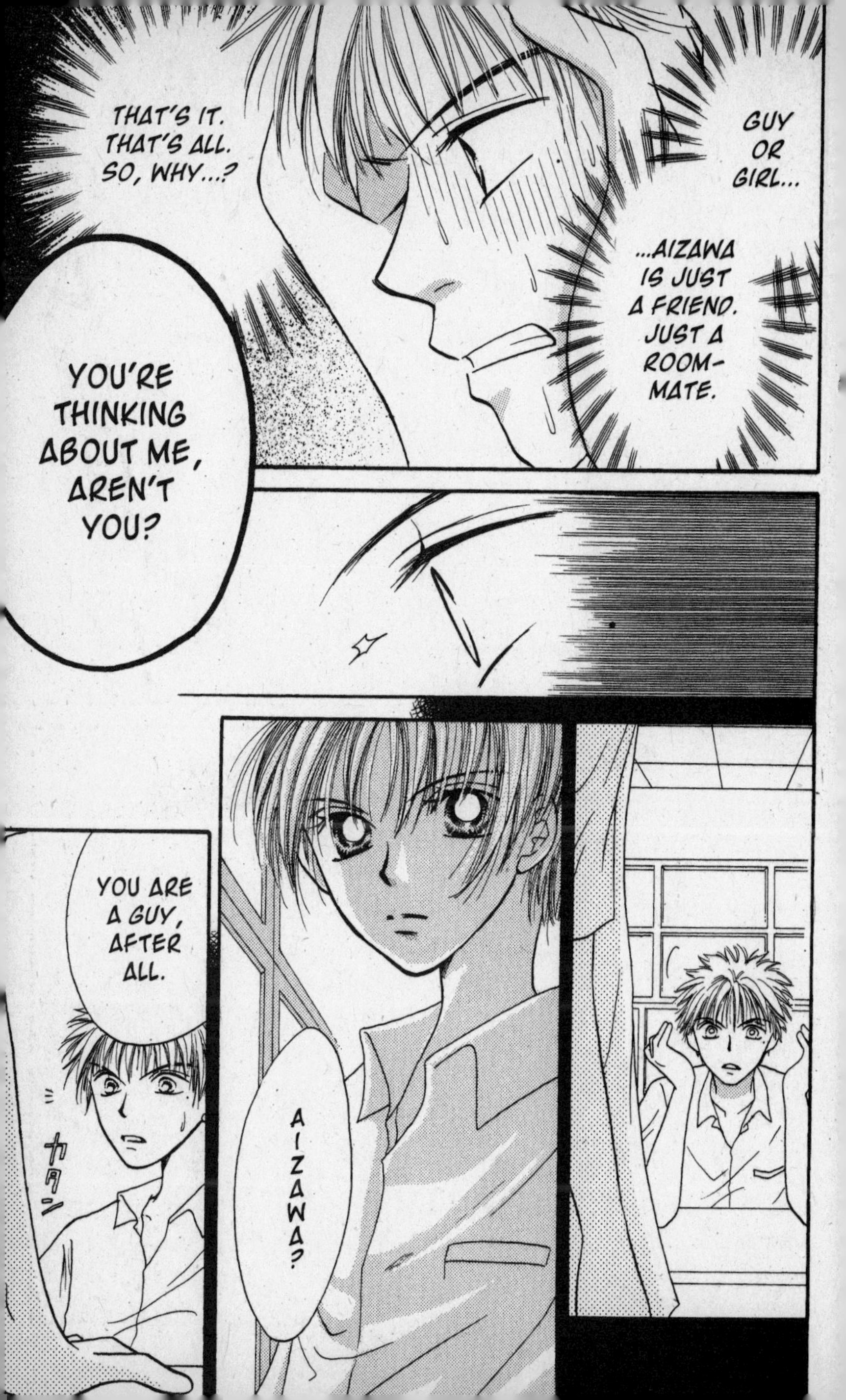
GUY OR GIRL...
...AIZAWA IS JUST A FRIEND. JUST A ROOM-MATE.
THAT'S IT. THAT'S ALL. SO, WHY...?
YOU'RE THINKING ABOUT ME, AREN'T YOU?
AIZAWA?
YOU ARE A GUY, AFTER ALL.

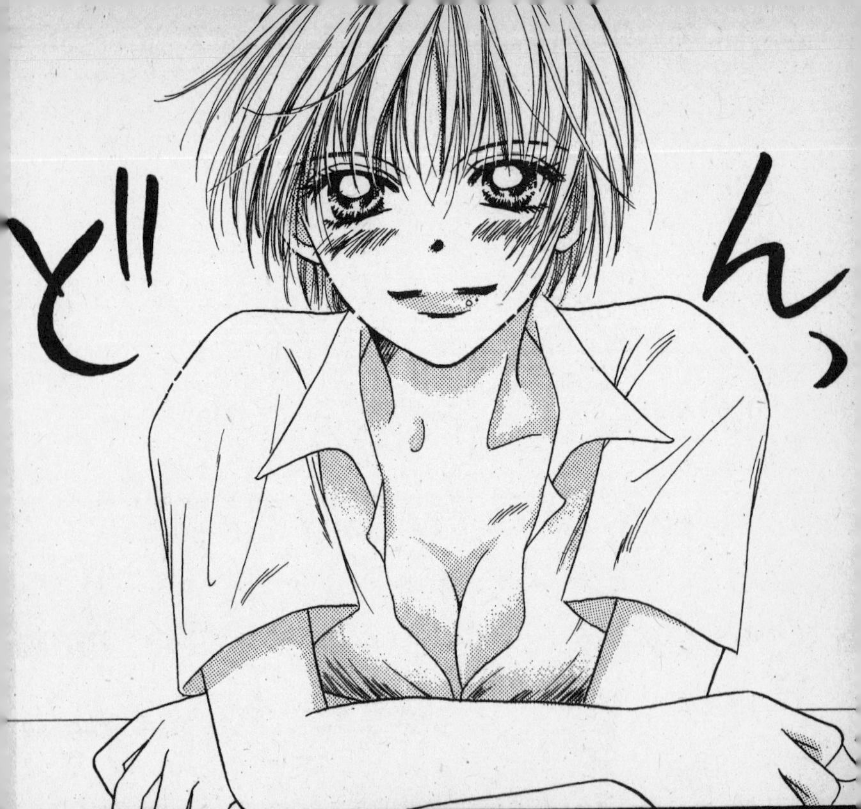
どん

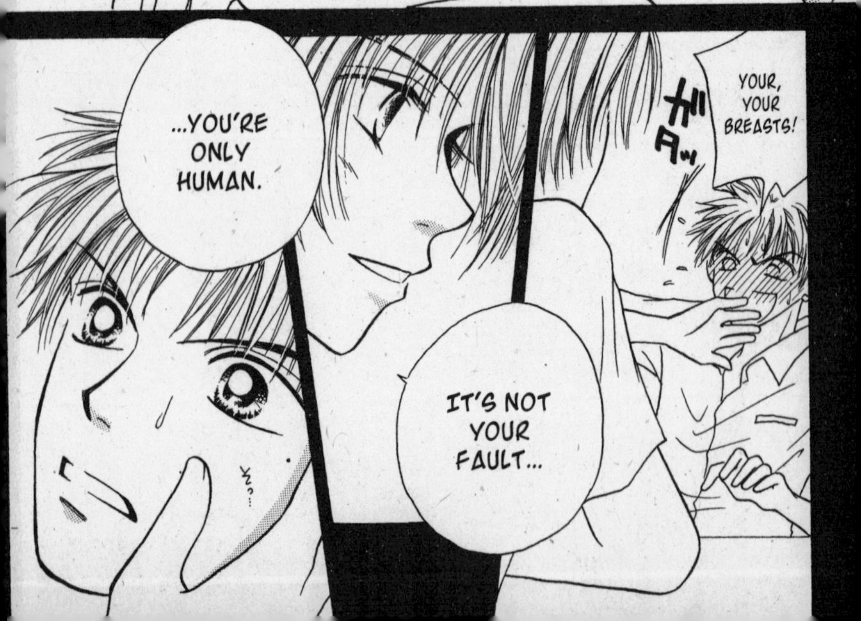
YOUR, YOUR BREASTS!
...YOU'RE ONLY HUMAN.
IT'S NOT YOUR FAULT...

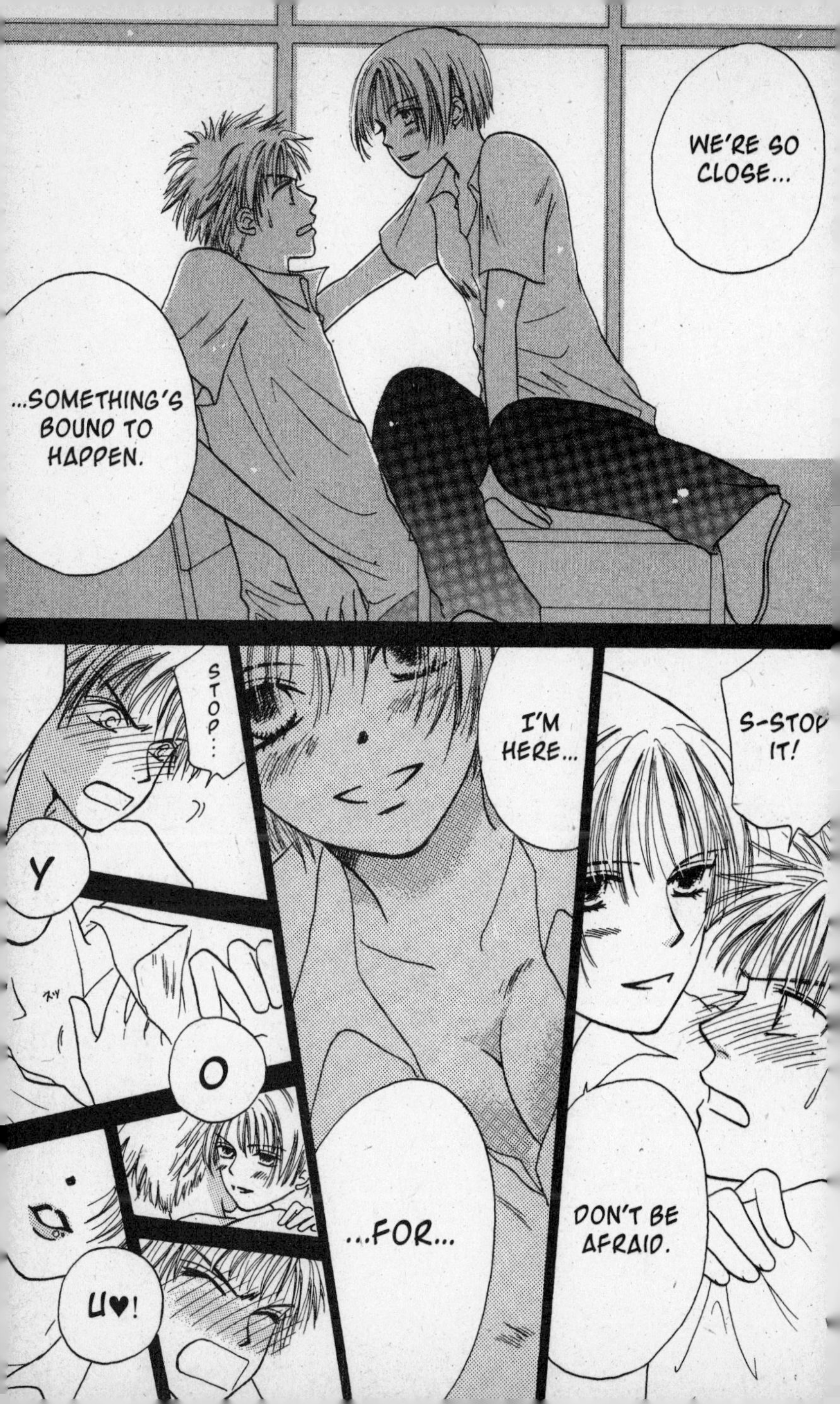

WE'RE SO CLOSE...
...SOMETHING'S BOUND TO HAPPEN.
S-STOP IT!
DON'T BE AFRAID.
I'M HERE...
...FOR...
STOP...
Y
O
U♥!

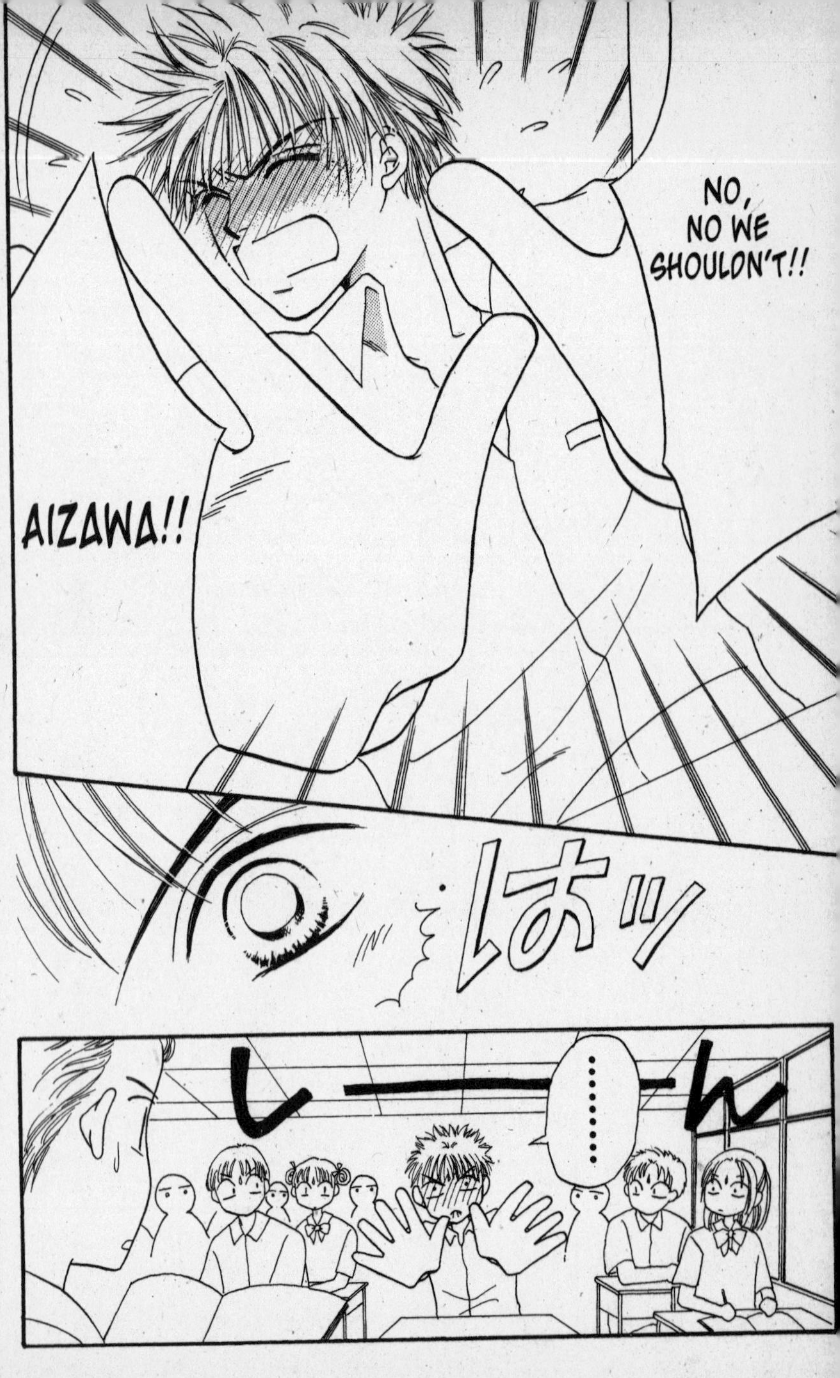
NO, NO WE SHOULDN'T!!
AIZAWA!!
はッ
しーーん
……

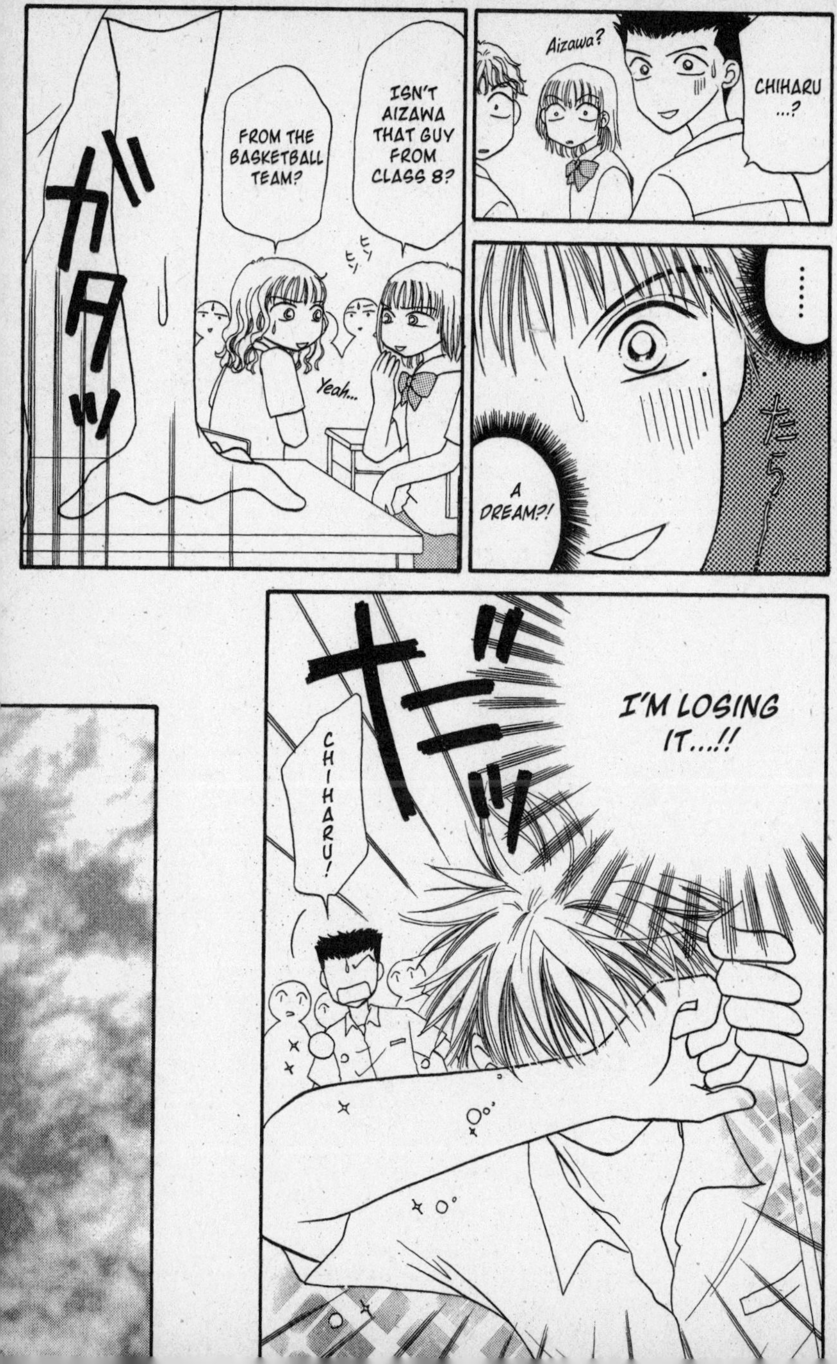
Aizawa?
CHIHARU ...?
......
A DREAM?!
たら
ISN'T AIZAWA THAT GUY FROM CLASS 8?
FROM THE BASKETBALL TEAM?
ヒソヒソ
Yeah...
ガタッ
ギュッ
I'M LOSING IT....!!
CHIHARU!

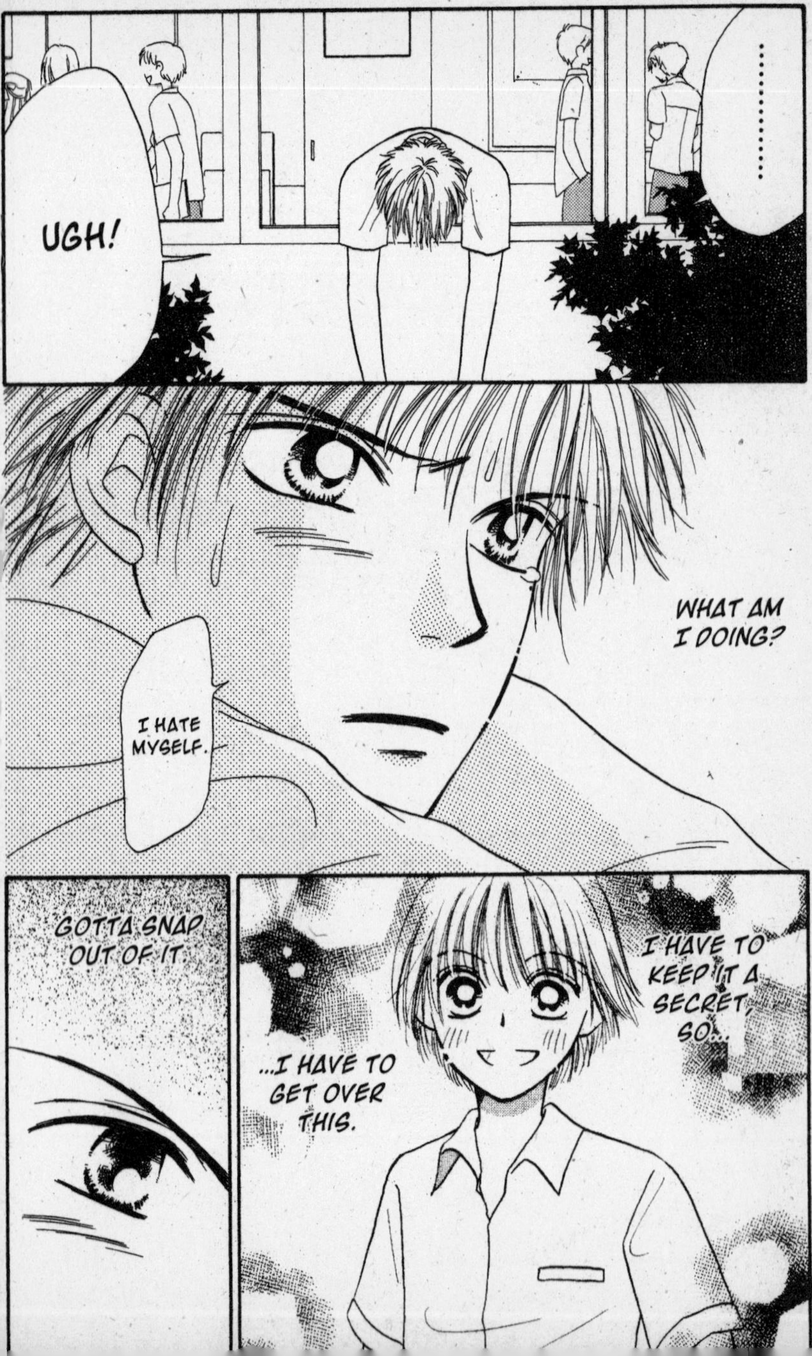
......
UGH!
WHAT AM I DOING?
I HATE MYSELF.
I HAVE TO KEEP IT A SECRET, SO...
...I HAVE TO GET OVER THIS.
GOTTA SNAP OUT OF IT.

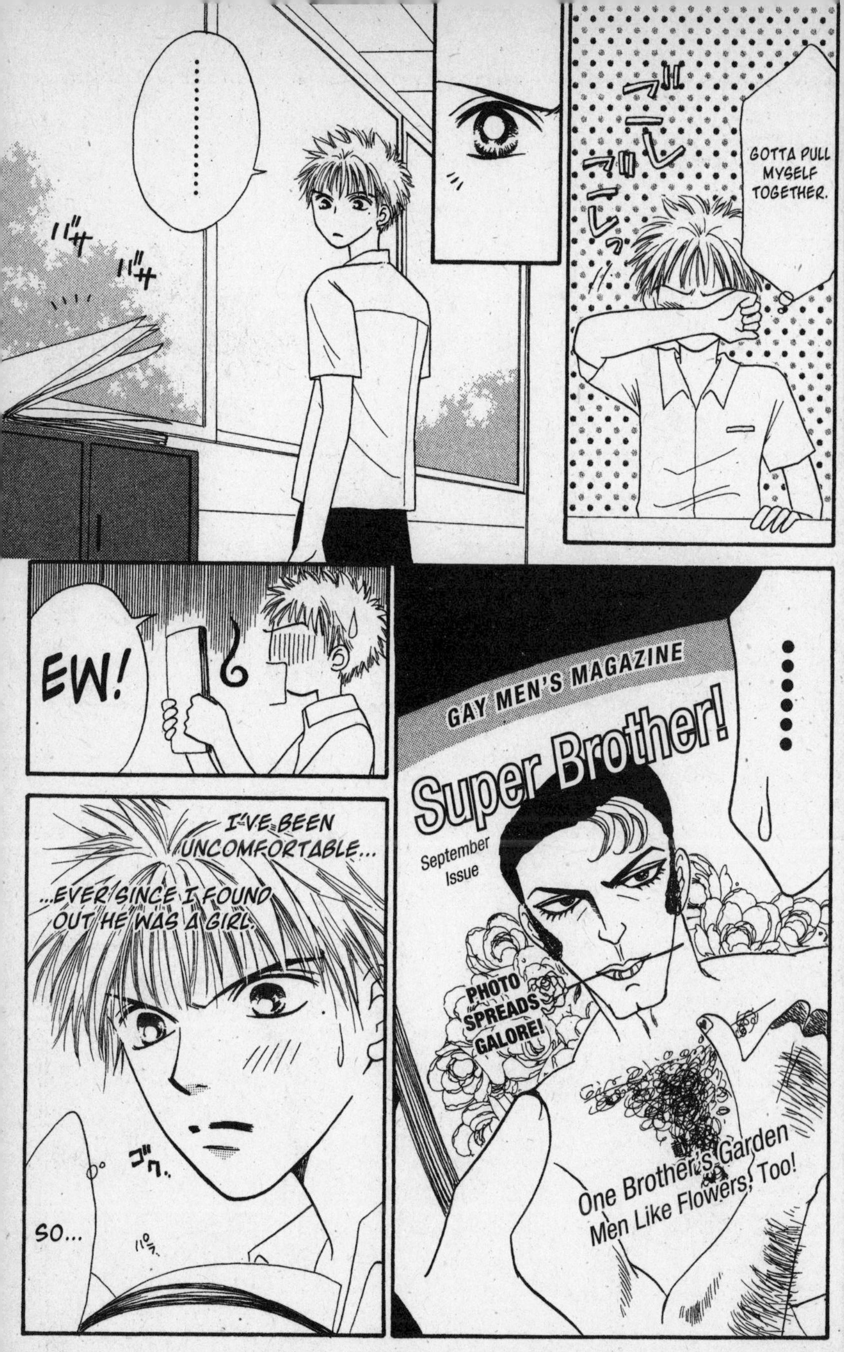
GOTTA PULL MYSELF TOGETHER.
......
バサ
バサ
......
GAY MEN'S MAGAZINE
Super Brother!
September Issue
PHOTO SPREADS GALORE!
One Brother's Garden
Men Like Flowers, Too!
EW!
I'VE BEEN UNCOMFORTABLE...
...EVER SINCE I FOUND OUT HE WAS A GIRL.
SO...

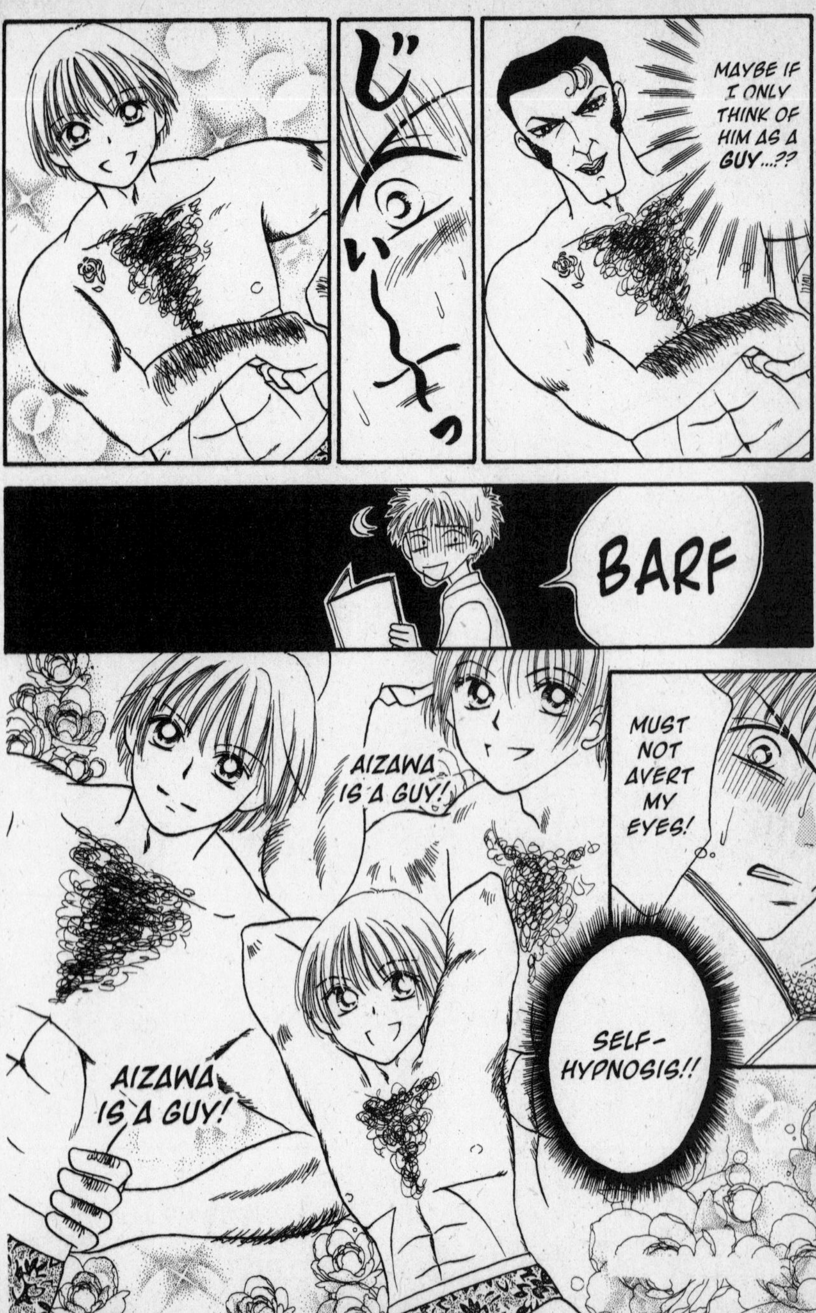
MAYBE IF I ONLY THINK OF HIM AS A GUY...??
じい〜っ
BARF
MUST NOT AVERT MY EYES!
AIZAWA IS A GUY!
SELF-HYPNOSIS!!
AIZAWA IS A GUY!

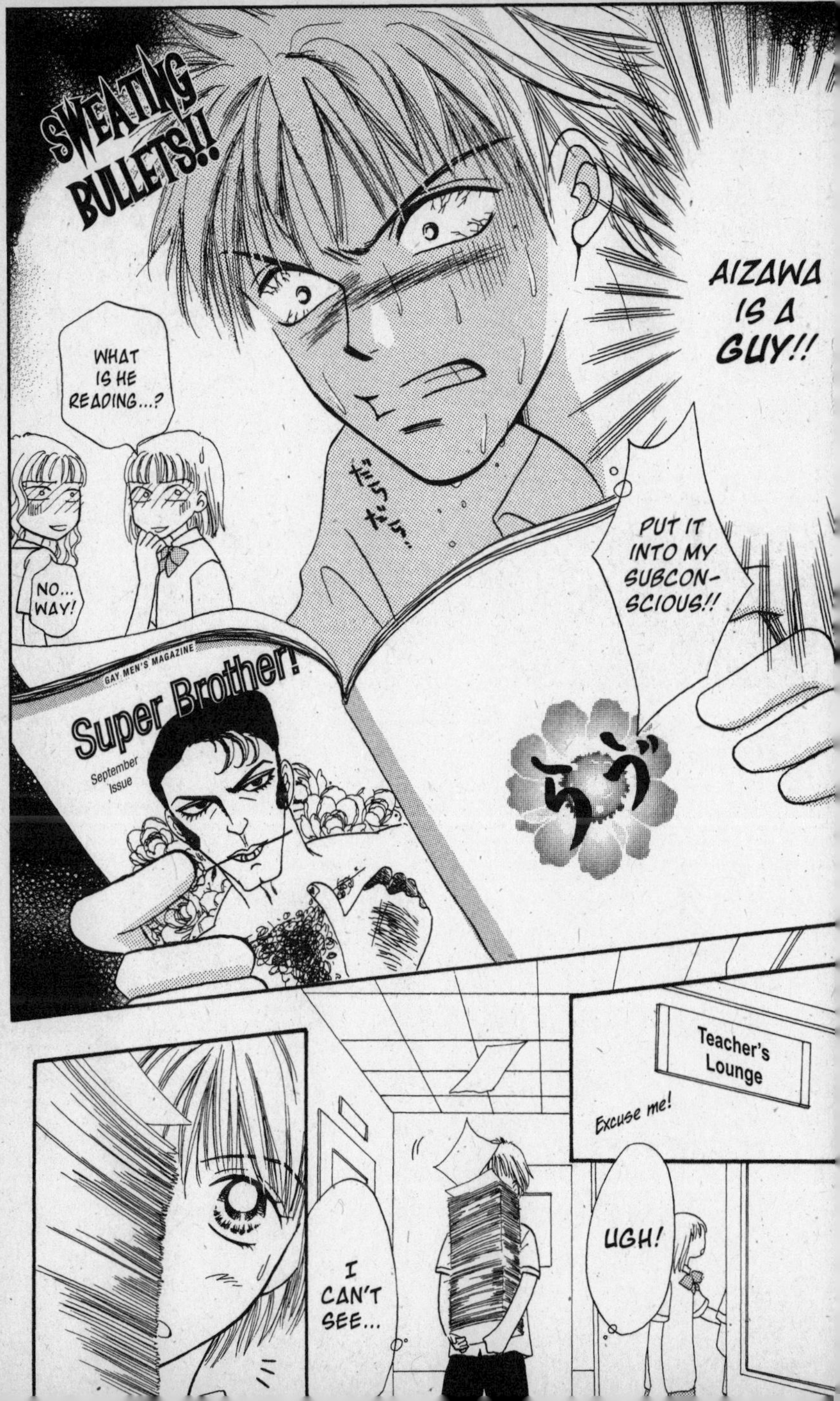
AIZAWA IS A GUY!!
PUT IT INTO MY SUBCONSCIOUS!!
SWEATING BULLETS!!
だらだら
WHAT IS HE READING...?
NO... WAY!
GAY MEN'S MAGAZINE
Super Brother!
September Issue
Teacher's Lounge
Excuse me!
UGH!
I CAN'T SEE...

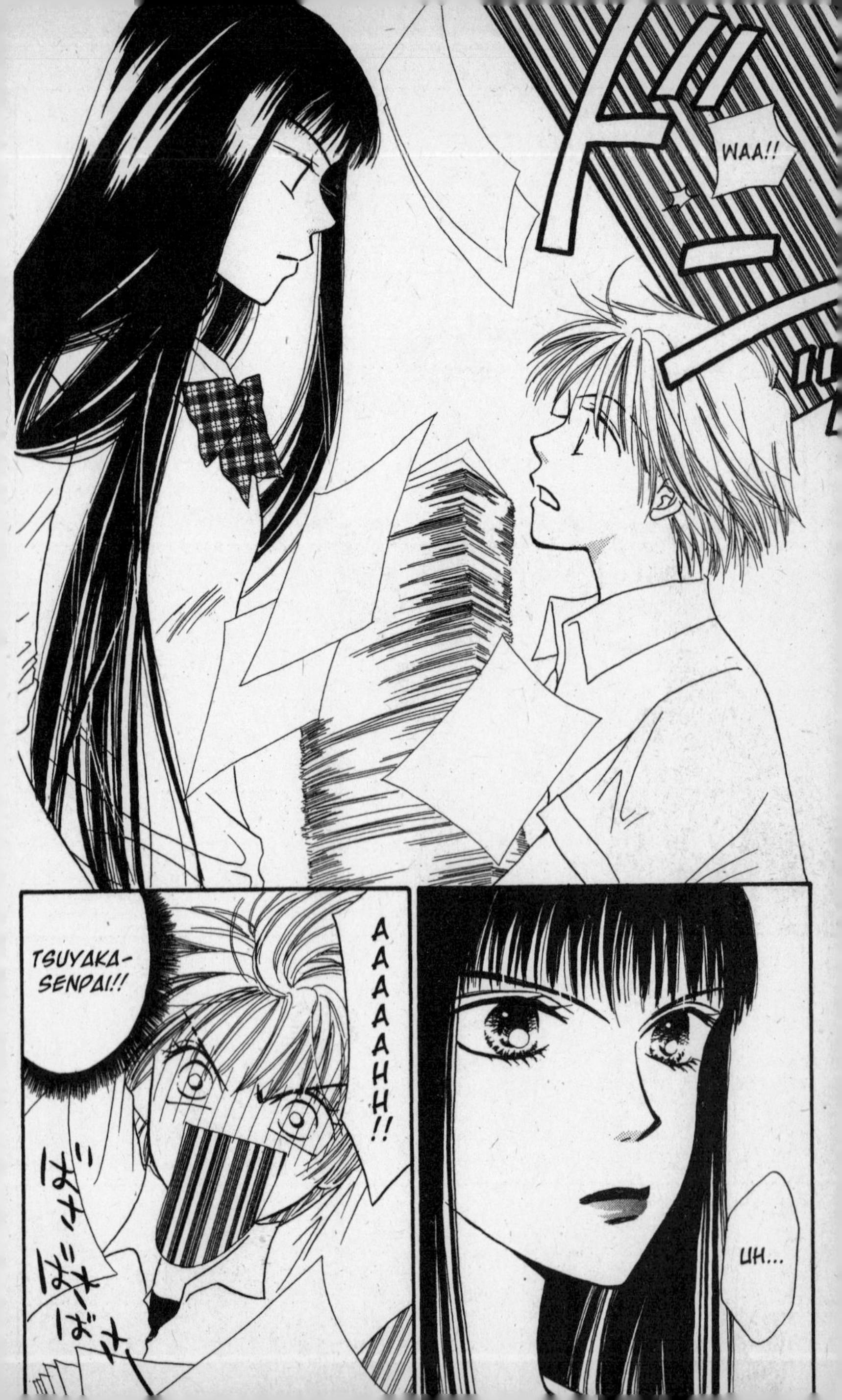
WAA!!
UH...
AAAAAAHH!!
TSUYAKA-SENPAI!!

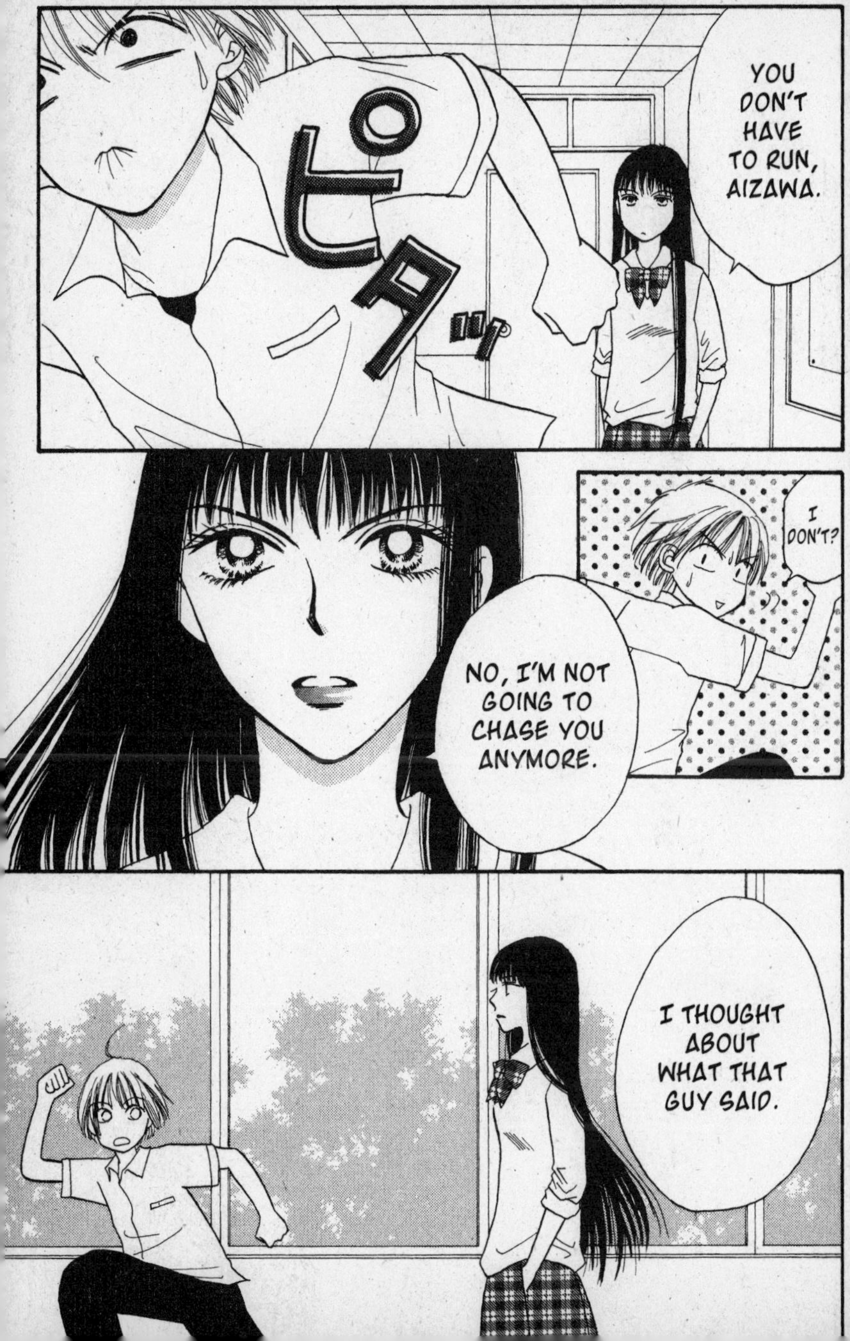
YOU DON'T HAVE TO RUN, AIZAWA.
ピタッ
I DON'T?
NO, I'M NOT GOING TO CHASE YOU ANYMORE.
I THOUGHT ABOUT WHAT THAT GUY SAID.

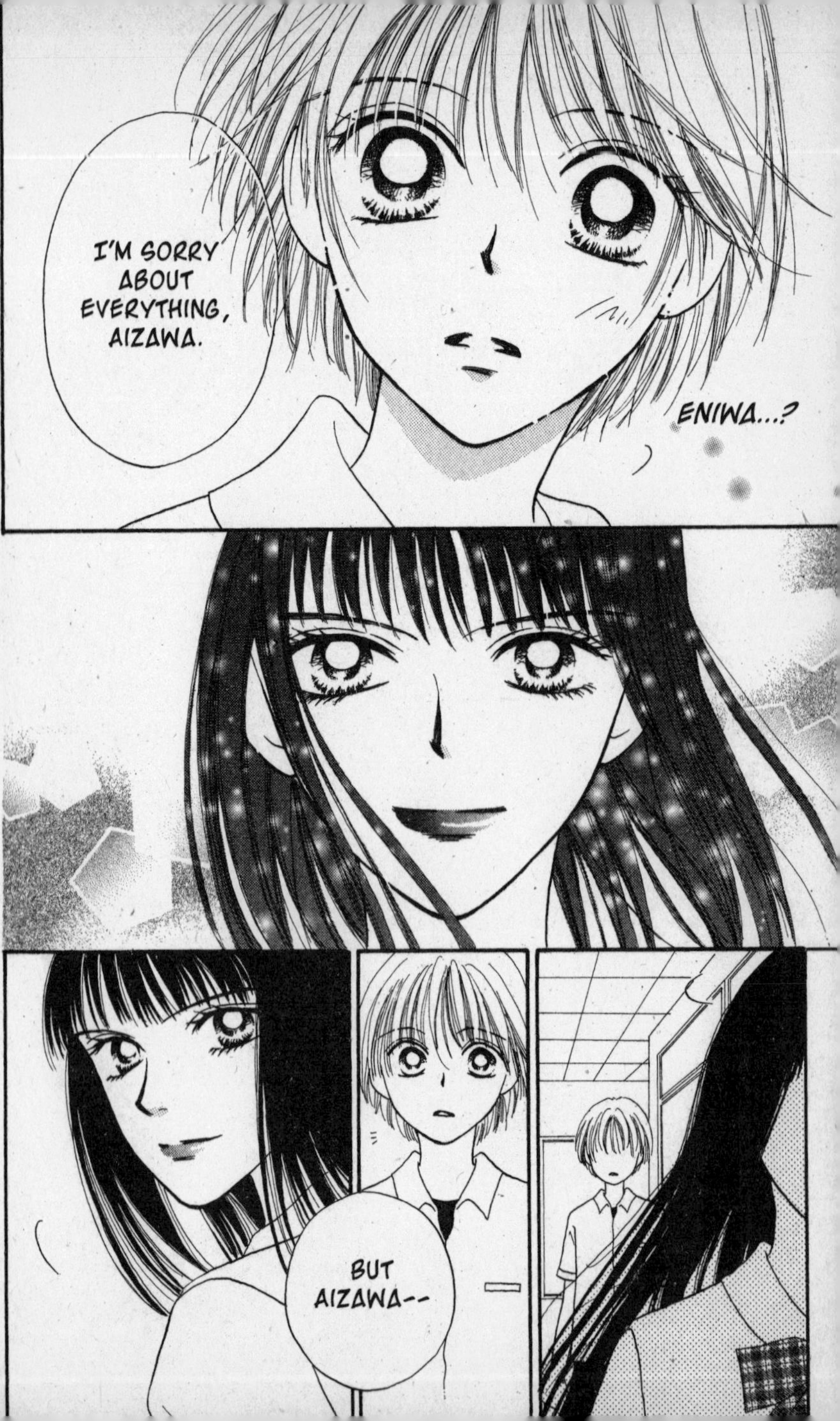
I'M SORRY ABOUT EVERYTHING, AIZAWA.
ENIWA...?
BUT AIZAWA--

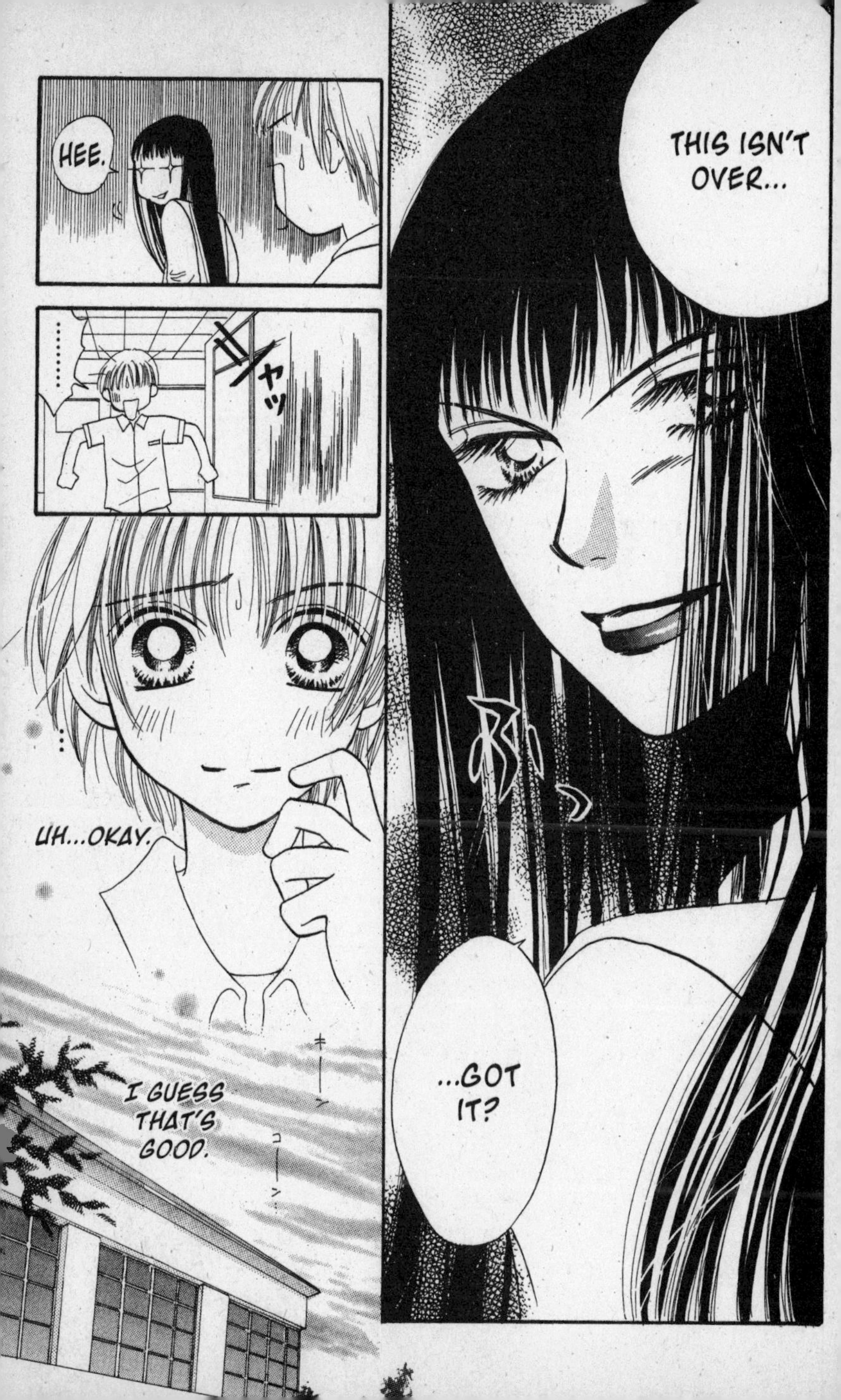
THIS ISN'T OVER...
...GOT IT?
HEE.
......
ニヤッ
......
UH...OKAY.
I GUESS THAT'S GOOD.
キーン
コーン…

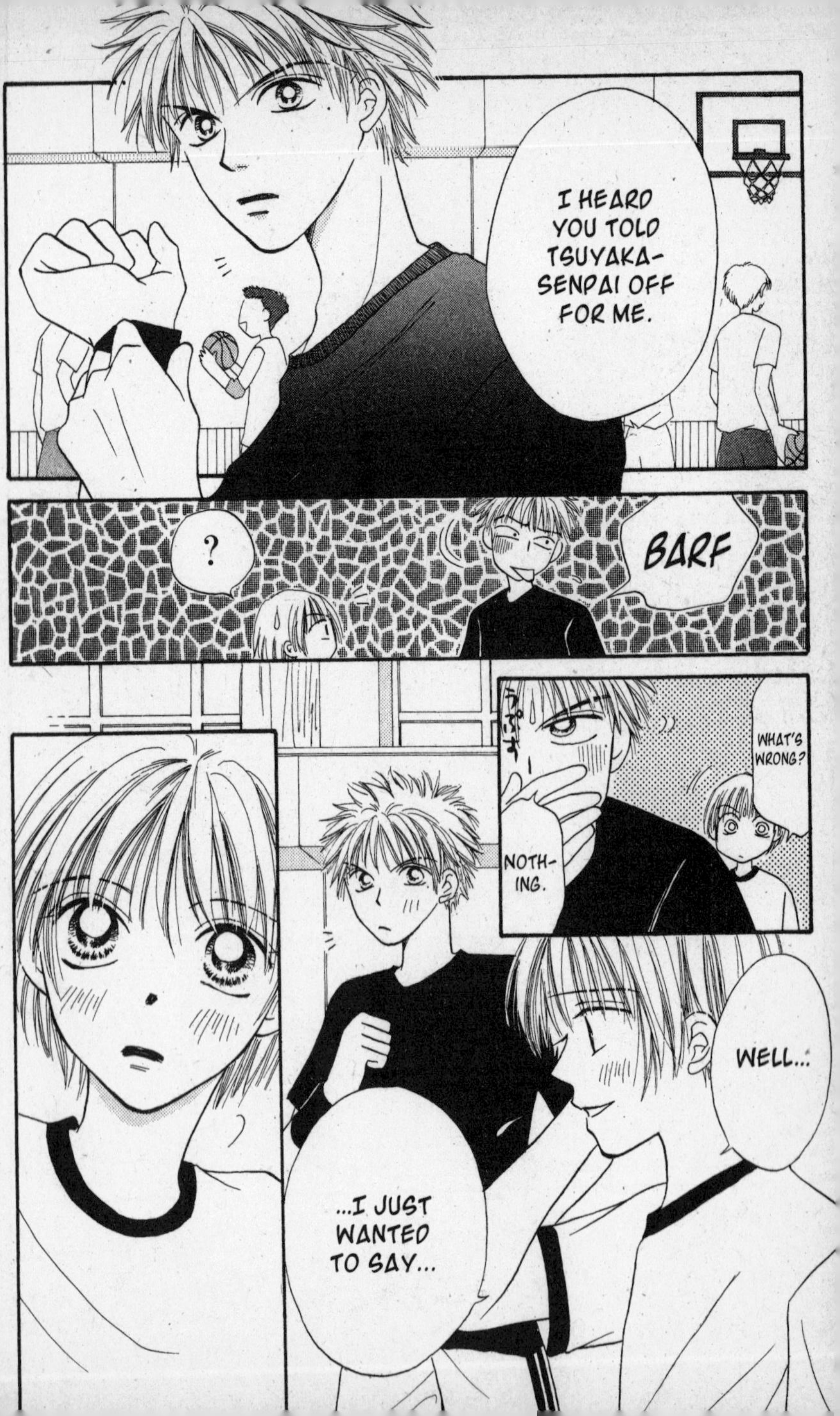
I HEARD YOU TOLD TSUYAKA-SENPAI OFF FOR ME.
BARF
?
WHAT'S WRONG?
NOTH-ING.
WELL...
...I JUST WANTED TO SAY...

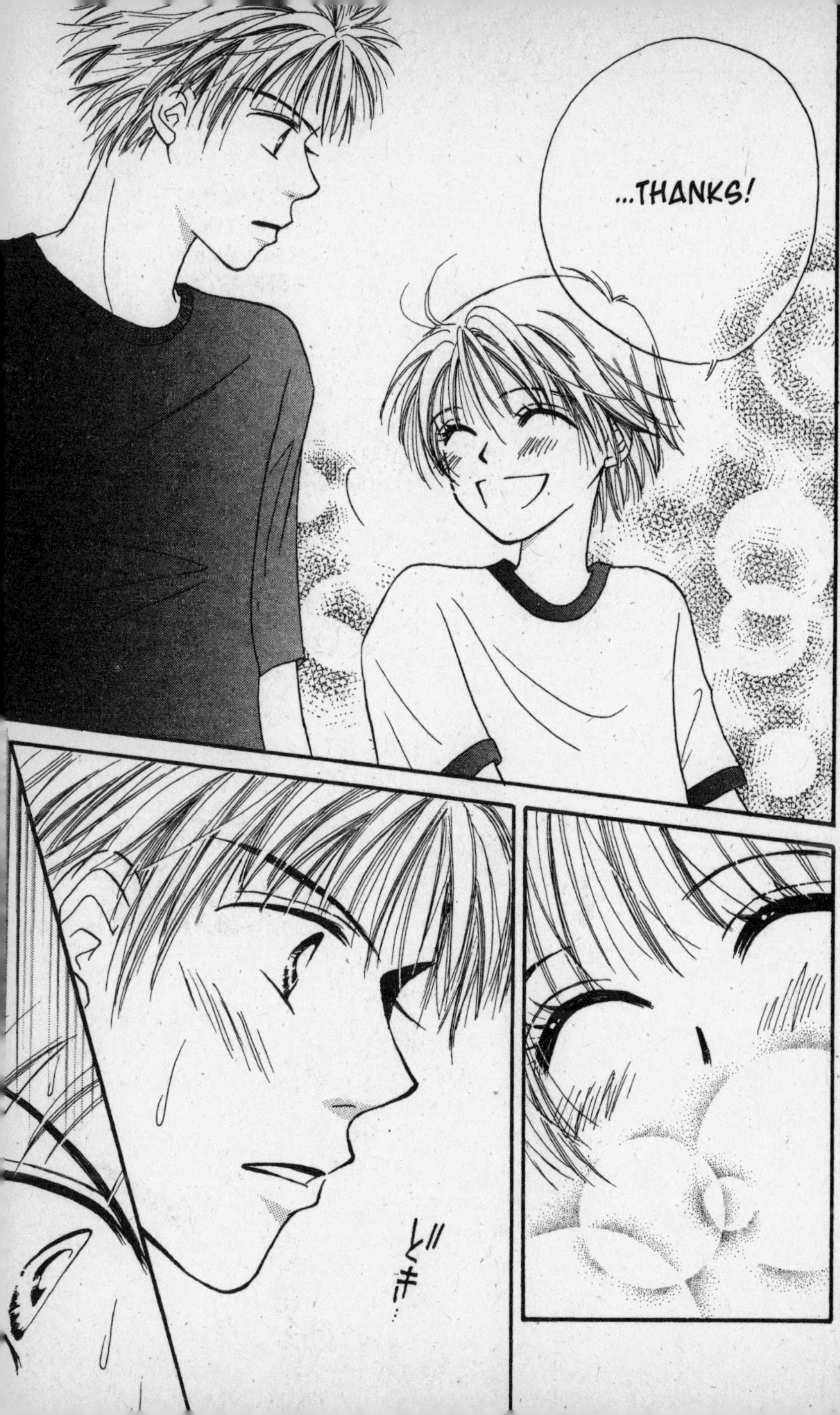
...THANKS!
どき...

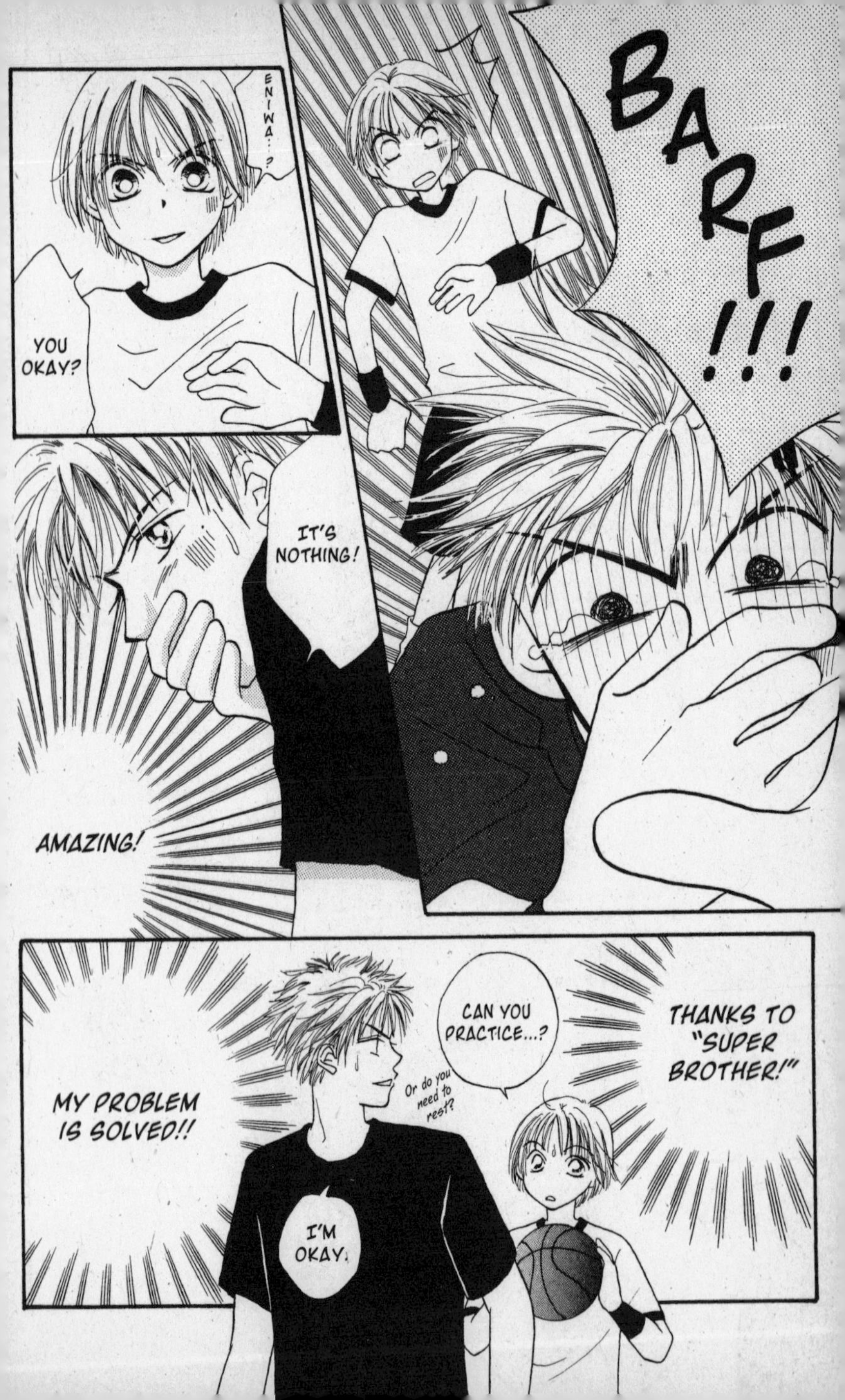
BARF!!!
ENIWA...?
YOU OKAY?
IT'S NOTHING!
AMAZING!
THANKS TO "SUPER BROTHER!"
CAN YOU PRACTICE...?
Or do you need to rest?
MY PROBLEM IS SOLVED!!
I'M OKAY.

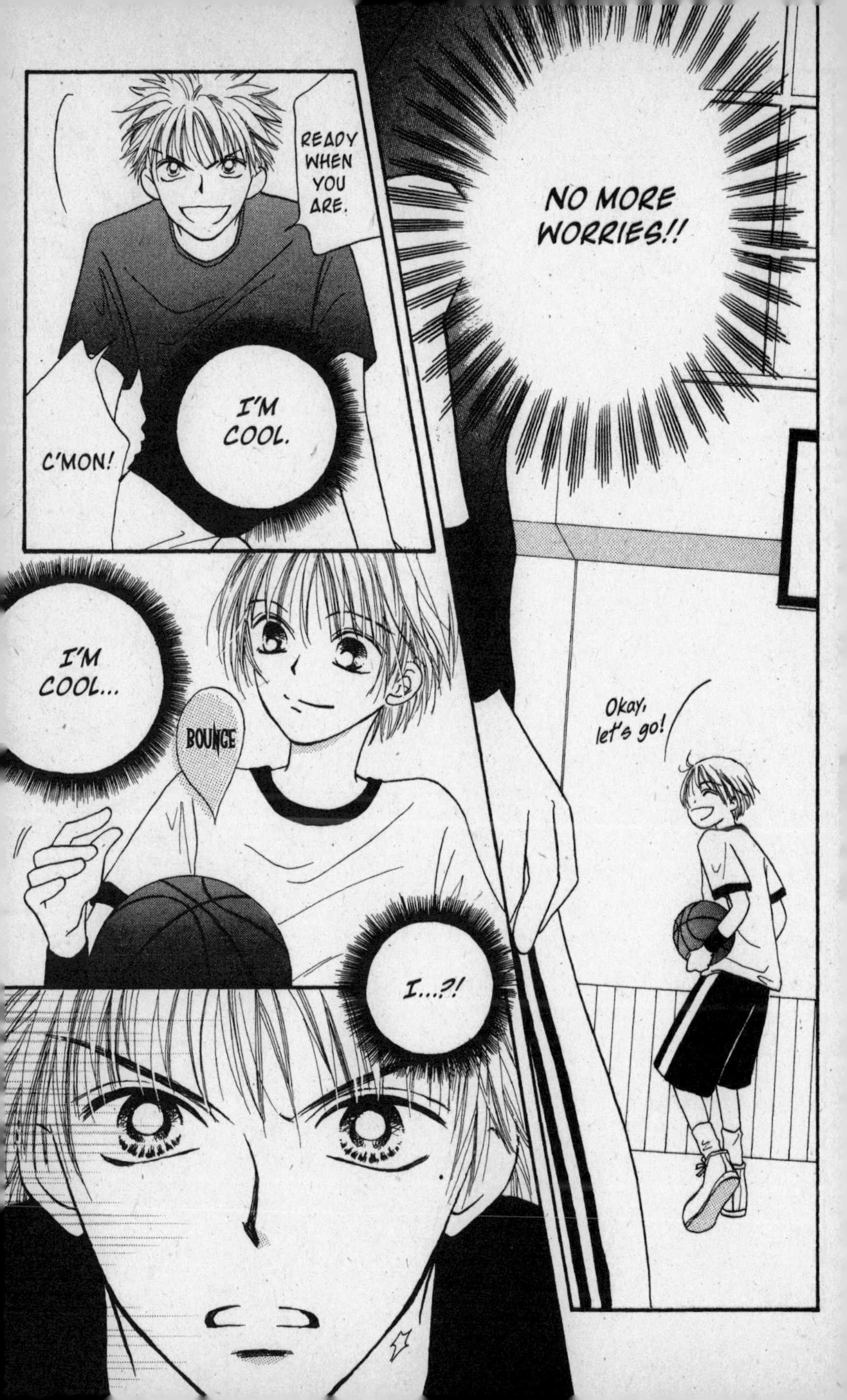
NO MORE WORRIES!!
Okay, let's go!
READY WHEN YOU ARE.
I'M COOL.
C'MON!
I'M COOL...
BOUNCE
I...?!

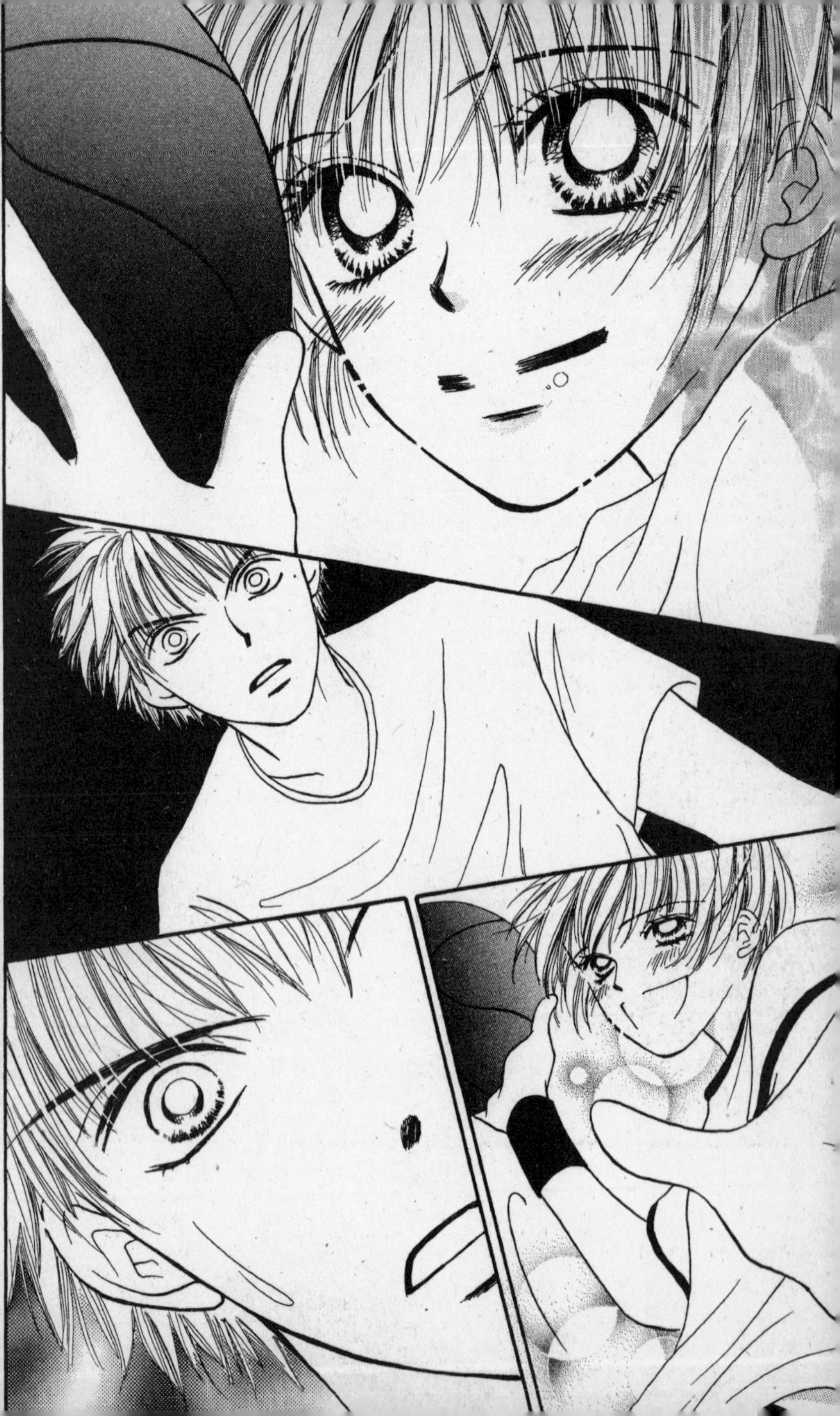

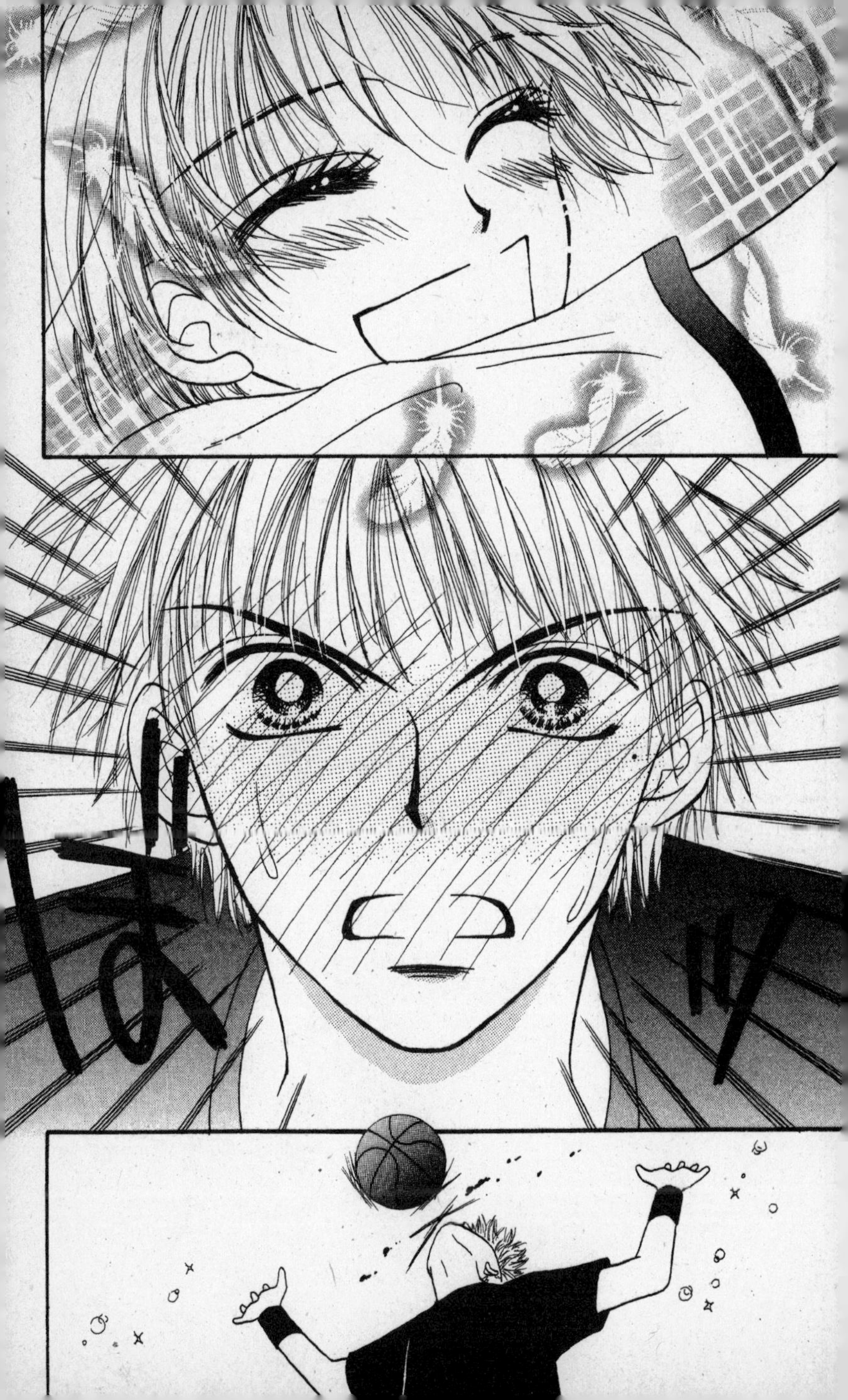
はッ

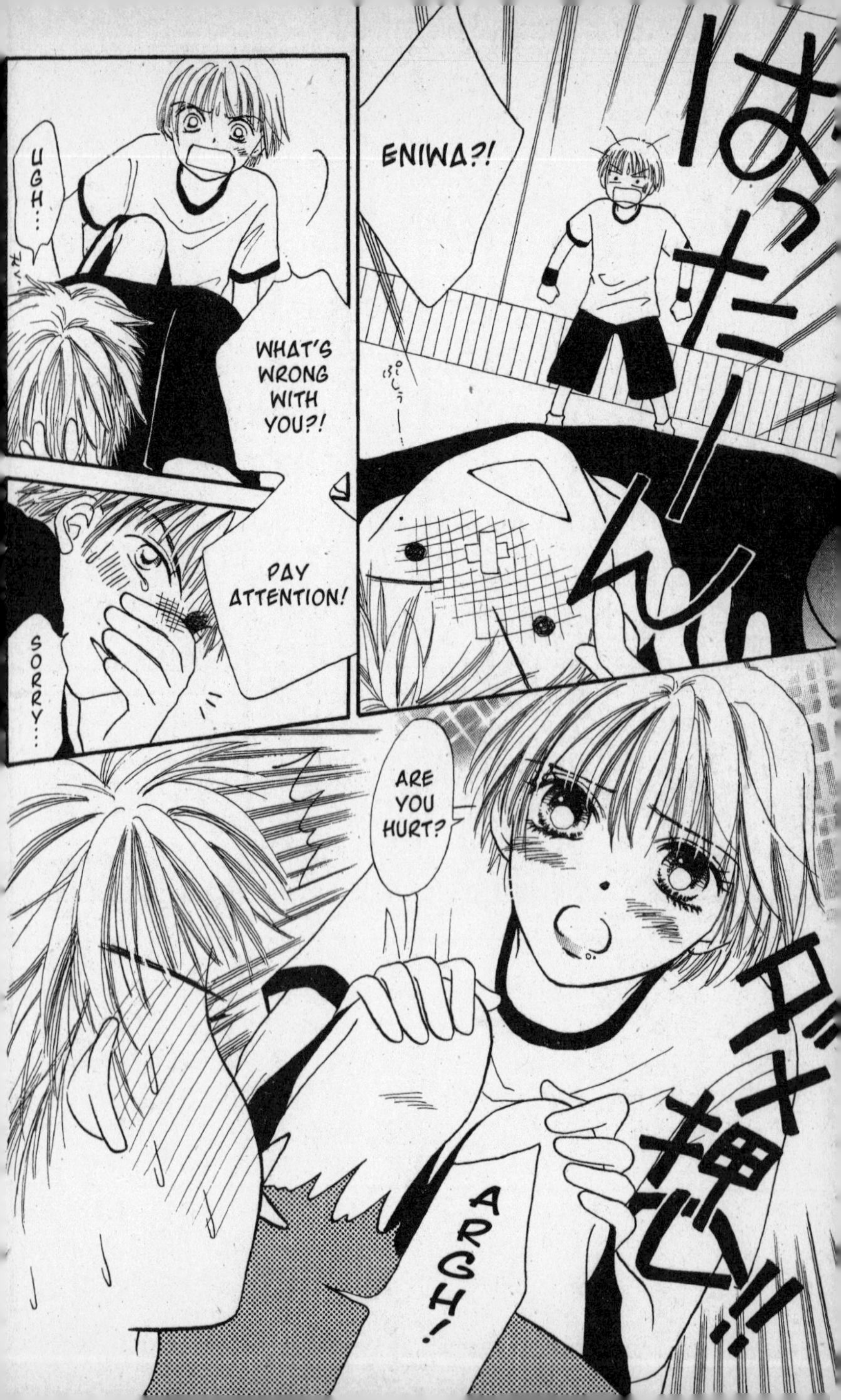
はったーん
ENIWA?!
WHAT'S WRONG WITH YOU?!
UGH...
PAY ATTENTION!
SORRY...
ダメ押し!!
ARE YOU HURT?
ARGH!

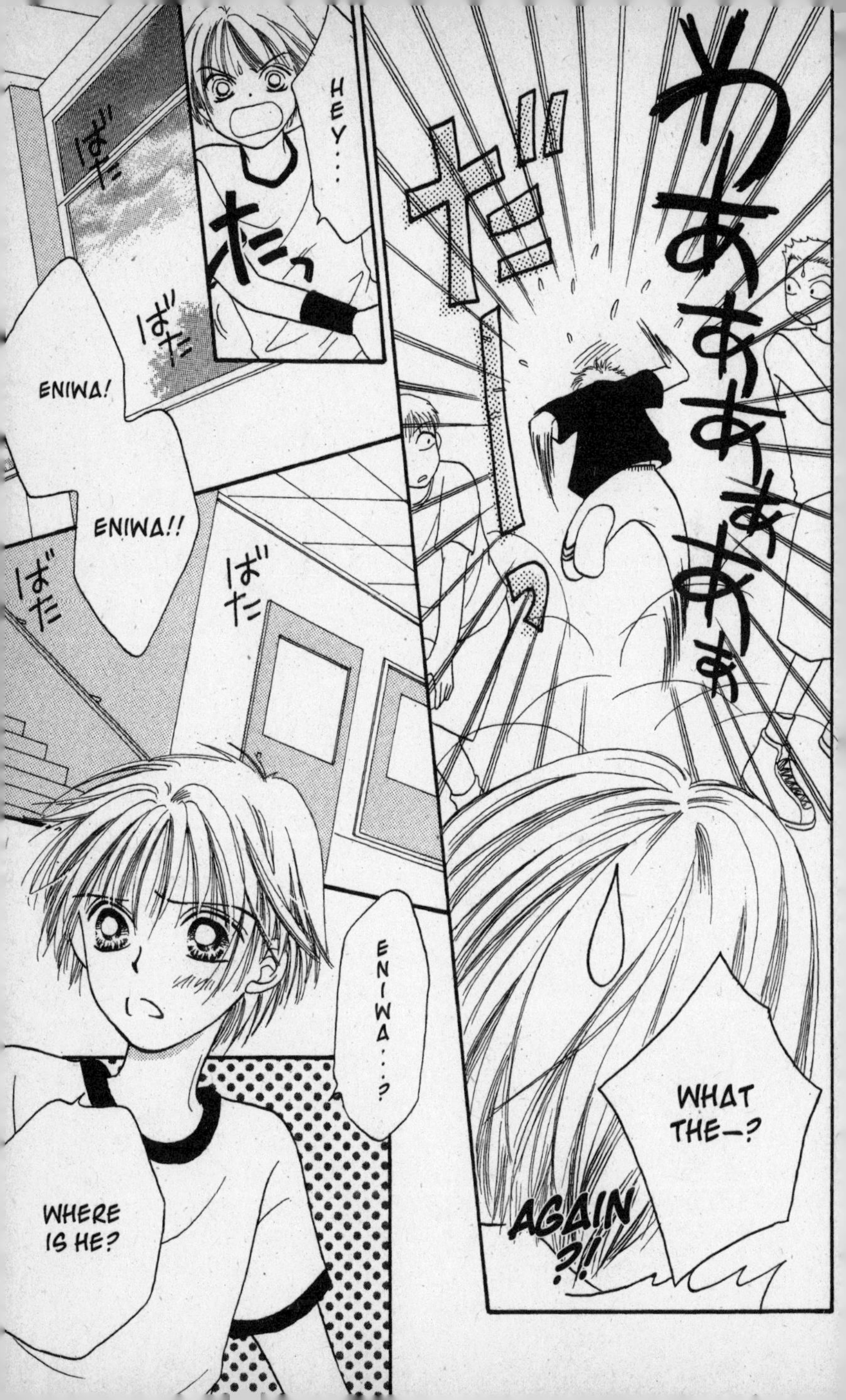

やあああああぁ
ガタン
WHAT THE—?
AGAIN ?!
HEY...
だっ
ばだ
ばだ
ENIWA!
ENIWA!!
ばだ
ばだ
ENIWA...?
WHERE IS HE?

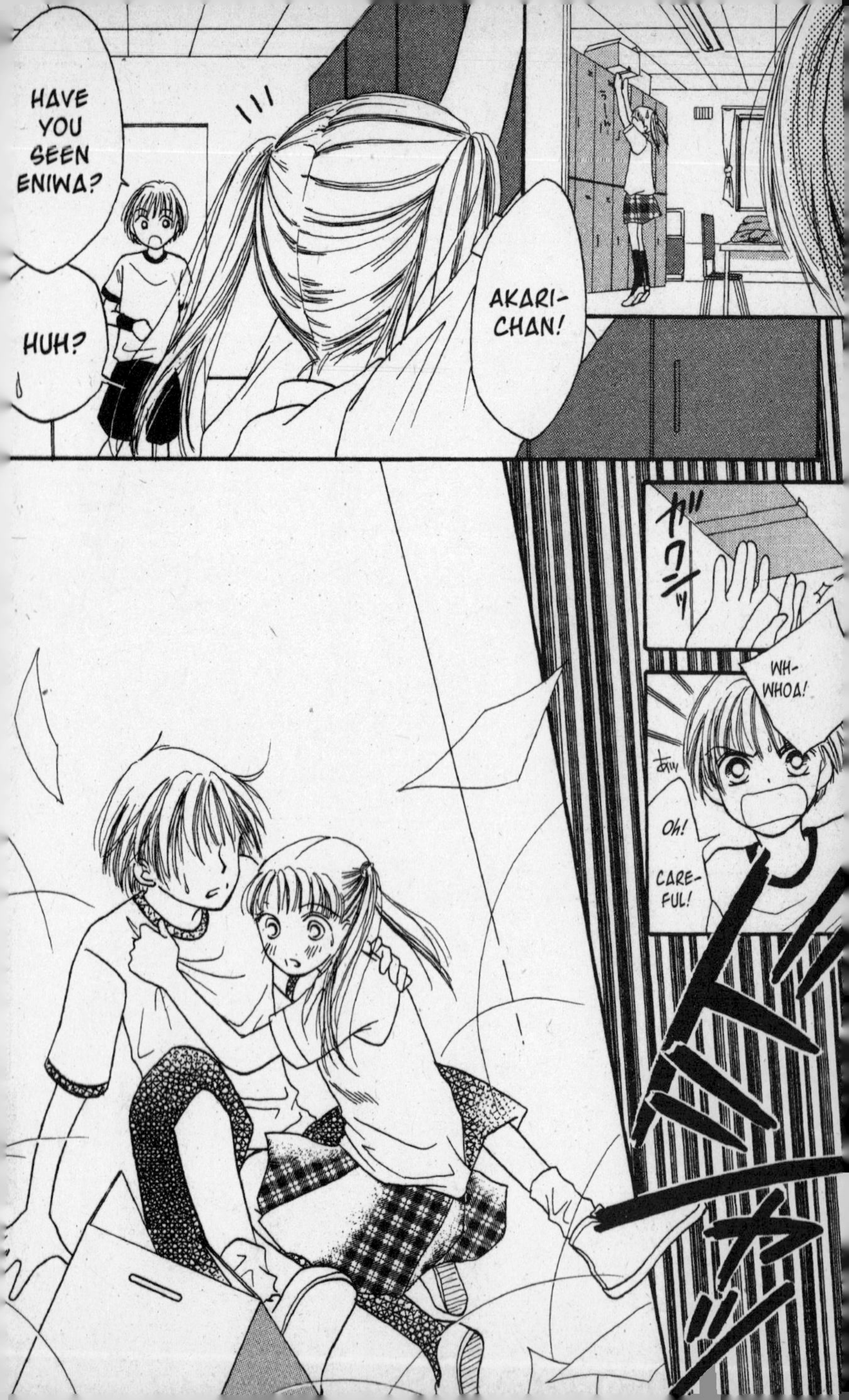
AKARI-CHAN!
HAVE YOU SEEN ENIWA?
HUH?
WH-WHOA!
Oh!
CARE-FUL!

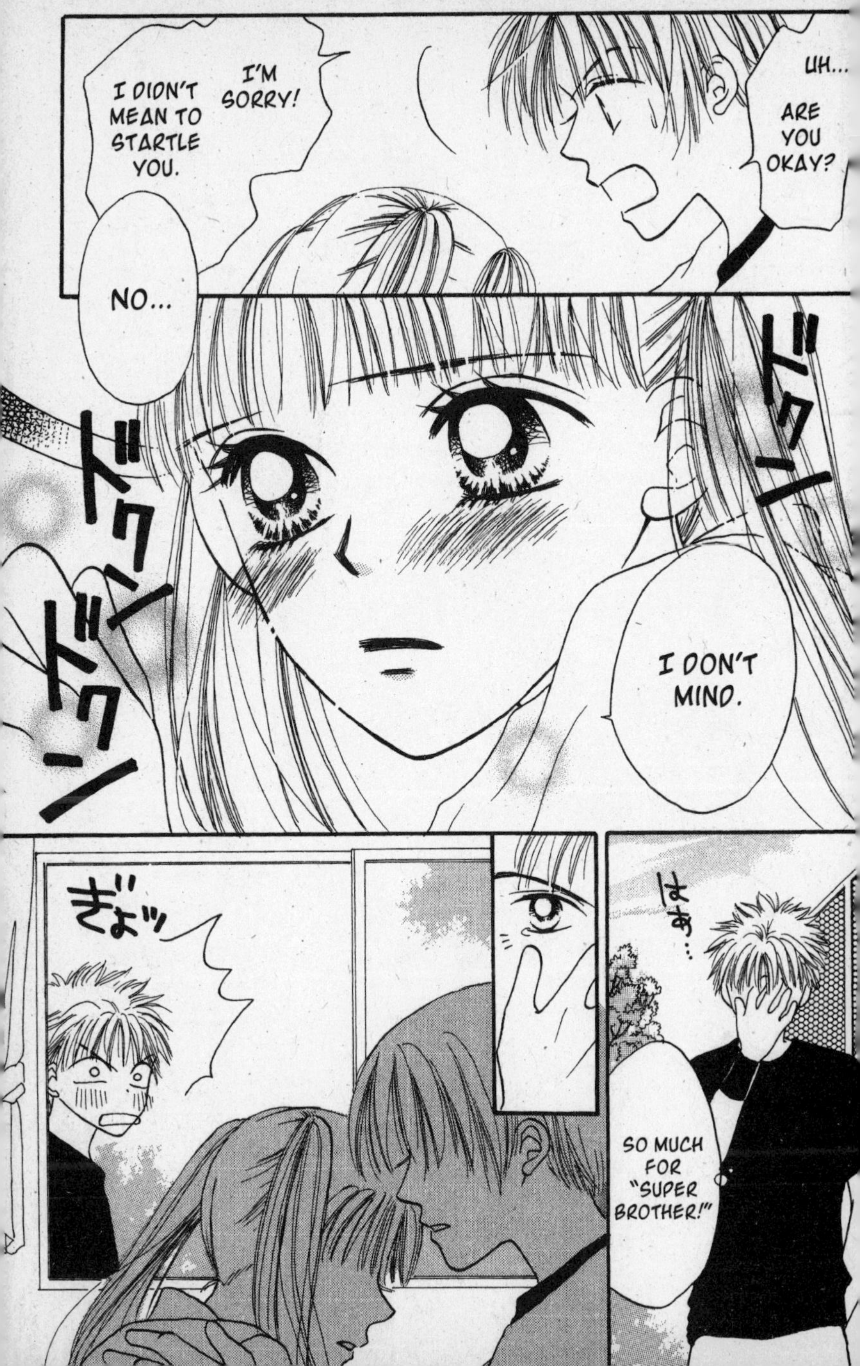

UH...
ARE YOU OKAY?
I'M SORRY!
I DIDN'T MEAN TO STARTLE YOU.
NO...
ドクン
I DON'T MIND.
ドクン
ドクン
はあ…
SO MUCH FOR "SUPER BROTHER!"
ぎょッ

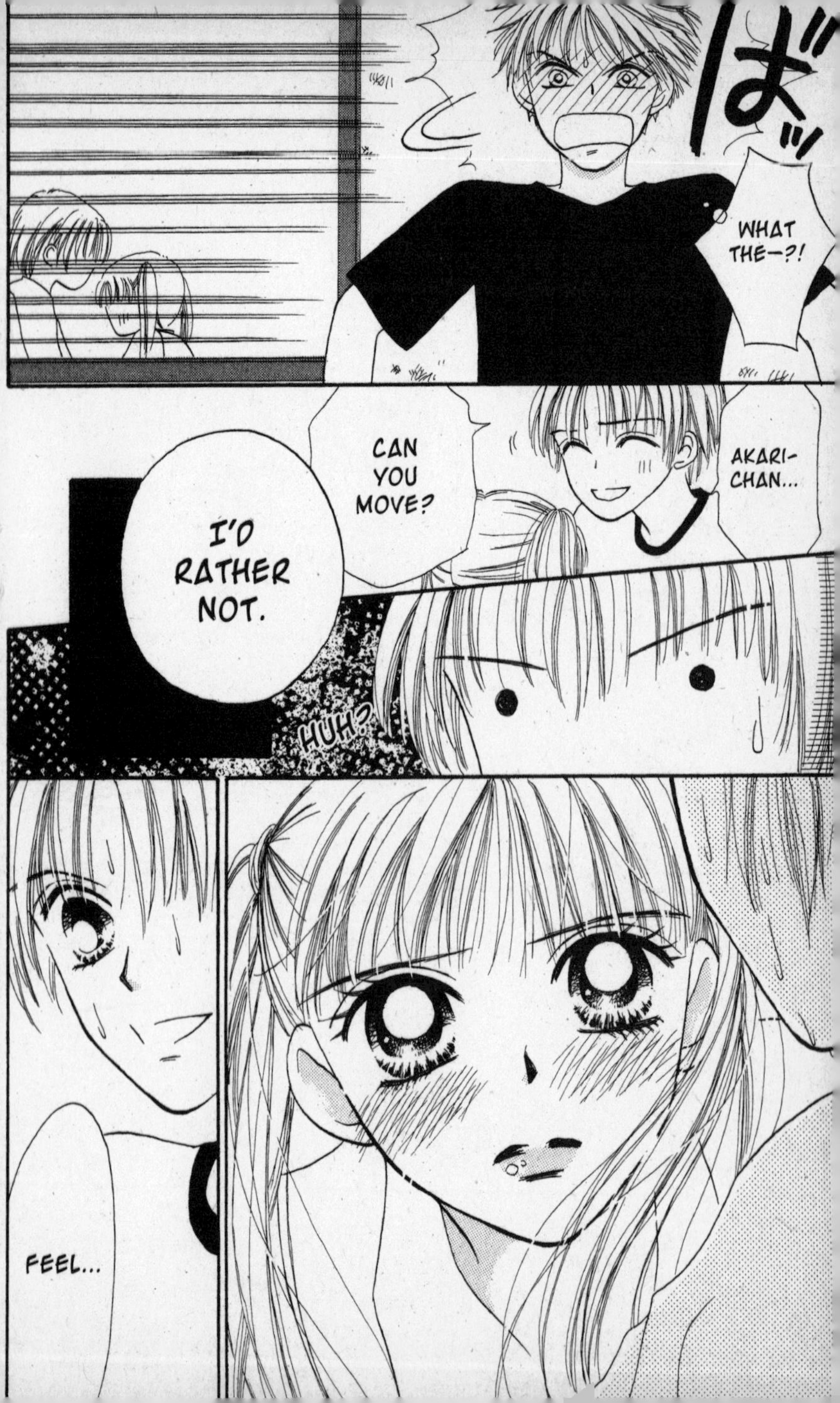
ばッ
WHAT THE--?!
AKARI-CHAN...
CAN YOU MOVE?
I'D RATHER NOT.
HUH?
FEEL...

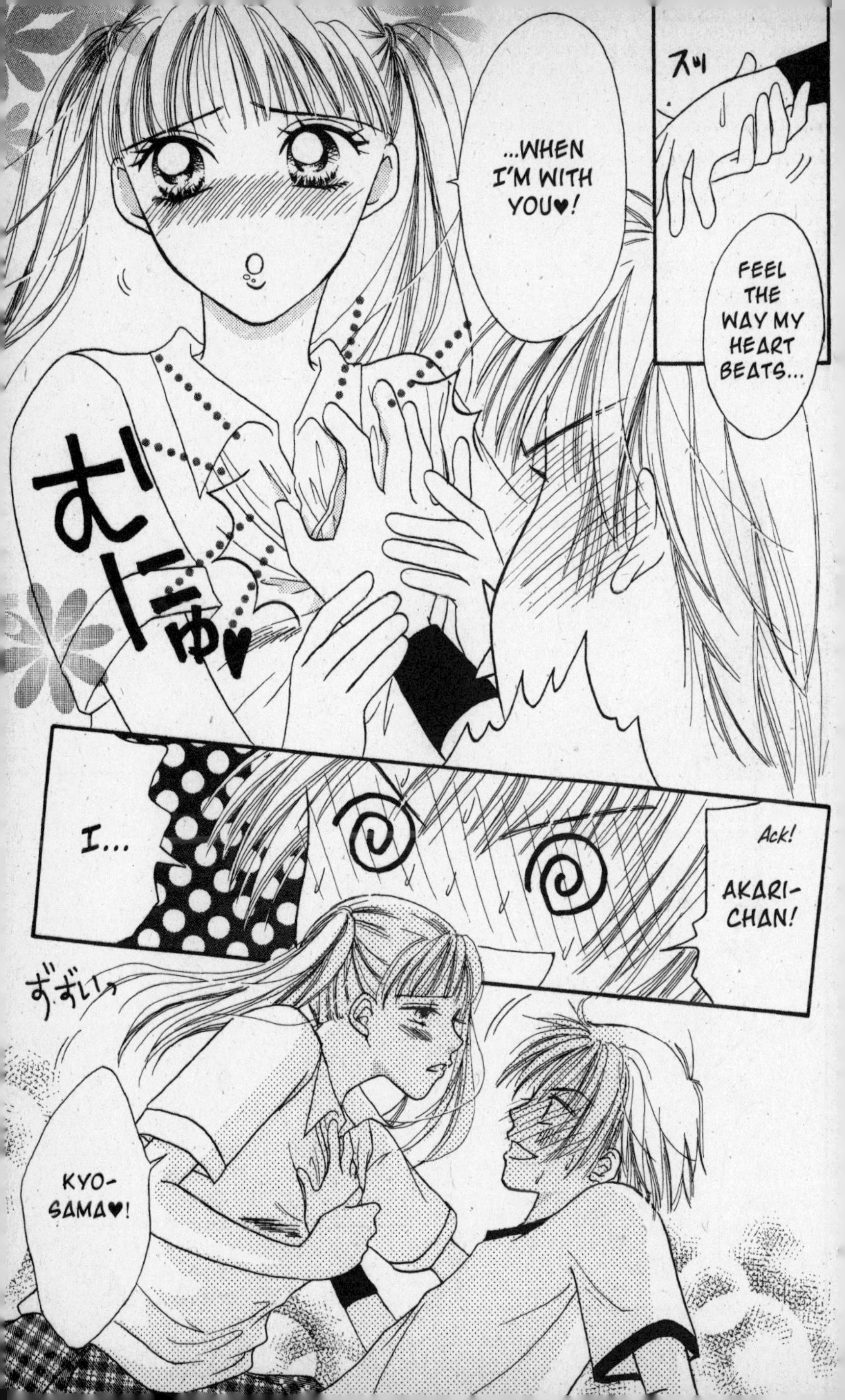
ズッ
FEEL THE WAY MY HEART BEATS...
...WHEN I'M WITH YOU♥!
むにゅ♥
Ack!
AKARI-CHAN!
I...
ずずいっ
KYO-SAMA♥!

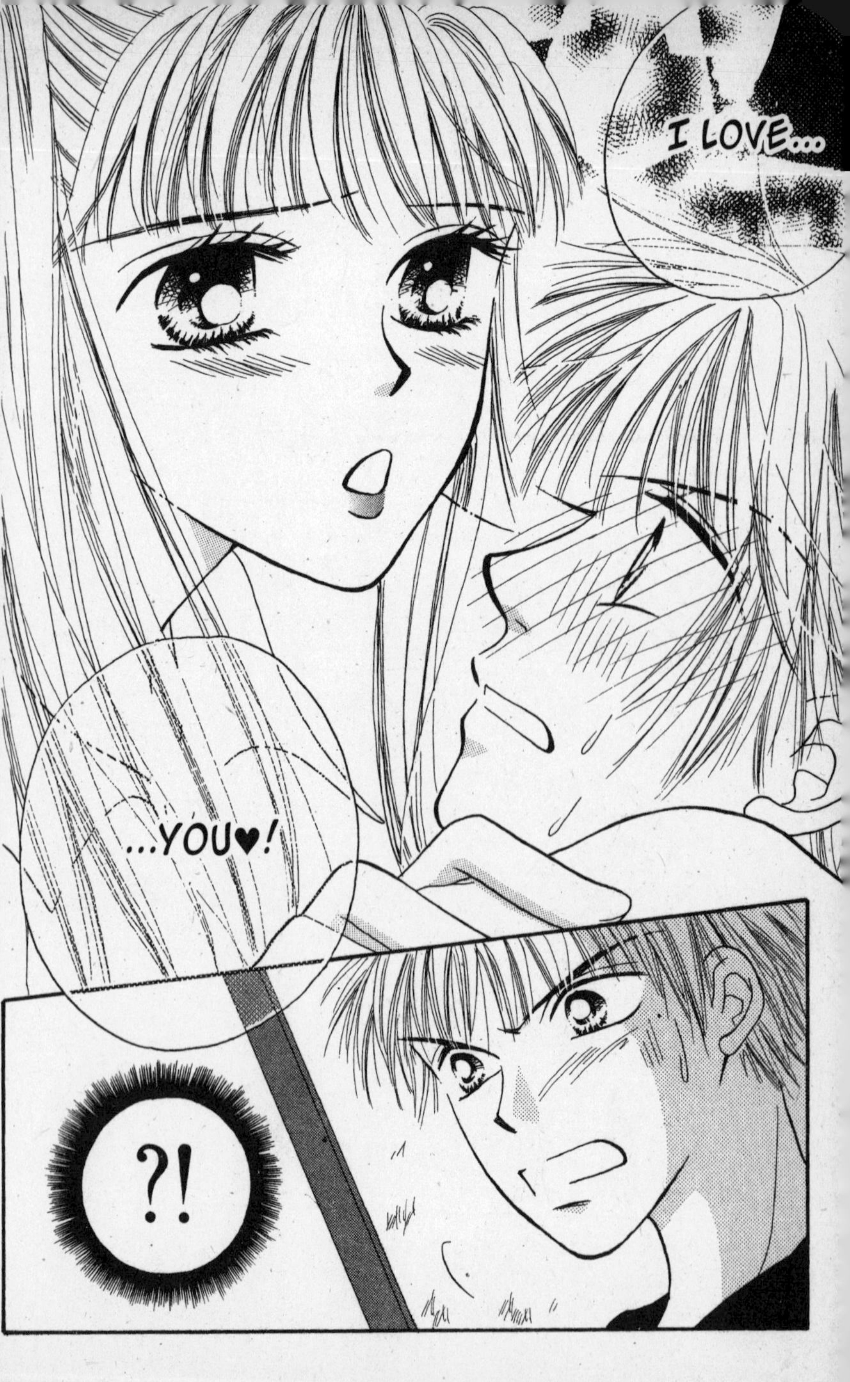
I LOVE...
...YOU♥!
?!

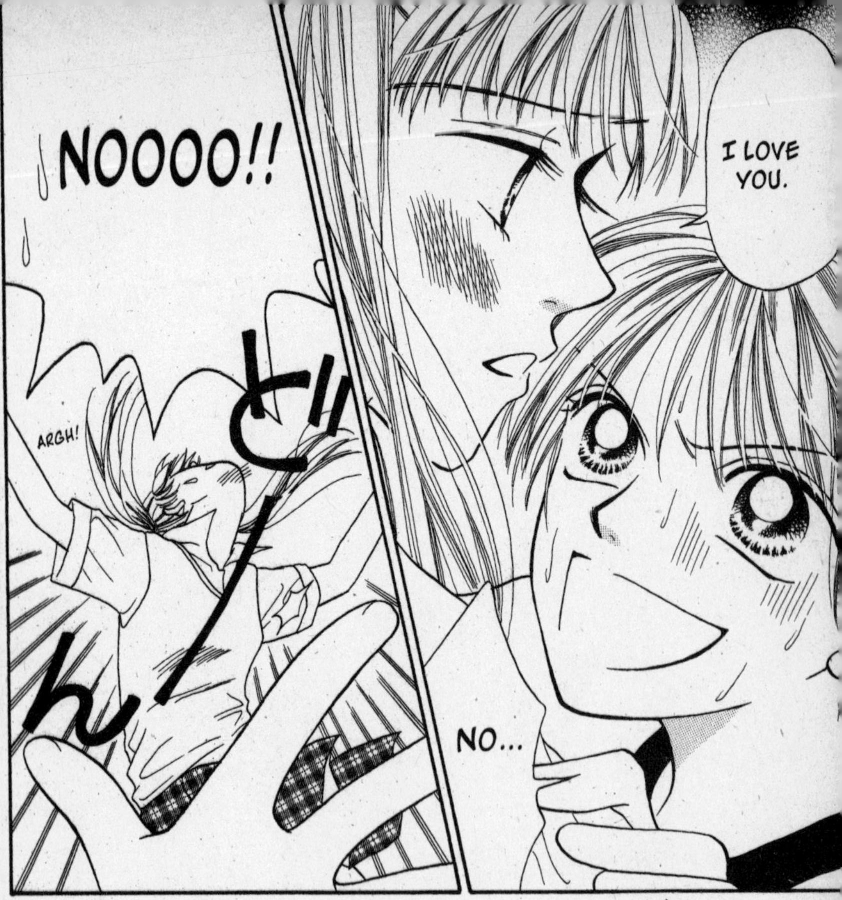
I LOVE YOU.
NO...
NOOOO!!
ARGH!
どーん

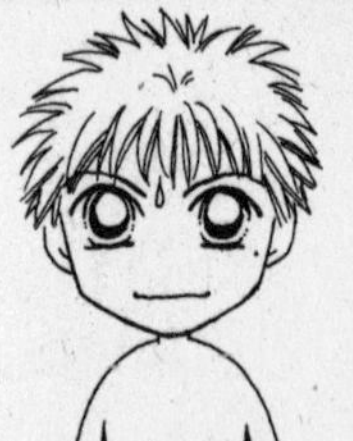

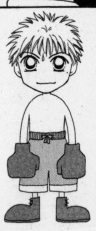

GIRL GOT GAME!

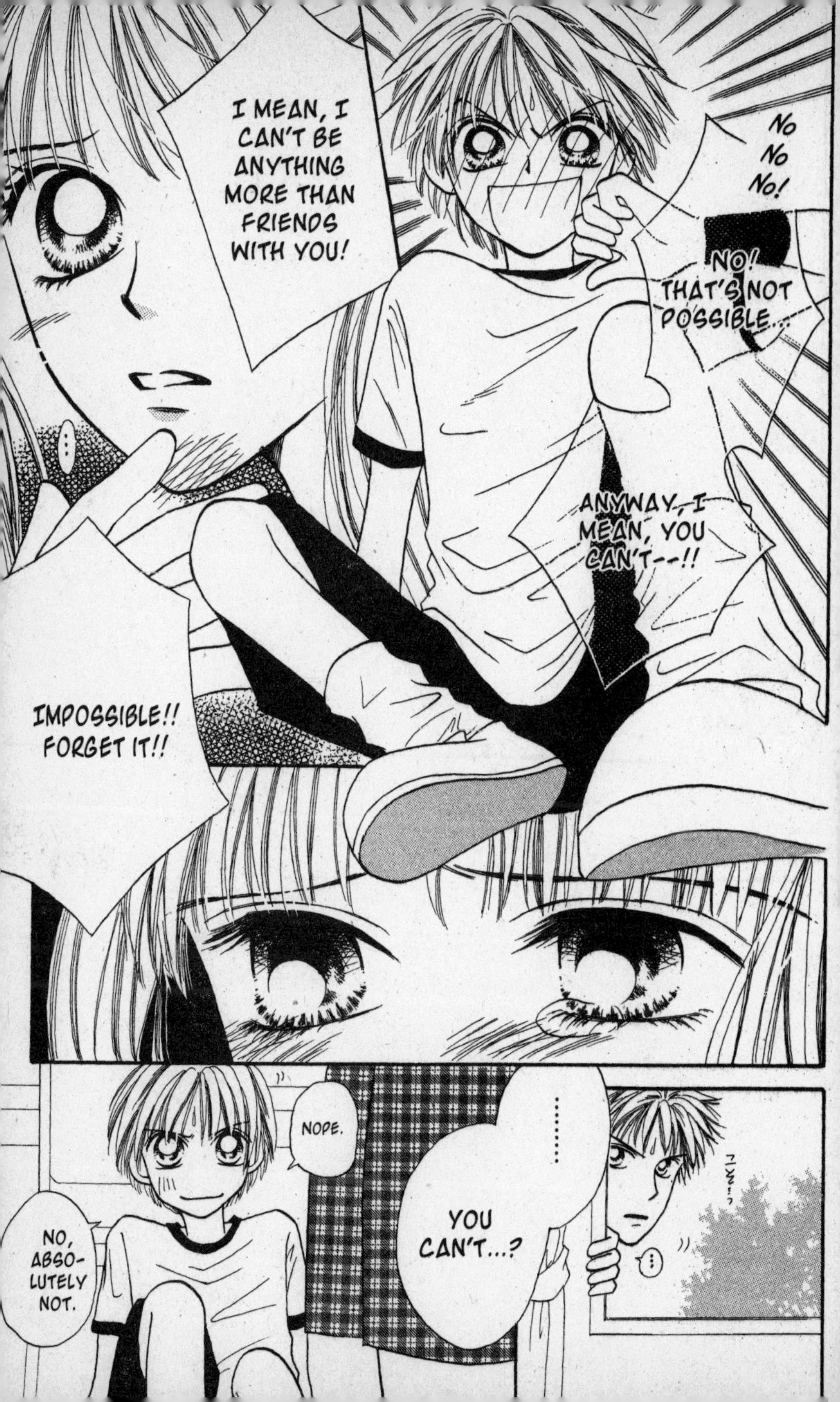
No No No!
NO! THAT'S NOT POSSIBLE...
I MEAN, I CAN'T BE ANYTHING MORE THAN FRIENDS WITH YOU!
...
ANYWAY, I MEAN, YOU CAN'T--!!
IMPOSSIBLE!! FORGET IT!!
......
YOU CAN'T...?
...
NOPE.
NO, ABSOLUTELY NOT.

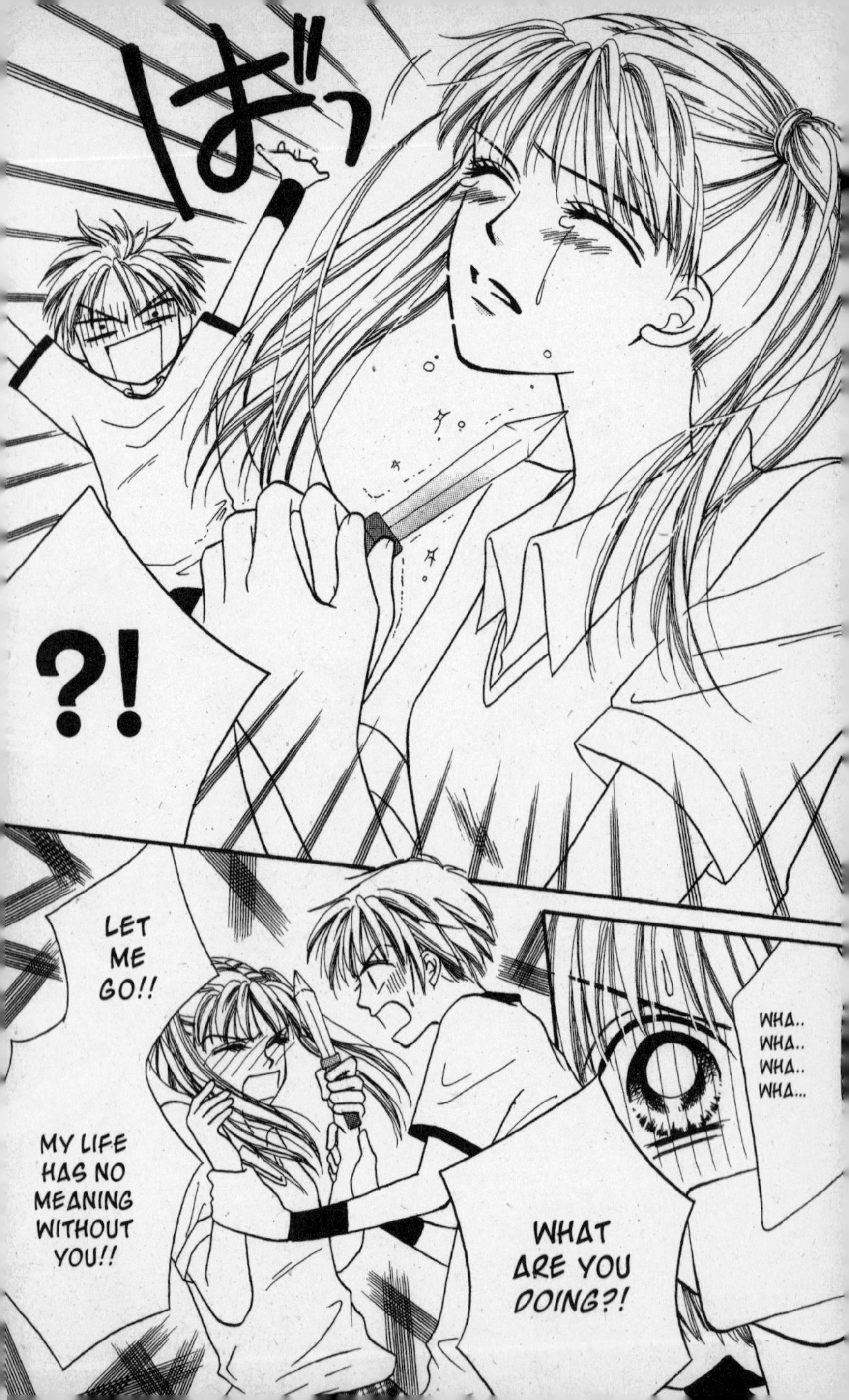
ばっ
?!
WHA.. WHA.. WHA.. WHA...
WHAT ARE YOU DOING?!
LET ME GO!!
MY LIFE HAS NO MEANING WITHOUT YOU!!

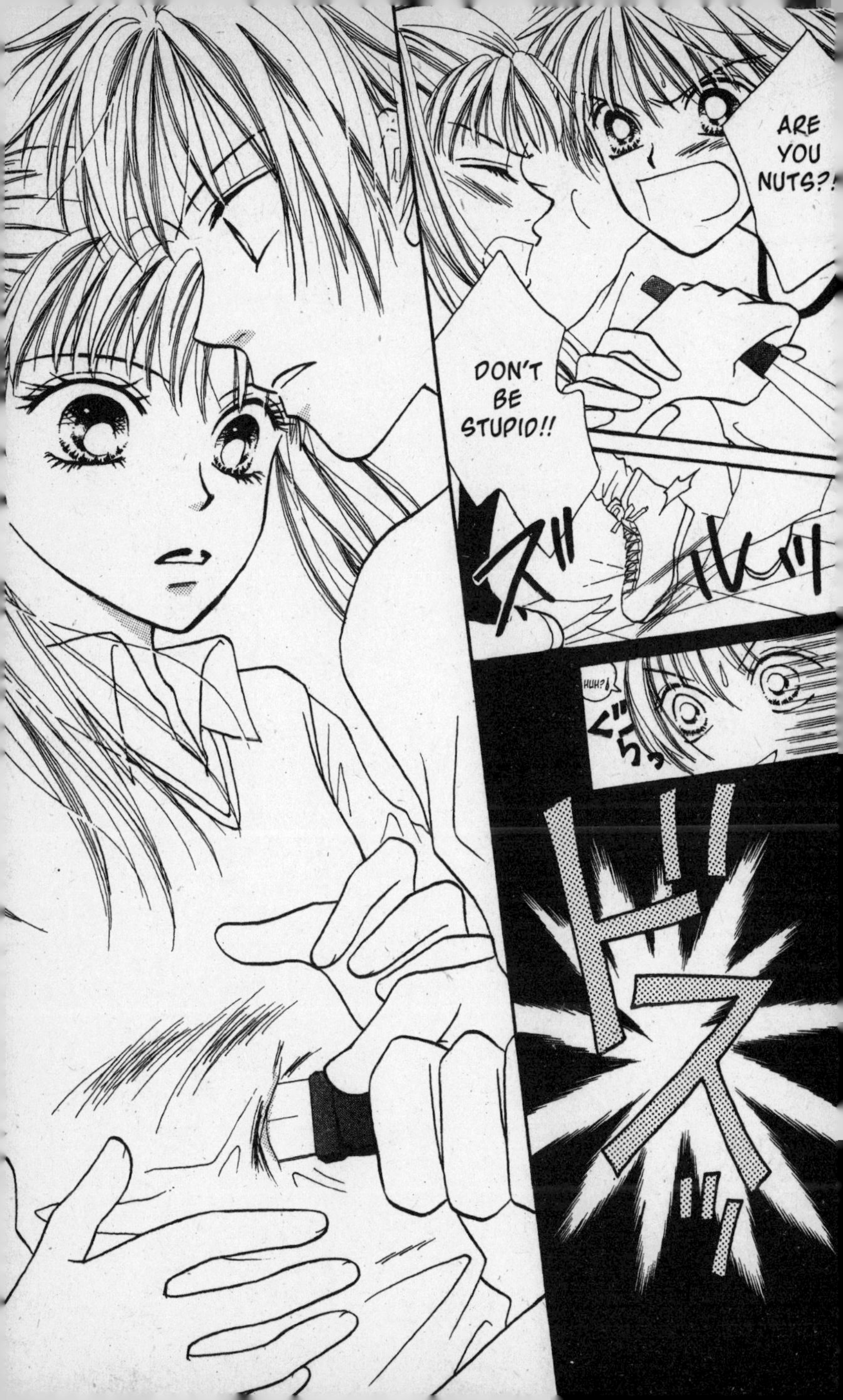
ARE YOU NUTS?!
DON'T BE STUPID!!
ズルッ
HUH?!
ぐらっ
ドスッ

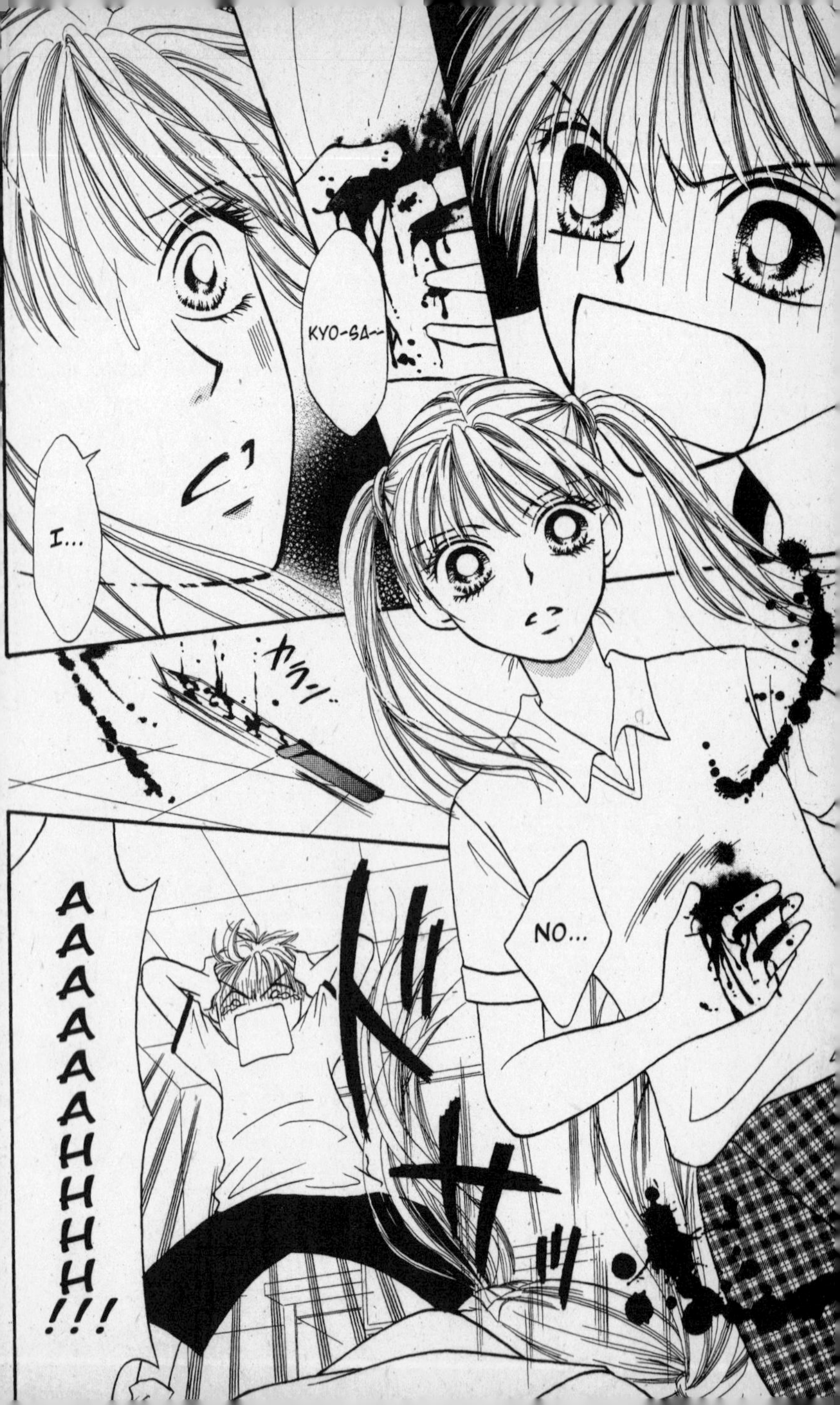
KYO-SA--
I...
NO...
AAAAAAHHHH!!!

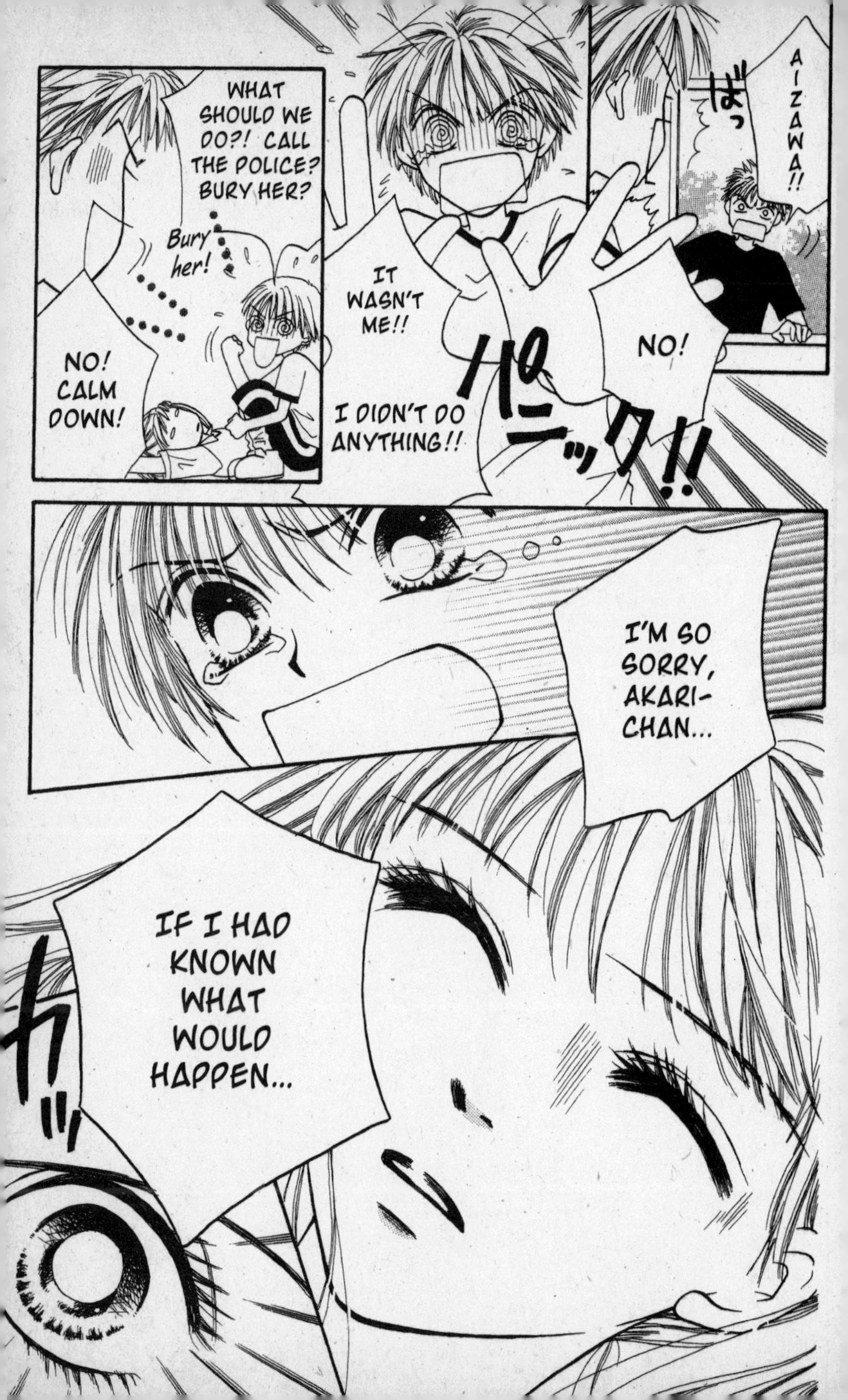
AIZAWA!!
ばっ
NO!
IT WASN'T ME!!
I DIDN'T DO ANYTHING!!
パニック!!
WHAT SHOULD WE DO?! CALL THE POLICE? BURY HER?
Bury her!
NO! CALM DOWN!
I'M SO SORRY, AKARI-CHAN...
IF I HAD KNOWN WHAT WOULD HAPPEN...

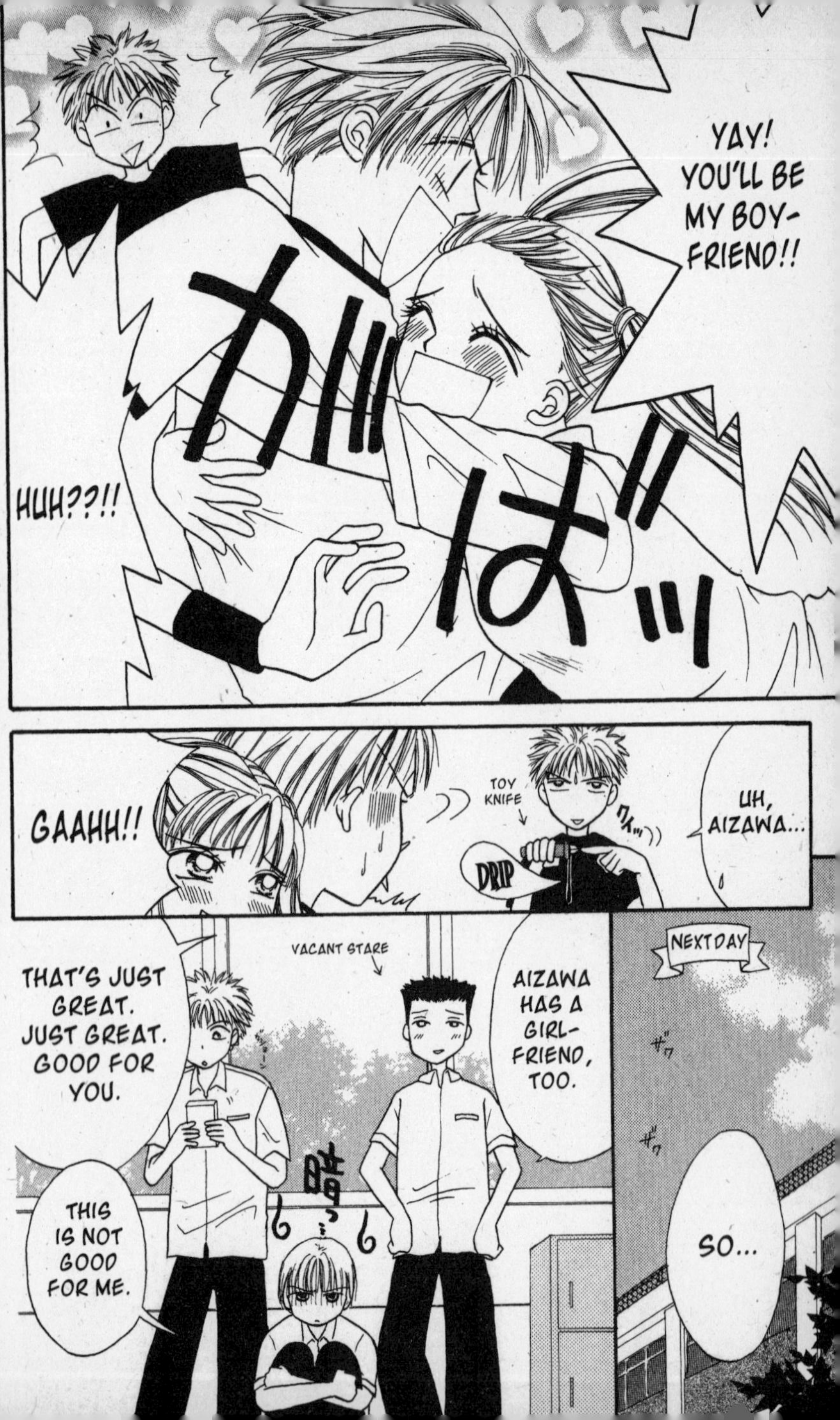
YAY! YOU'LL BE MY BOY-FRIEND!!
かばッ
HUH??!!
UH, AIZAWA...
TOY KNIFE
DRIP
GAAHH!!
NEXT DAY
SO...
AIZAWA HAS A GIRL-FRIEND, TOO.
VACANT STARE
THAT'S JUST GREAT. JUST GREAT. GOOD FOR YOU.
THIS IS NOT GOOD FOR ME.

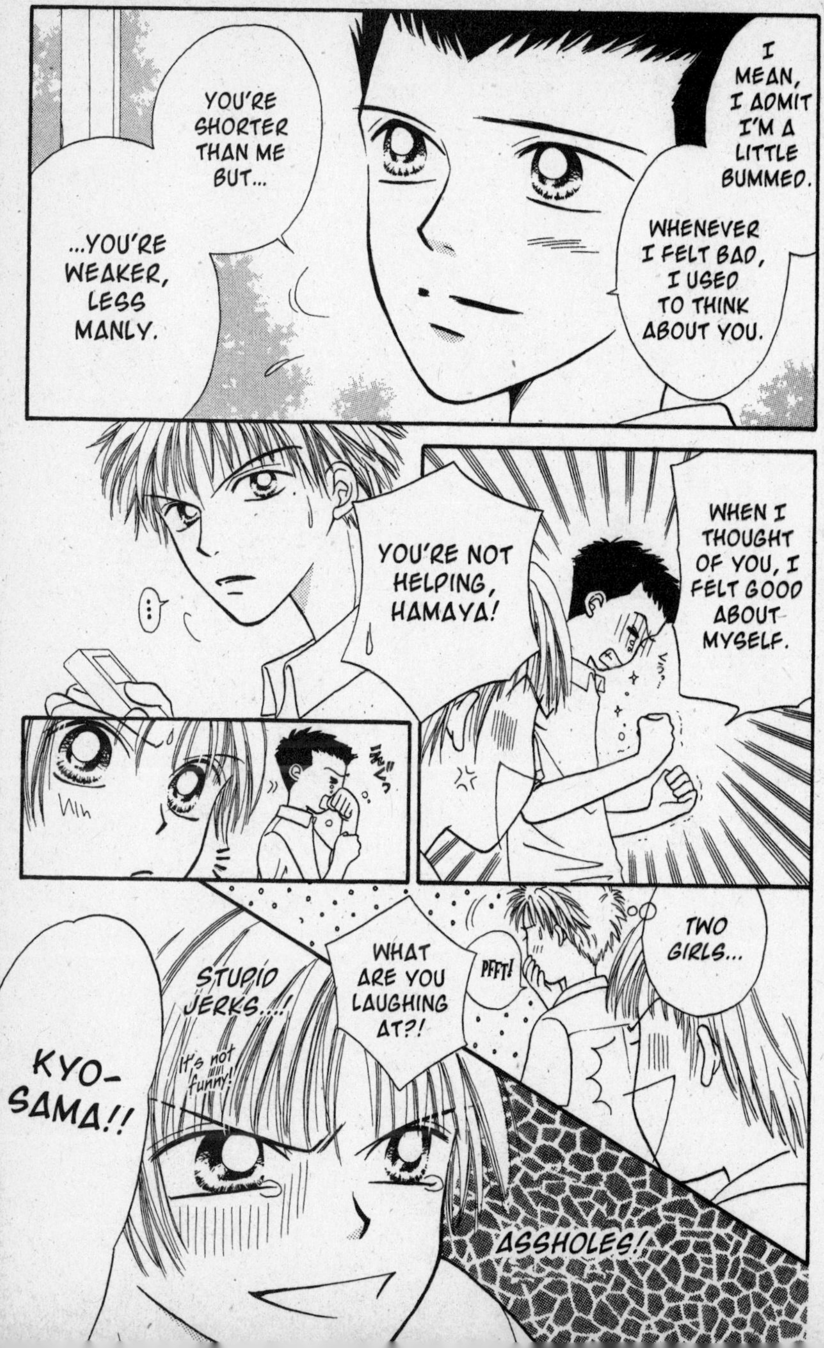
I MEAN, I ADMIT I'M A LITTLE BUMMED.
WHENEVER I FELT BAD, I USED TO THINK ABOUT YOU.
YOU'RE SHORTER THAN ME BUT...
...YOU'RE WEAKER, LESS MANLY.
WHEN I THOUGHT OF YOU, I FELT GOOD ABOUT MYSELF.
YOU'RE NOT HELPING, HAMAYA!
...
TWO GIRLS...
PFFT!
WHAT ARE YOU LAUGHING AT?!
STUPID JERKS...!
It's not funny!
KYO-SAMA!!
ASSHOLES!

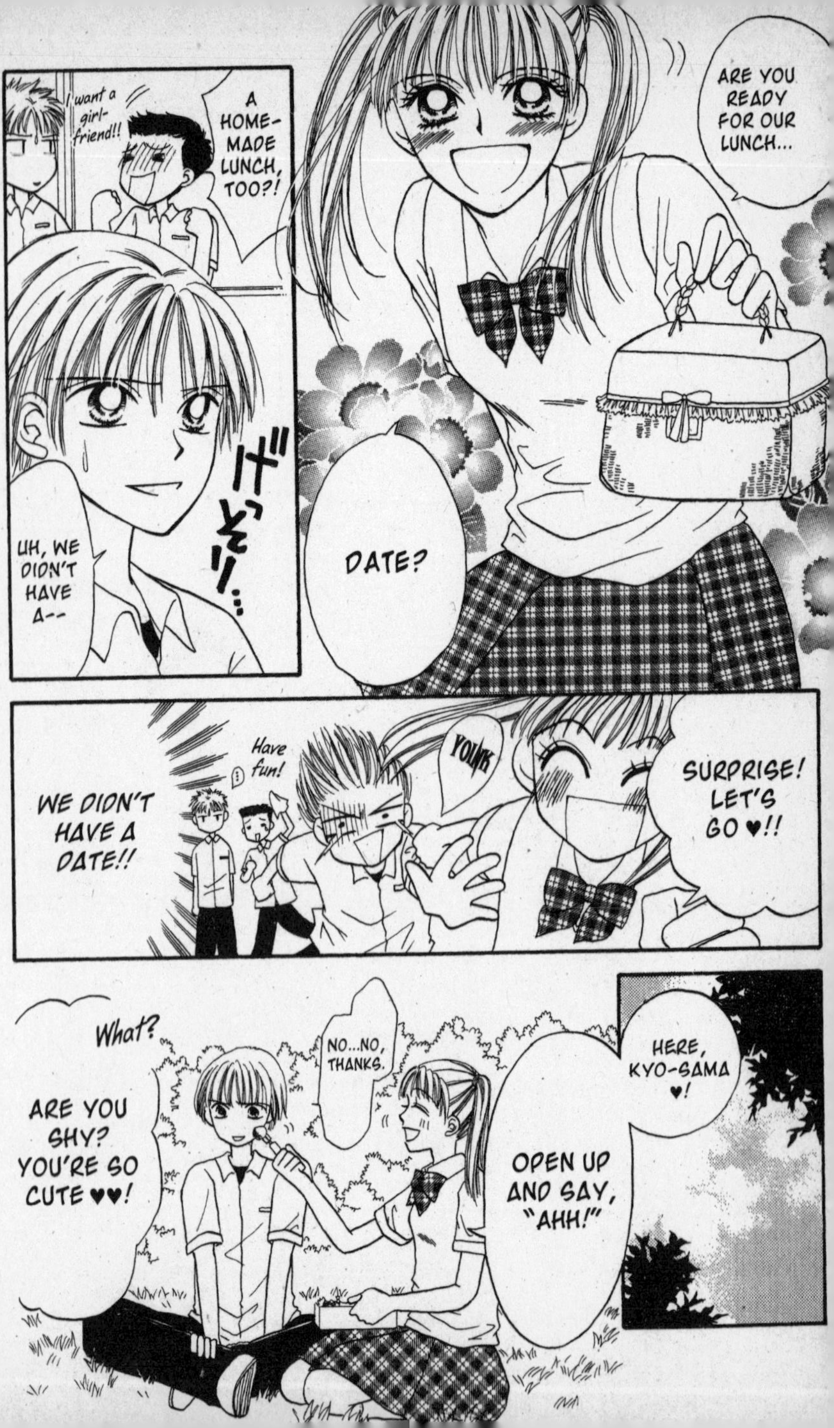

ARE YOU READY FOR OUR LUNCH...
DATE?
A HOME-MADE LUNCH, TOO?!
I want a girl-friend!!
げっそり…
UH, WE DIDN'T HAVE A--
SURPRISE! LET'S GO ♥!!
YOINK
Have fun!
WE DIDN'T HAVE A DATE!!
HERE, KYO-SAMA ♥!
OPEN UP AND SAY, "AHH!"
NO...NO, THANKS.
What?
ARE YOU SHY? YOU'RE SO CUTE ♥♥!

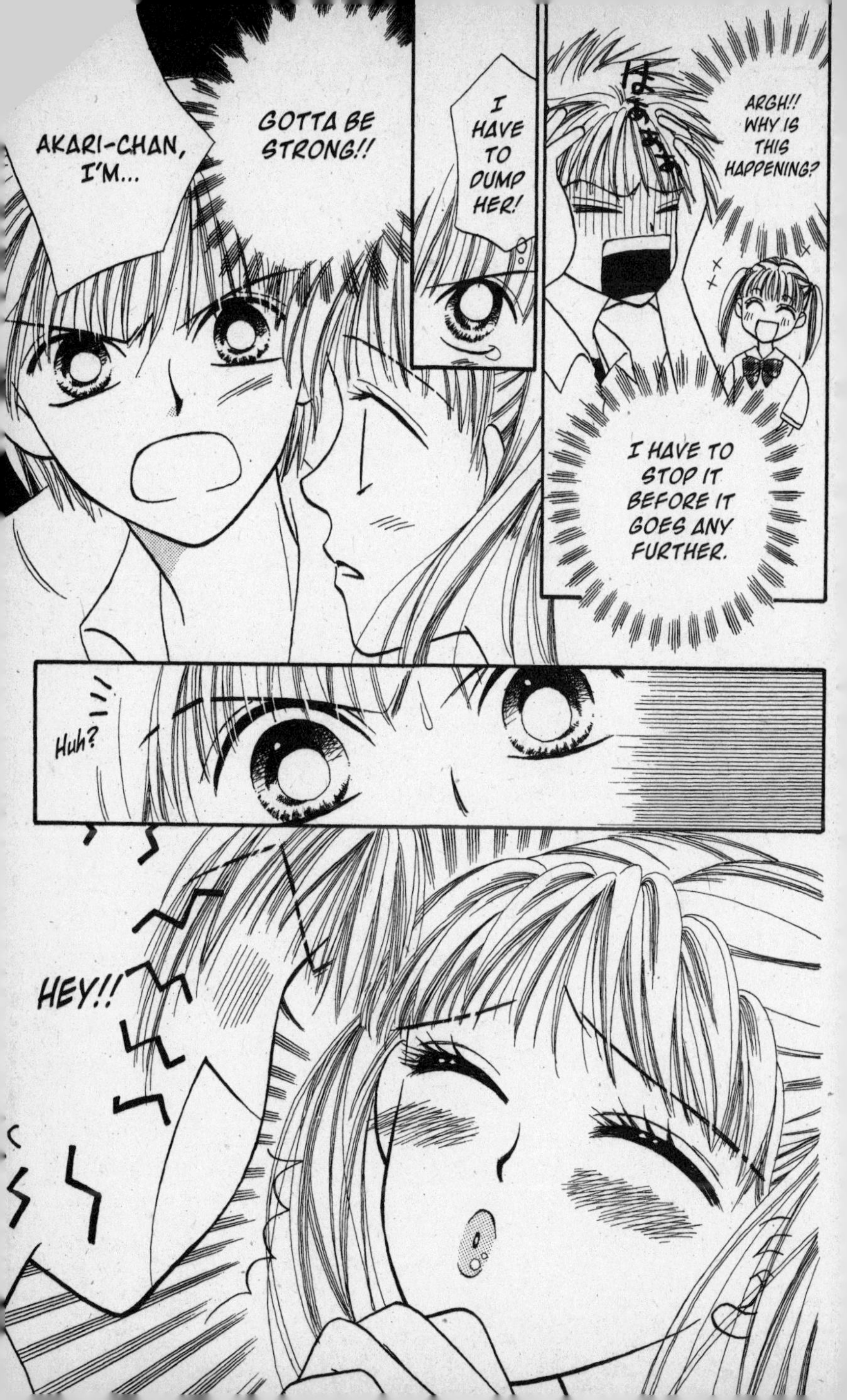

ARGH!! WHY IS THIS HAPPENING?
I HAVE TO STOP IT BEFORE IT GOES ANY FURTHER.
I HAVE TO DUMP HER!
GOTTA BE STRONG!!
AKARI-CHAN, I'M...
Huh?
HEY!!

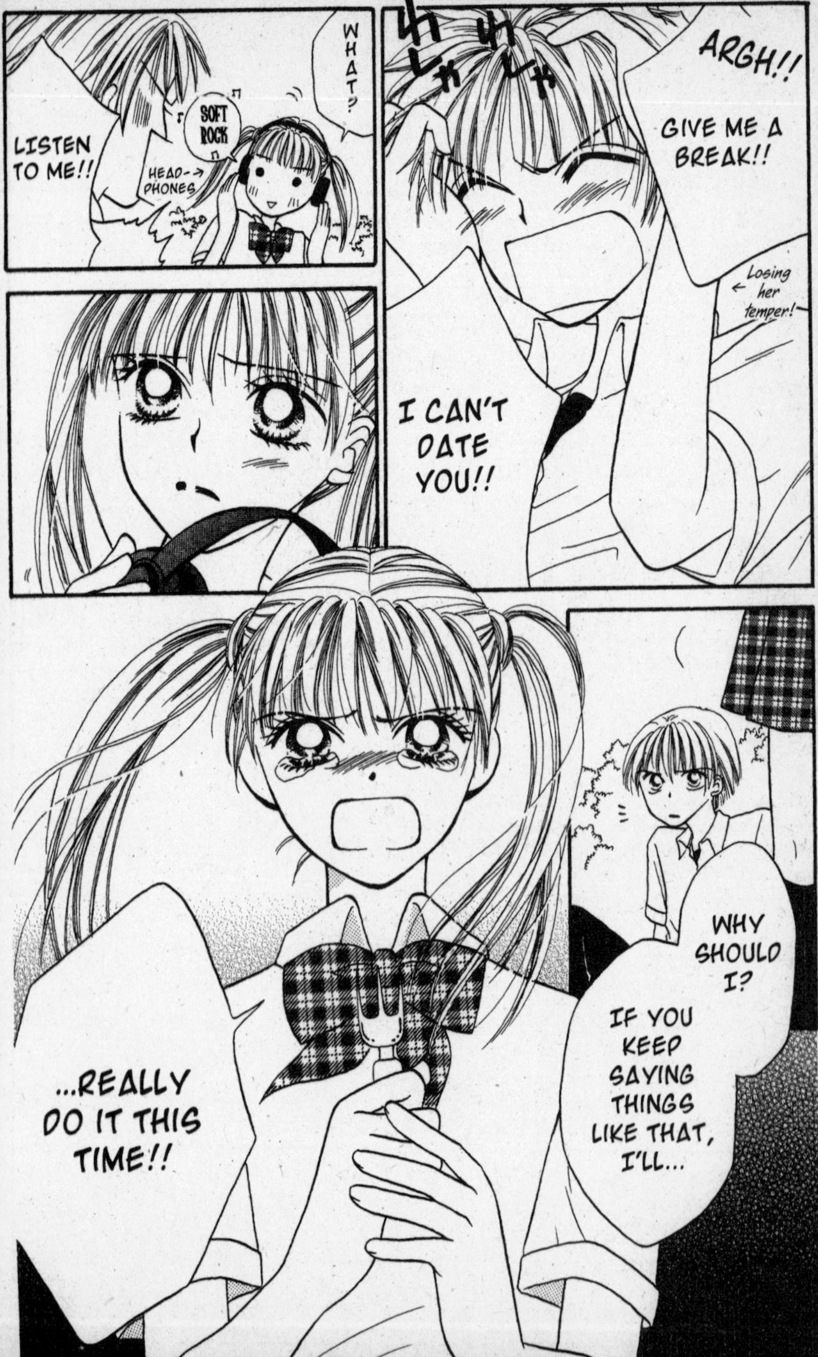
ARGH!!
GIVE ME A BREAK!!
Losing her temper!
I CAN'T DATE YOU!!
WHAT?
SOFT ROCK
LISTEN TO ME!!
HEAD-PHONES
WHY SHOULD I?
IF YOU KEEP SAYING THINGS LIKE THAT, I'LL...
...REALLY DO IT THIS TIME!!

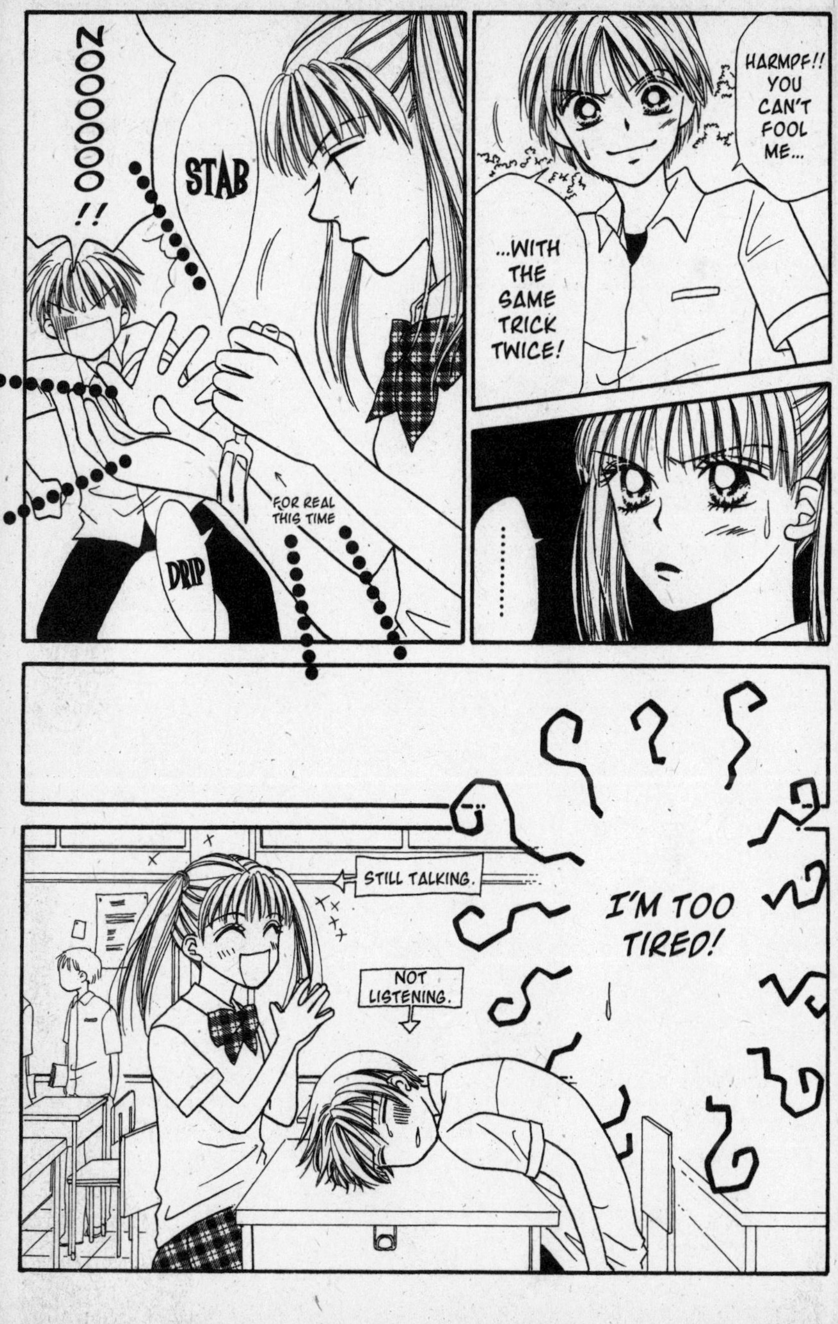
HARMPF!! YOU CAN'T FOOL ME...
...WITH THE SAME TRICK TWICE!
......
STAB
NOOOOOOO!!
FOR REAL THIS TIME
DRIP
I'M TOO TIRED!
STILL TALKING.
NOT LISTENING.

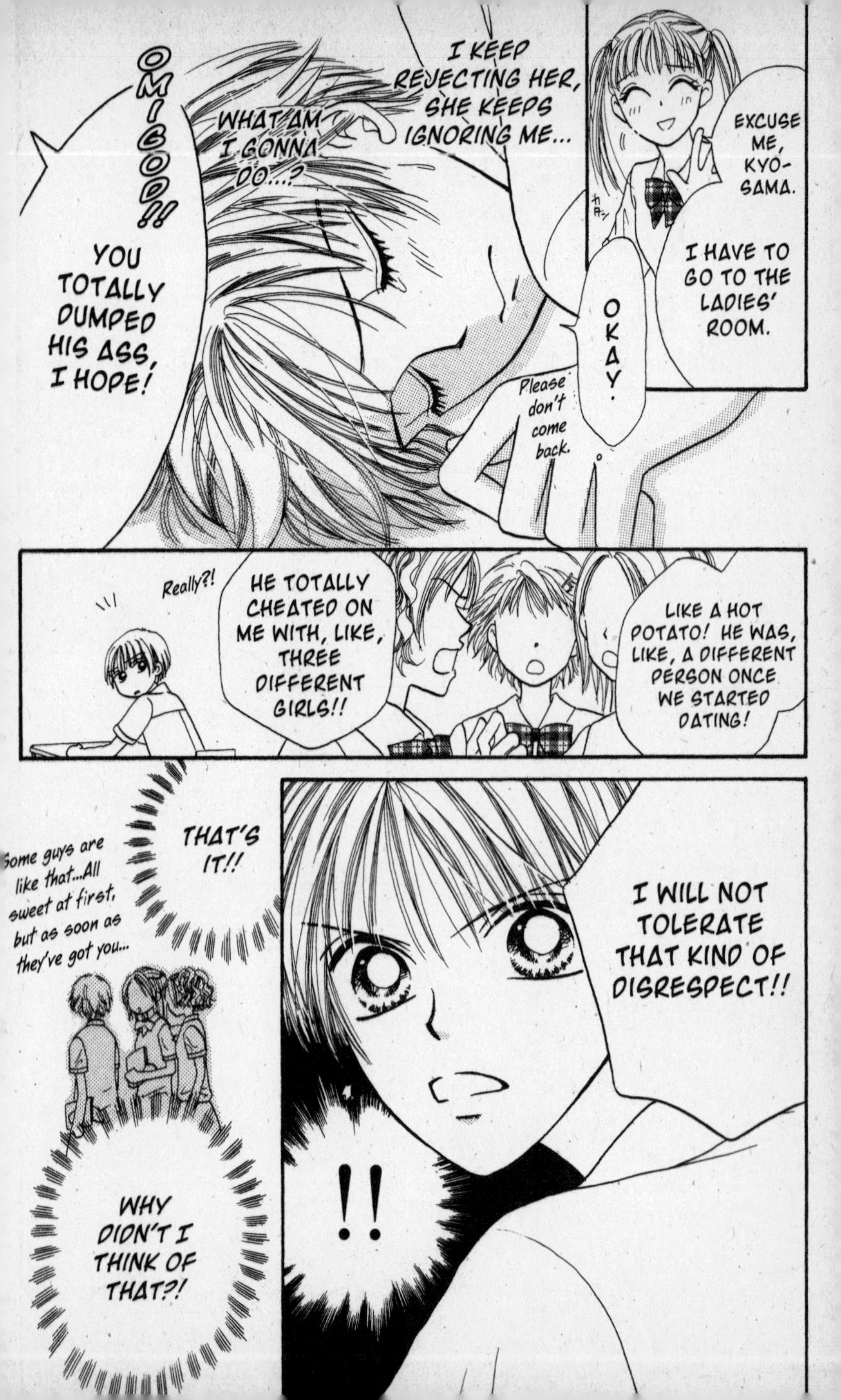

EXCUSE ME, KYO-SAMA.
I HAVE TO GO TO THE LADIES' ROOM.
OKAY.
Please don't come back.
I KEEP REJECTING HER, SHE KEEPS IGNORING ME...
WHAT AM I GONNA DO...?
OMIGOD!!
YOU TOTALLY DUMPED HIS ASS, I HOPE!
LIKE A HOT POTATO! HE WAS, LIKE, A DIFFERENT PERSON ONCE WE STARTED DATING!
HE TOTALLY CHEATED ON ME WITH, LIKE, THREE DIFFERENT GIRLS!!
Really?!
I WILL NOT TOLERATE THAT KIND OF DISRESPECT!!
!!
THAT'S IT!!
Some guys are like that...All sweet at first, but as soon as they've got you...
WHY DIDN'T I THINK OF THAT?!

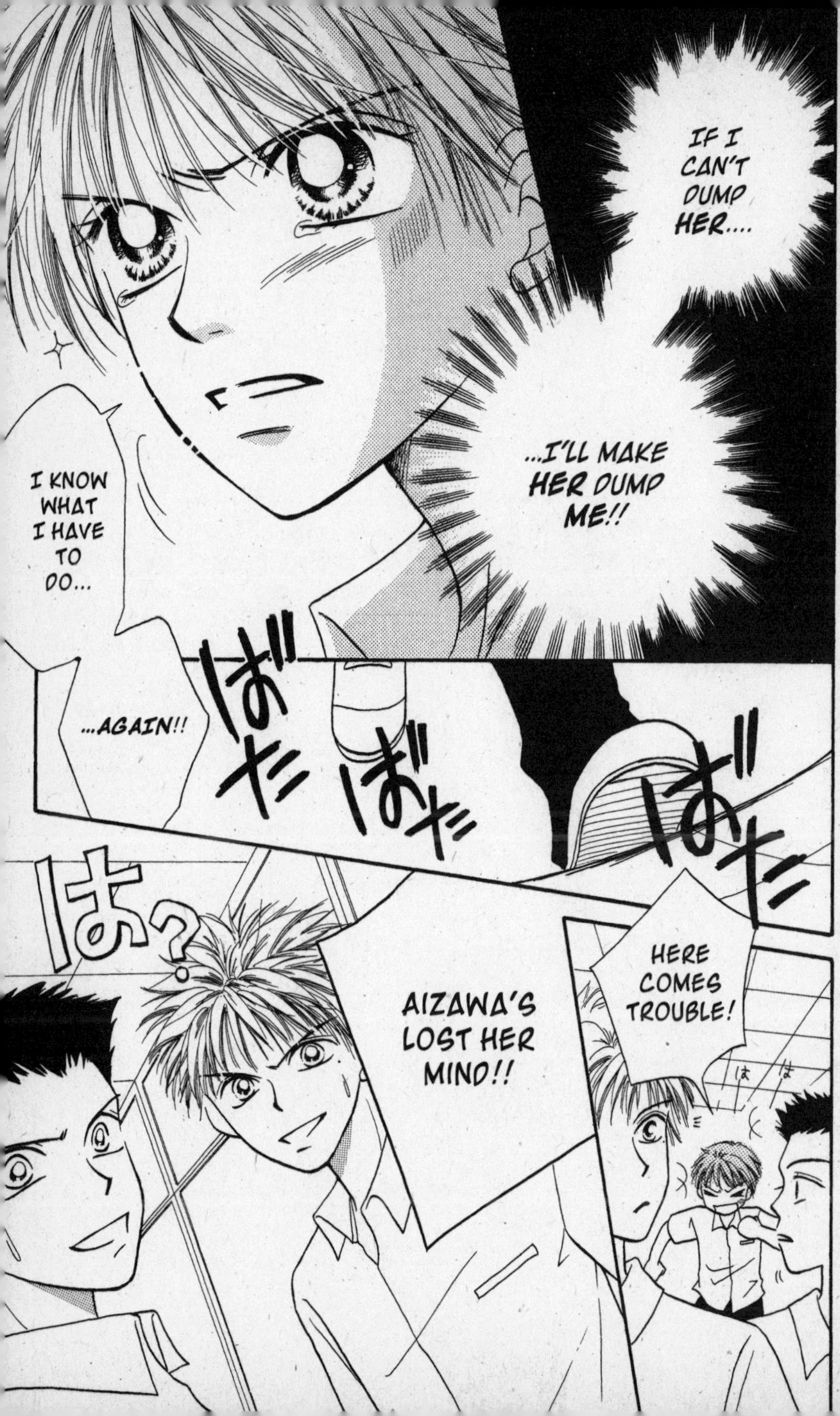

IF I CAN'T DUMP HER....
...I'LL MAKE HER DUMP ME!!
I KNOW WHAT I HAVE TO DO...
...AGAIN!!
ばた ばた ばた
HERE COMES TROUBLE!
はは
AIZAWA'S LOST HER MIND!!
は？

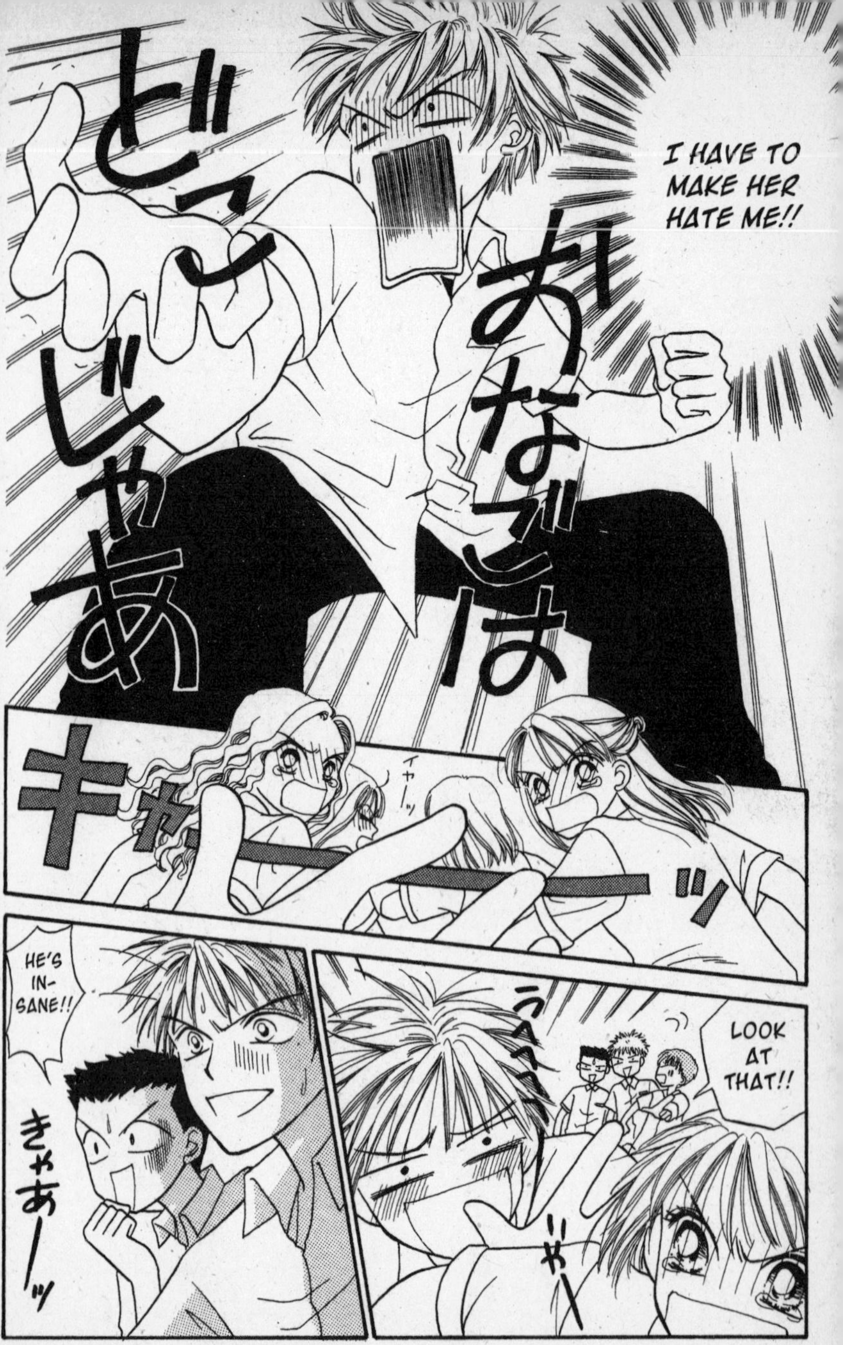
I HAVE TO MAKE HER HATE ME!!
キャーッ
LOOK AT THAT!!
HE'S IN-SANE!!
きゃあーッ

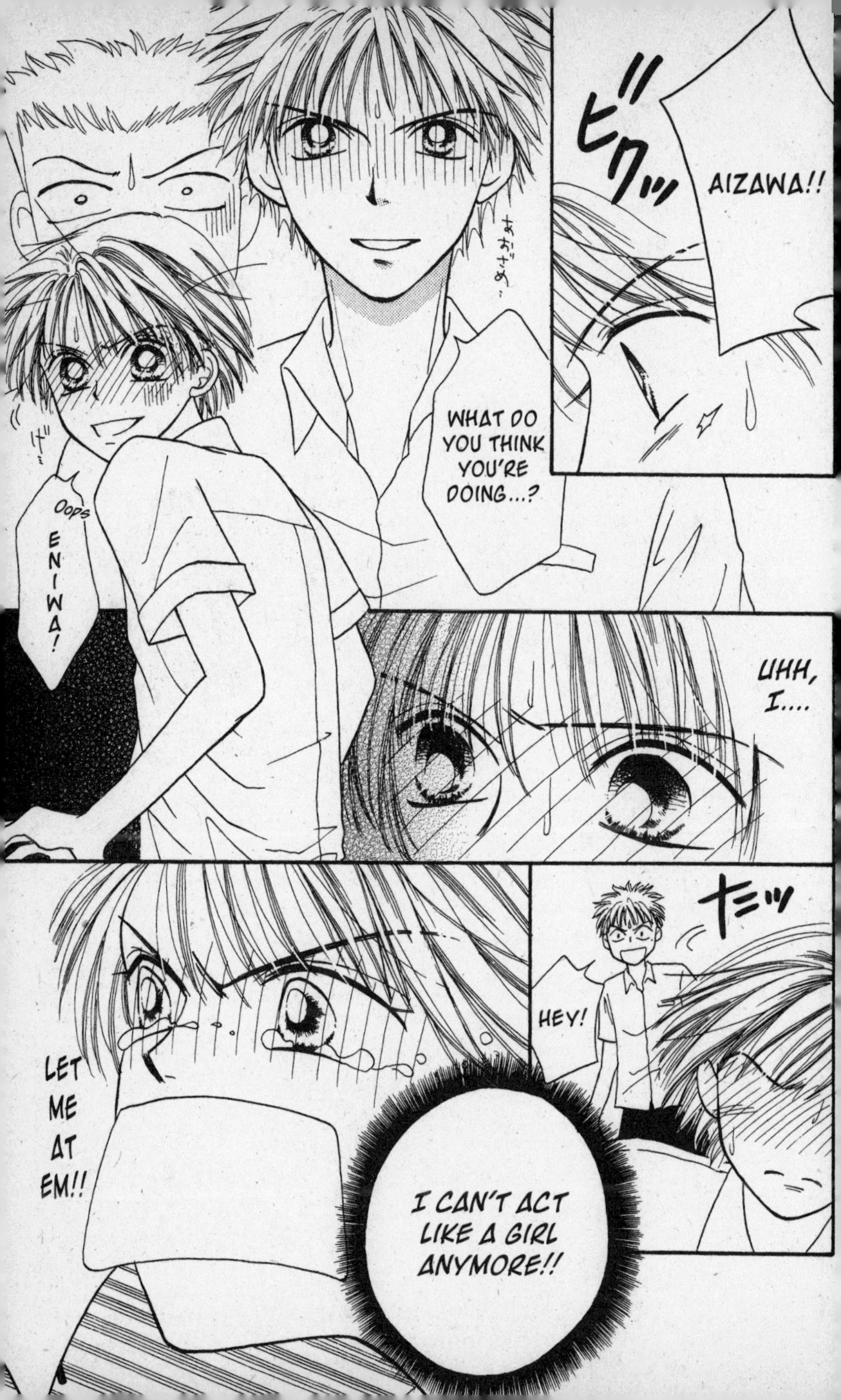

ビクッ
AIZAWA!!
UHH, I....
WHAT DO YOU THINK YOU'RE DOING...?
あおざめ
げ
Oops
ENIWA!
ダッ
HEY!
I CAN'T ACT LIKE A GIRL ANYMORE!!
LET ME AT EM!!

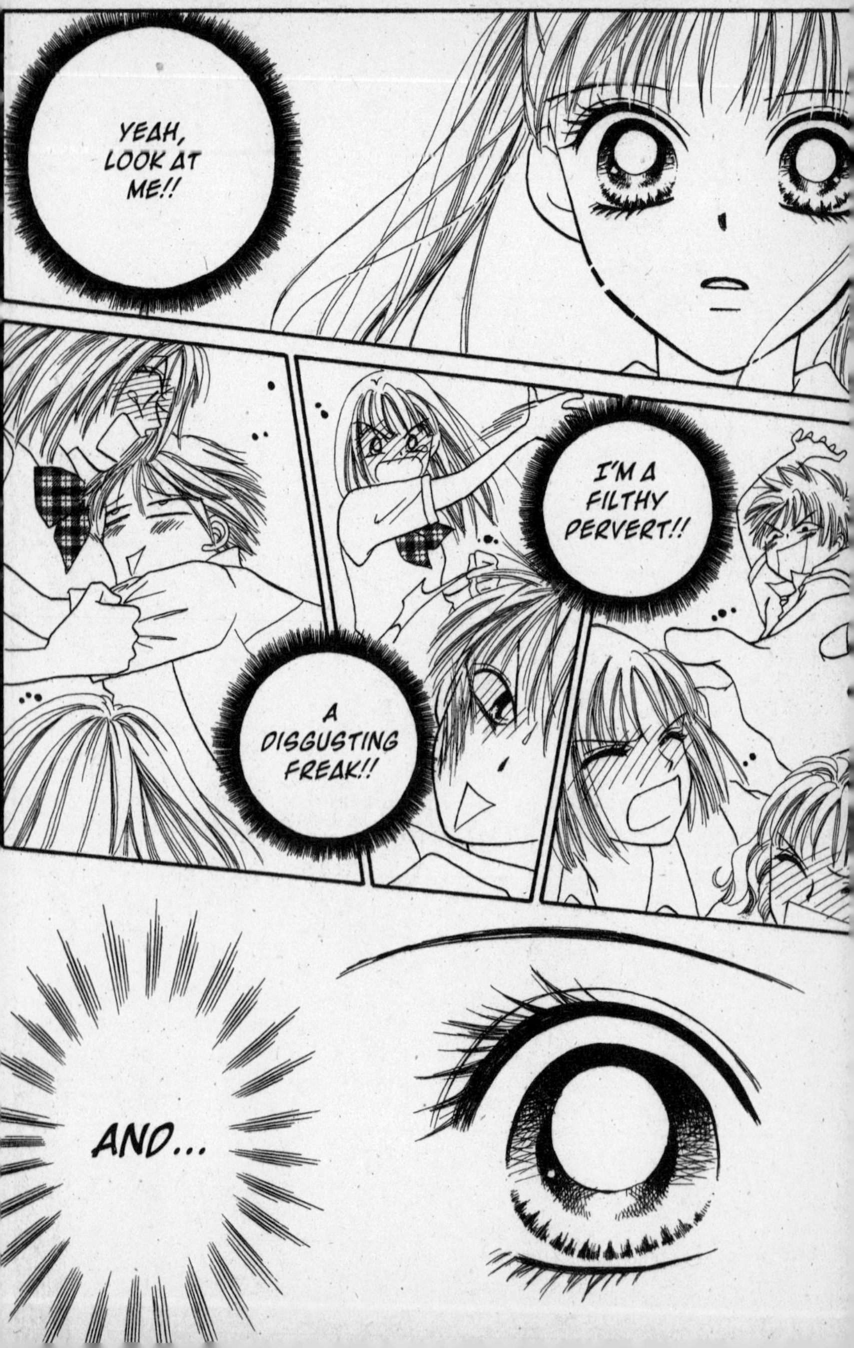
YEAH, LOOK AT ME!!
I'M A FILTHY PERVERT!!
A DISGUSTING FREAK!!
AND...

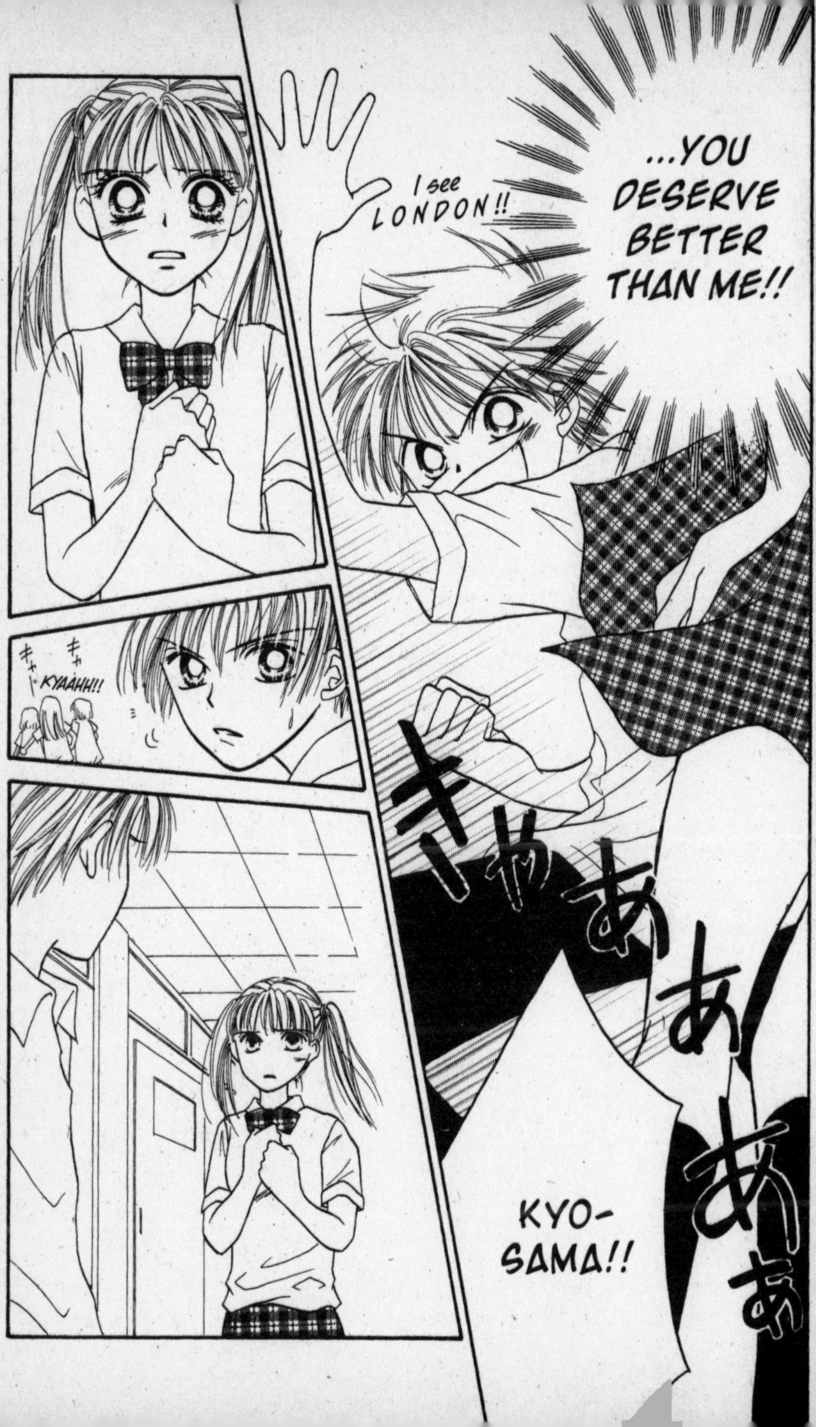
...YOU DESERVE BETTER THAN ME!!
I see LONDON!!
きゃああああ
KYO-SAMA!!
キャー キャ
KYAAHH!!

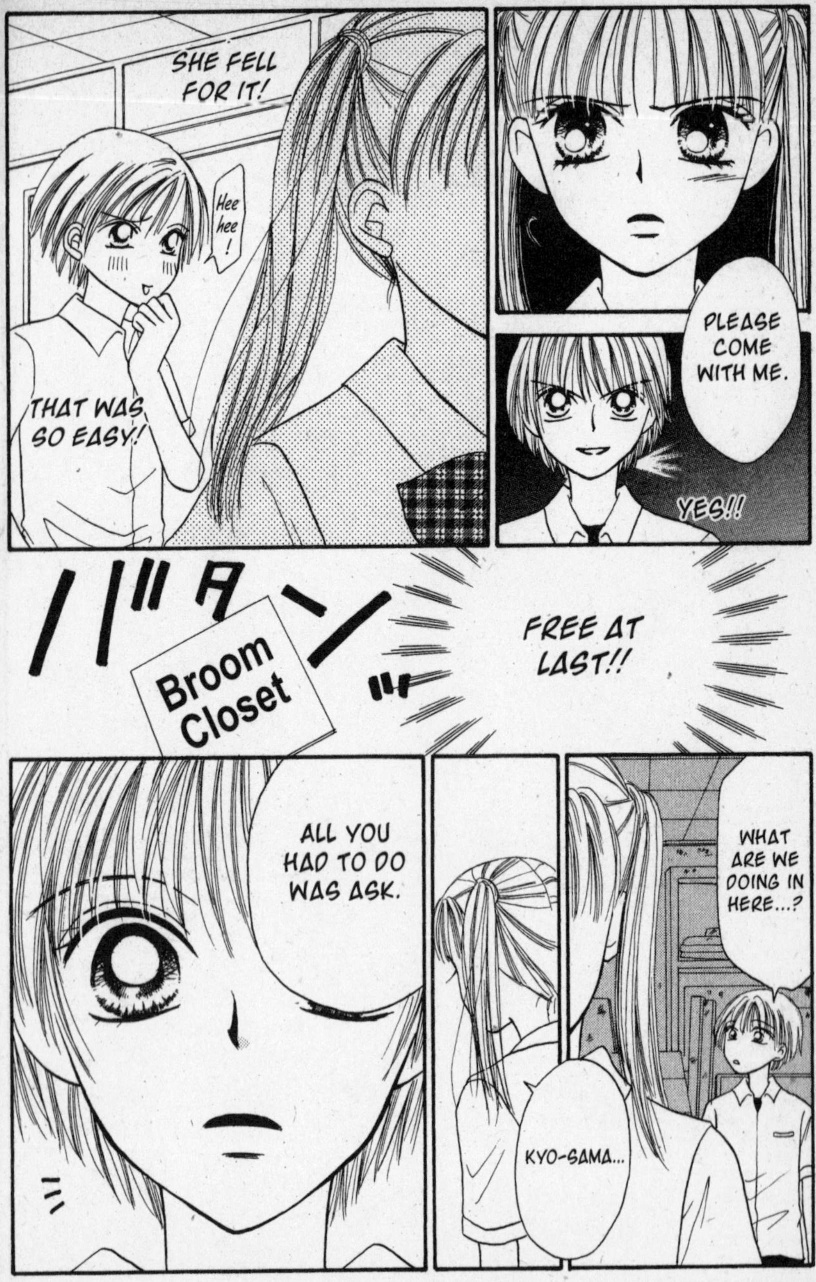
PLEASE COME WITH ME.
YES!!
SHE FELL FOR IT!
Hee hee!
THAT WAS SO EASY!
バタン
Broom Closet
FREE AT LAST!!
WHAT ARE WE DOING IN HERE...?
KYO-SAMA...
ALL YOU HAD TO DO WAS ASK.

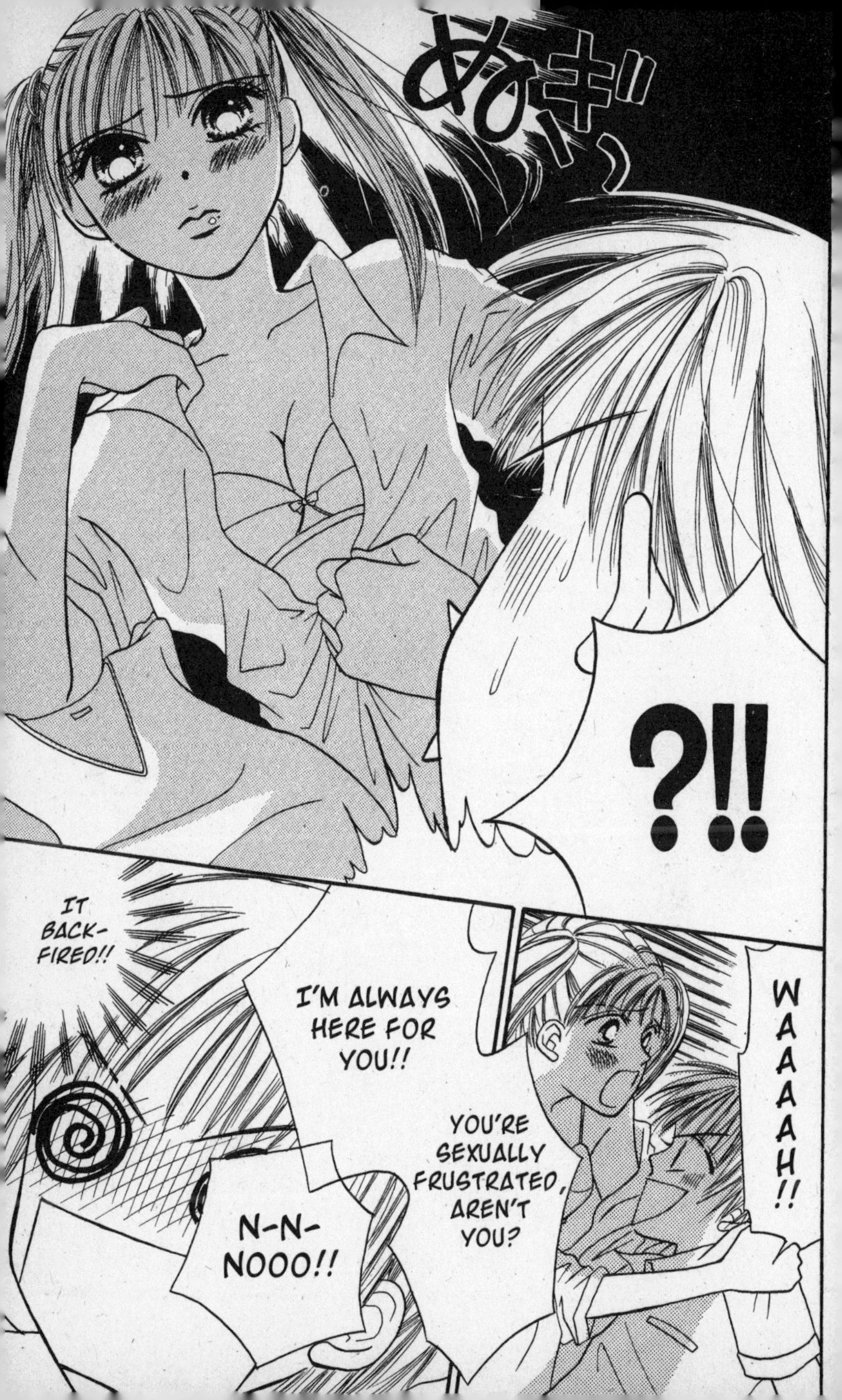
めぎ
?!!
WAAAAAH!!
YOU'RE SEXUALLY FRUSTRATED, AREN'T YOU?
I'M ALWAYS HERE FOR YOU!!
IT BACK-FIRED!!
N-N-NOOO!!

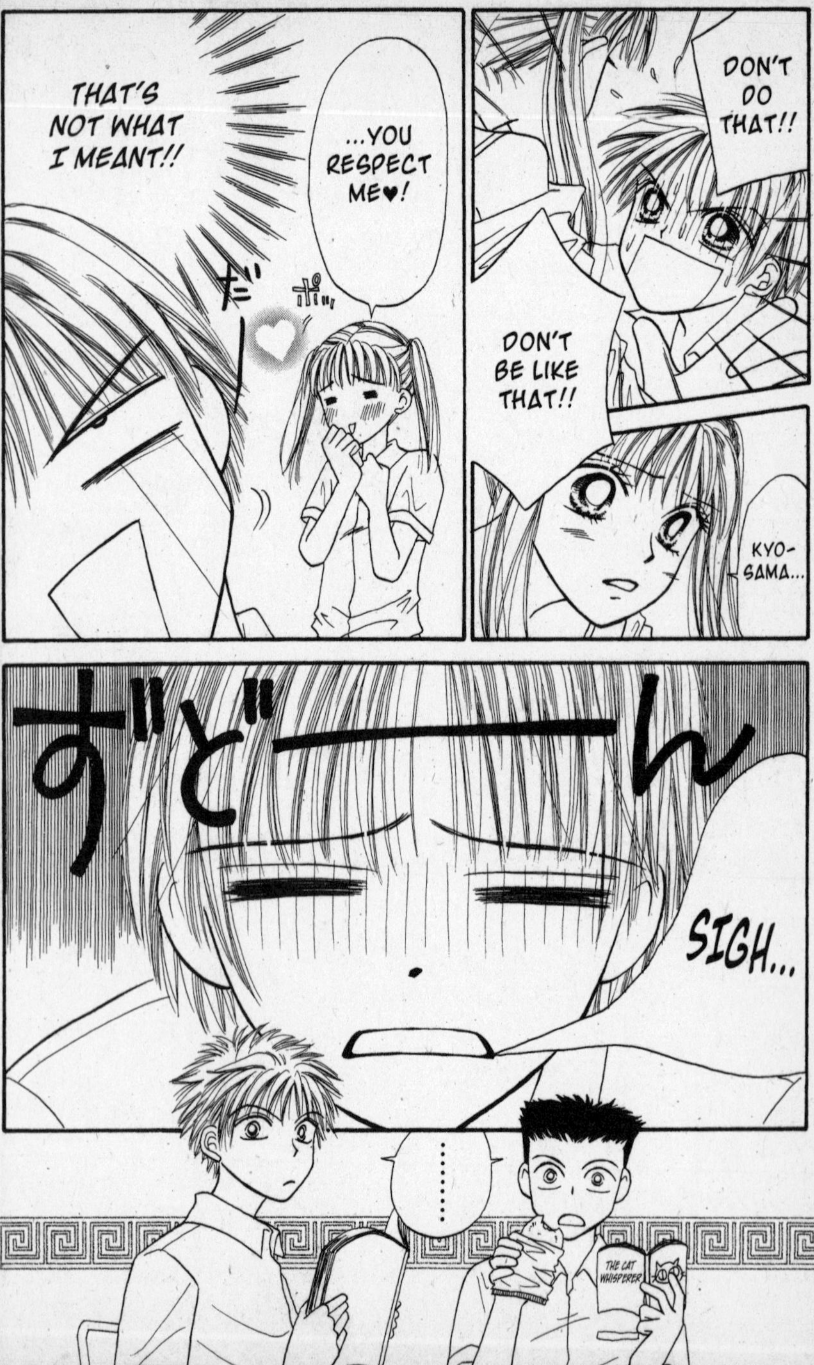
DON'T DO THAT!!
DON'T BE LIKE THAT!!
KYO-SAMA...
...YOU RESPECT ME♥!
THAT'S NOT WHAT I MEANT!!
ずどーーん
SIGH...
......
THE CAT WHISPERER

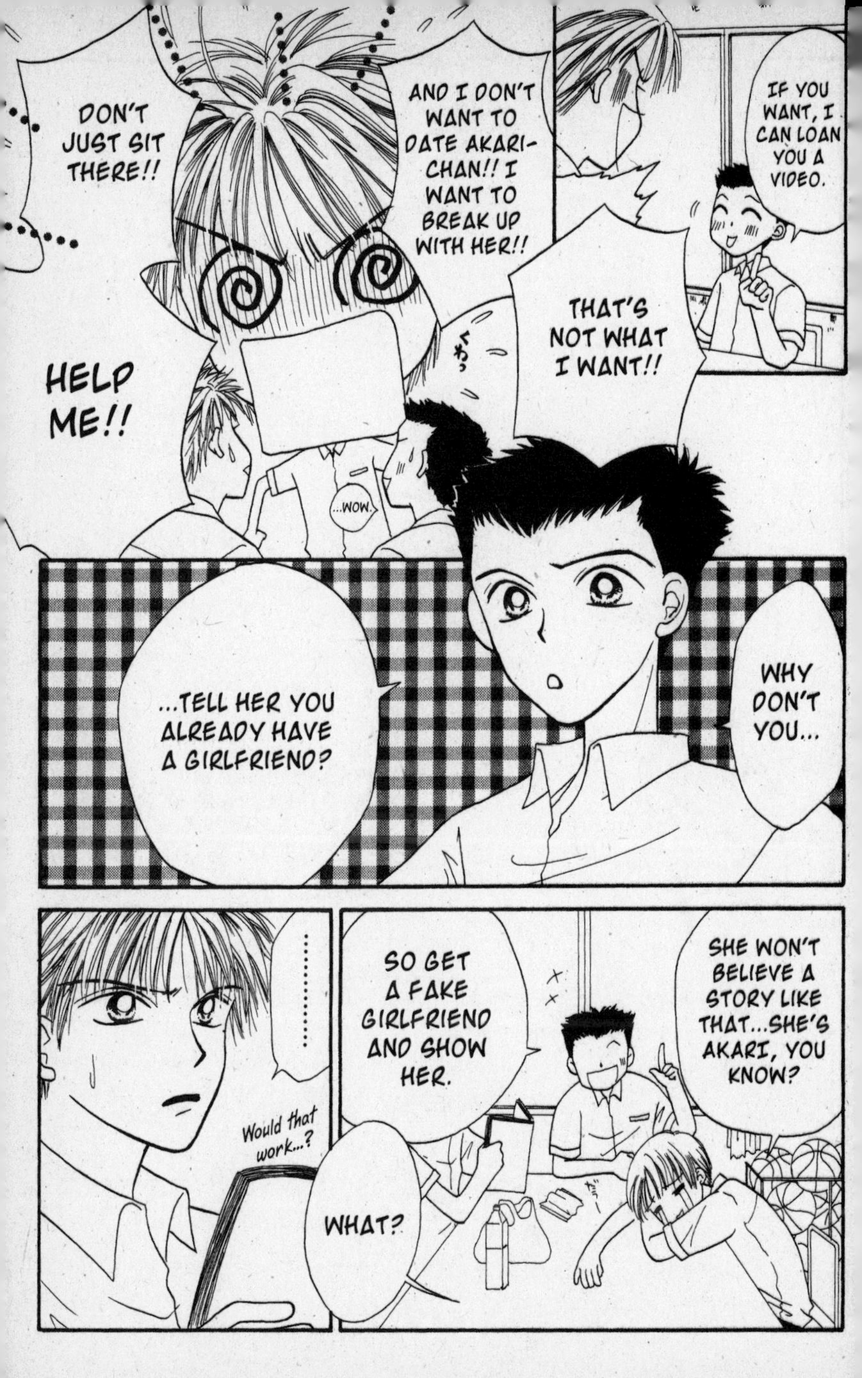
IF YOU WANT, I CAN LOAN YOU A VIDEO.
THAT'S NOT WHAT I WANT!!
AND I DON'T WANT TO DATE AKARI-CHAN!! I WANT TO BREAK UP WITH HER!!
DON'T JUST SIT THERE!!
HELP ME!!
...WOW.
WHY DON'T YOU...
...TELL HER YOU ALREADY HAVE A GIRLFRIEND?
SHE WON'T BELIEVE A STORY LIKE THAT...SHE'S AKARI, YOU KNOW?
SO GET A FAKE GIRLFRIEND AND SHOW HER.
WHAT?
......
Would that work...?

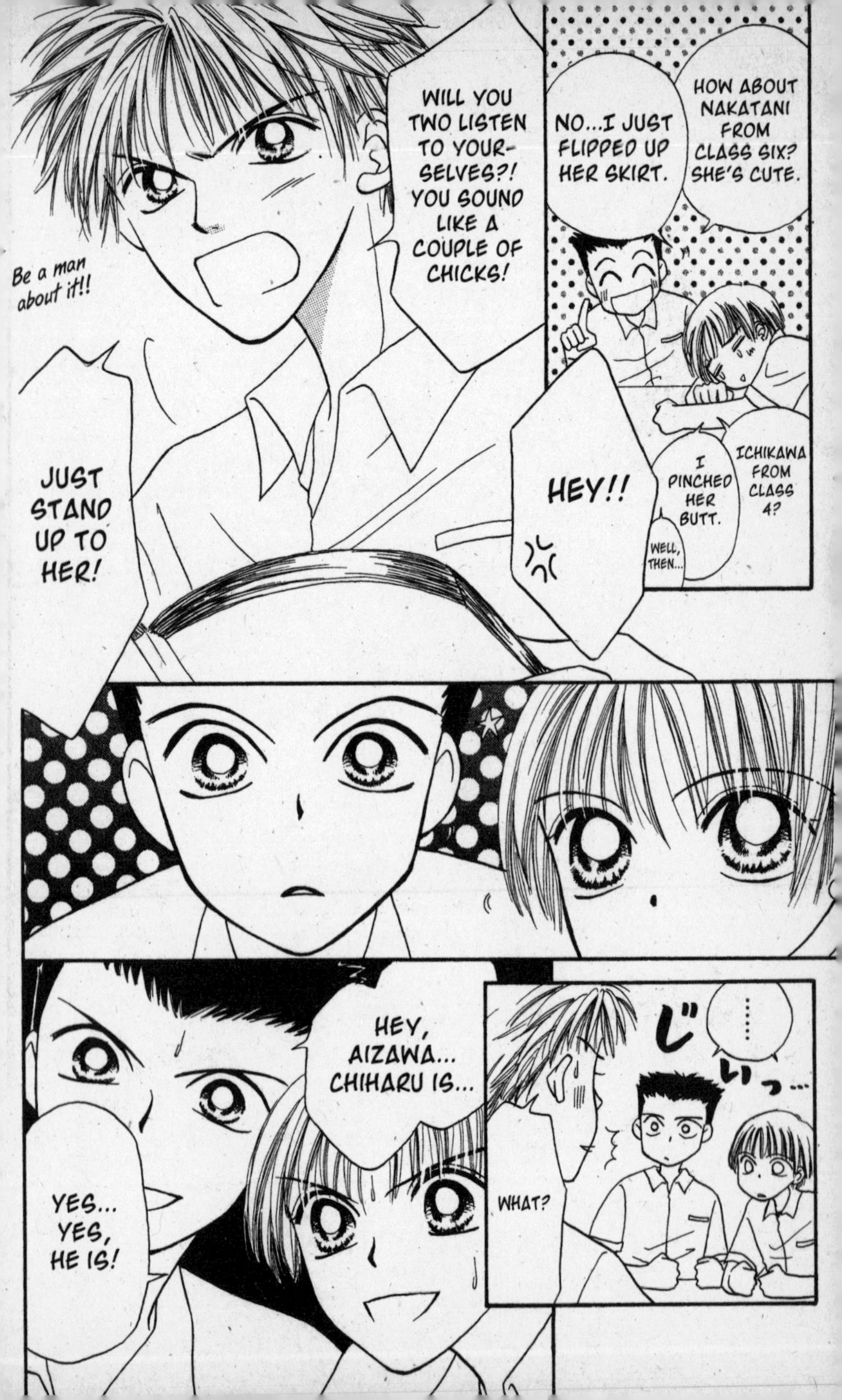
HOW ABOUT NAKATANI FROM CLASS SIX? SHE'S CUTE.
NO...I JUST FLIPPED UP HER SKIRT.
ICHIKAWA FROM CLASS 4?
WELL, THEN...
I PINCHED HER BUTT.
HEY!!
WILL YOU TWO LISTEN TO YOURSELVES?! YOU SOUND LIKE A COUPLE OF CHICKS!
JUST STAND UP TO HER!
Be a man about it!!
......
じいっ...
WHAT?
HEY, AIZAWA... CHIHARU IS...
YES... YES, HE IS!

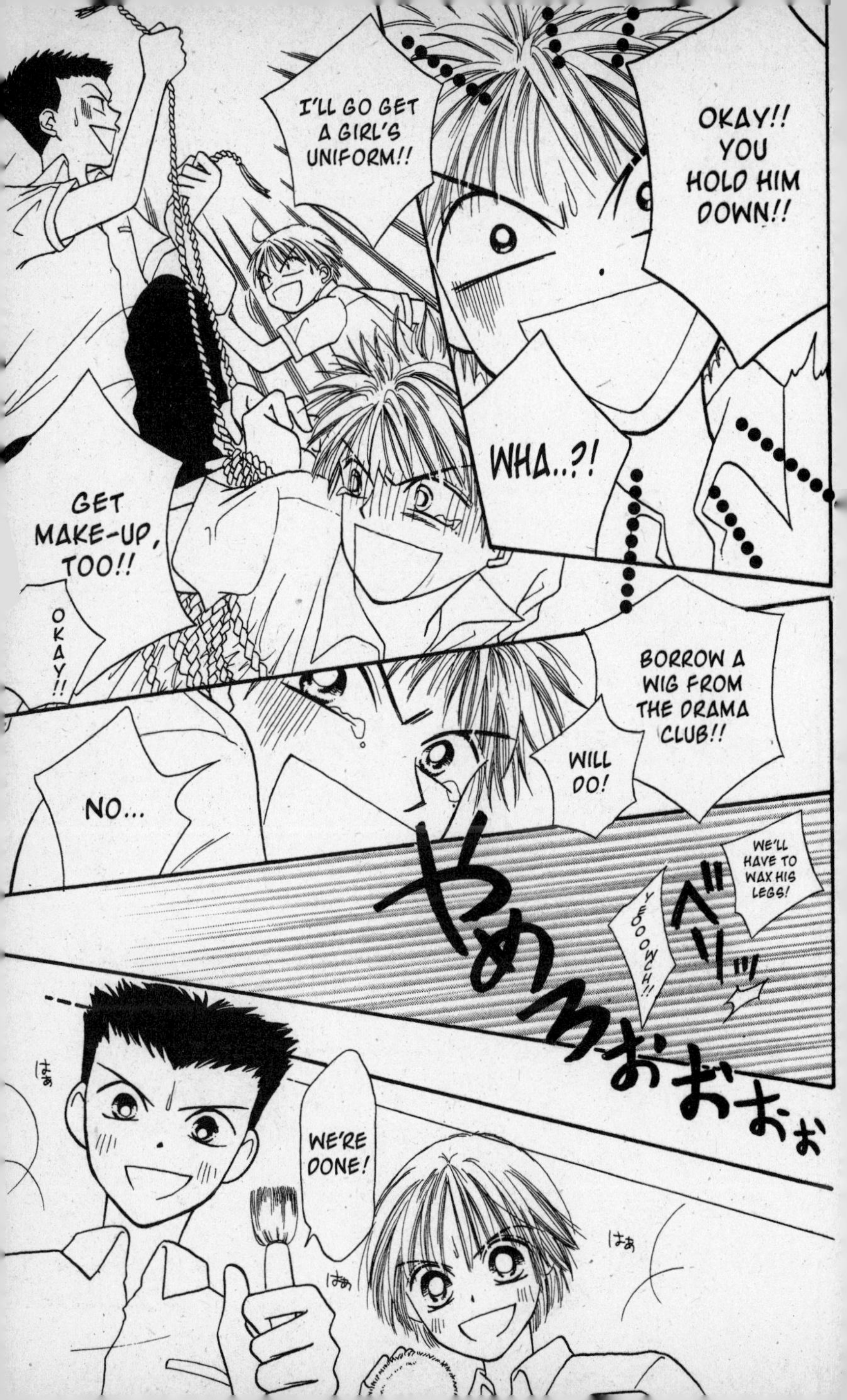

OKAY!! YOU HOLD HIM DOWN!!
WHA..?!
I'LL GO GET A GIRL'S UNIFORM!!
GET MAKE-UP, TOO!!
OKAY!!
BORROW A WIG FROM THE DRAMA CLUB!!
WILL DO!
NO...
WE'LL HAVE TO WAX HIS LEGS!
ベリッ
YEOOOWCH!!
やめろおおおぉ
WE'RE DONE!
はあ
はあ
はあ

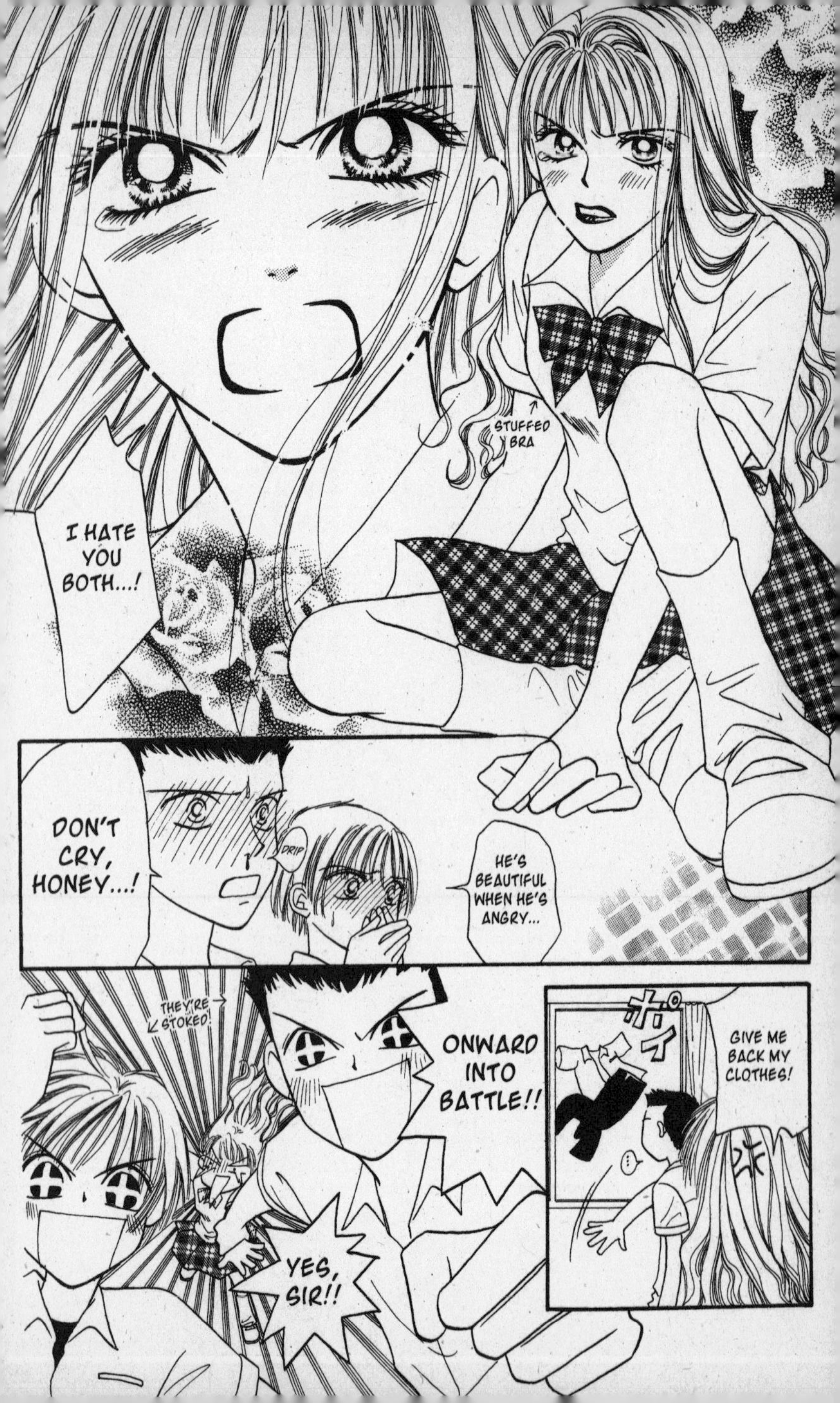
STUFFED BRA
I HATE YOU BOTH...!
HE'S BEAUTIFUL WHEN HE'S ANGRY...
DRIP
DON'T CRY, HONEY...!
ポイ
GIVE ME BACK MY CLOTHES!
ONWARD INTO BATTLE!!
THEY'RE STOKED!
YES, SIR!!

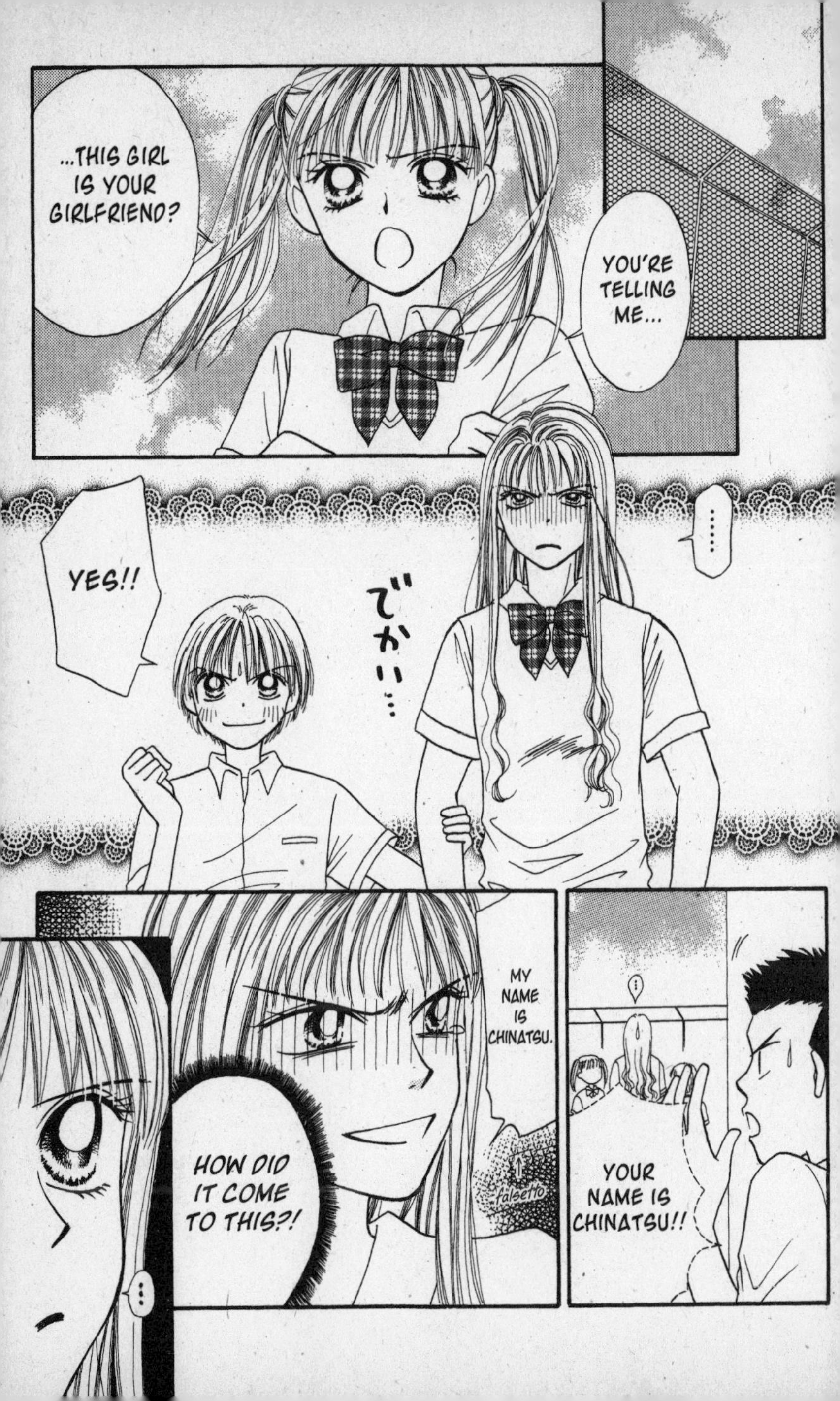
...THIS GIRL IS YOUR GIRLFRIEND?
YOU'RE TELLING ME...
......
でかい…
YES!!
YOUR NAME IS CHINATSU!!
!
MY NAME IS CHINATSU.
↑ falsetto
HOW DID IT COME TO THIS?!
...

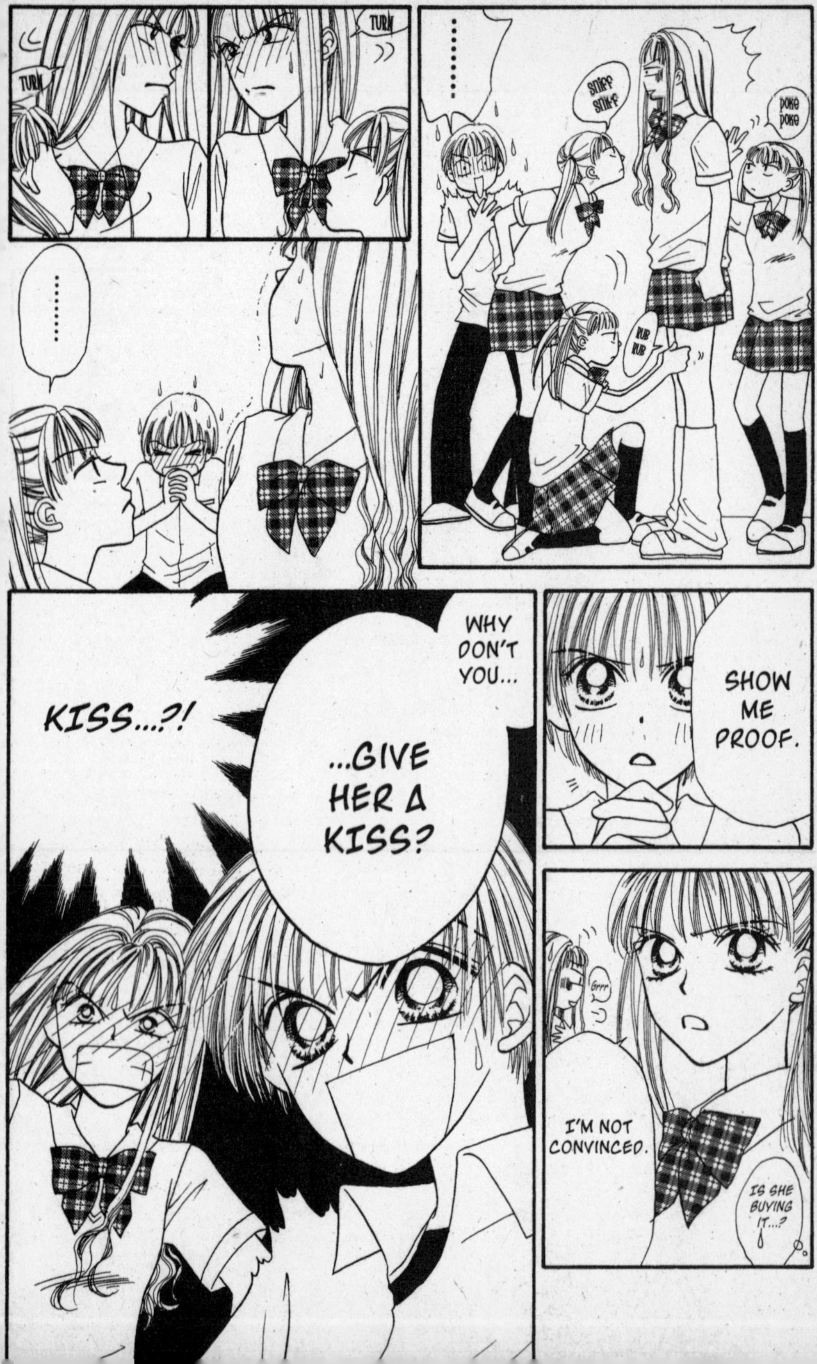
......
SNIFF SNIFF
POKE POKE
RUB RUB
TURN
TURN
......
SHOW ME PROOF.
I'M NOT CONVINCED.
Grrr
IS SHE BUYING IT...?
WHY DON'T YOU...
...GIVE HER A KISS?
KISS...?!

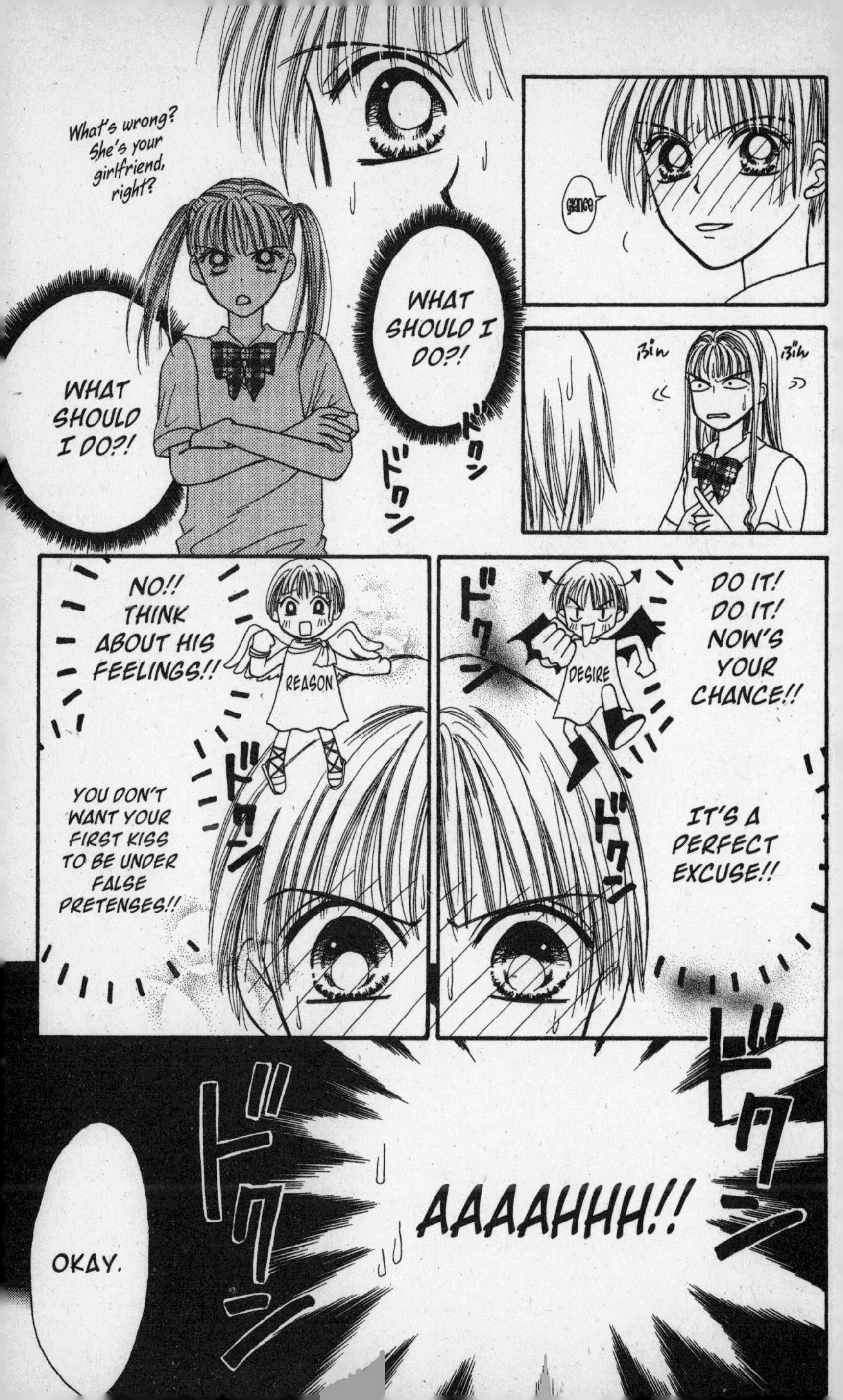
Glance
WHAT SHOULD I DO?!
ドクン
ドクン
What's wrong? She's your girlfriend, right?
WHAT SHOULD I DO?!
DO IT! DO IT! NOW'S YOUR CHANCE!!
DESIRE
ドクン
ドクン
IT'S A PERFECT EXCUSE!!
NO!! THINK ABOUT HIS FEELINGS!!
REASON
ドクン
YOU DON'T WANT YOUR FIRST KISS TO BE UNDER FALSE PRETENSES!!
ビクン
AAAAHHH!!
ドクン
OKAY.

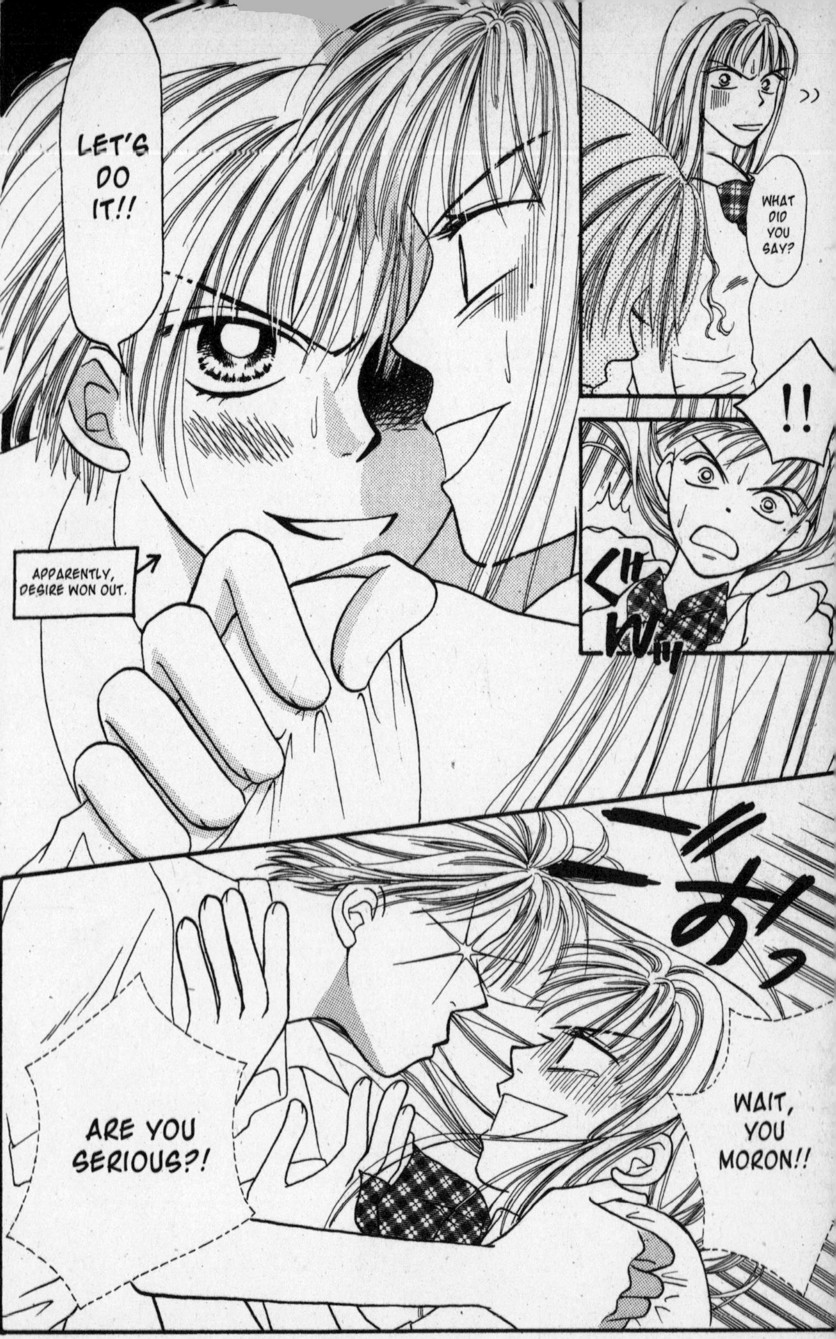

WHAT DID YOU SAY?
!!
ぐいっ
LET'S DO IT!!
APPARENTLY, DESIRE WON OUT.
おっ
WAIT, YOU MORON!!
ARE YOU SERIOUS?!

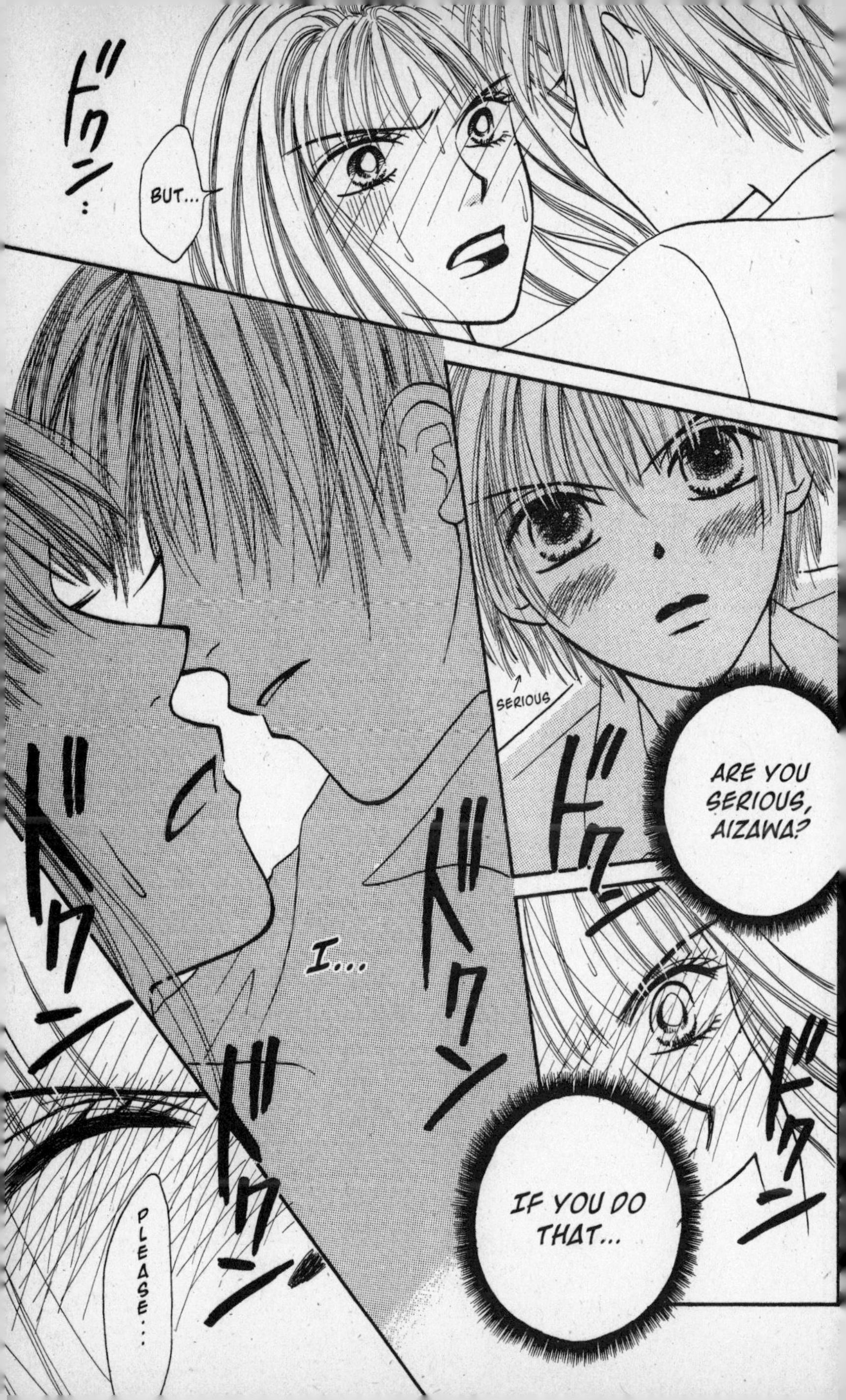
BUT...
ドクン…
SERIOUS
ARE YOU SERIOUS, AIZAWA?
ドクン
ドクン
I...
ドクン
ドクン
IF YOU DO THAT...
ドクン
PLEASE...

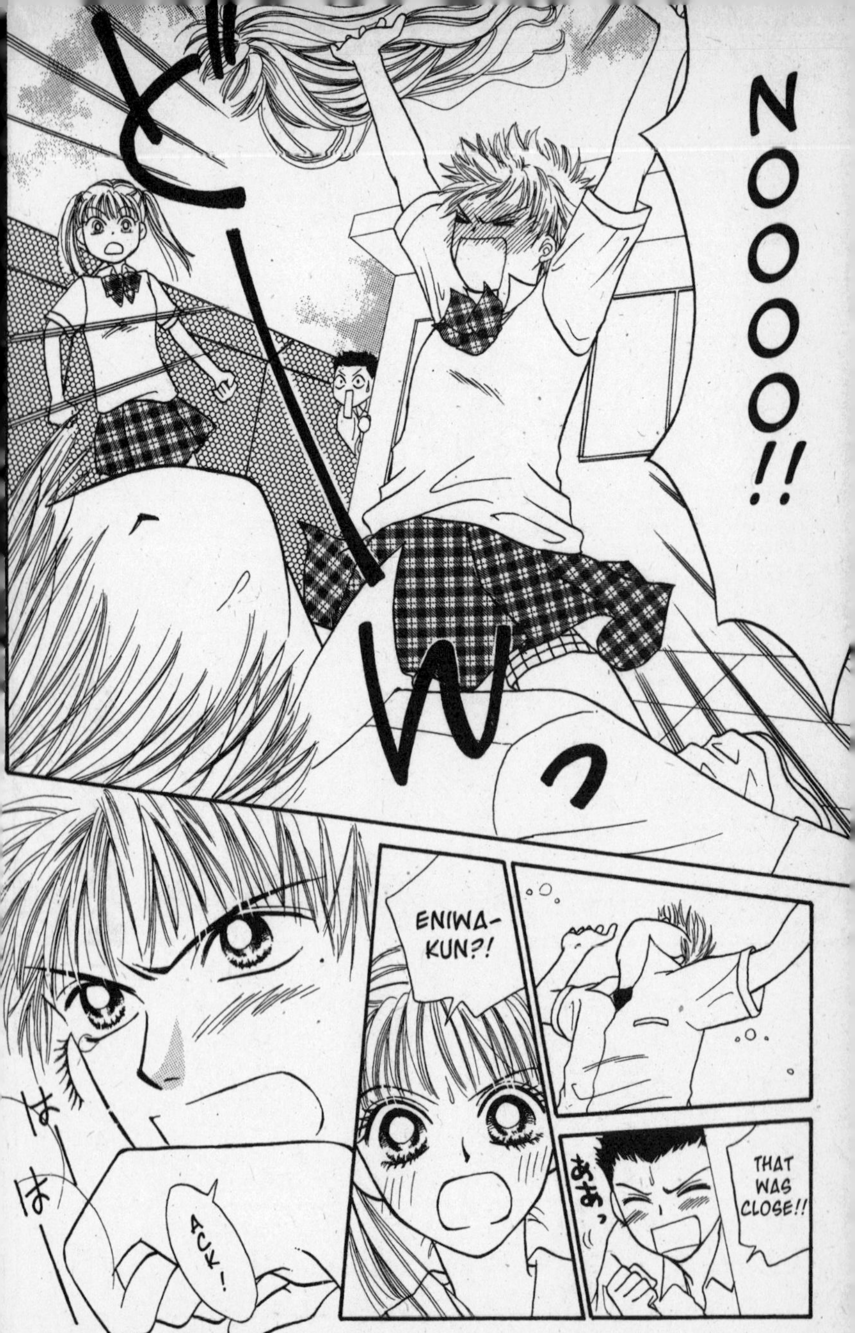
NOOOOO!!
どーんっ
ああっ
THAT WAS CLOSE!!
ENIWA-KUN?!
ACK!
はーはー

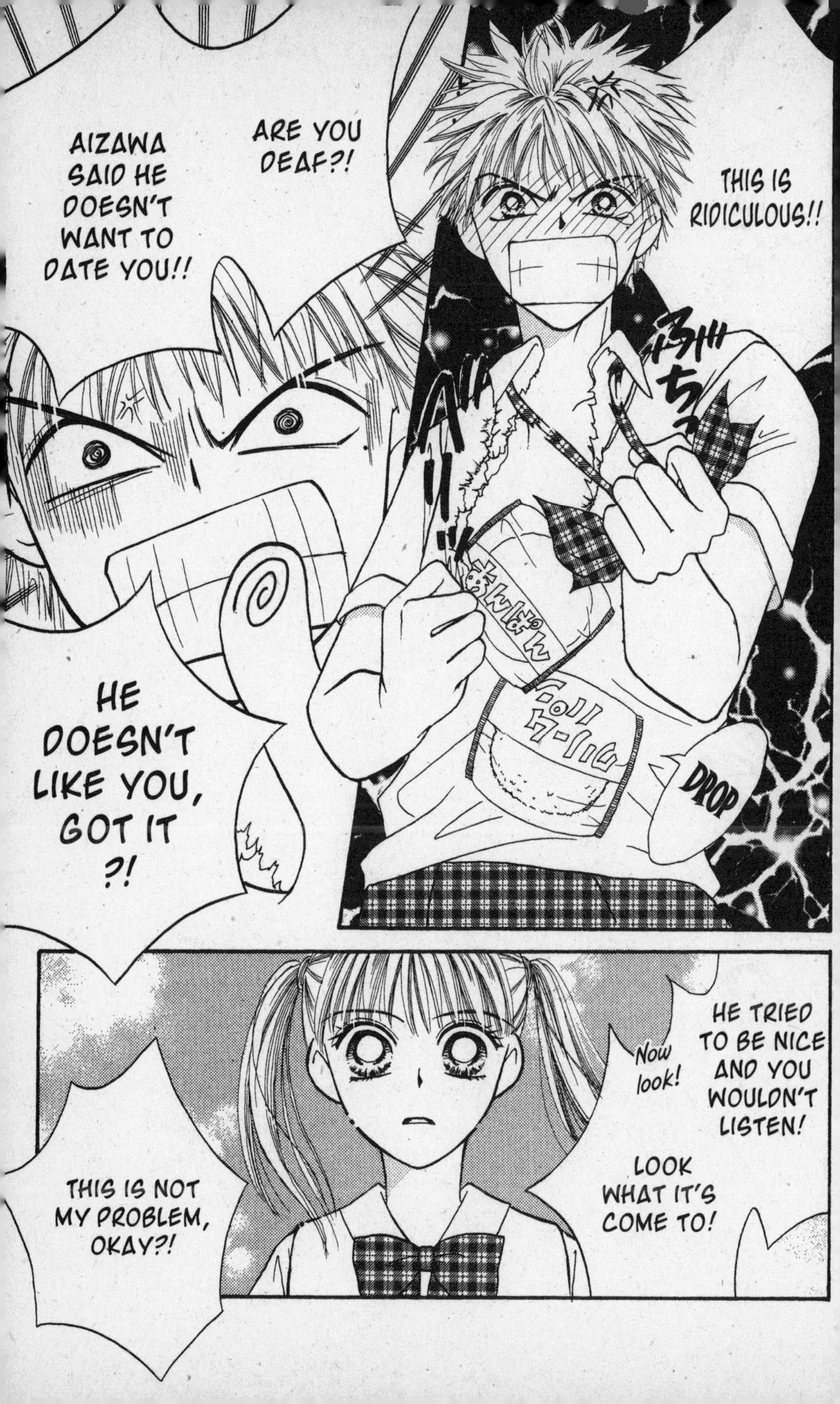
THIS IS RIDICULOUS!!
ARE YOU DEAF?!
AIZAWA SAID HE DOESN'T WANT TO DATE YOU!!
DROP
HE DOESN'T LIKE YOU, GOT IT ?!
HE TRIED TO BE NICE AND YOU WOULDN'T LISTEN!
Now look!
LOOK WHAT IT'S COME TO!
THIS IS NOT MY PROBLEM, OKAY?!

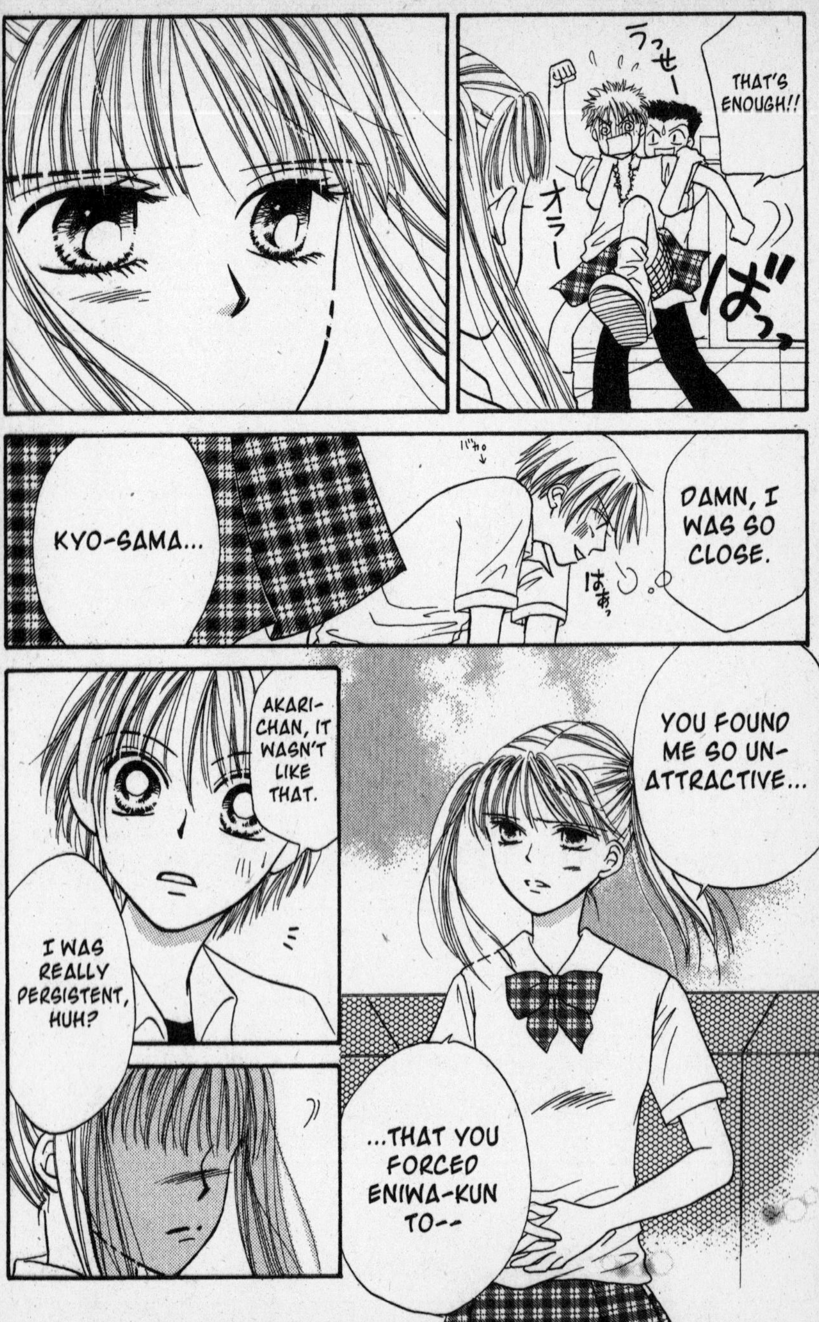
ラッせー
THAT'S ENOUGH!!
オラー
ばっ
DAMN, I WAS SO CLOSE.
はぁっ
KYO-SAMA...
YOU FOUND ME SO UN-ATTRACTIVE...
...THAT YOU FORCED ENIWA-KUN TO--
AKARI-CHAN, IT WASN'T LIKE THAT.
I WAS REALLY PERSISTENT, HUH?

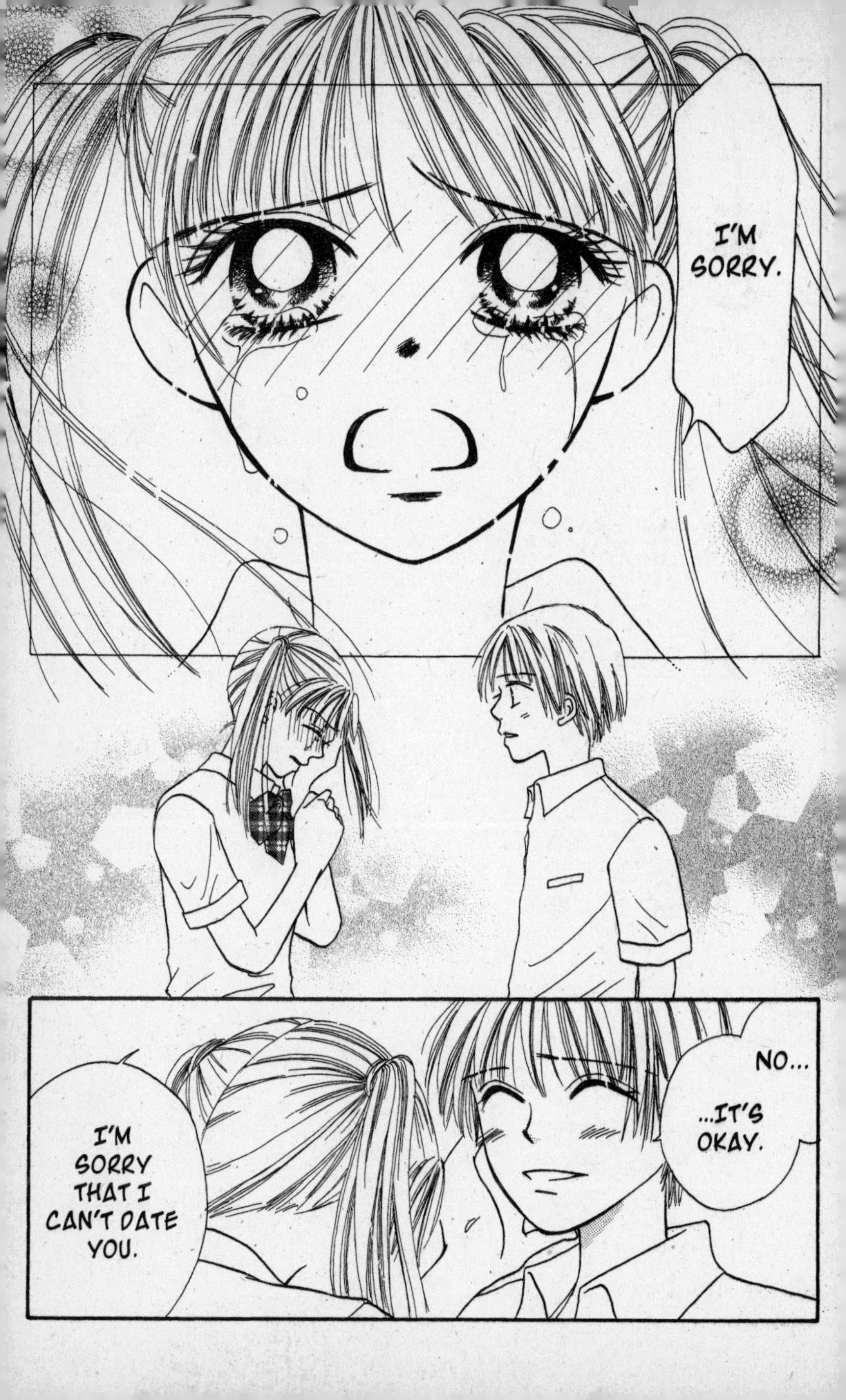
I'M SORRY.
NO... ...IT'S OKAY.
I'M SORRY THAT I CAN'T DATE YOU.

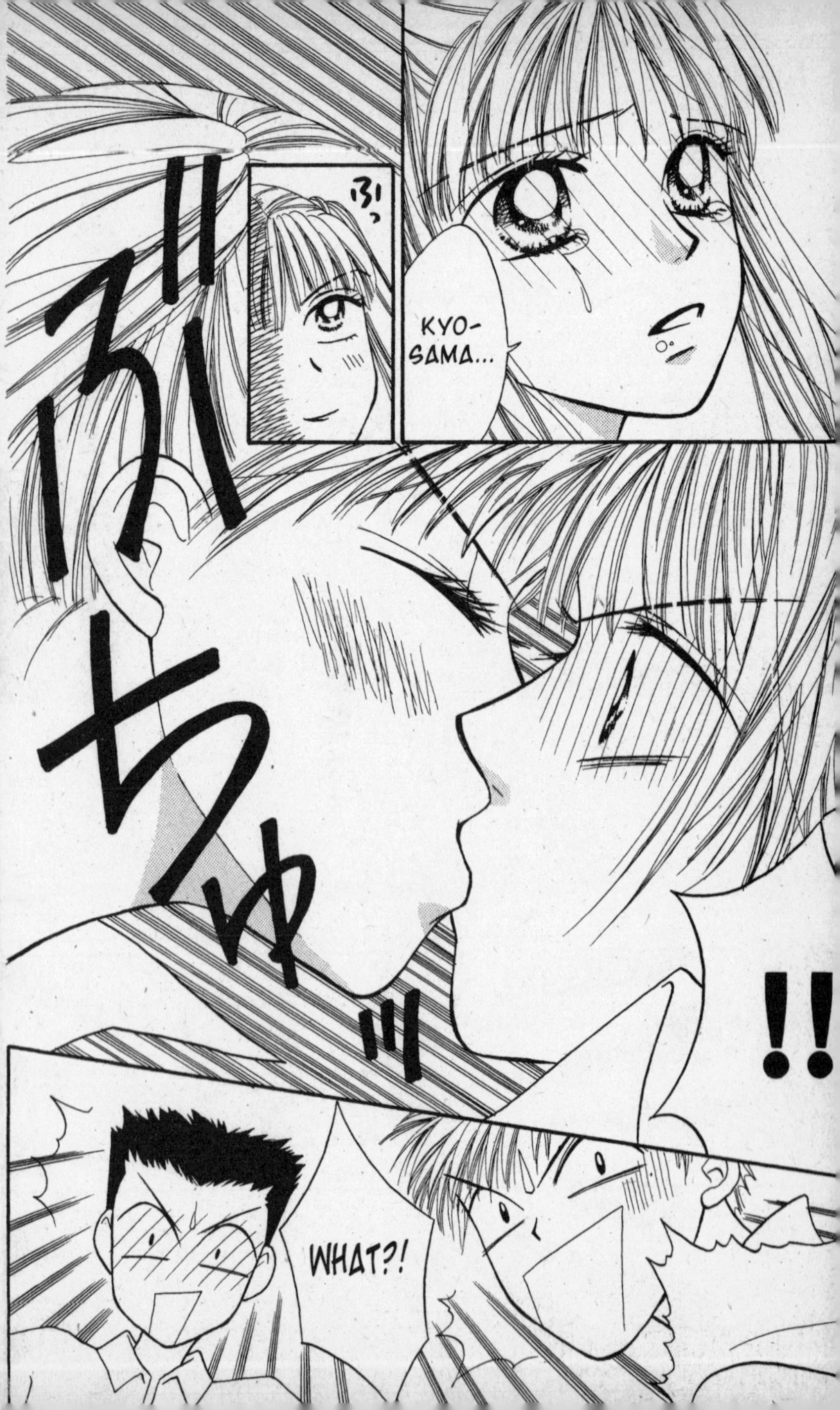
KYO-SAMA...
ふっ
ぶちゅ
!!
WHAT?!

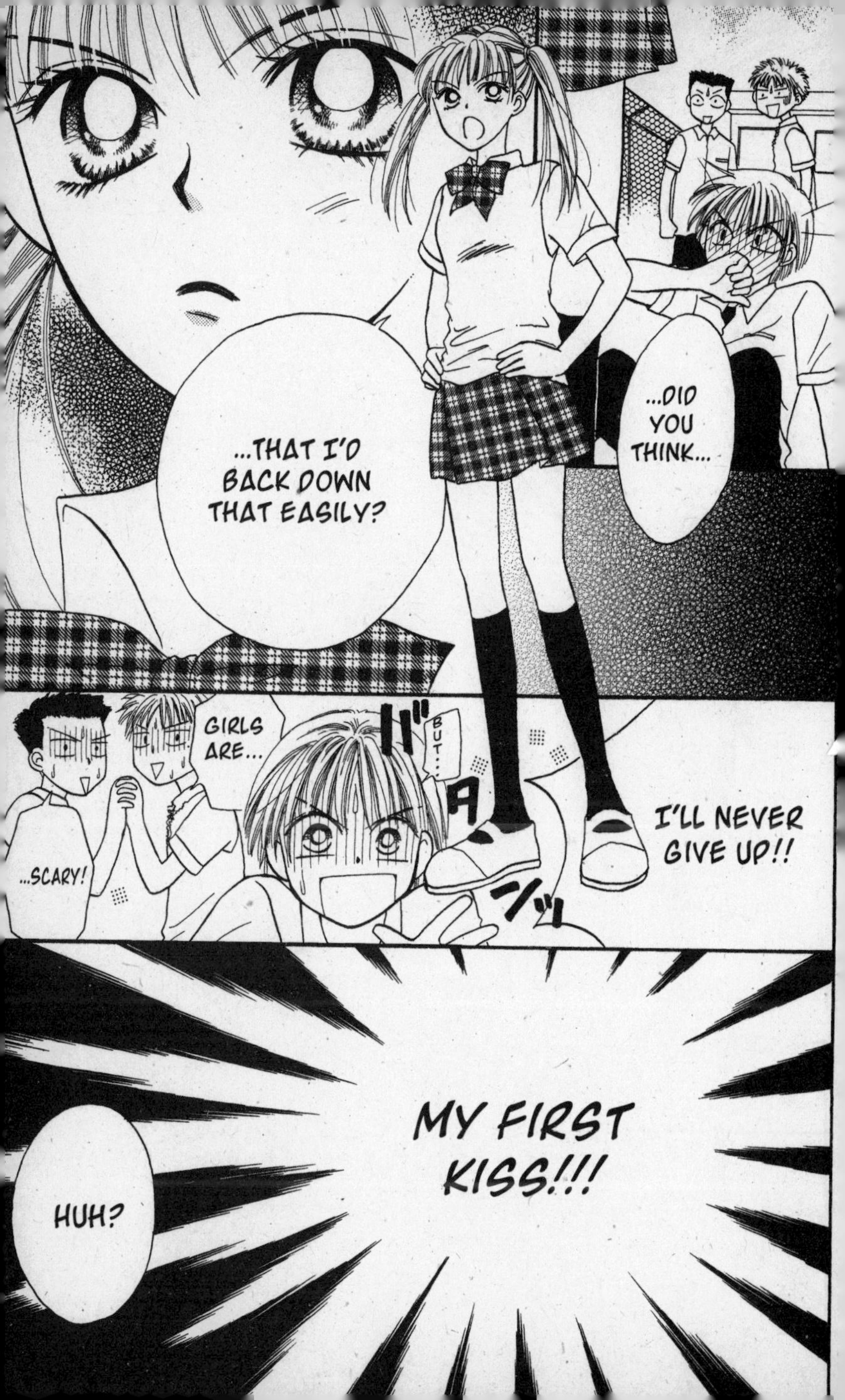
...DID YOU THINK...
...THAT I'D BACK DOWN THAT EASILY?
I'LL NEVER GIVE UP!!
BUT...
GIRLS ARE...
...SCARY!
MY FIRST KISS!!!
HUH?

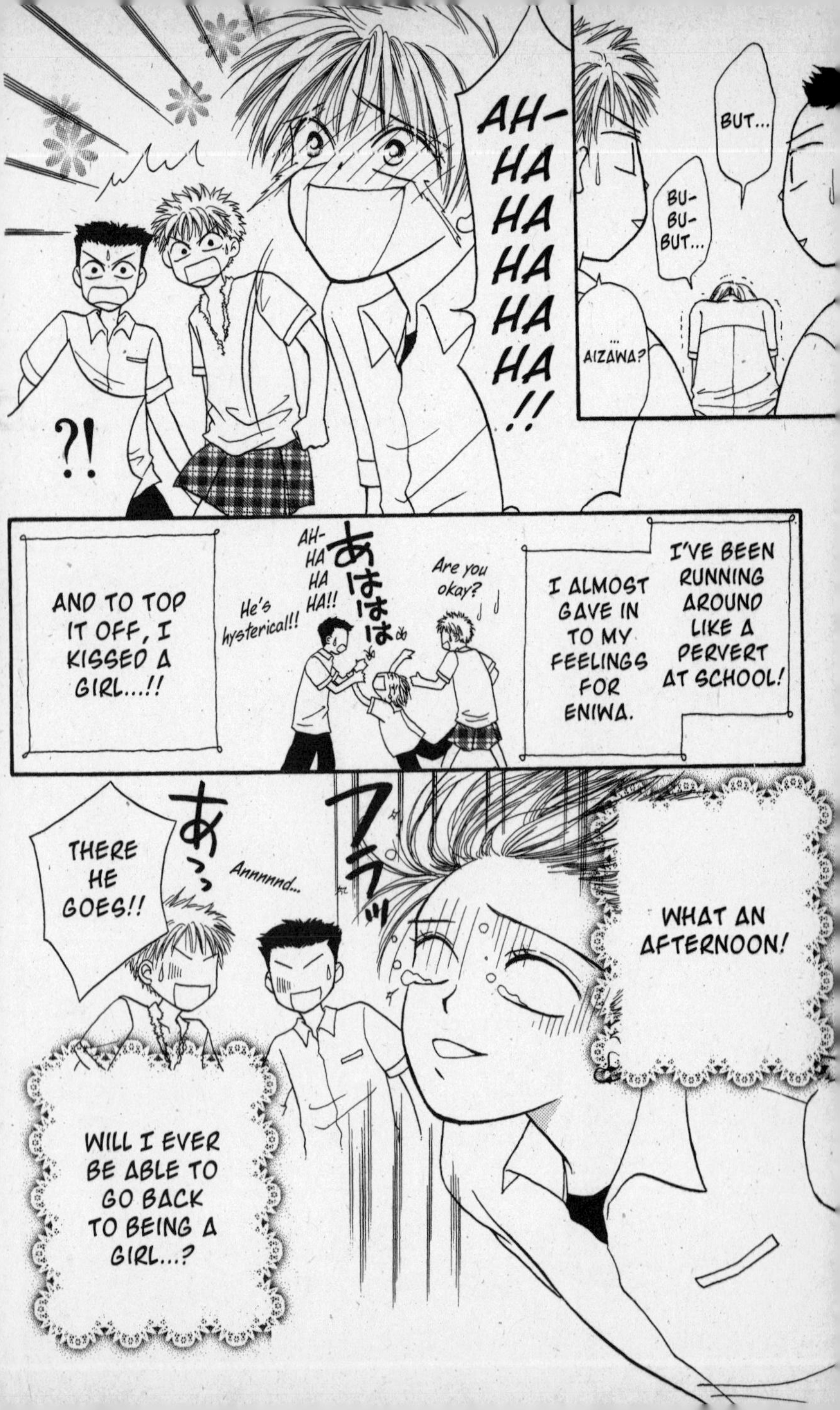

BUT...
BU-BU-BUT...
...AIZAWA?
AH-HA HA HA HA HA HA!!
?!
I'VE BEEN RUNNING AROUND LIKE A PERVERT AT SCHOOL!
I ALMOST GAVE IN TO MY FEELINGS FOR ENIWA.
Are you okay?
あははは
AH-HA HA HA!!
He's hysterical!!
AND TO TOP IT OFF, I KISSED A GIRL...!!
WHAT AN AFTERNOON!
フラッ
Annnnnd...
あっ
THERE HE GOES!!
WILL I EVER BE ABLE TO GO BACK TO BEING A GIRL...?

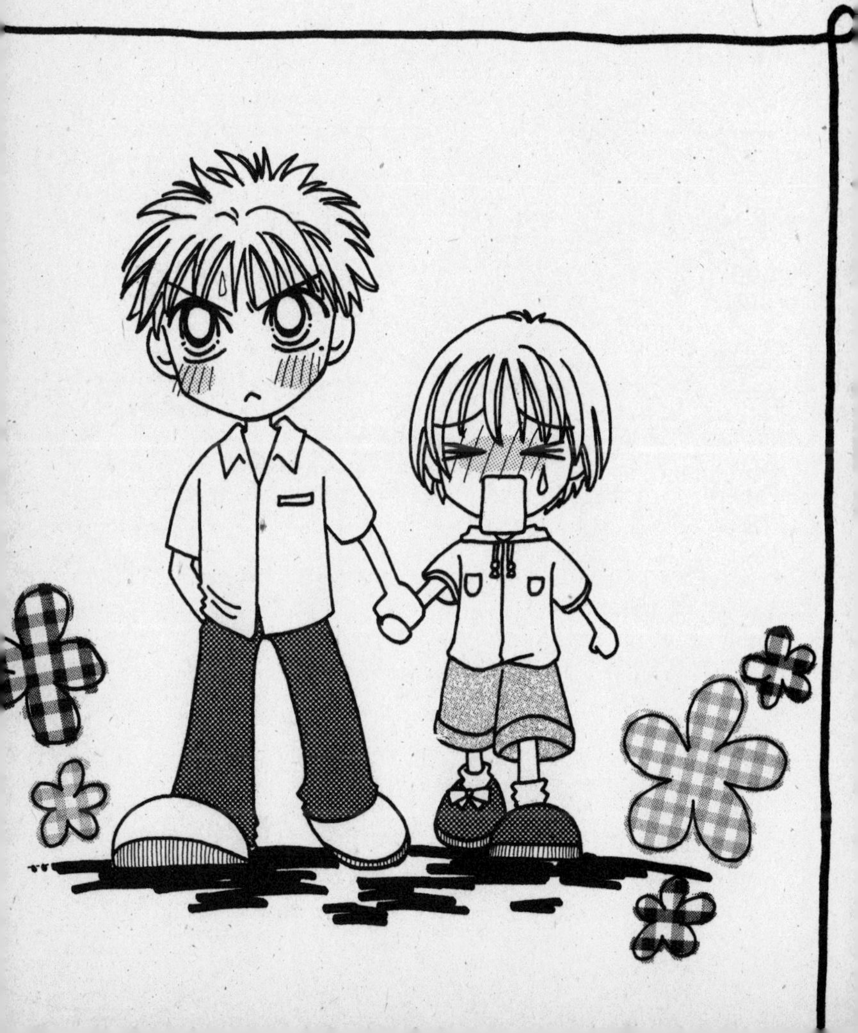

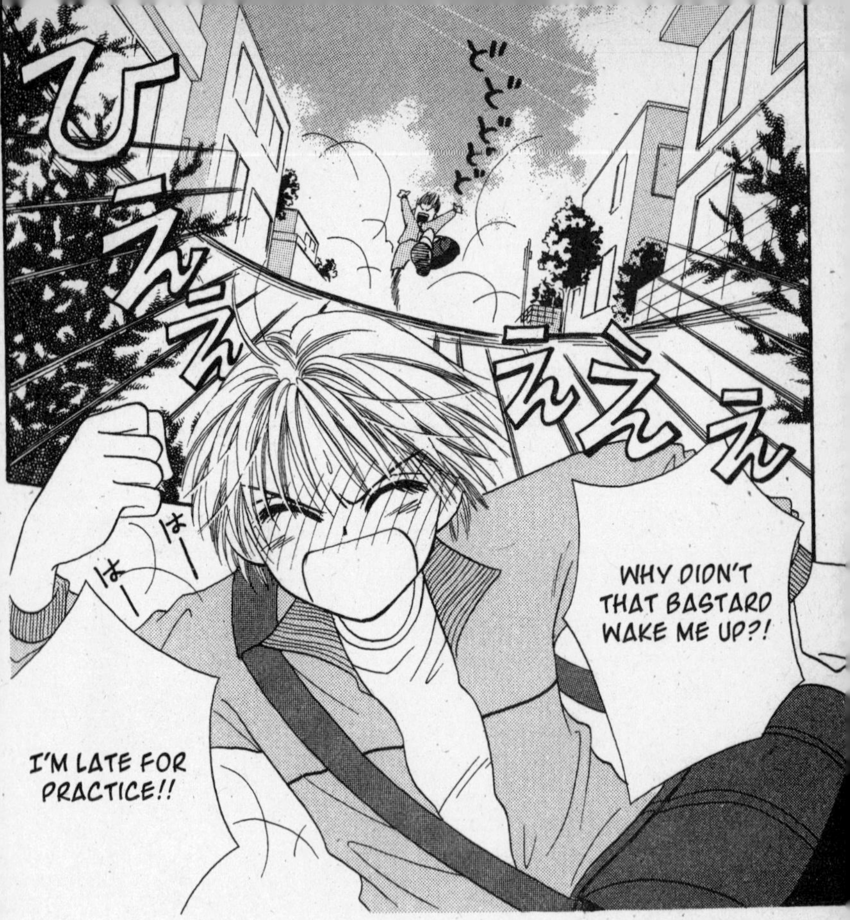
どどどど
ひえええ
ええええ
WHY DIDN'T THAT BASTARD WAKE ME UP?!
はーはー
I'M LATE FOR PRACTICE!!

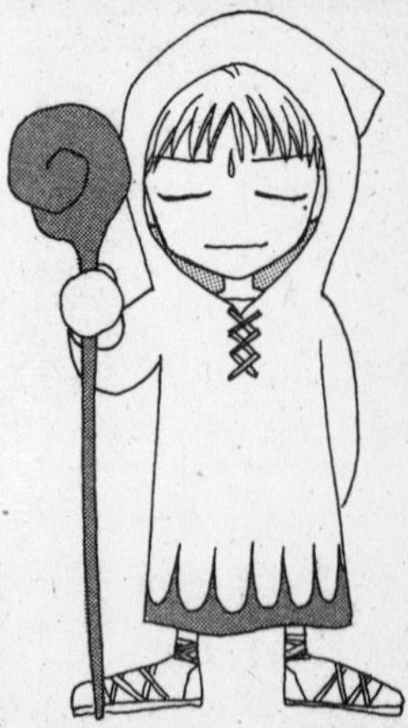

GIRL GOT GAME!

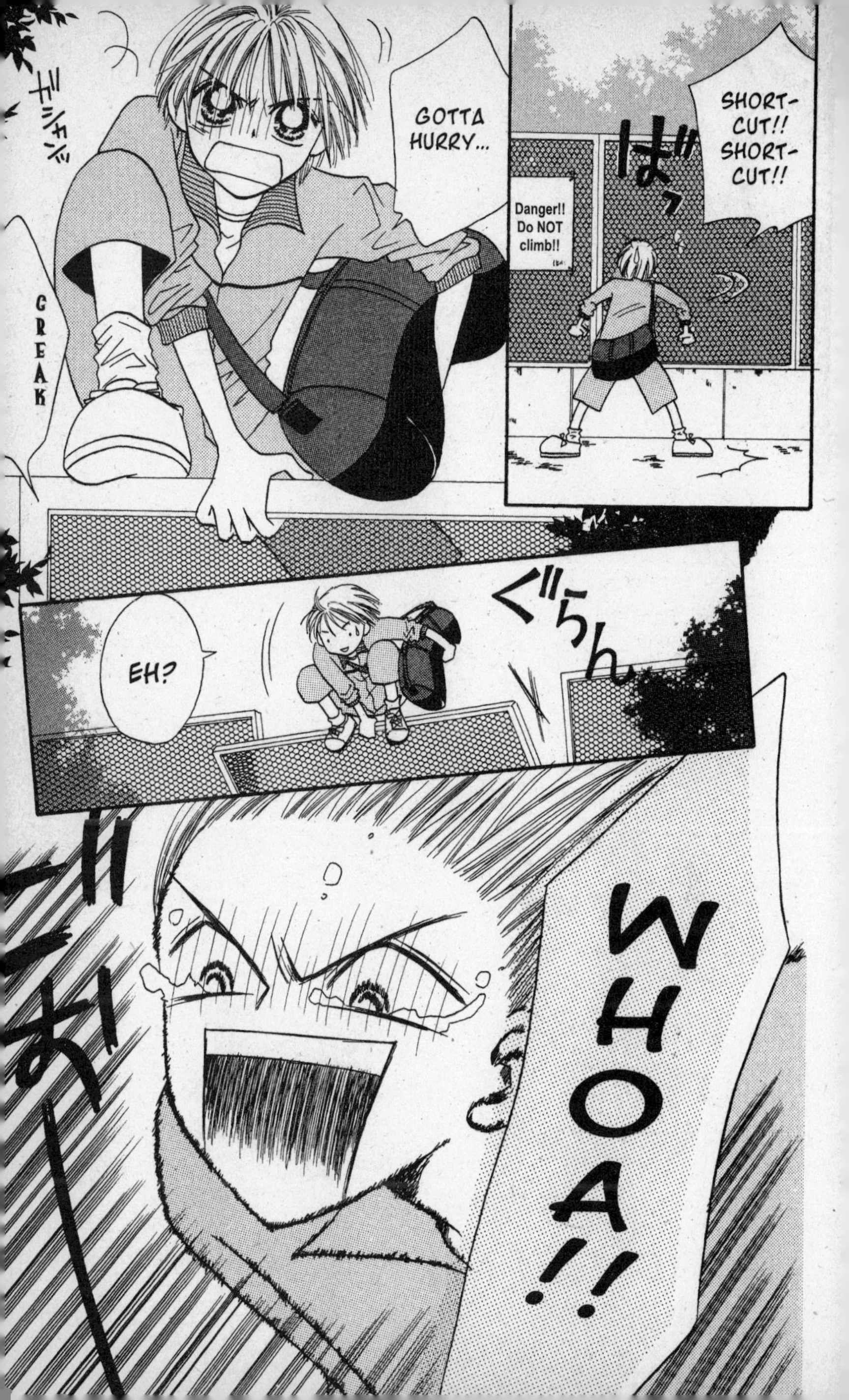
ばっ
Danger!! Do NOT climb!!
SHORT-CUT!! SHORT-CUT!!
GOTTA HURRY...
GREAK
ぐらん
EH?
WHOA!!

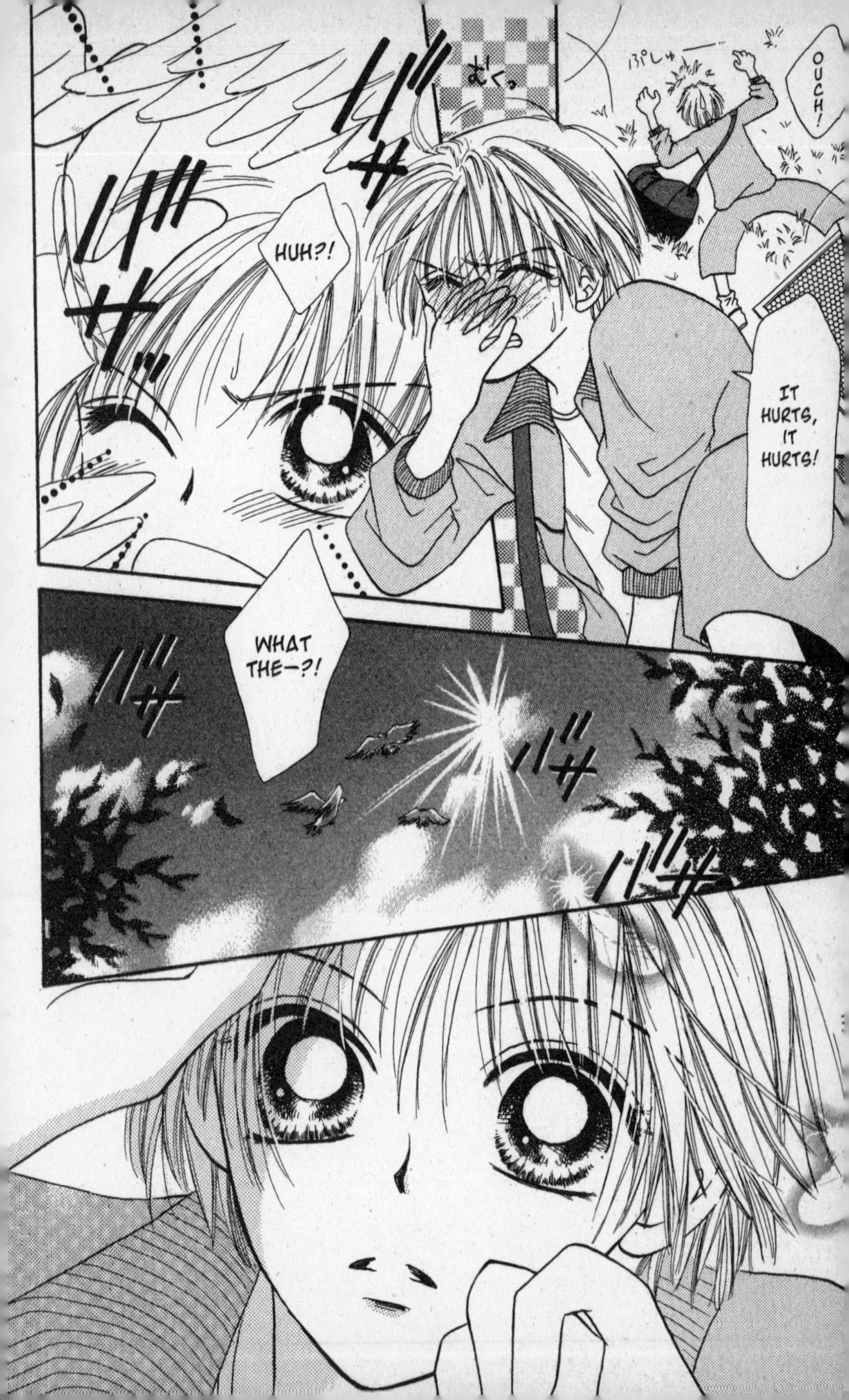
OUCH!
ぷしゅー
むくっ
IT HURTS, IT HURTS!
HUH?!
WHAT THE—?!

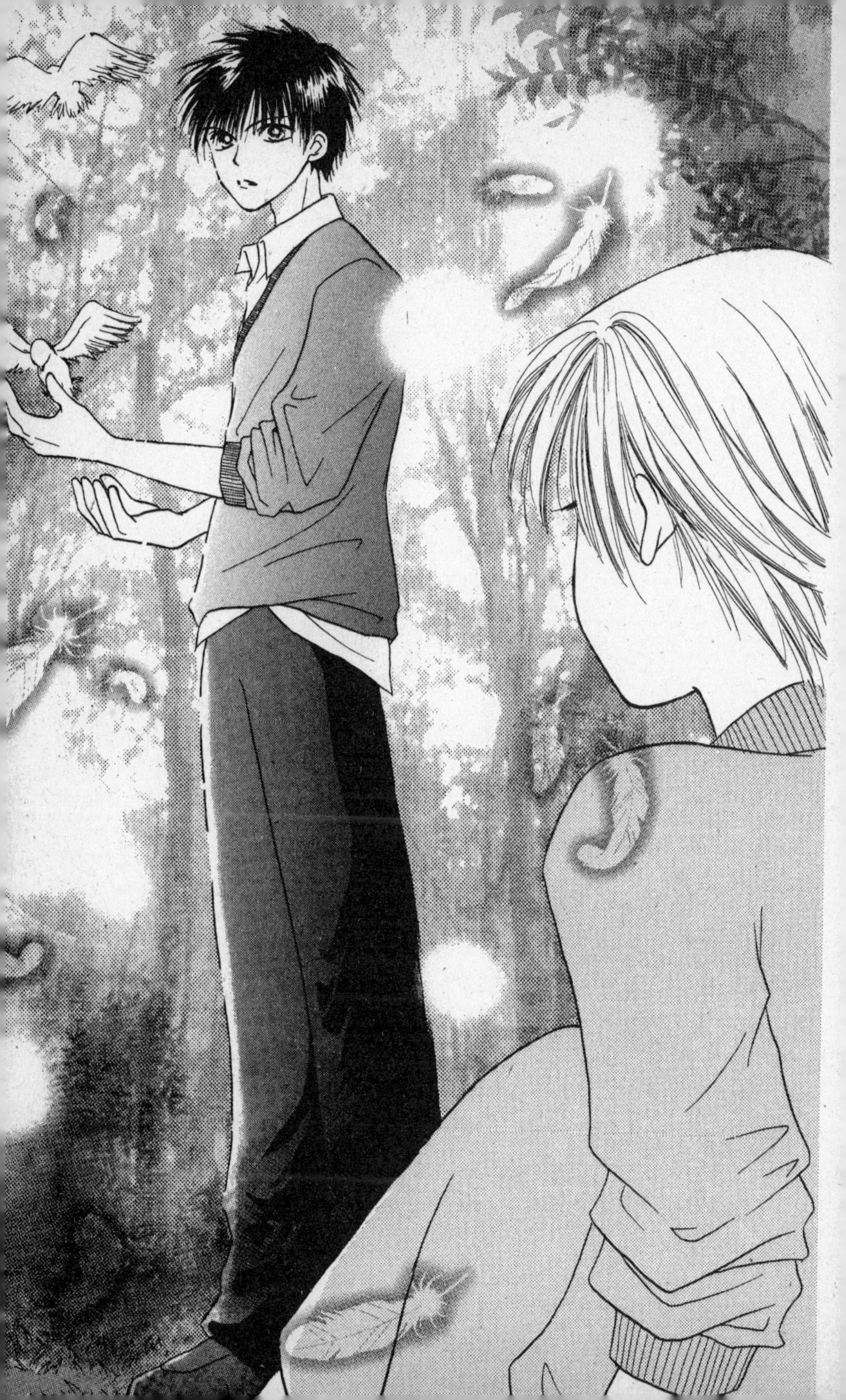

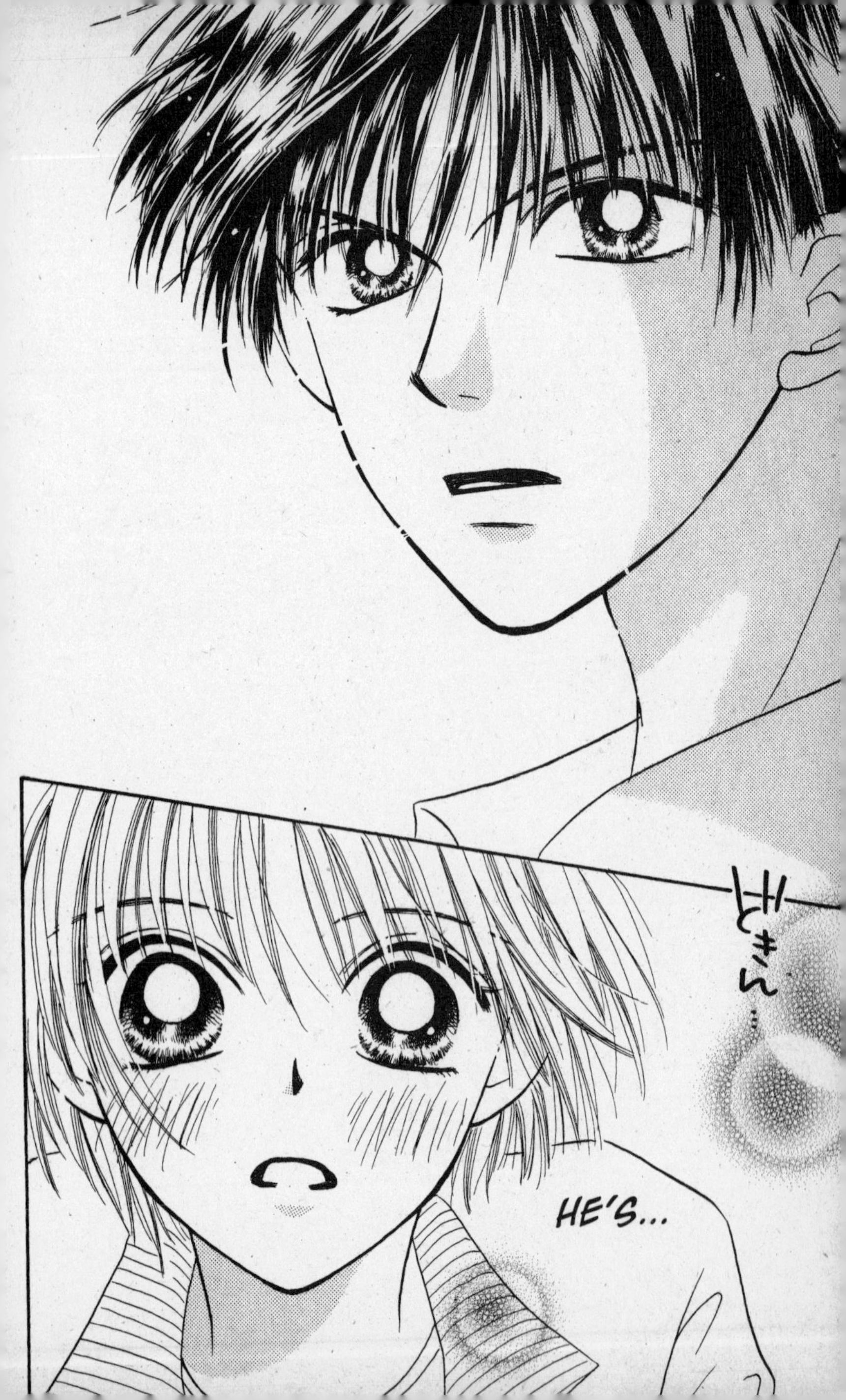
どきん…
HE'S...

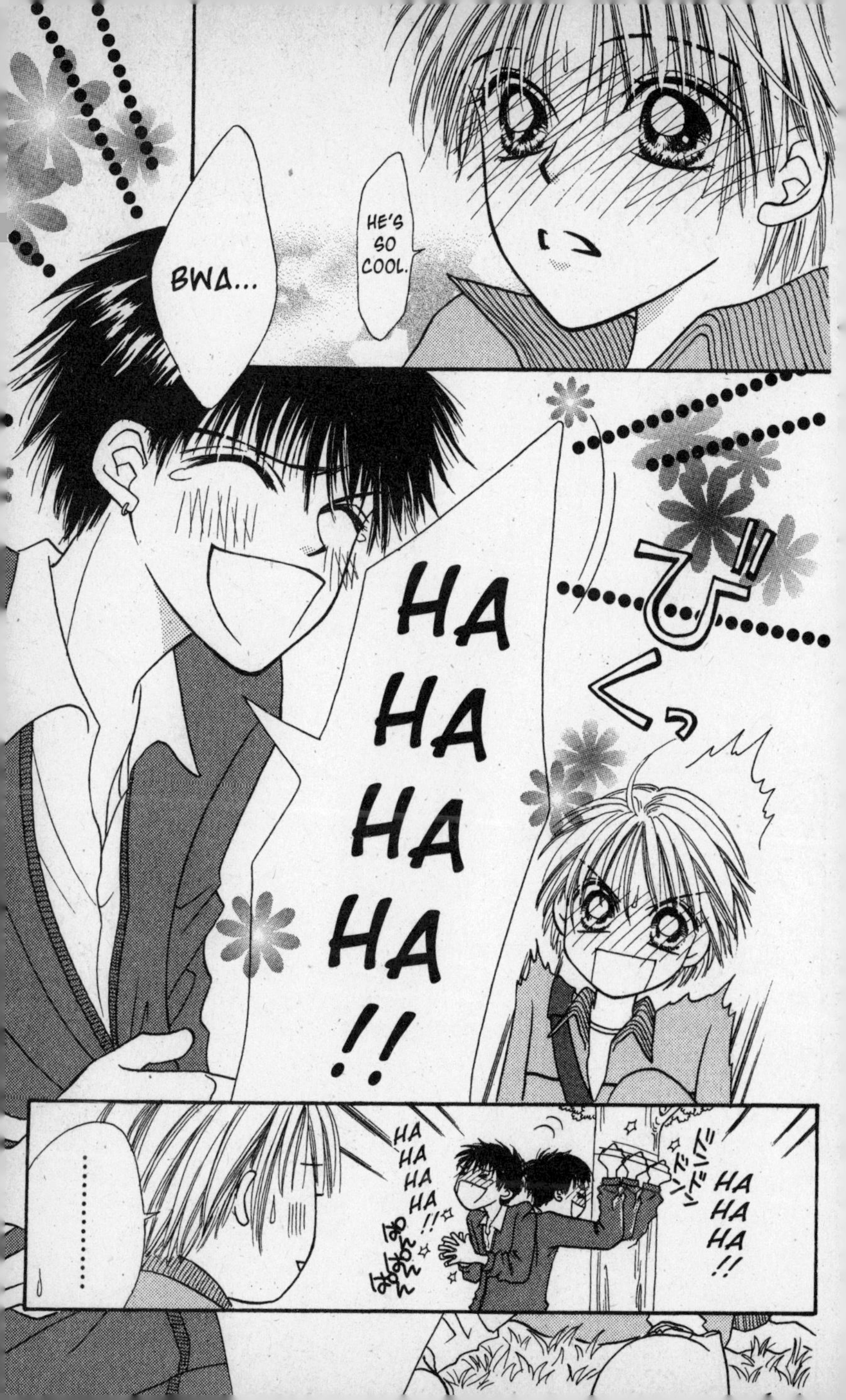
HE'S SO COOL.
BWA...
びくっ
HA HA HA HA!!
HA HA HA!!
HA HA HA HA!!
......

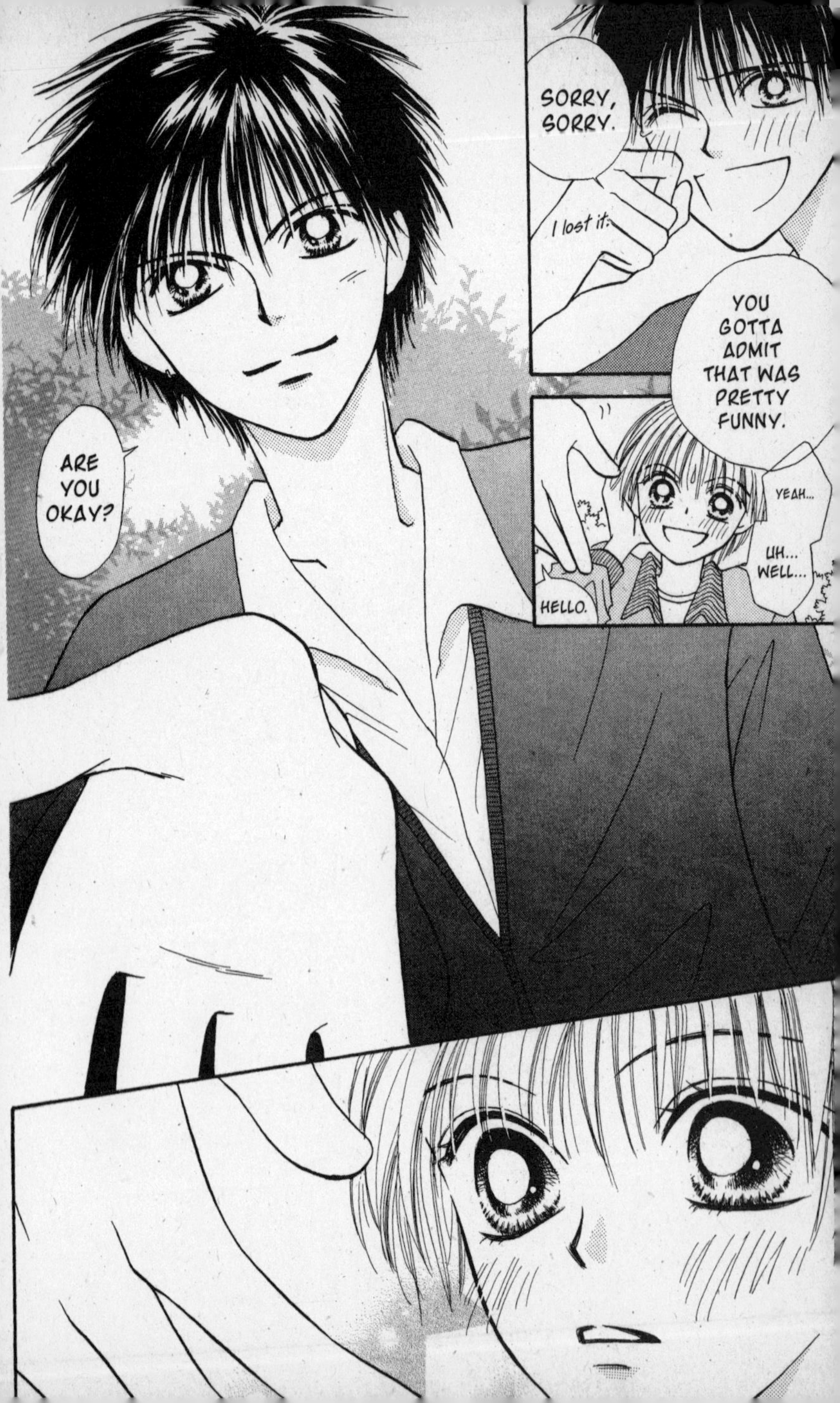
SORRY, SORRY.
I lost it.
YOU GOTTA ADMIT THAT WAS PRETTY FUNNY.
YEAH...
UH... WELL...
HELLO.
ARE YOU OKAY?

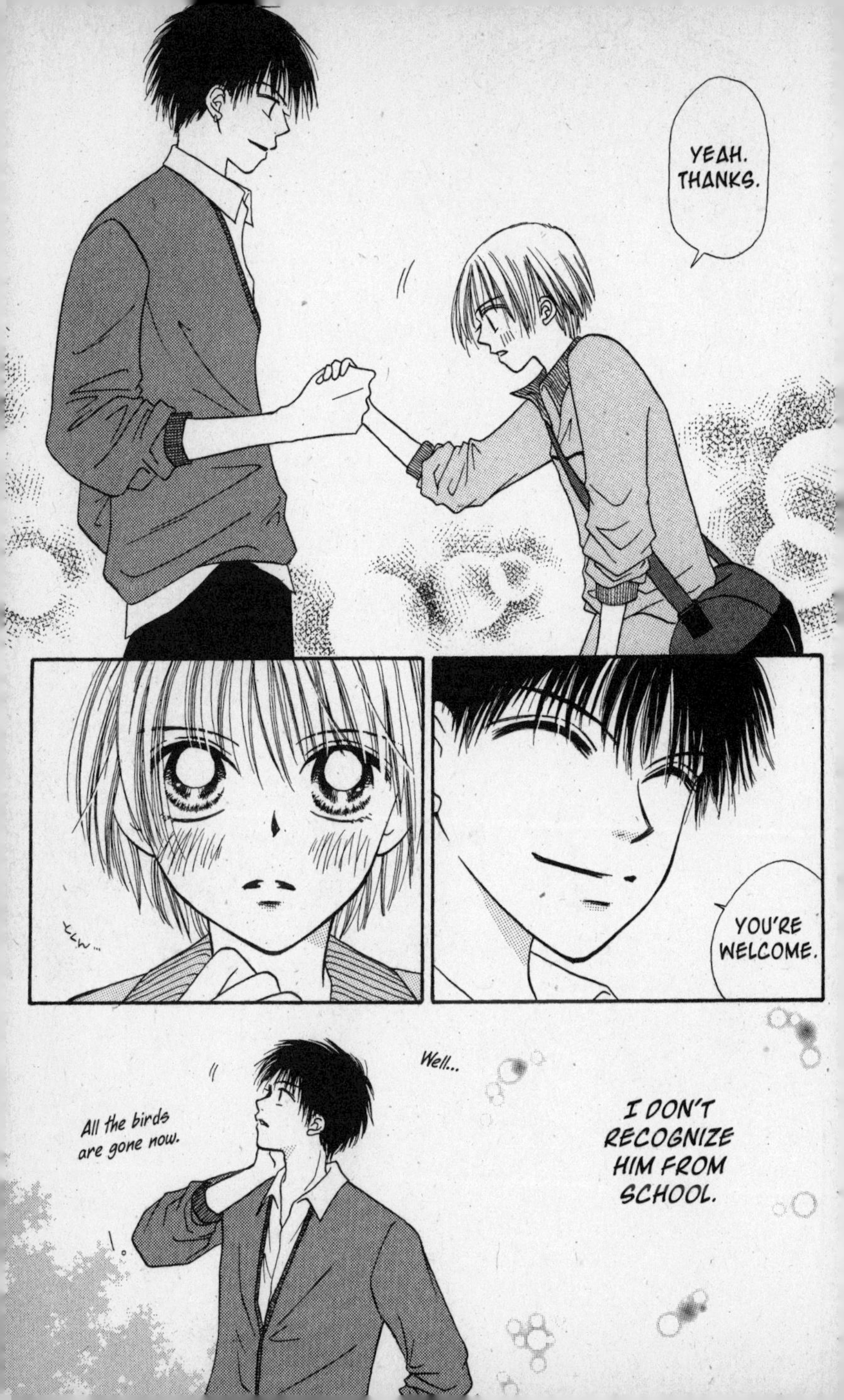
YEAH. THANKS.
YOU'RE WELCOME.
とくん…
Well...
I DON'T RECOGNIZE HIM FROM SCHOOL.
All the birds are gone now.

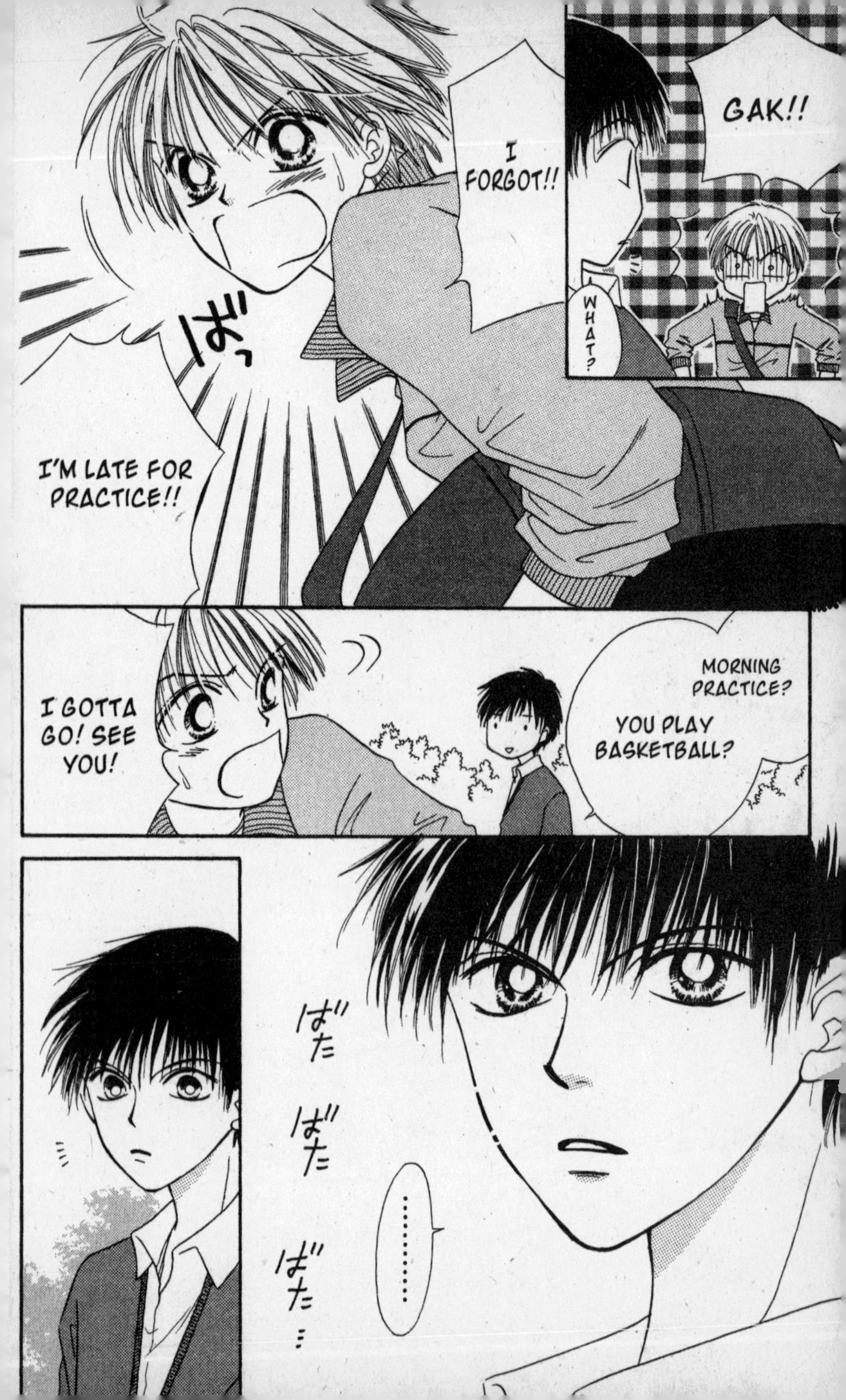
GAK!!
WHAT?
I FORGOT!!
ぱっ
I'M LATE FOR PRACTICE!!
MORNING PRACTICE?
YOU PLAY BASKETBALL?
I GOTTA GO! SEE YOU!
ばた
ばた
ばた
......

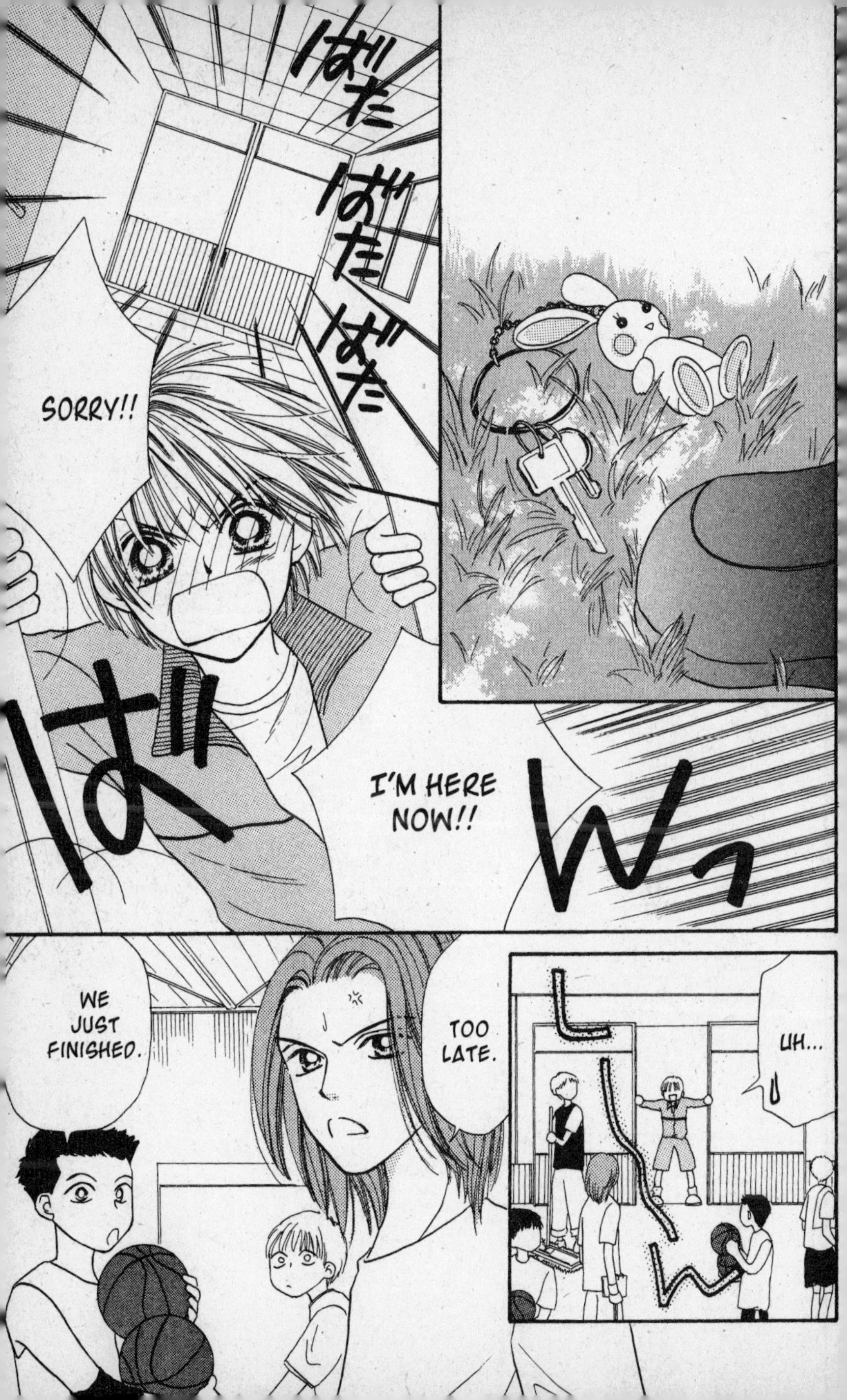
ばたばたばた
SORRY!!
ばっ
I'M HERE NOW!!
UH...
TOO LATE.
WE JUST FINISHED.

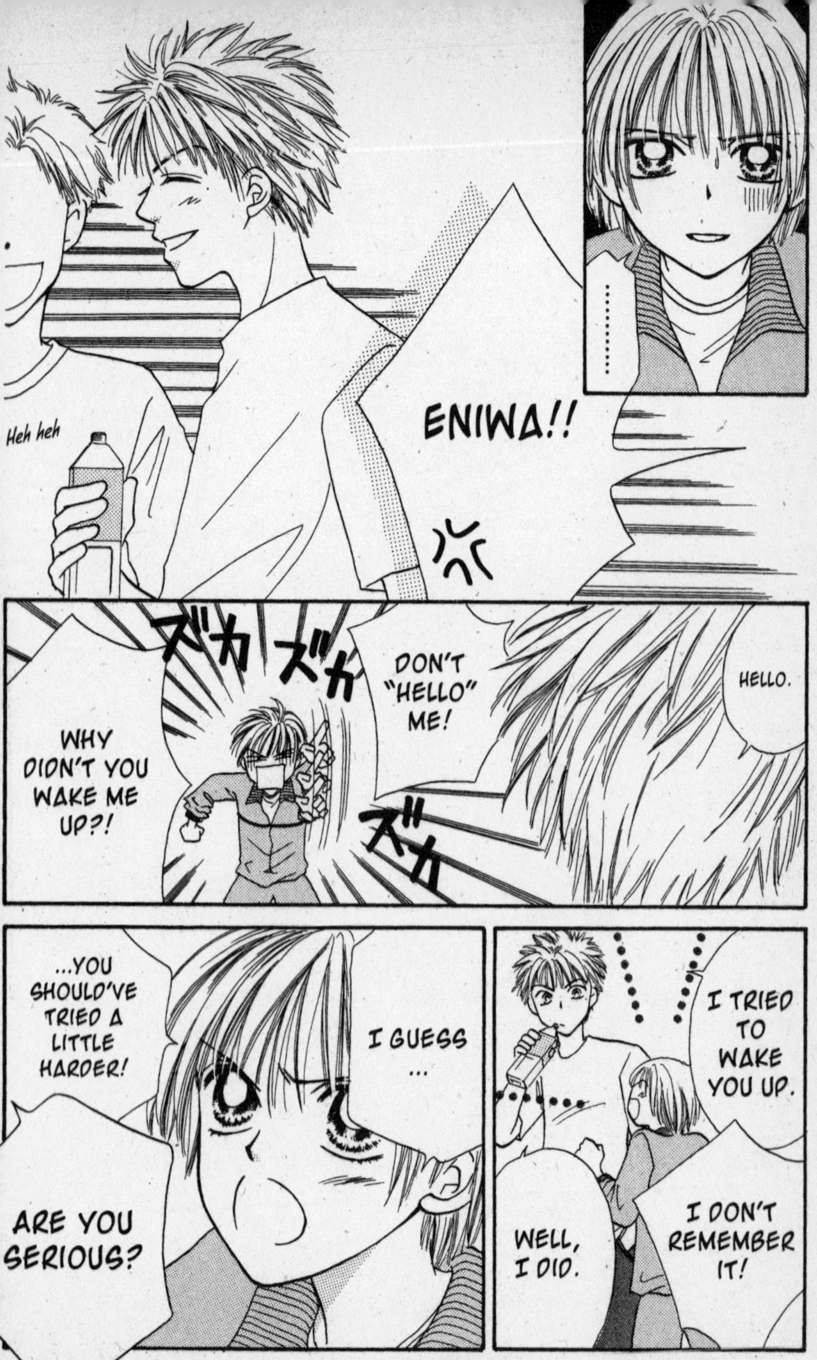
......
ENIWA!!
Heh heh
HELLO.
DON'T "HELLO" ME!
ズカズカ
WHY DIDN'T YOU WAKE ME UP?!
ズカ
I TRIED TO WAKE YOU UP.
I DON'T REMEMBER IT!
WELL, I DID.
I GUESS ...
...YOU SHOULD'VE TRIED A LITTLE HARDER!
ARE YOU SERIOUS?

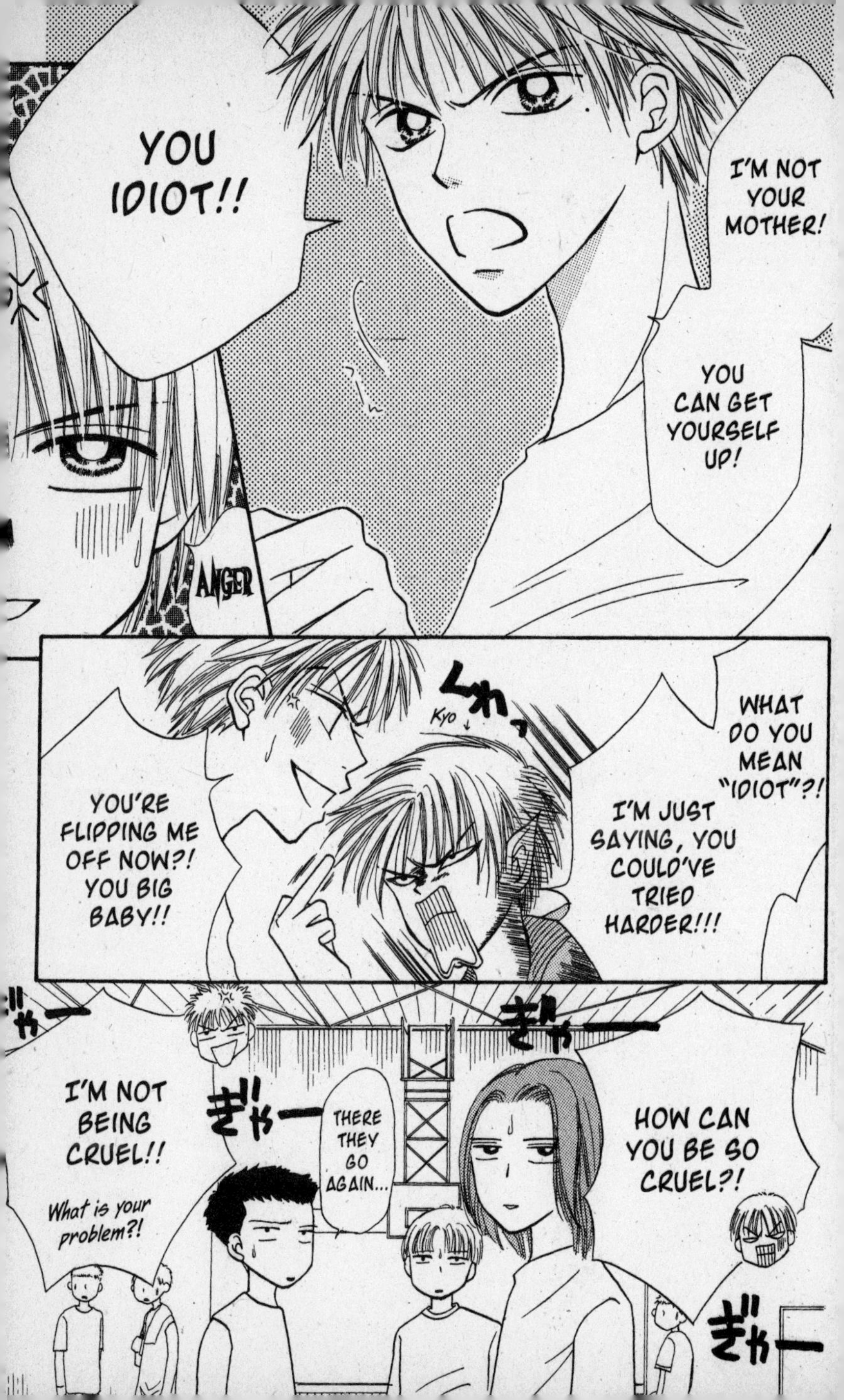
I'M NOT YOUR MOTHER!
YOU CAN GET YOURSELF UP!
YOU IDIOT!!
ANGER
WHAT DO YOU MEAN "IDIOT"?!
I'M JUST SAYING, YOU COULD'VE TRIED HARDER!!!
Kyo
YOU'RE FLIPPING ME OFF NOW?! YOU BIG BABY!!
ぎゃー
HOW CAN YOU BE SO CRUEL?!
ぎゃー
THERE THEY GO AGAIN...
ぎゃー
I'M NOT BEING CRUEL!!
What is your problem?!
ぎゃー

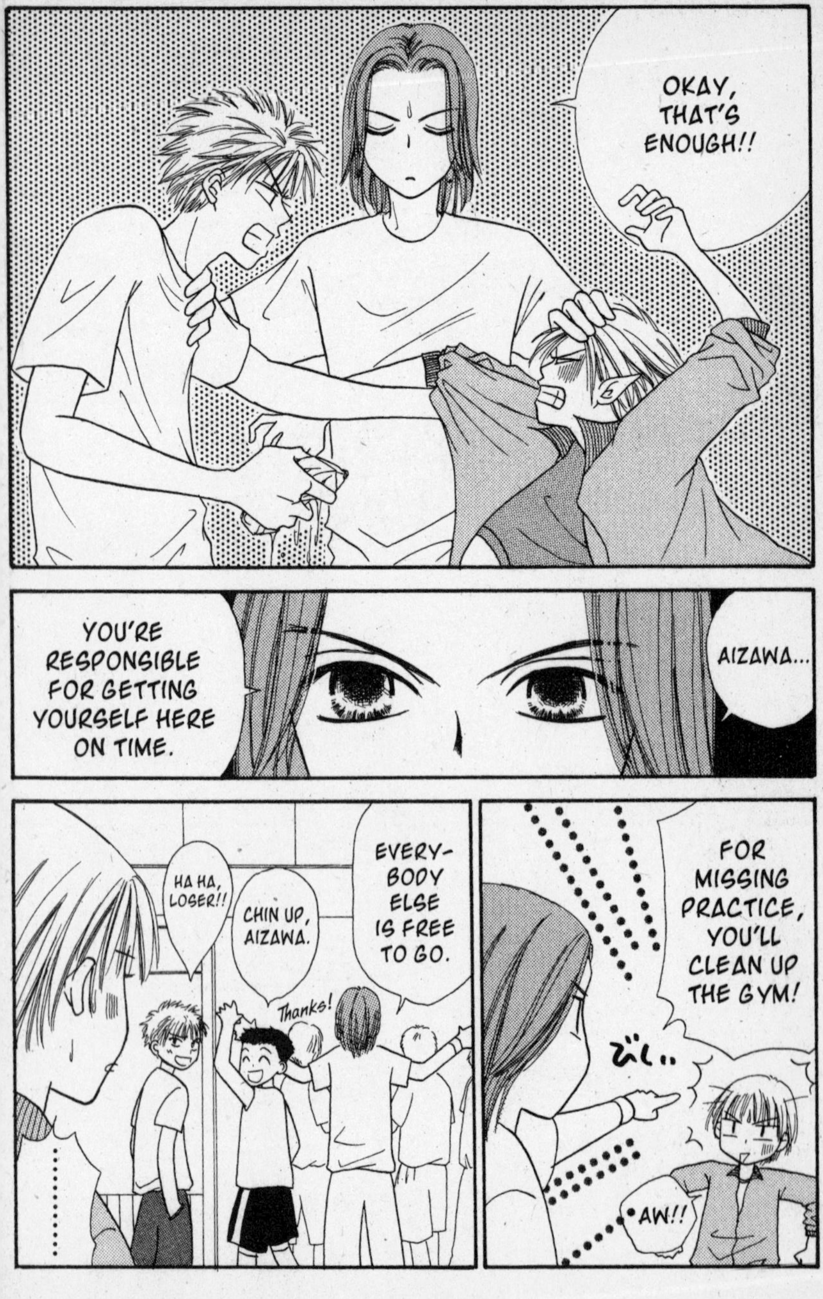
OKAY, THAT'S ENOUGH!!
AIZAWA...
YOU'RE RESPONSIBLE FOR GETTING YOURSELF HERE ON TIME.
FOR MISSING PRACTICE, YOU'LL CLEAN UP THE GYM!
びし..
AW!!
EVERY-BODY ELSE IS FREE TO GO.
Thanks!
CHIN UP, AIZAWA.
HA HA, LOSER!!
....

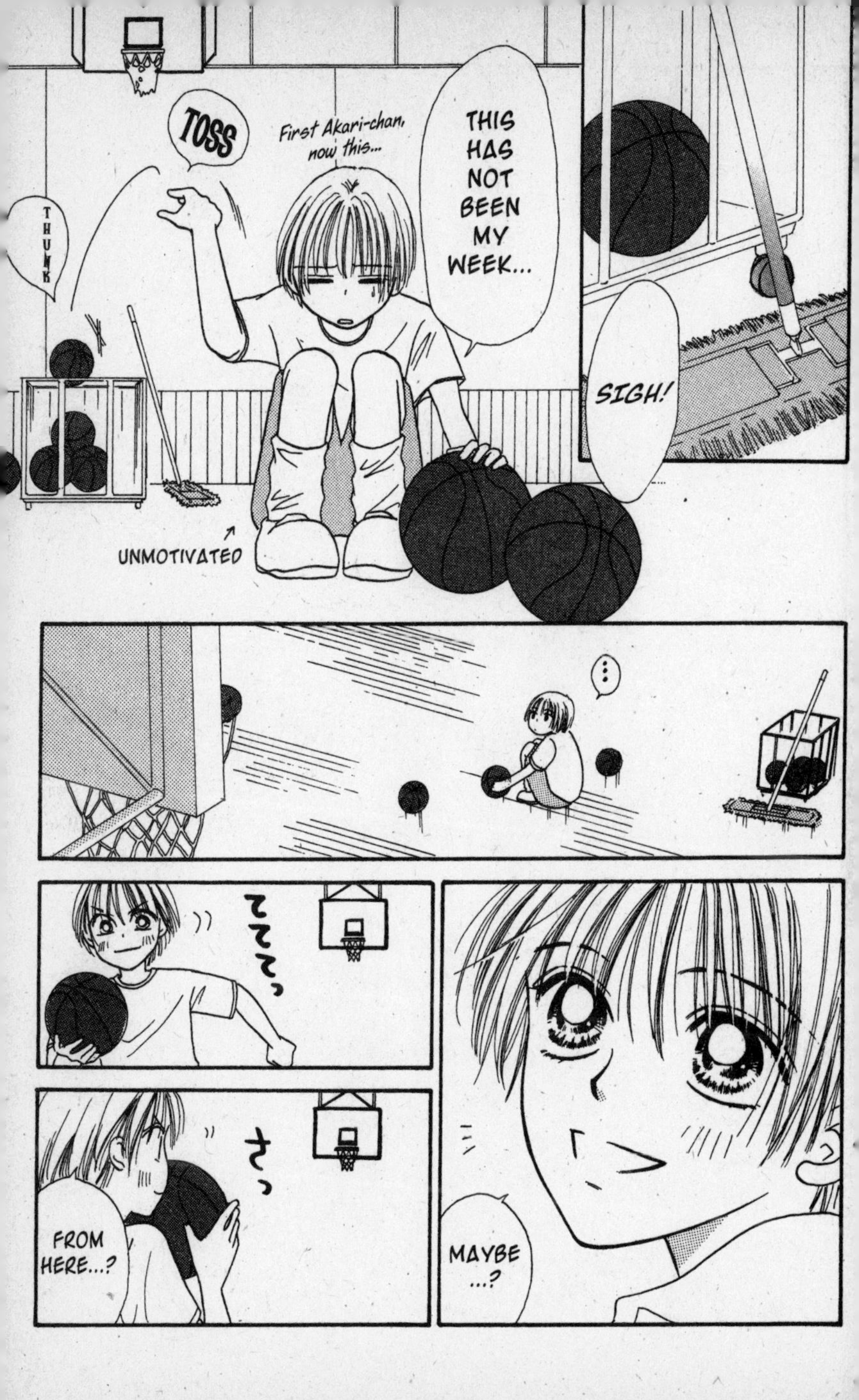
THIS HAS NOT BEEN MY WEEK...
First Akari-chan, now this...
TOSS
THUNK
UNMOTIVATED
SIGH!
...
MAYBE ...?
てててっ
さっ
FROM HERE...?

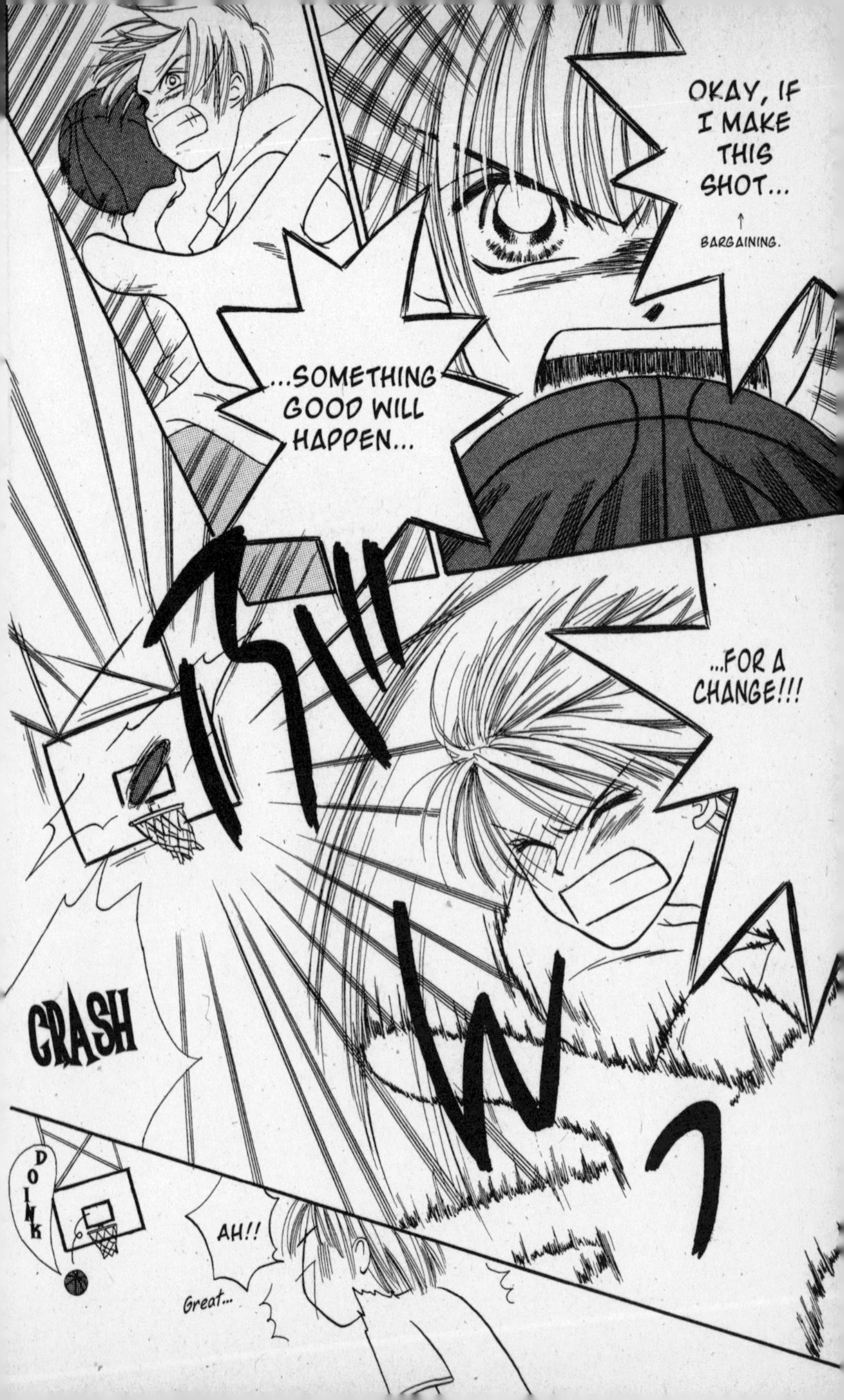
OKAY, IF I MAKE THIS SHOT...
BARGAINING.
...SOMETHING GOOD WILL HAPPEN...
...FOR A CHANGE!!!
CRASH
AH!!
Great...
DOINK

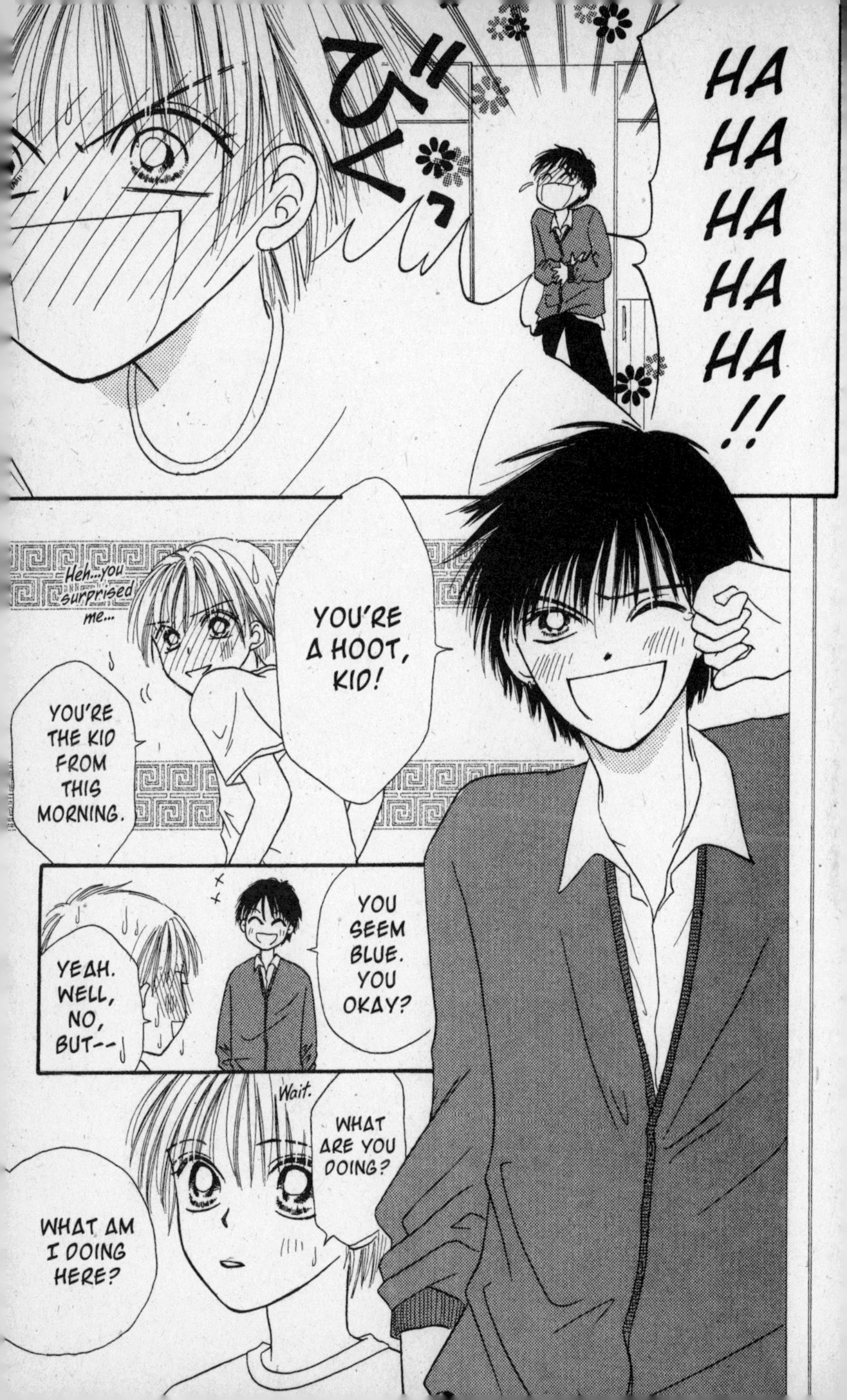
HA HA HA HA HA HA!!
びくっ
YOU'RE A HOOT, KID!
Heh...you surprised me...
YOU'RE THE KID FROM THIS MORNING.
YOU SEEM BLUE. YOU OKAY?
YEAH. WELL, NO, BUT--
Wait.
WHAT ARE YOU DOING?
WHAT AM I DOING HERE?

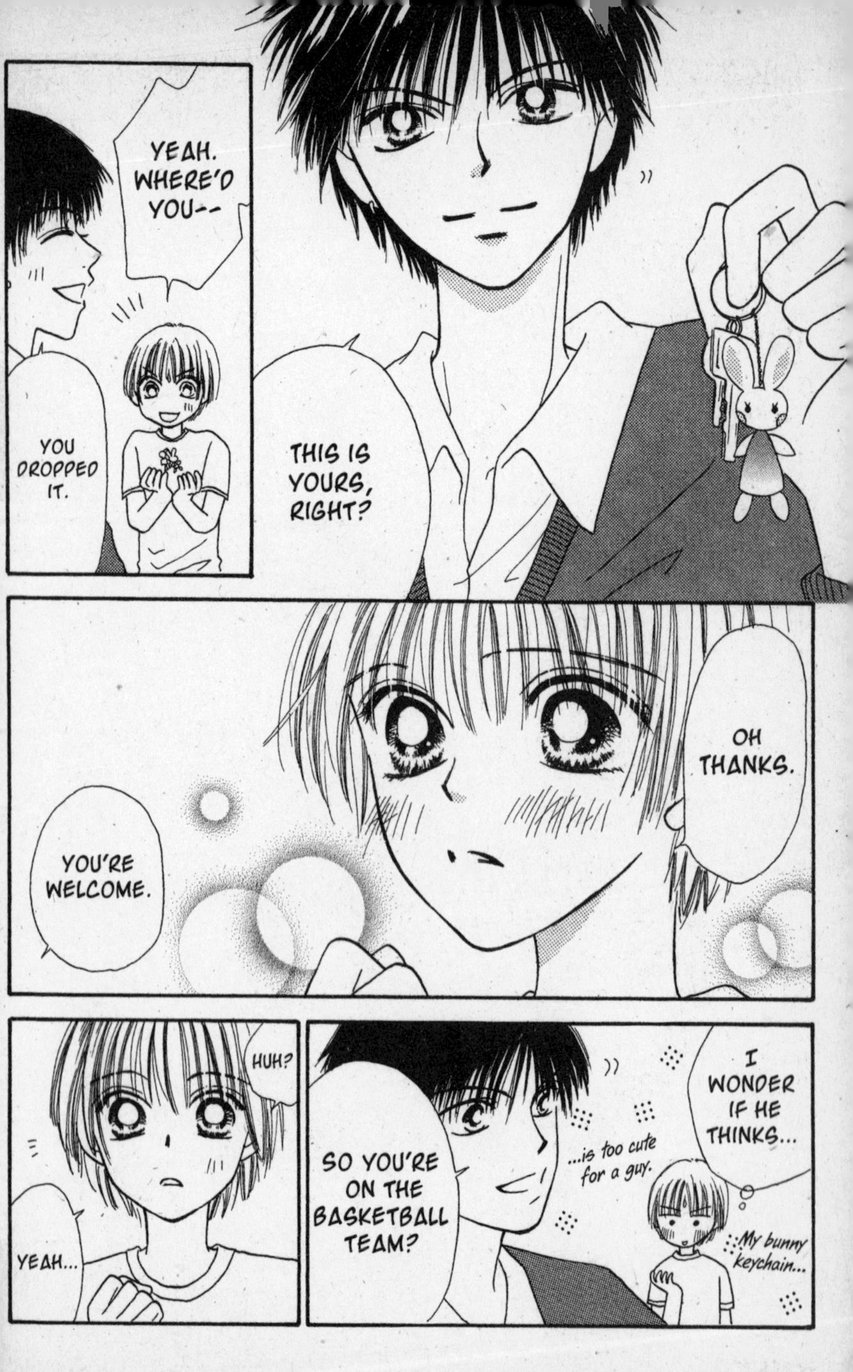
THIS IS YOURS, RIGHT?
YEAH. WHERE'D YOU--
YOU DROPPED IT.
OH THANKS.
YOU'RE WELCOME.
I WONDER IF HE THINKS...
My bunny keychain...
...is too cute for a guy.
SO YOU'RE ON THE BASKETBALL TEAM?
HUH?
YEAH...

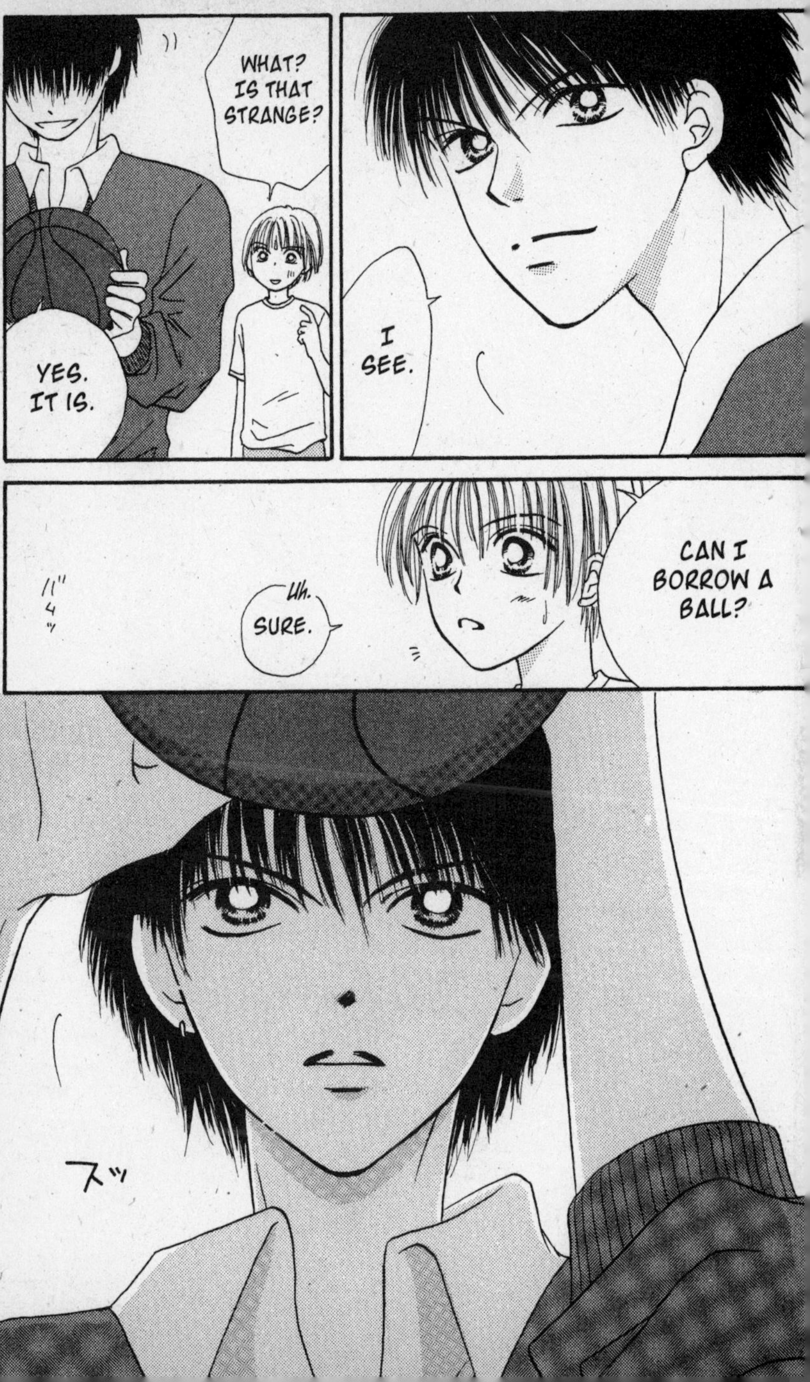
I SEE.
WHAT? IS THAT STRANGE?
YES. IT IS.
CAN I BORROW A BALL?
Uh. SURE.
バムッ
ズッ

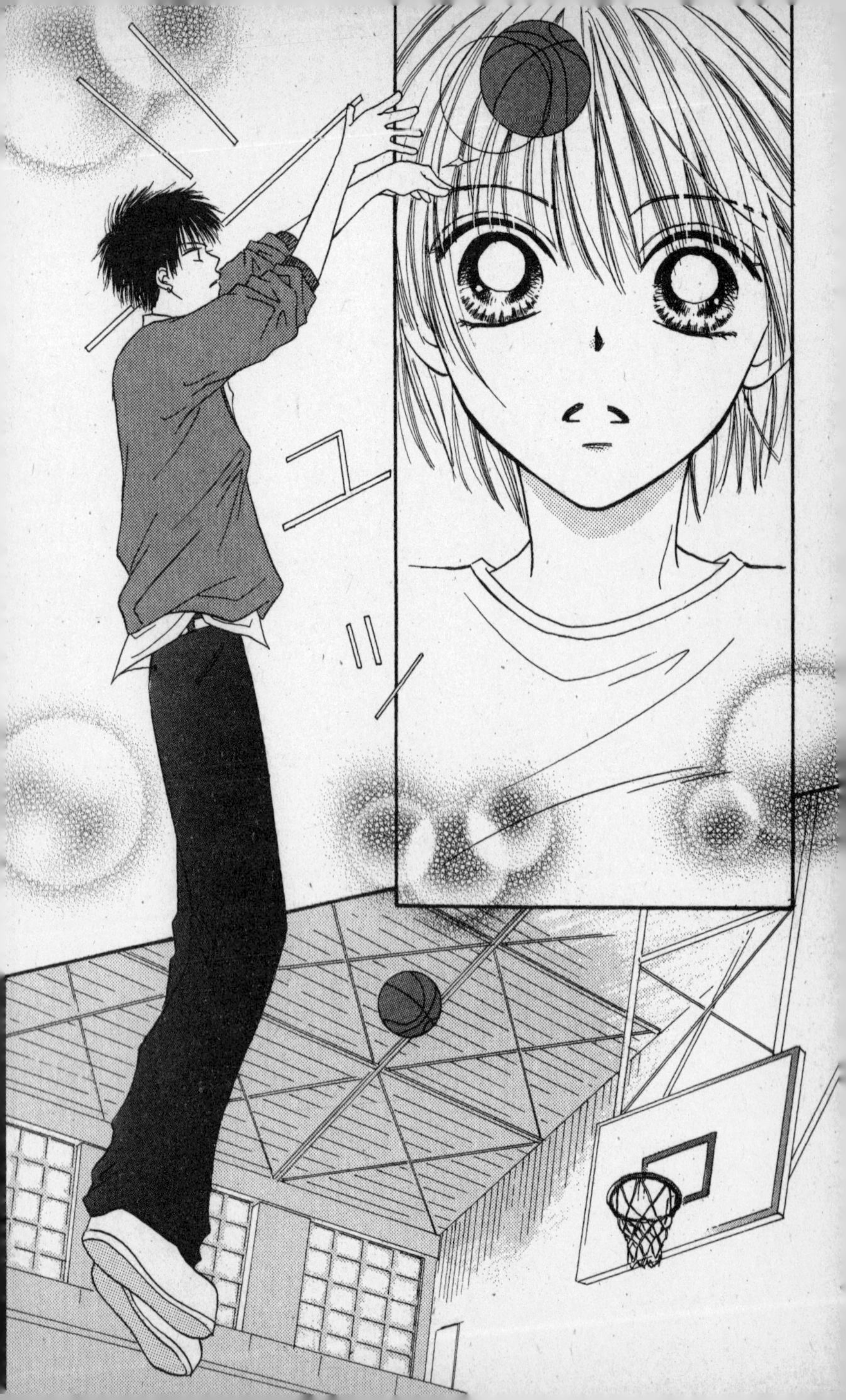

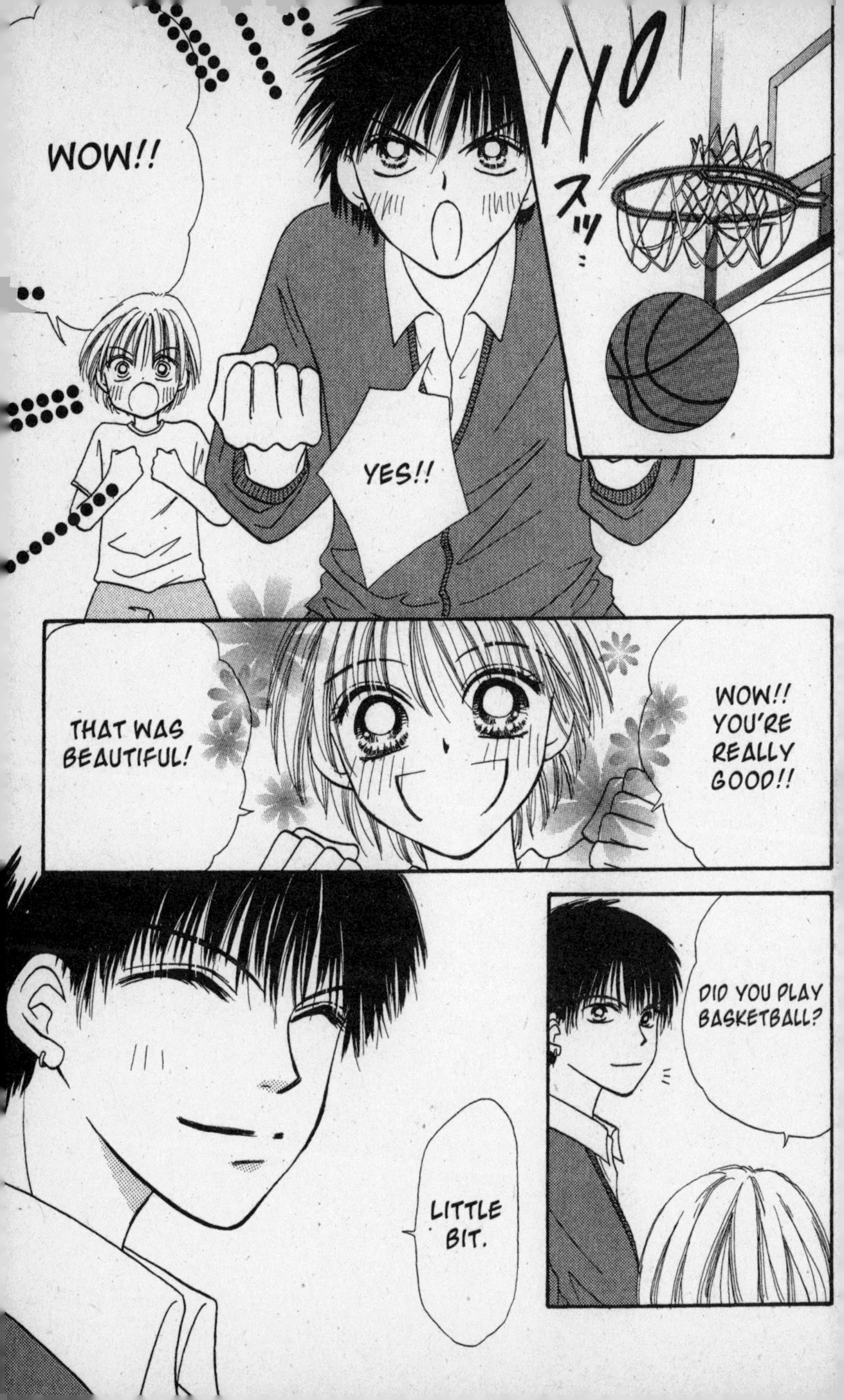
スッ
YES!!
WOW!!
WOW!! YOU'RE REALLY GOOD!!
THAT WAS BEAUTIFUL!
DID YOU PLAY BASKETBALL?
LITTLE BIT.

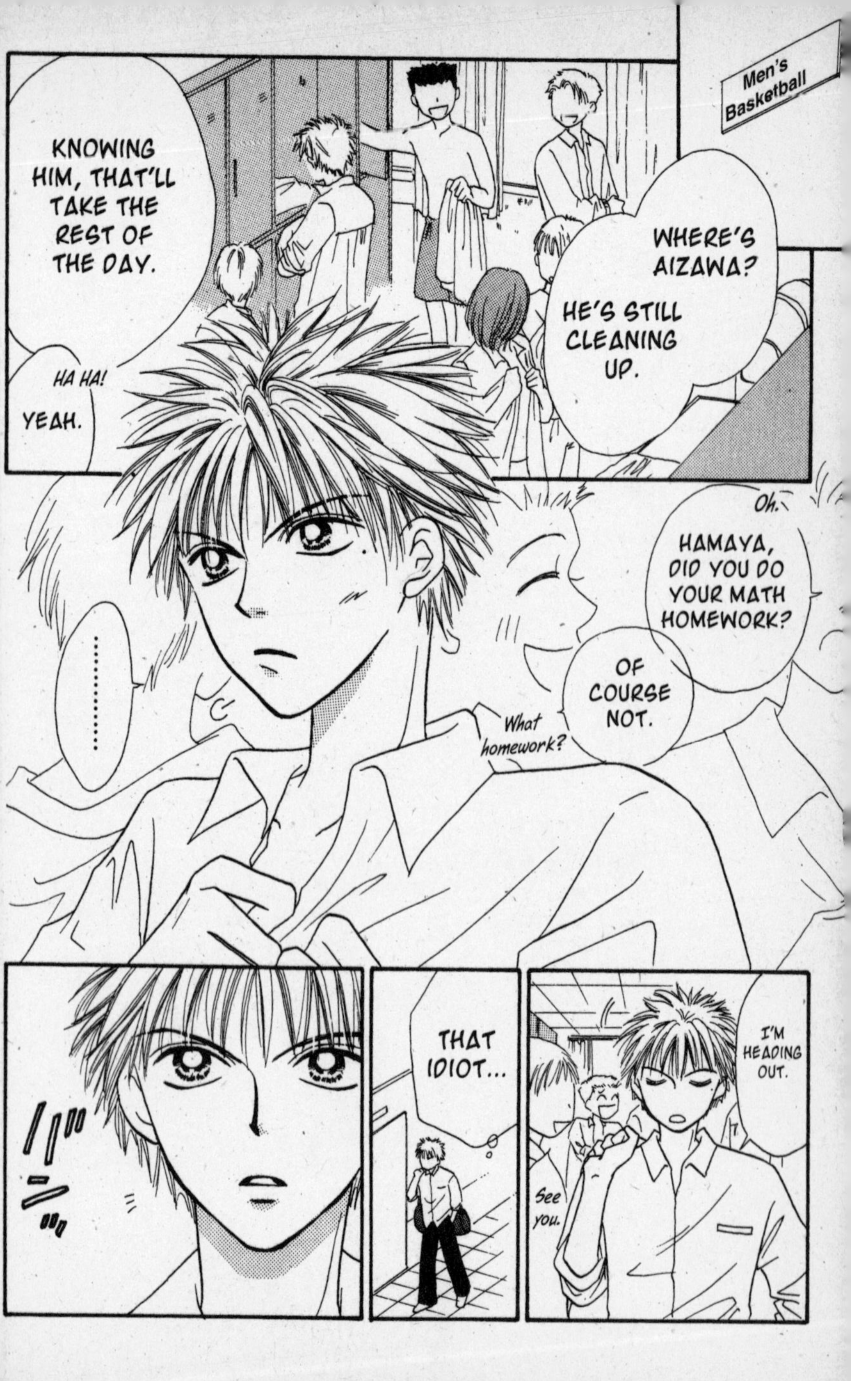
Men's Basketball
WHERE'S AIZAWA?
HE'S STILL CLEANING UP.
KNOWING HIM, THAT'LL TAKE THE REST OF THE DAY.
HA HA!
YEAH.
Oh.
HAMAYA, DID YOU DO YOUR MATH HOMEWORK?
OF COURSE NOT.
What homework?
......
I'M HEADING OUT.
See you.
THAT IDIOT...

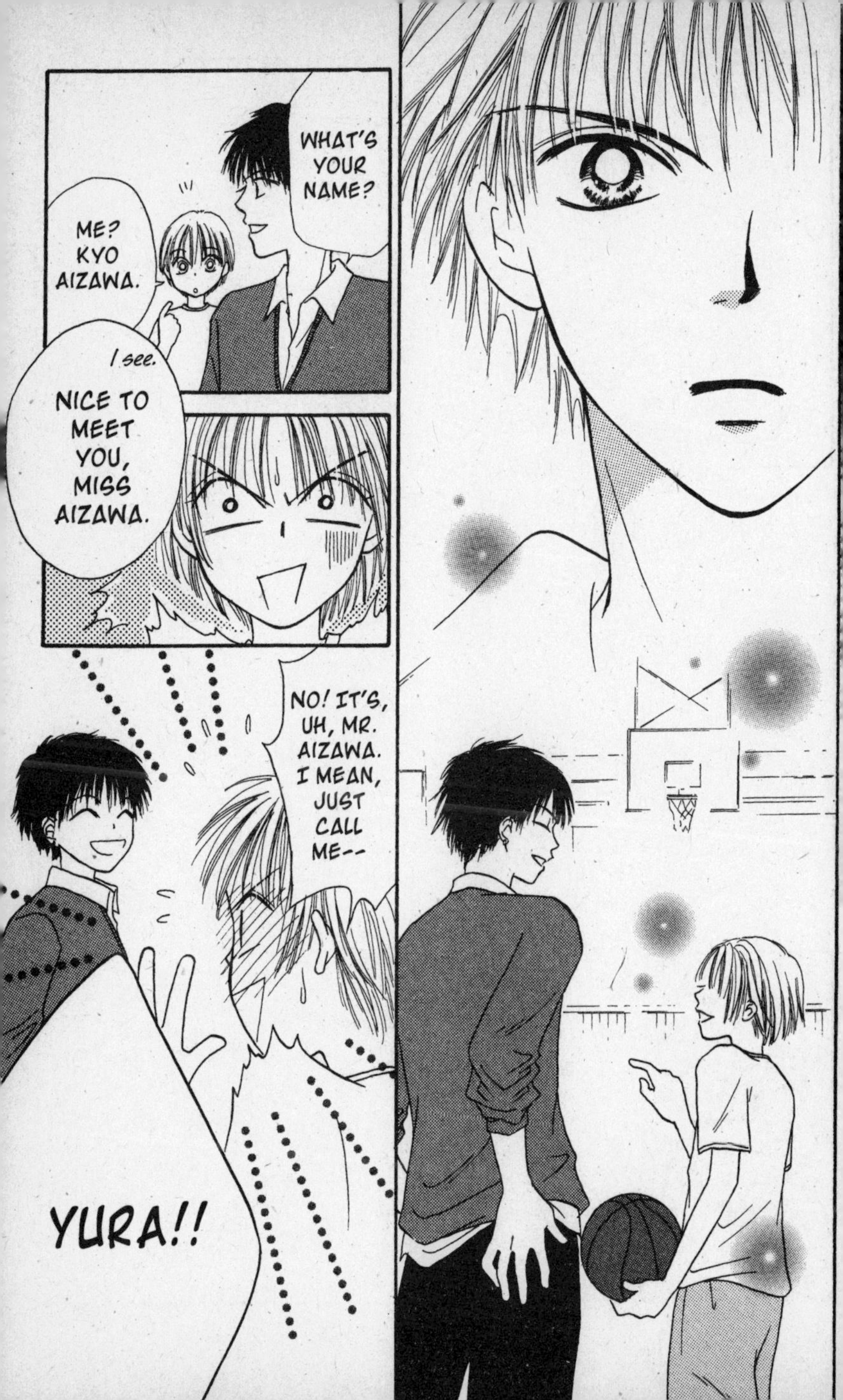
WHAT'S YOUR NAME?
ME? KYO AIZAWA.
I see.
NICE TO MEET YOU, MISS AIZAWA.
NO! IT'S, UH, MR. AIZAWA. I MEAN, JUST CALL ME--
YURA!!

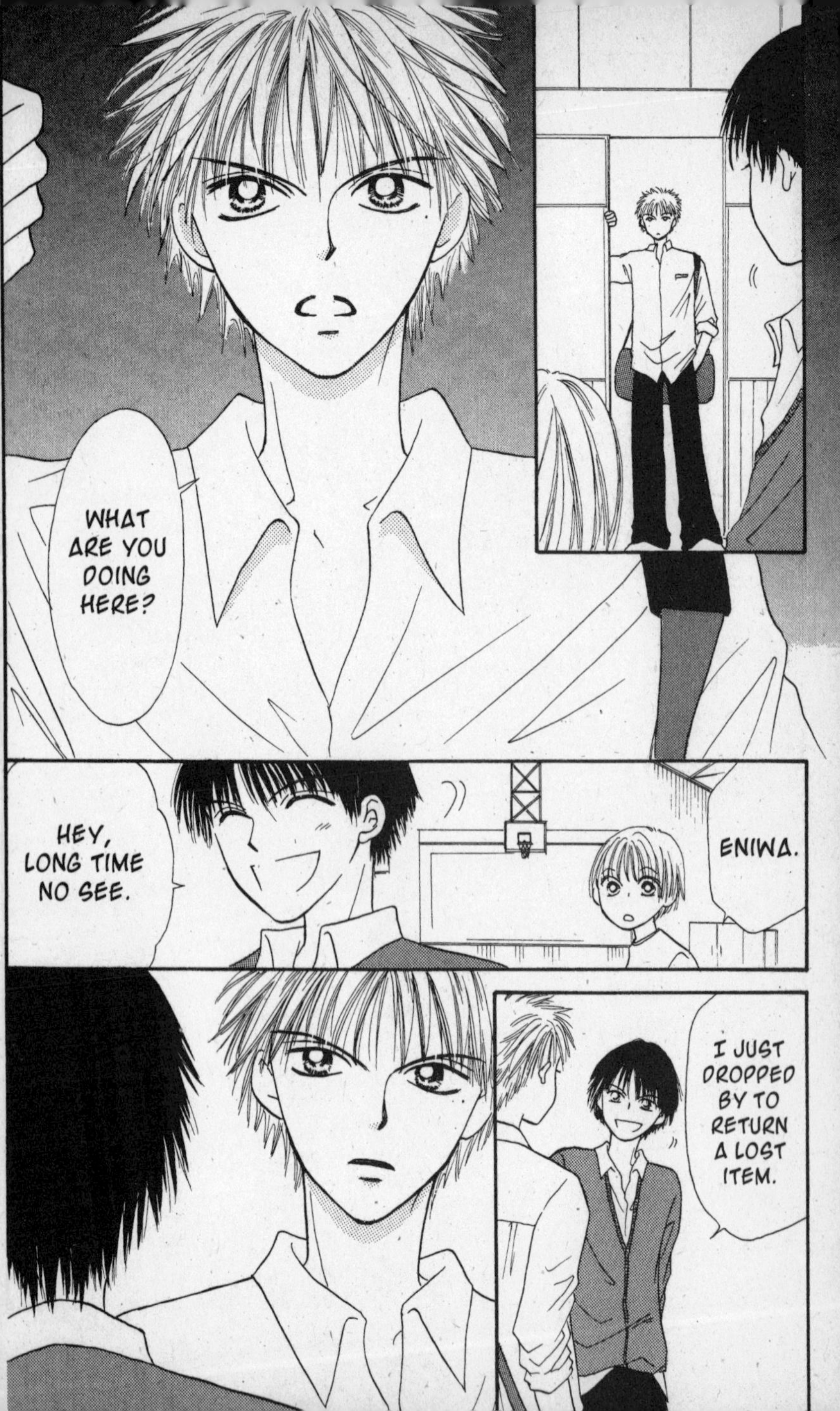
WHAT ARE YOU DOING HERE?
ENIWA.
HEY, LONG TIME NO SEE.
I JUST DROPPED BY TO RETURN A LOST ITEM.

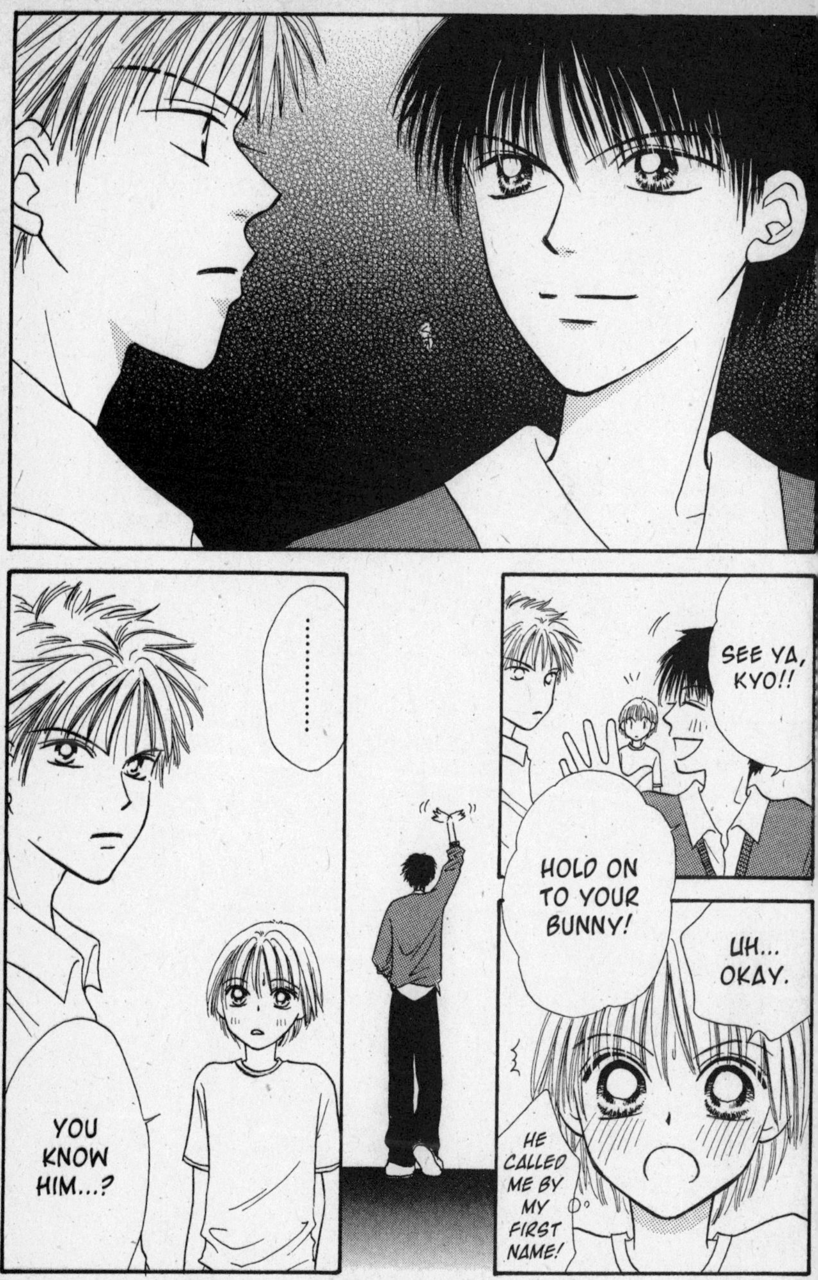

SEE YA, KYO!!
HOLD ON TO YOUR BUNNY!
UH... OKAY.
HE CALLED ME BY MY FIRST NAME!
....
YOU KNOW HIM...?

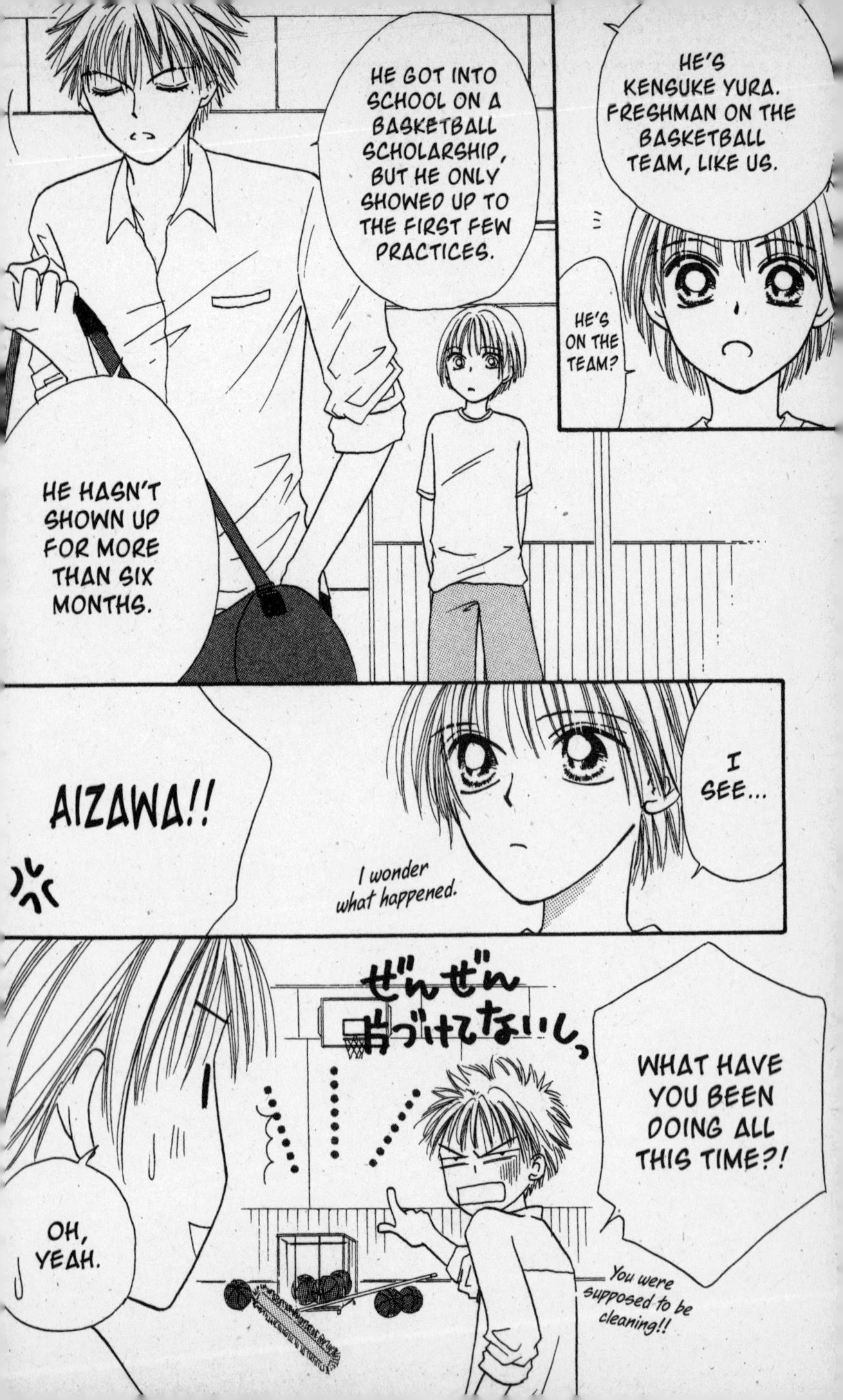
HE'S KENSUKE YURA. FRESHMAN ON THE BASKETBALL TEAM, LIKE US.
HE'S ON THE TEAM?
HE GOT INTO SCHOOL ON A BASKETBALL SCHOLARSHIP, BUT HE ONLY SHOWED UP TO THE FIRST FEW PRACTICES.
HE HASN'T SHOWN UP FOR MORE THAN SIX MONTHS.
I SEE...
I wonder what happened.
AIZAWA!!
WHAT HAVE YOU BEEN DOING ALL THIS TIME?!
ぜんぜん片づけてないし、
You were supposed to be cleaning!!
OH, YEAH.

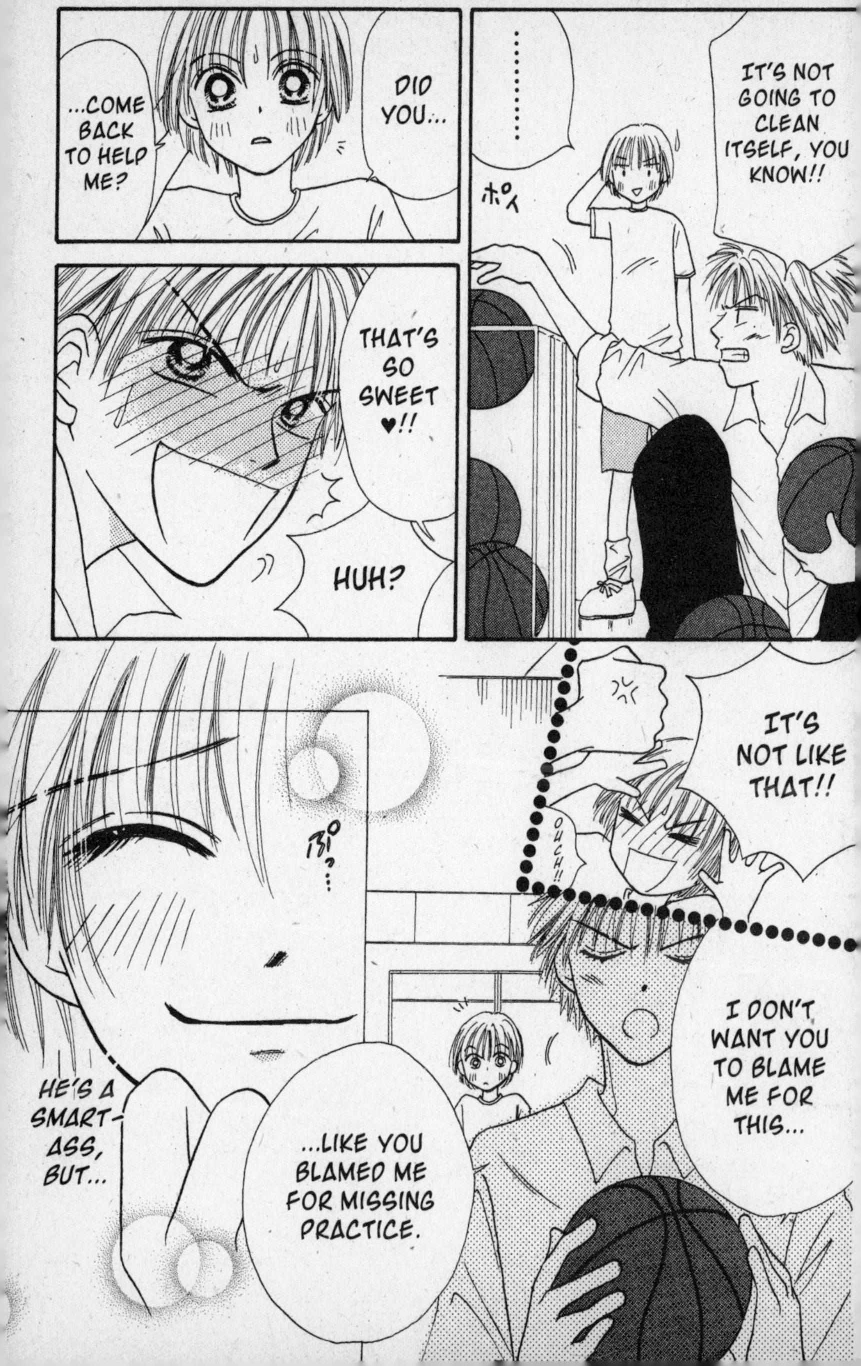
IT'S NOT GOING TO CLEAN ITSELF, YOU KNOW!!
......
ポイ
DID YOU...
...COME BACK TO HELP ME?
THAT'S SO SWEET♥!!
HUH?
IT'S NOT LIKE THAT!!
OUCH!!
I DON'T WANT YOU TO BLAME ME FOR THIS...
...LIKE YOU BLAMED ME FOR MISSING PRACTICE.
ぷっ…
HE'S A SMART-ASS, BUT...

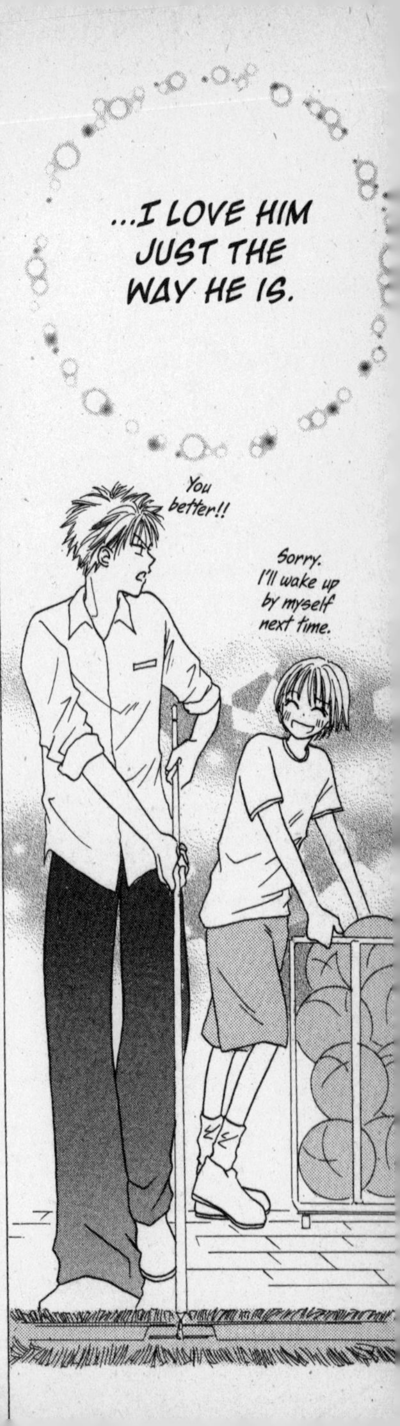
...I LOVE HIM JUST THE WAY HE IS.
Sorry. I'll wake up by myself next time.
You better!!
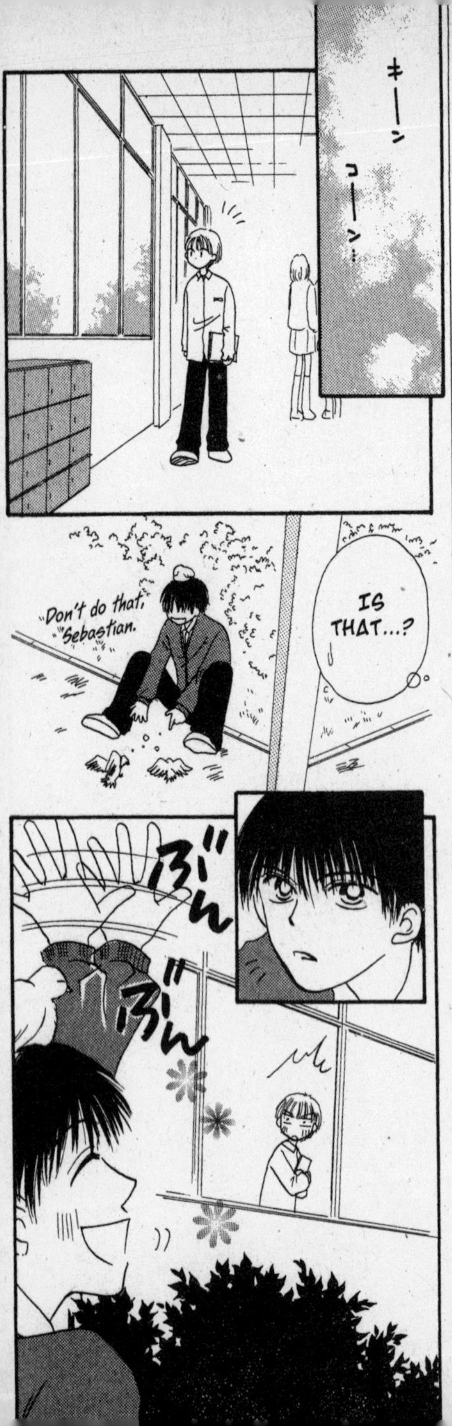
キーン　コーン…
IS THAT...?
Don't do that, Sebastian.
ぶん
ぶん

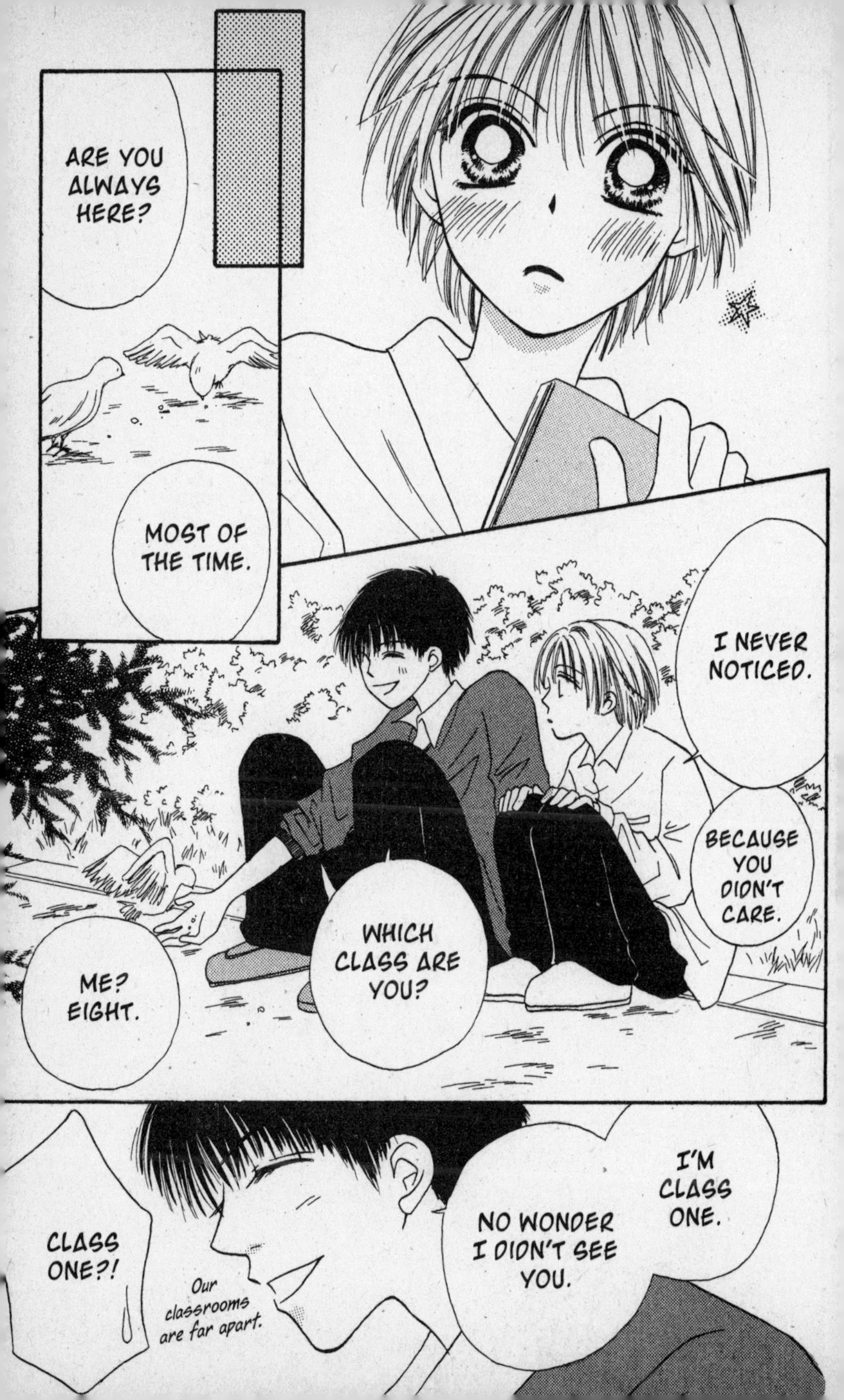
ARE YOU ALWAYS HERE?
MOST OF THE TIME.
I NEVER NOTICED.
BECAUSE YOU DIDN'T CARE.
WHICH CLASS ARE YOU?
ME? EIGHT.
I'M CLASS ONE.
NO WONDER I DIDN'T SEE YOU.
CLASS ONE?!
Our classrooms are far apart.

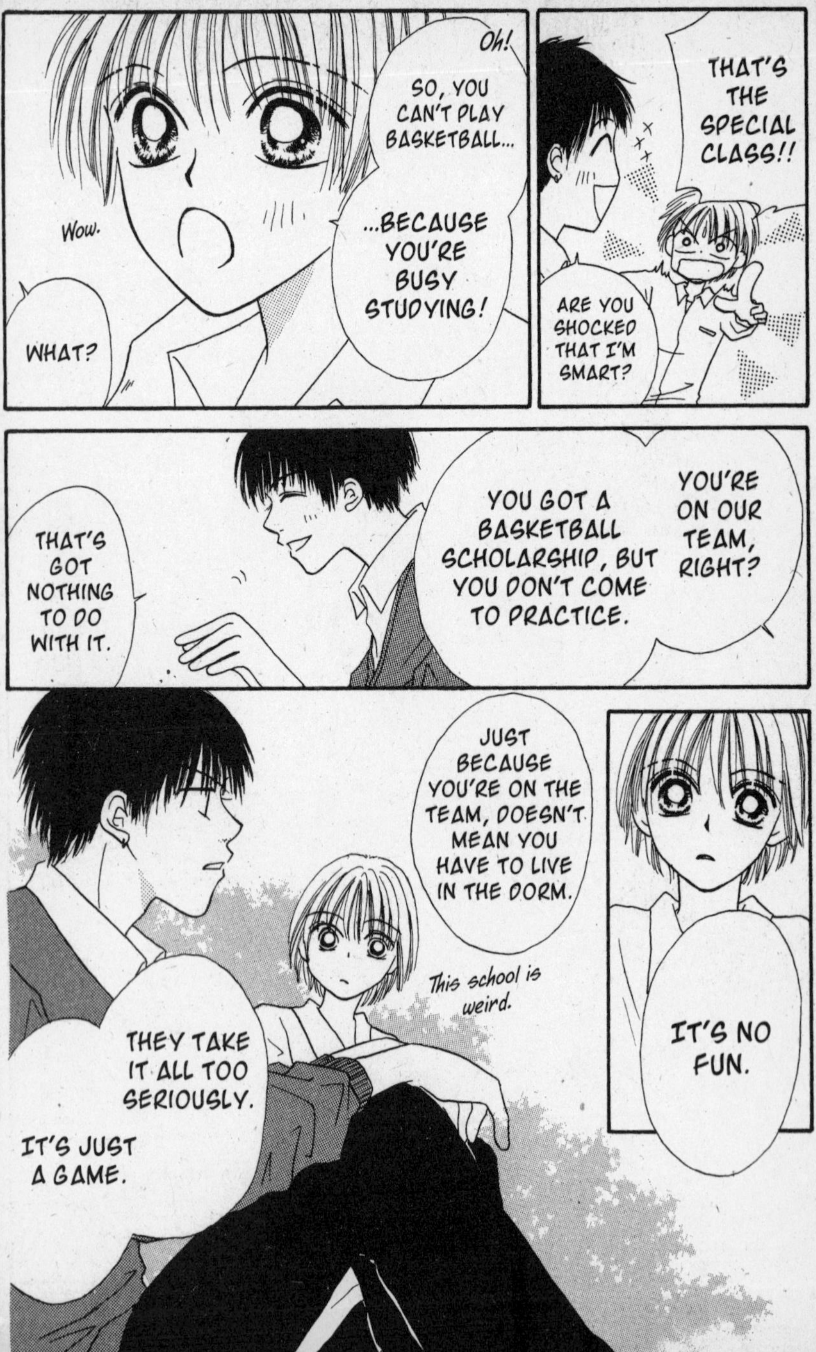
THAT'S THE SPECIAL CLASS!!
ARE YOU SHOCKED THAT I'M SMART?
Oh!
SO, YOU CAN'T PLAY BASKETBALL...
...BECAUSE YOU'RE BUSY STUDYING!
Wow.
WHAT?
YOU'RE ON OUR TEAM, RIGHT?
YOU GOT A BASKETBALL SCHOLARSHIP, BUT YOU DON'T COME TO PRACTICE.
THAT'S GOT NOTHING TO DO WITH IT.
IT'S NO FUN.
JUST BECAUSE YOU'RE ON THE TEAM, DOESN'T MEAN YOU HAVE TO LIVE IN THE DORM.
This school is weird.
THEY TAKE IT ALL TOO SERIOUSLY.
IT'S JUST A GAME.

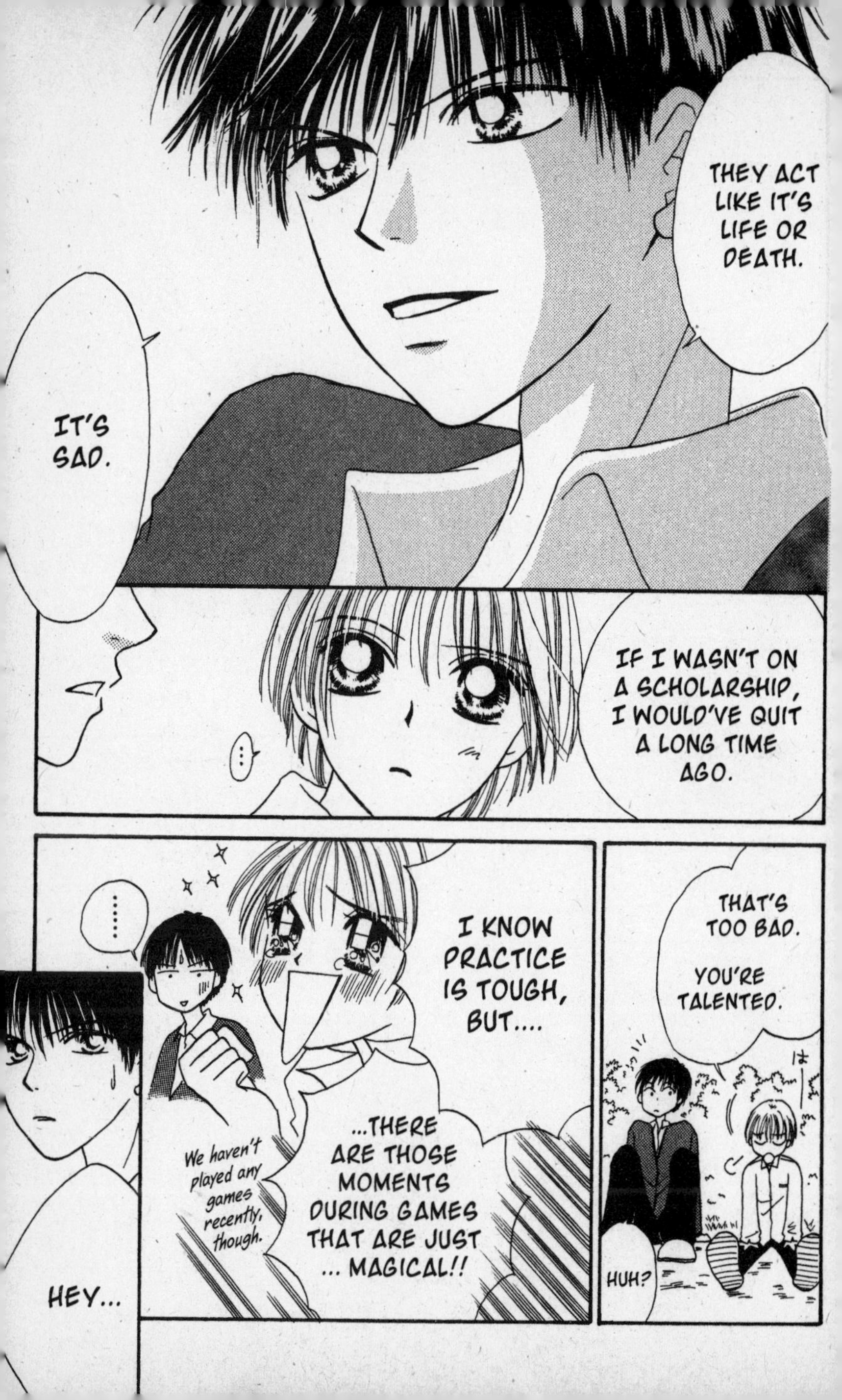
THEY ACT LIKE IT'S LIFE OR DEATH.
IT'S SAD.
IF I WASN'T ON A SCHOLARSHIP, I WOULD'VE QUIT A LONG TIME AGO.
...
THAT'S TOO BAD.
YOU'RE TALENTED.
HUH?
I KNOW PRACTICE IS TOUGH, BUT....
...THERE ARE THOSE MOMENTS DURING GAMES THAT ARE JUST ... MAGICAL!!
We haven't played any games recently, though.
......
HEY...

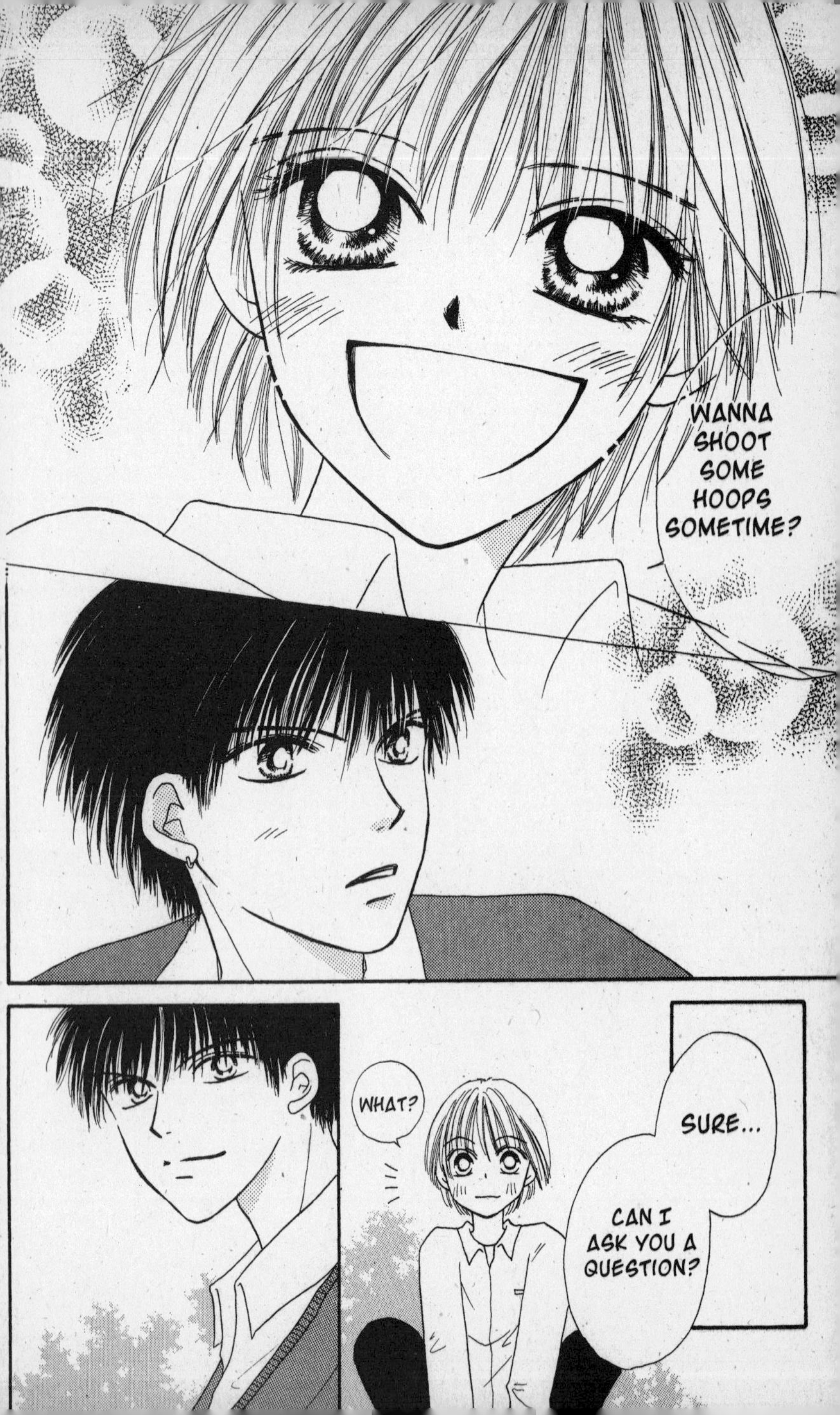
WANNA SHOOT SOME HOOPS SOMETIME?
SURE...
CAN I ASK YOU A QUESTION?
WHAT?

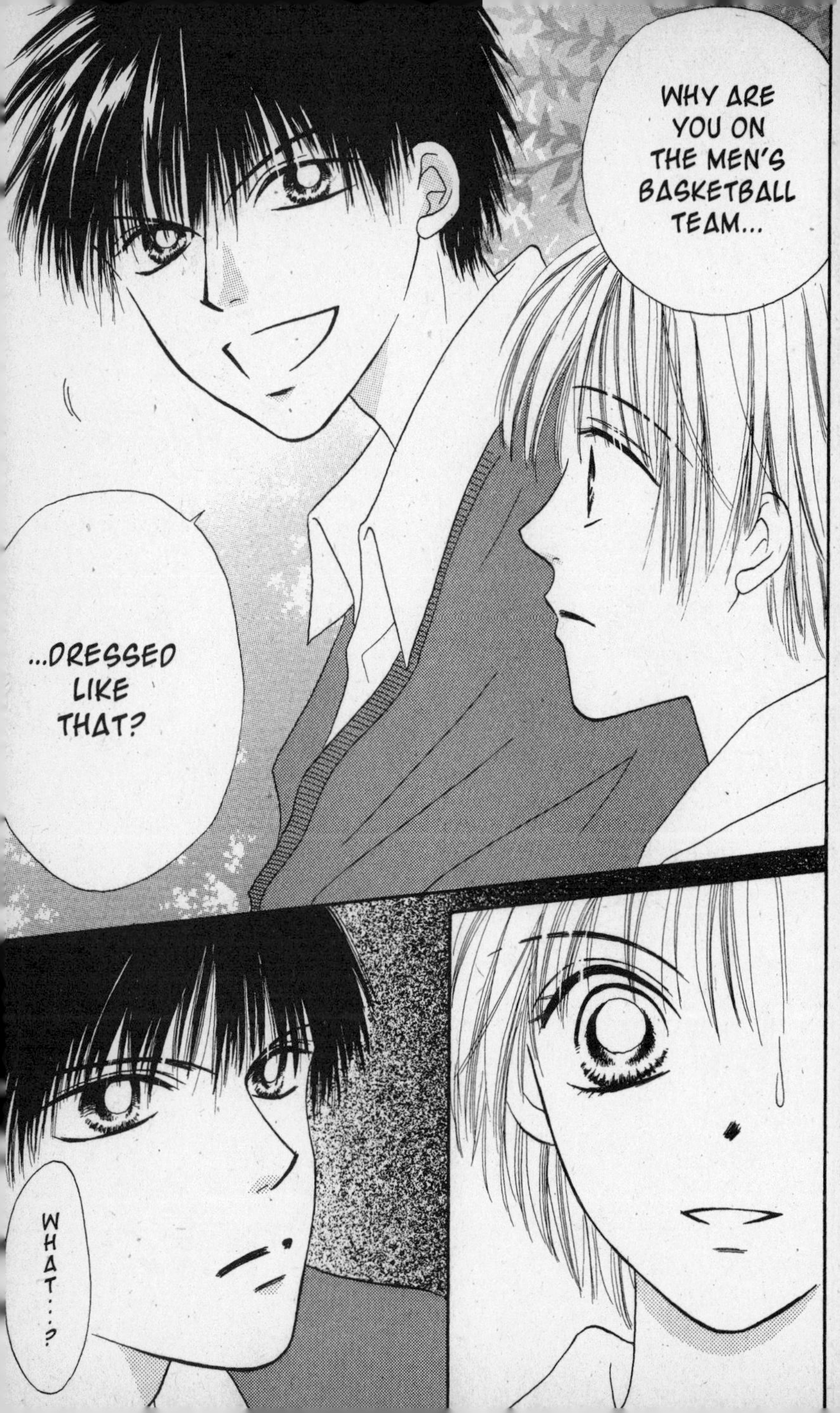
WHY ARE YOU ON THE MEN'S BASKETBALL TEAM...
...DRESSED LIKE THAT?
WHAT...?

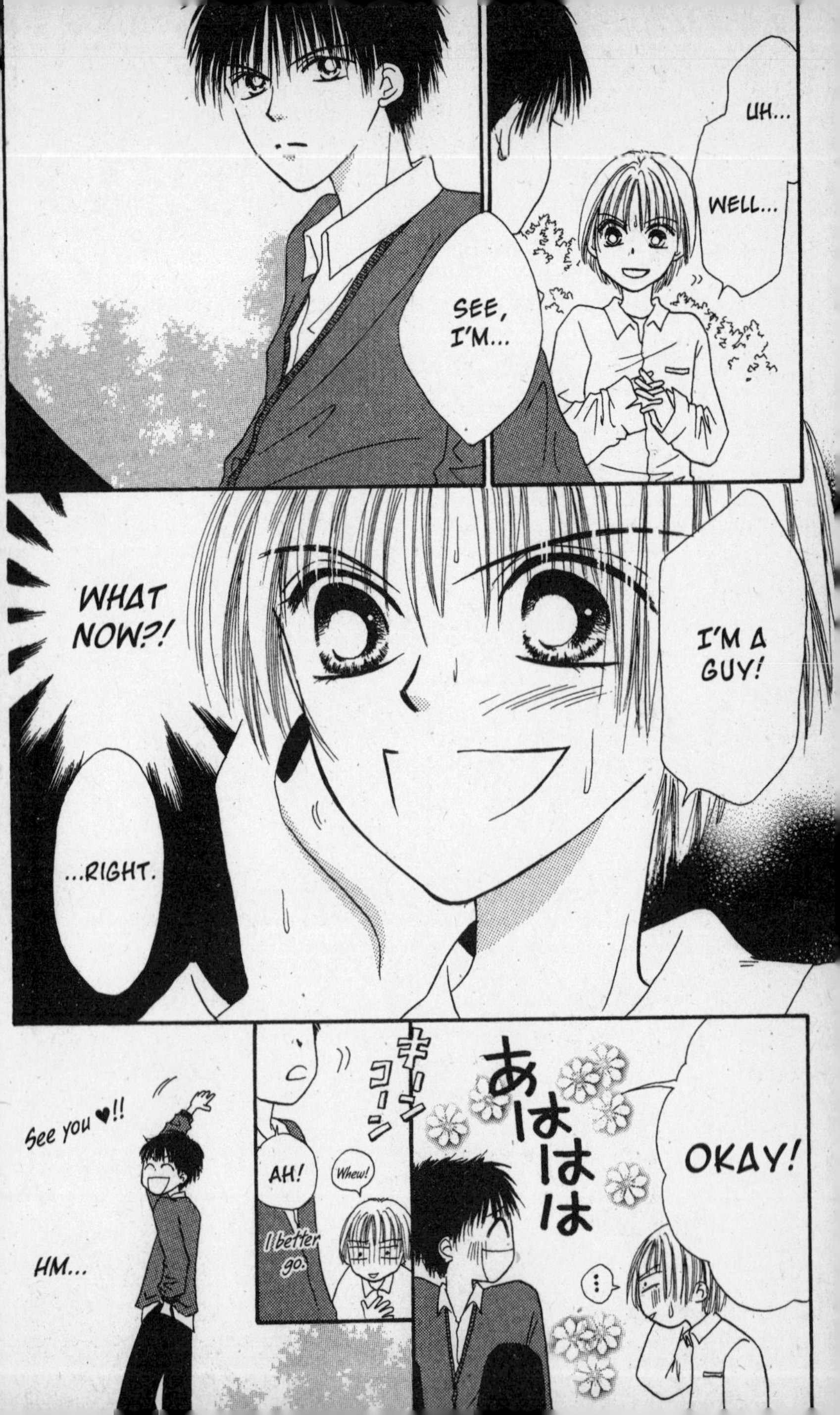
UH...
WELL...
SEE, I'M...
I'M A GUY!
WHAT NOW?!
...RIGHT.
OKAY!
あははは
...
キーンコーン
AH!
Whew!
I better go.
See you♥!!
HM...

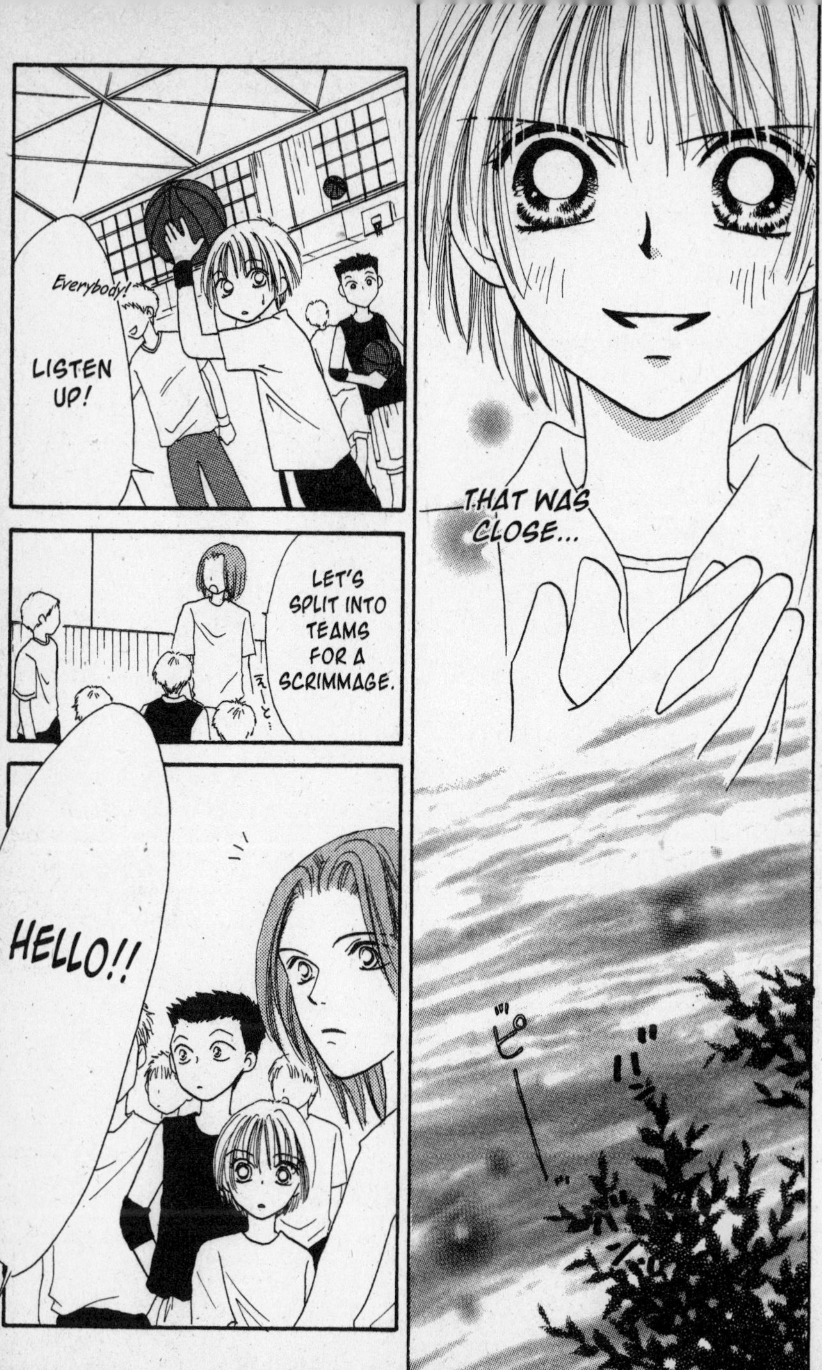
THAT WAS CLOSE...
ピー
Everybody!
LISTEN UP!
LET'S SPLIT INTO TEAMS FOR A SCRIMMAGE.
えーと…
HELLO!!

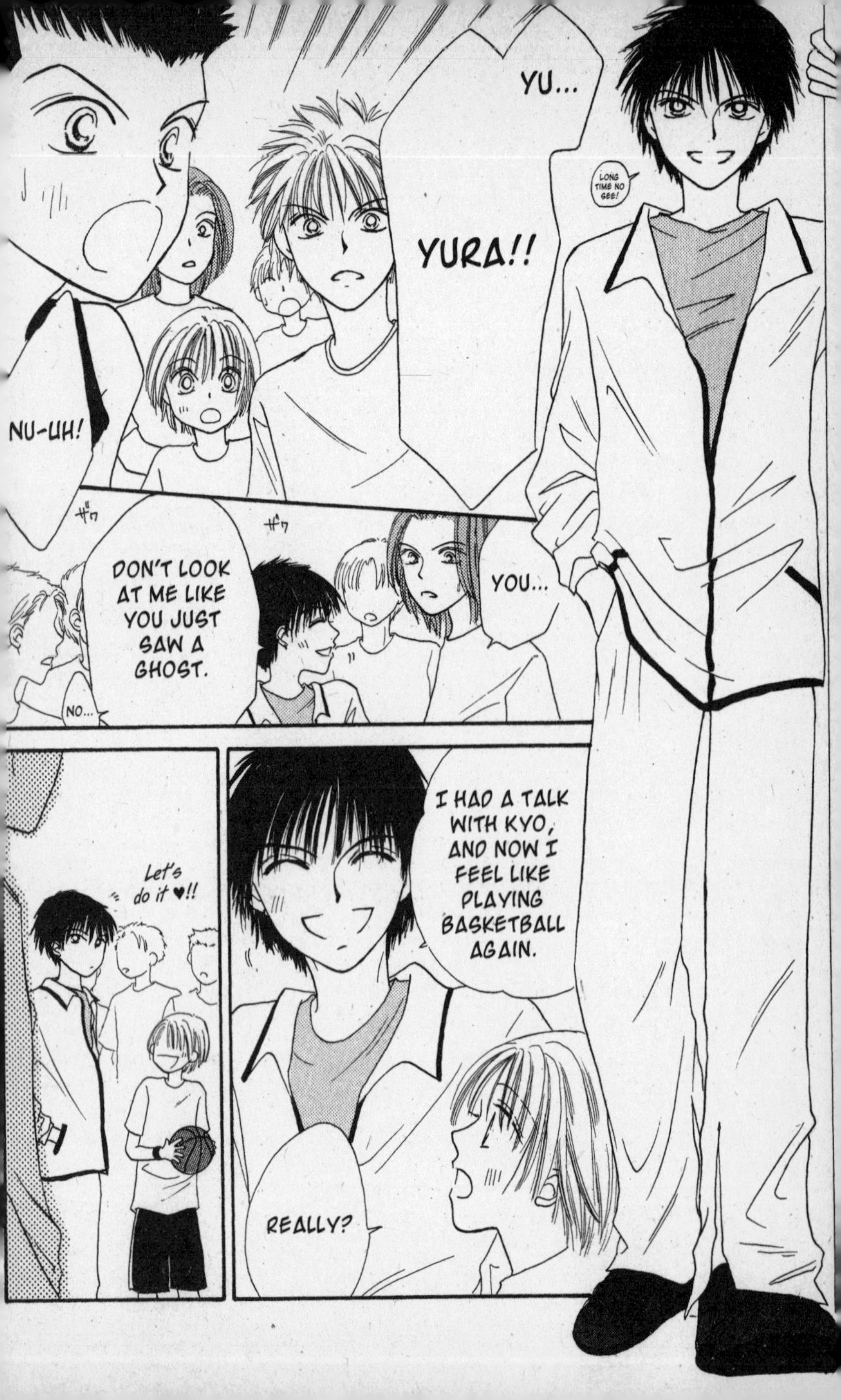
LONG TIME NO SEE!
YU...
YURA!!
NU-UH!
ザワ
YOU...
ザワ
DON'T LOOK AT ME LIKE YOU JUST SAW A GHOST.
NO...
I HAD A TALK WITH KYO, AND NOW I FEEL LIKE PLAYING BASKETBALL AGAIN.
REALLY?
Let's do it ♥!!

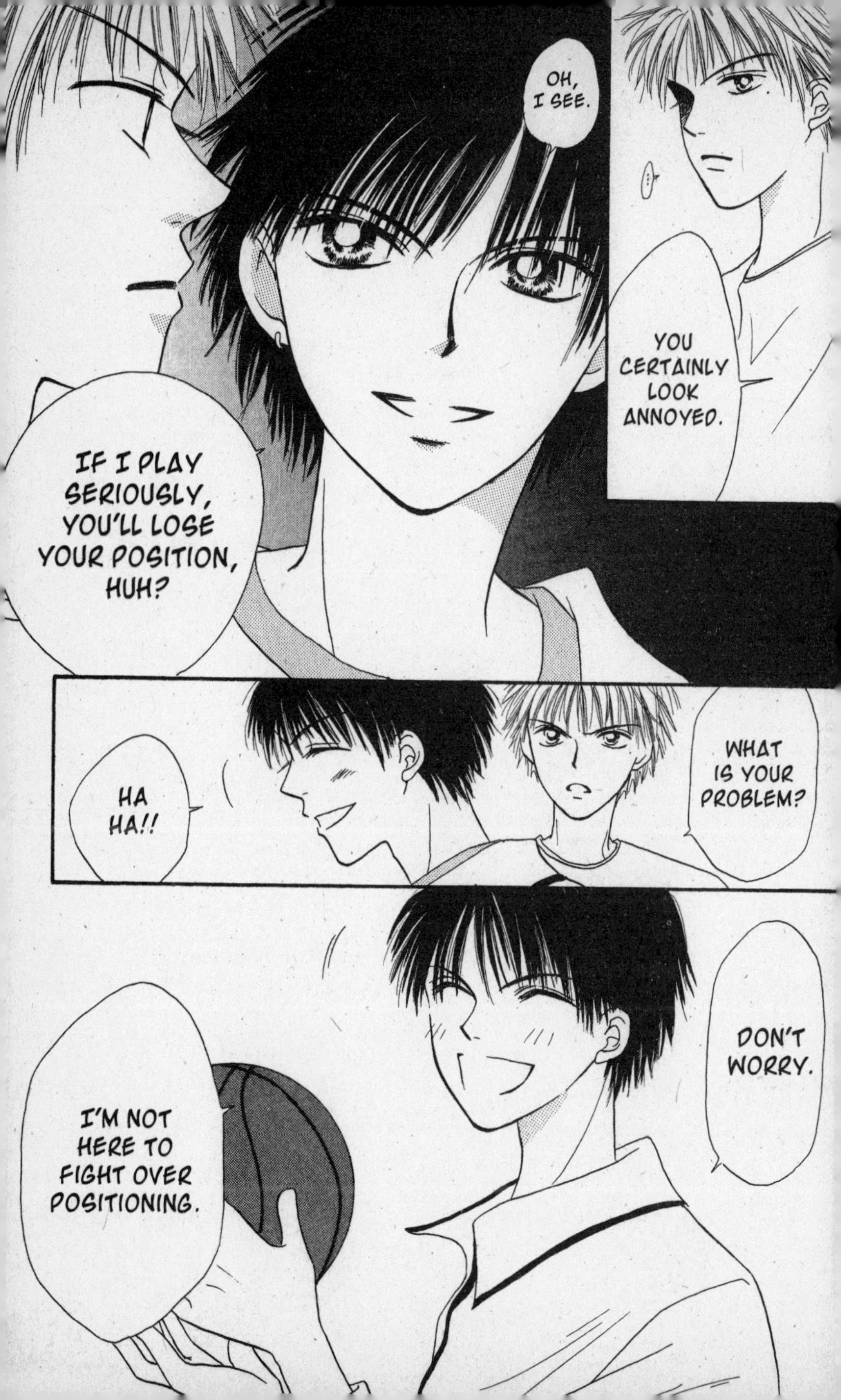
...
YOU CERTAINLY LOOK ANNOYED.
OH, I SEE.
IF I PLAY SERIOUSLY, YOU'LL LOSE YOUR POSITION, HUH?
WHAT IS YOUR PROBLEM?
HA HA!!
DON'T WORRY.
I'M NOT HERE TO FIGHT OVER POSITIONING.

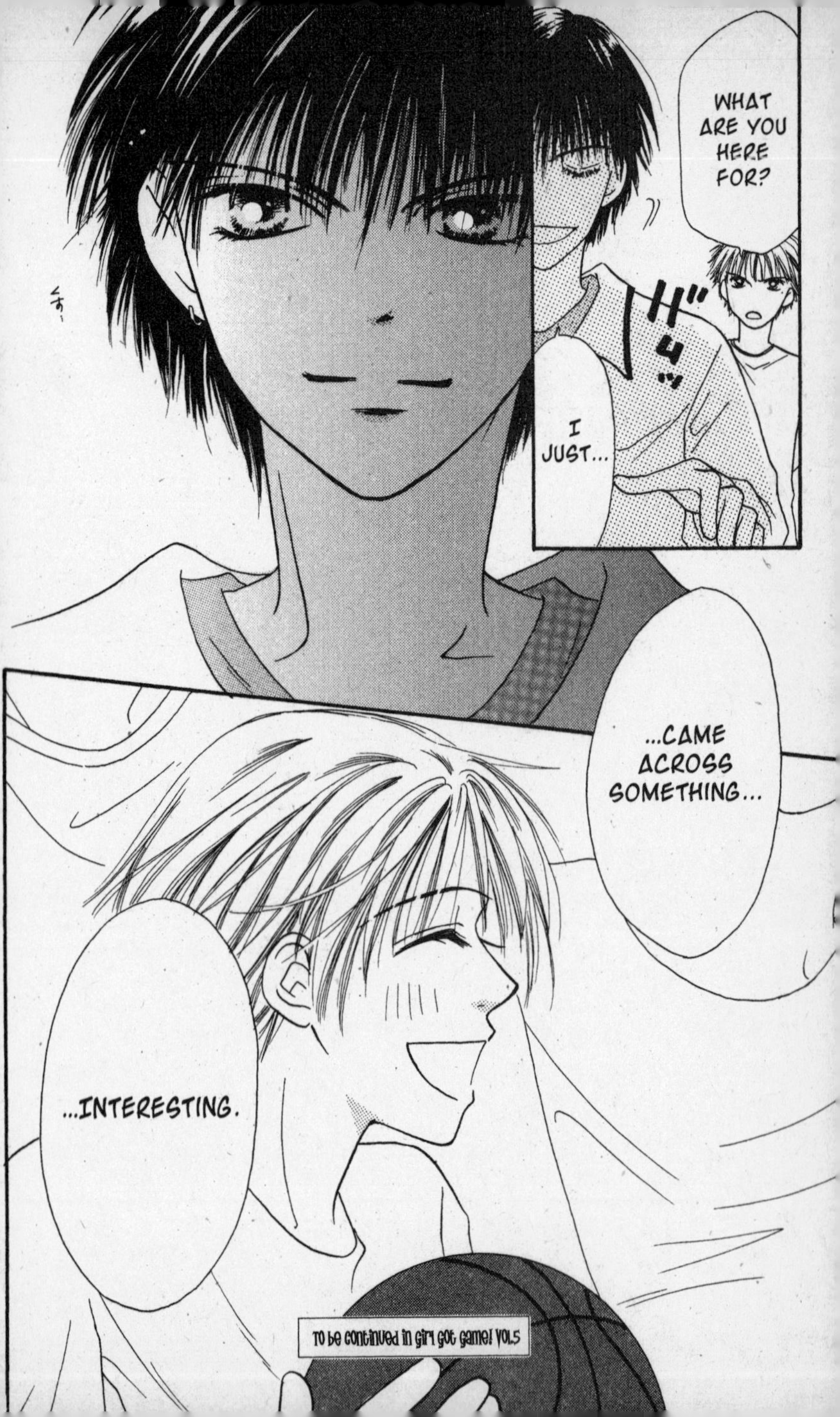
WHAT ARE YOU HERE FOR?
I JUST...
...CAME ACROSS SOMETHING...
...INTERESTING.
TO BE CONTINUED IN GIRL GOT GAME! VOL.5

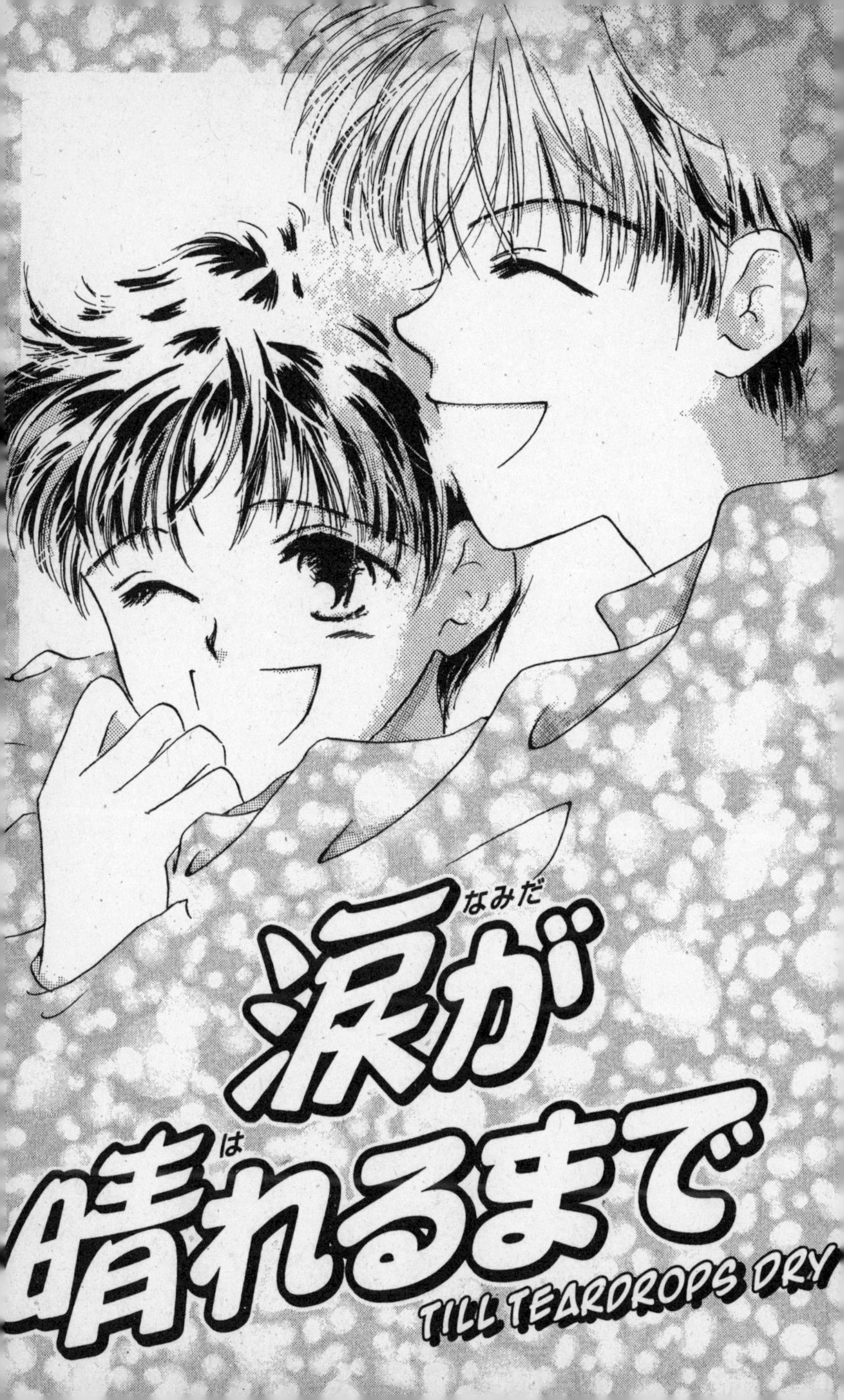
涙が晴れるまで
TILL TEARDROPS DRY

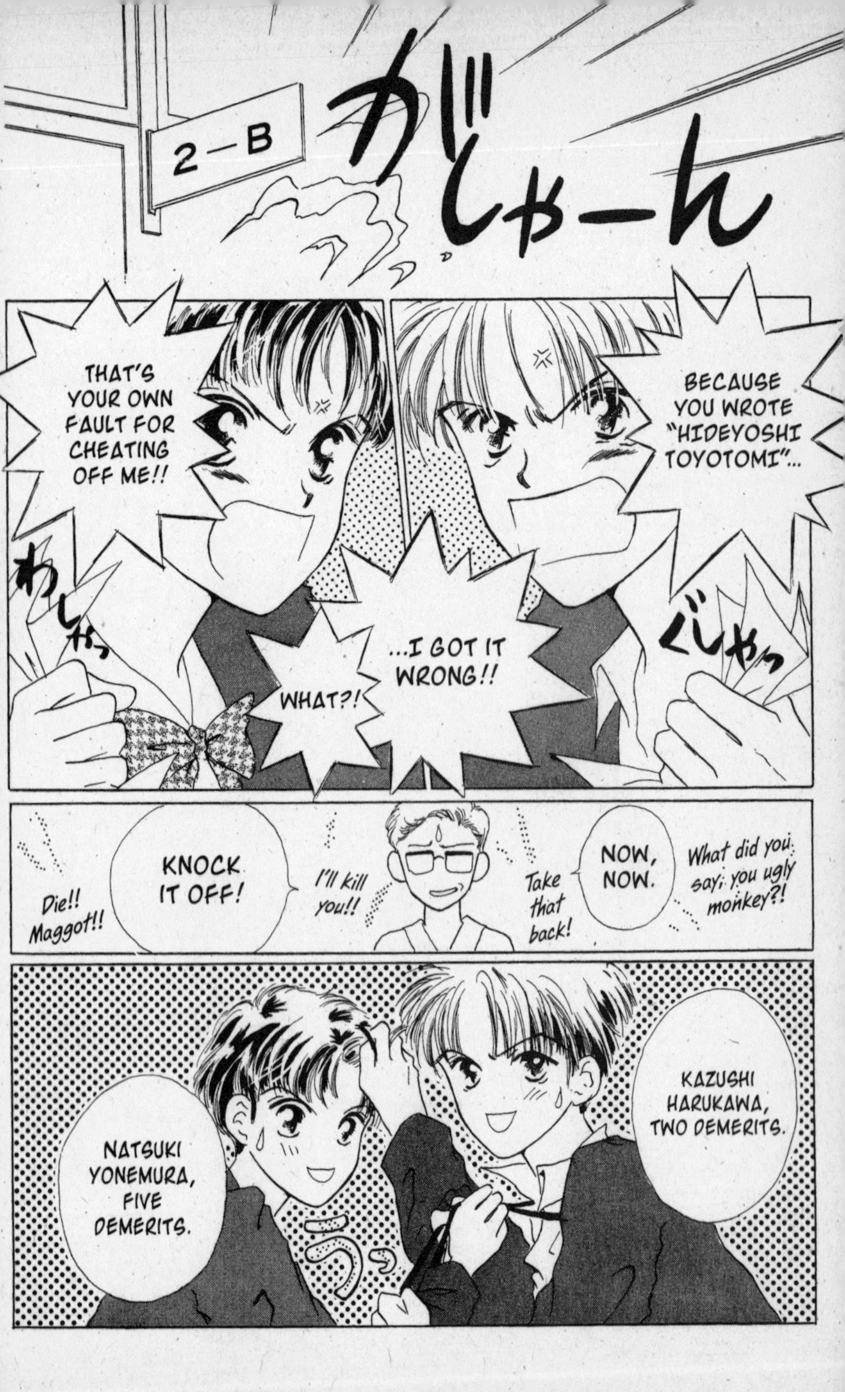
2—B
がじゃーん
BECAUSE YOU WROTE "HIDEYOSHI TOYOTOMI"...
くしゃっ
THAT'S YOUR OWN FAULT FOR CHEATING OFF ME!!
わしゃっ
...I GOT IT WRONG!!
WHAT?!
What did you say, you ugly monkey?!
NOW, NOW.
Take that back!
I'll kill you!!
KNOCK IT OFF!
Die!! Maggot!!
KAZUSHI HARUKAWA, TWO DEMERITS.
NATSUKI YONEMURA, FIVE DEMERITS.

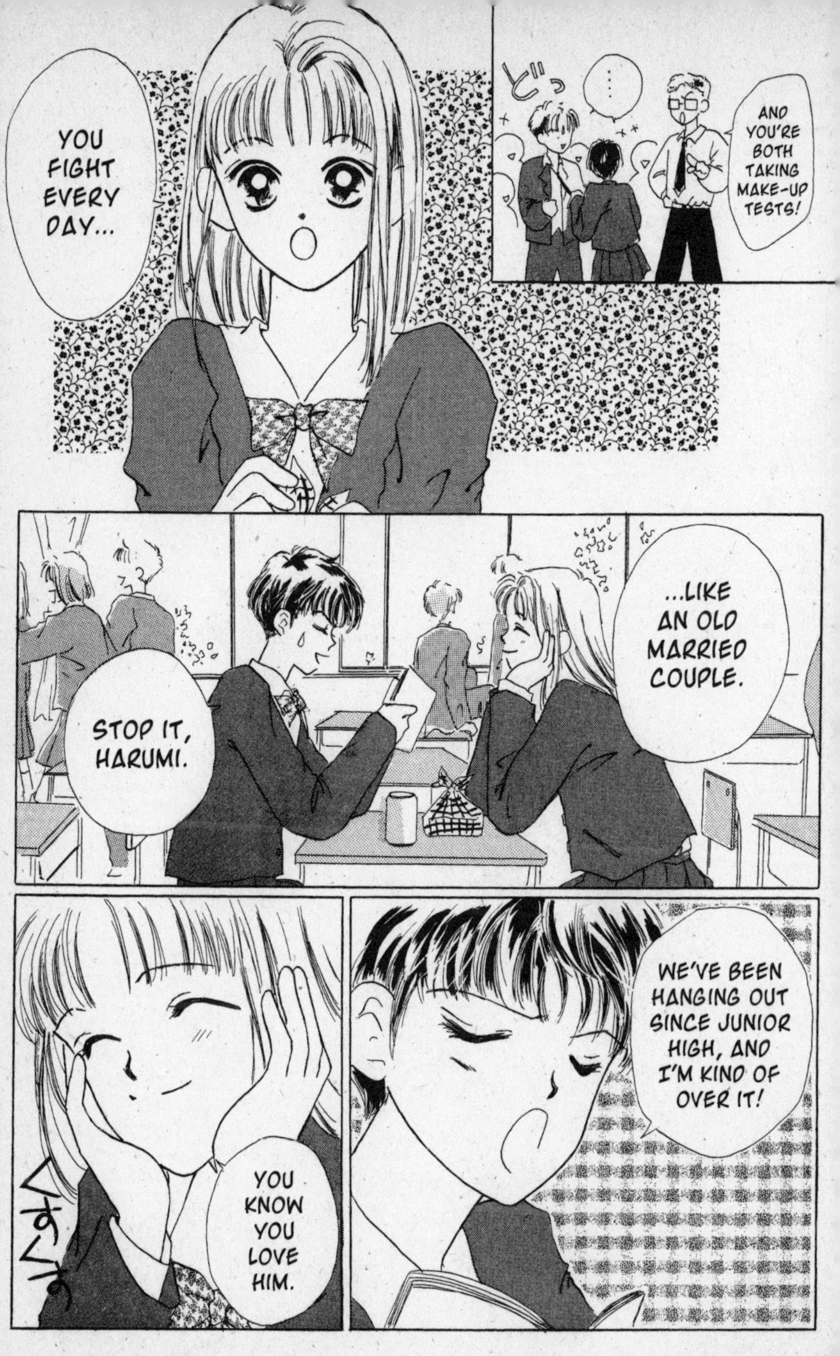
AND YOU'RE BOTH TAKING MAKE-UP TESTS!
どっ
YOU FIGHT EVERY DAY...
...LIKE AN OLD MARRIED COUPLE.
STOP IT, HARUMI.
WE'VE BEEN HANGING OUT SINCE JUNIOR HIGH, AND I'M KIND OF OVER IT!
YOU KNOW YOU LOVE HIM.
くすくす

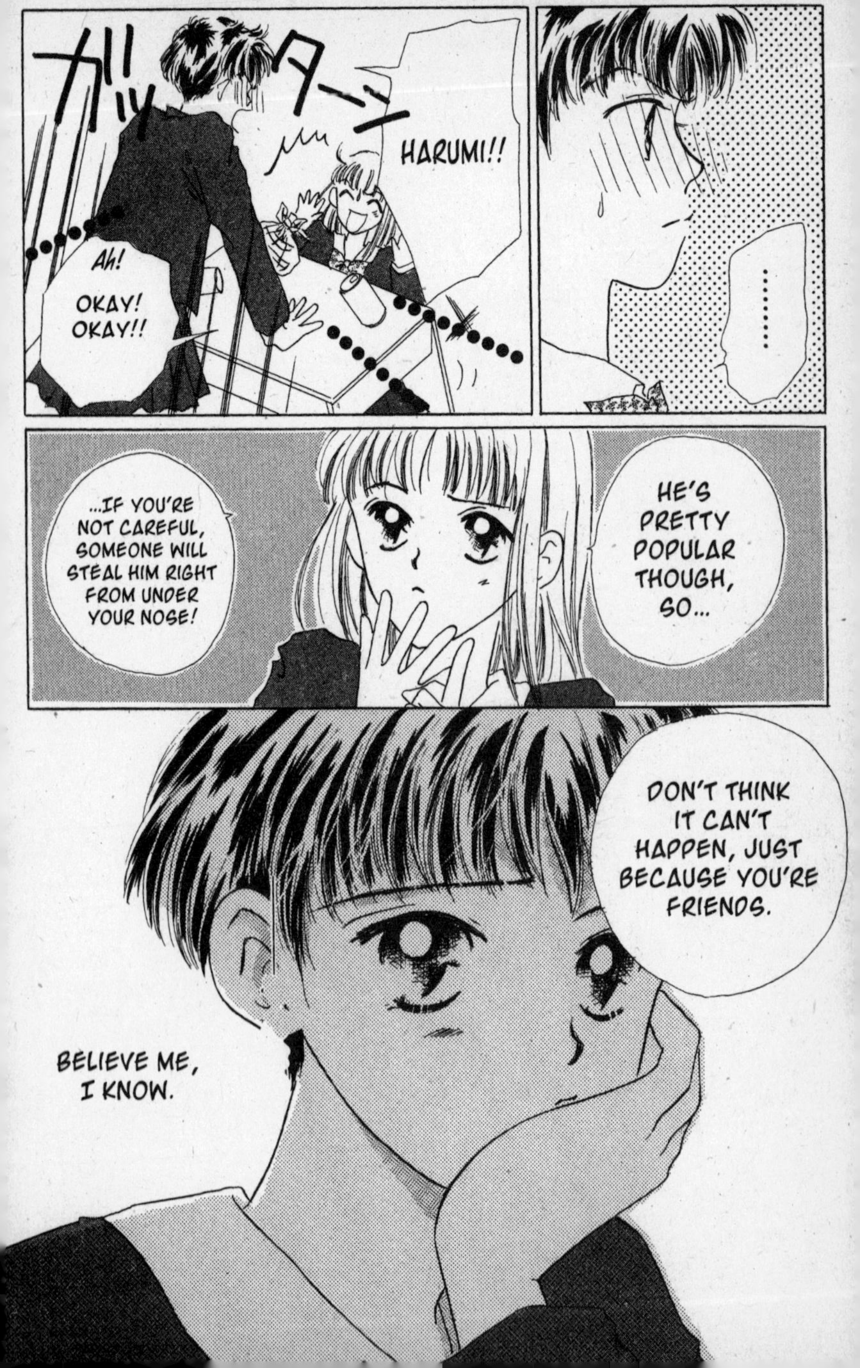
......
ガッターン
HARUMI!!
Ah!
OKAY! OKAY!!
HE'S PRETTY POPULAR THOUGH, SO...
...IF YOU'RE NOT CAREFUL, SOMEONE WILL STEAL HIM RIGHT FROM UNDER YOUR NOSE!
DON'T THINK IT CAN'T HAPPEN, JUST BECAUSE YOU'RE FRIENDS.
BELIEVE ME, I KNOW.

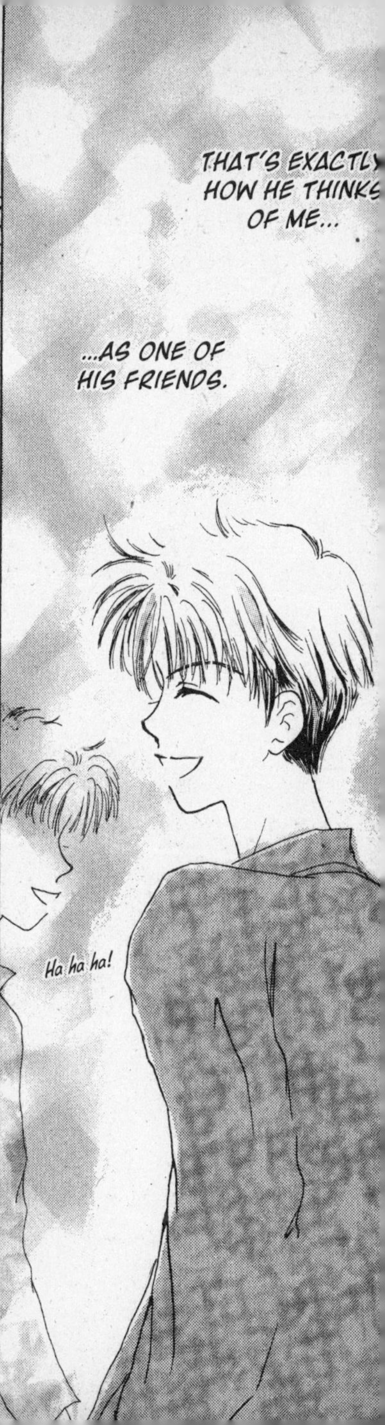
THAT'S EXACTLY HOW HE THINKS OF ME...
...AS ONE OF HIS FRIENDS.
Ha ha ha!

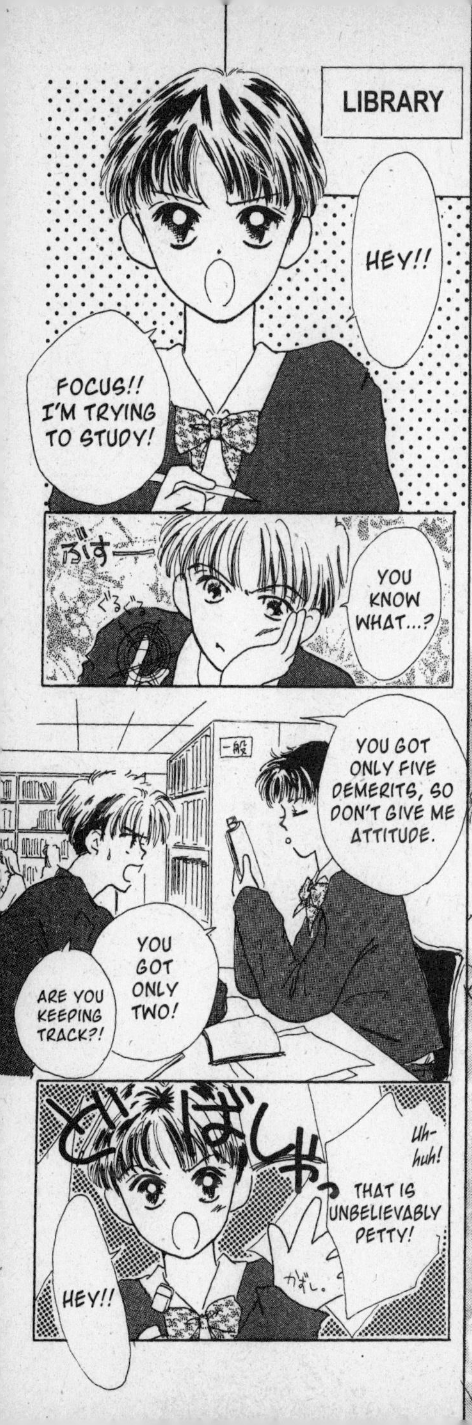
LIBRARY
HEY!!
FOCUS!! I'M TRYING TO STUDY!
YOU KNOW WHAT...?
ぶすー
ぐるぐる
YOU GOT ONLY FIVE DEMERITS, SO DON'T GIVE ME ATTITUDE.
一般
YOU GOT ONLY TWO!
ARE YOU KEEPING TRACK?!
Uh-huh!
THAT IS UNBELIEVABLY PETTY!
どばしゃっ
かざし。
HEY!!

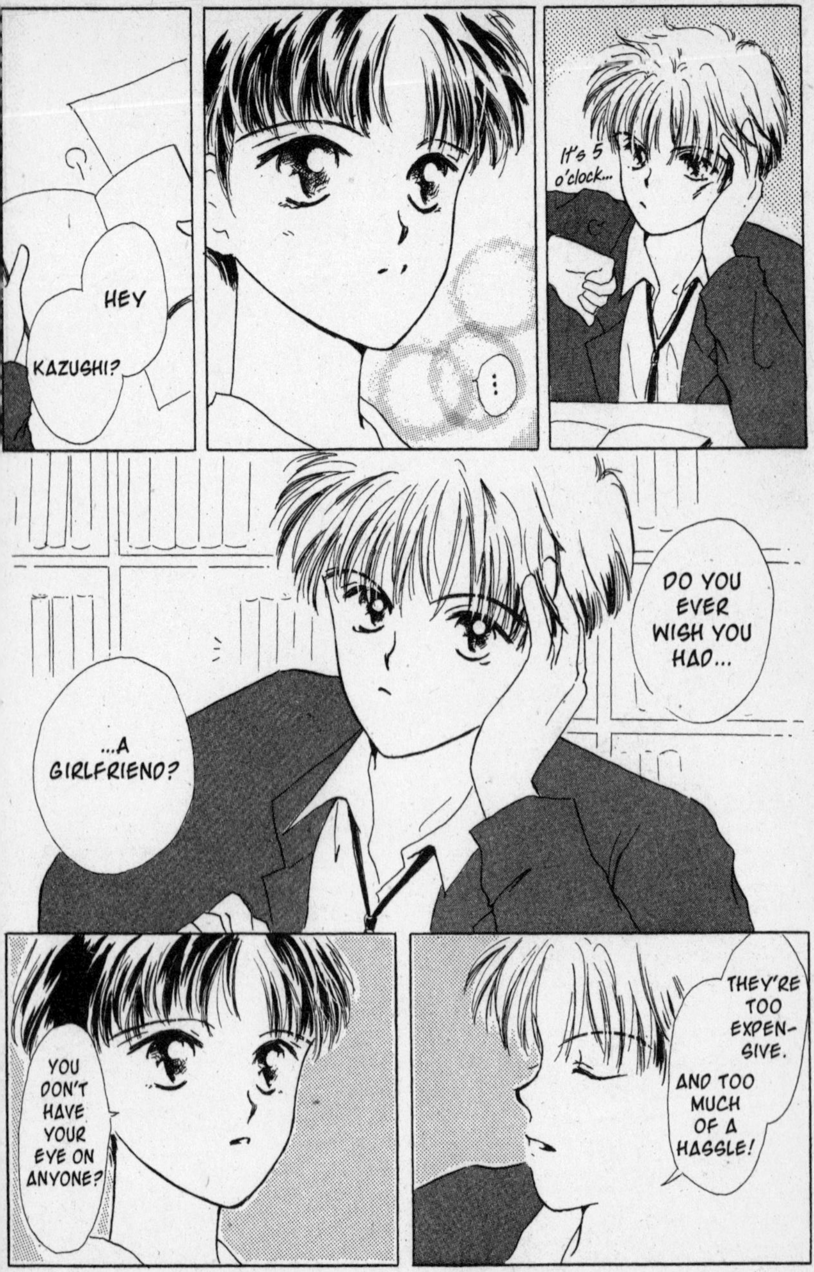
It's 5 o'clock...
...
HEY KAZUSHI?
DO YOU EVER WISH YOU HAD...
...A GIRLFRIEND?
THEY'RE TOO EXPEN-SIVE.
AND TOO MUCH OF A HASSLE!
YOU DON'T HAVE YOUR EYE ON ANYONE?

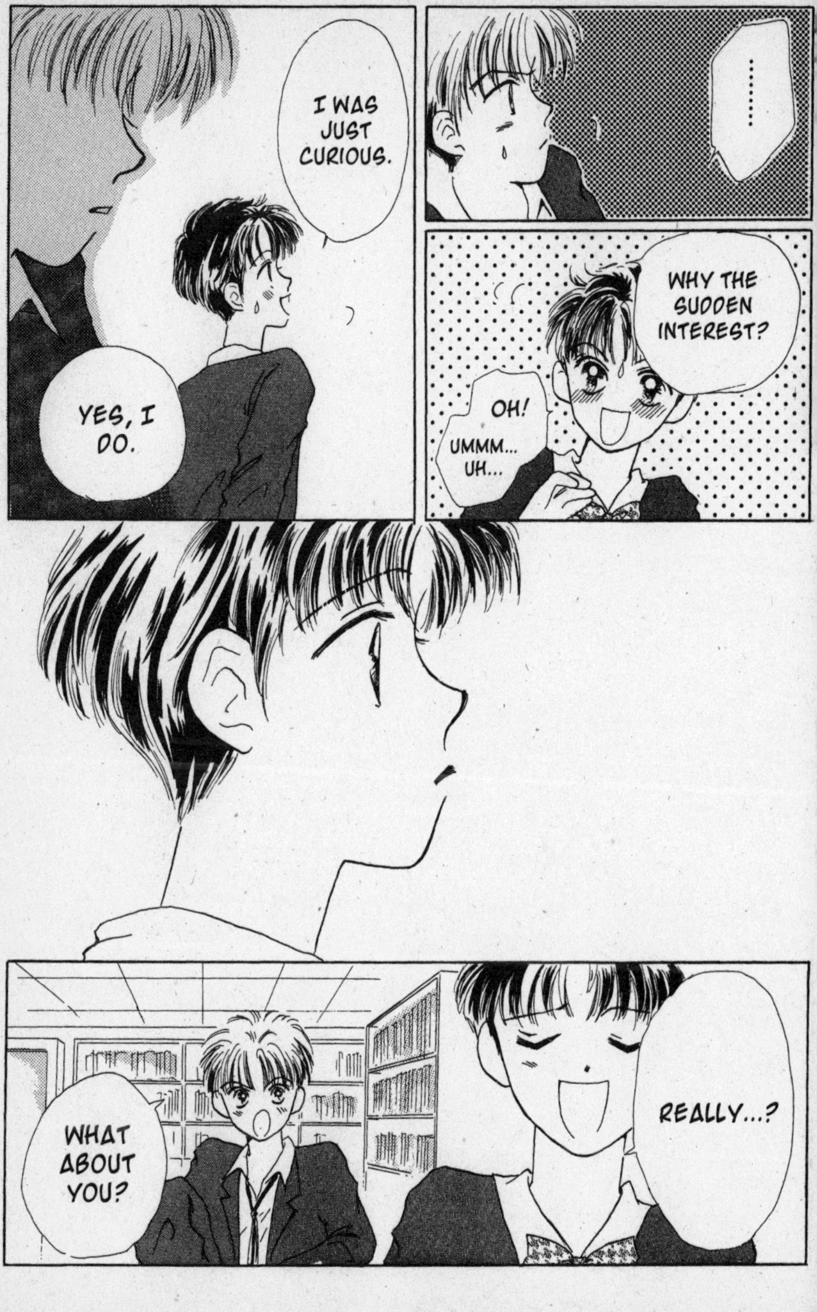
……
WHY THE SUDDEN INTEREST?
OH!
UMMM... UH...
I WAS JUST CURIOUS.
YES, I DO.
REALLY...?
WHAT ABOUT YOU?

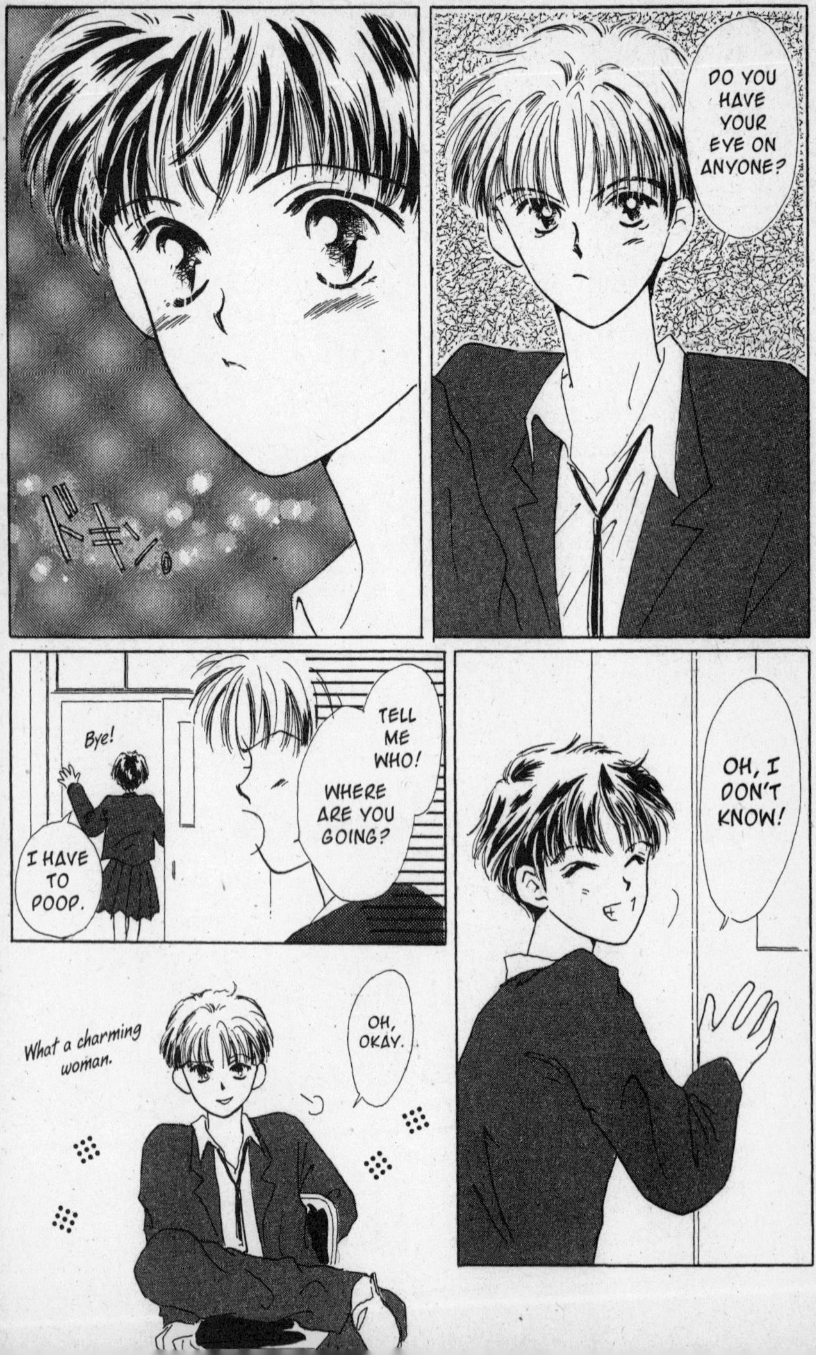
DO YOU HAVE YOUR EYE ON ANYONE?
ドキン。
OH, I DON'T KNOW!
TELL ME WHO!
WHERE ARE YOU GOING?
Bye!
I HAVE TO POOP.
OH, OKAY.
What a charming woman.

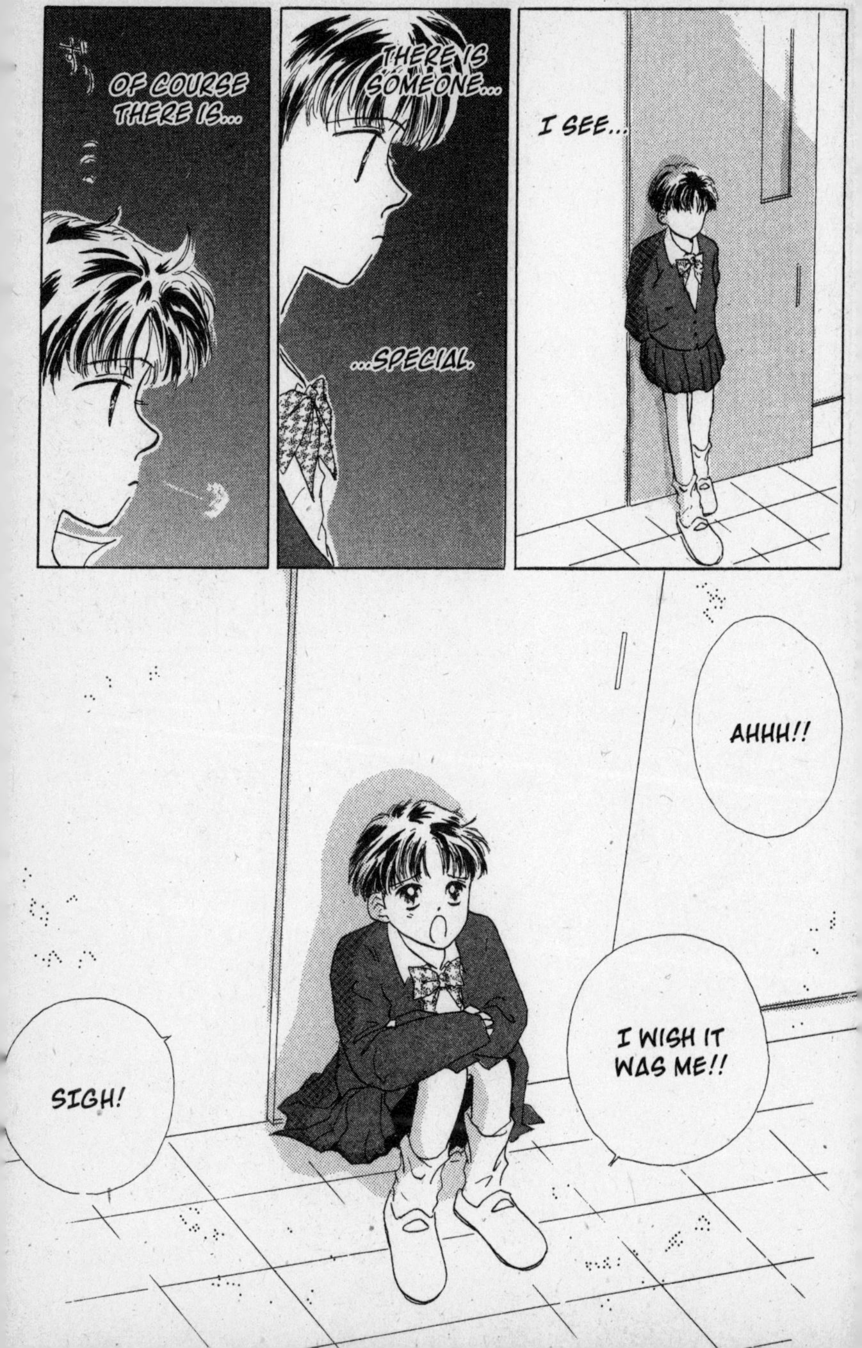
I SEE...
THERE IS SOMEONE...
...SPECIAL.
OF COURSE THERE IS...
AHHH!!
I WISH IT WAS ME!!
SIGH!

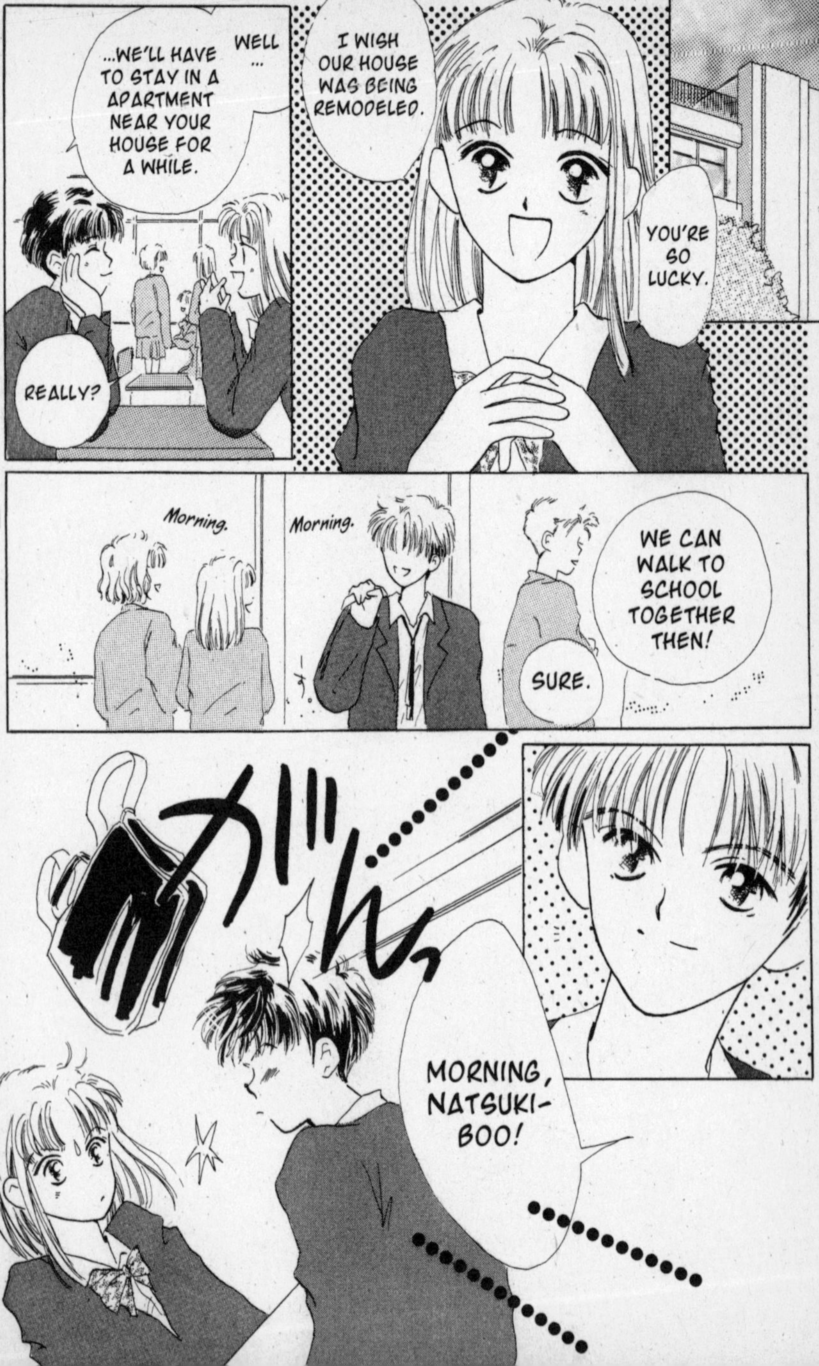
I WISH OUR HOUSE WAS BEING REMODELED.
YOU'RE SO LUCKY.
WELL ...
...WE'LL HAVE TO STAY IN A APARTMENT NEAR YOUR HOUSE FOR A WHILE.
REALLY?
WE CAN WALK TO SCHOOL TOGETHER THEN!
SURE.
Morning.
Morning.
MORNING, NATSUKI-BOO!

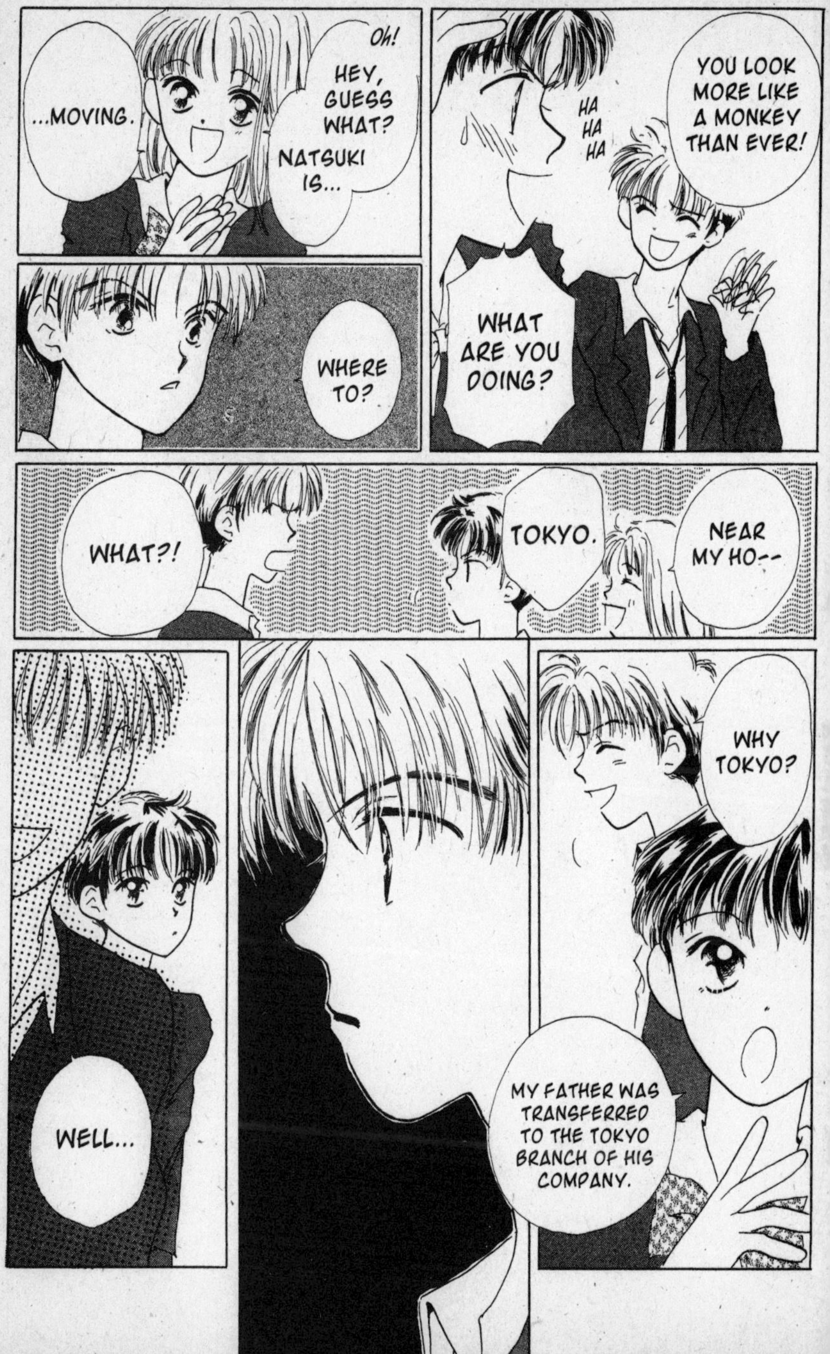
YOU LOOK MORE LIKE A MONKEY THAN EVER!
HA HA HA
WHAT ARE YOU DOING?
Oh!
HEY, GUESS WHAT?
NATSUKI IS...
...MOVING.
WHERE TO?
NEAR MY HO--
TOKYO.
WHAT?!
WHY TOKYO?
MY FATHER WAS TRANSFERRED TO THE TOKYO BRANCH OF HIS COMPANY.
WELL...

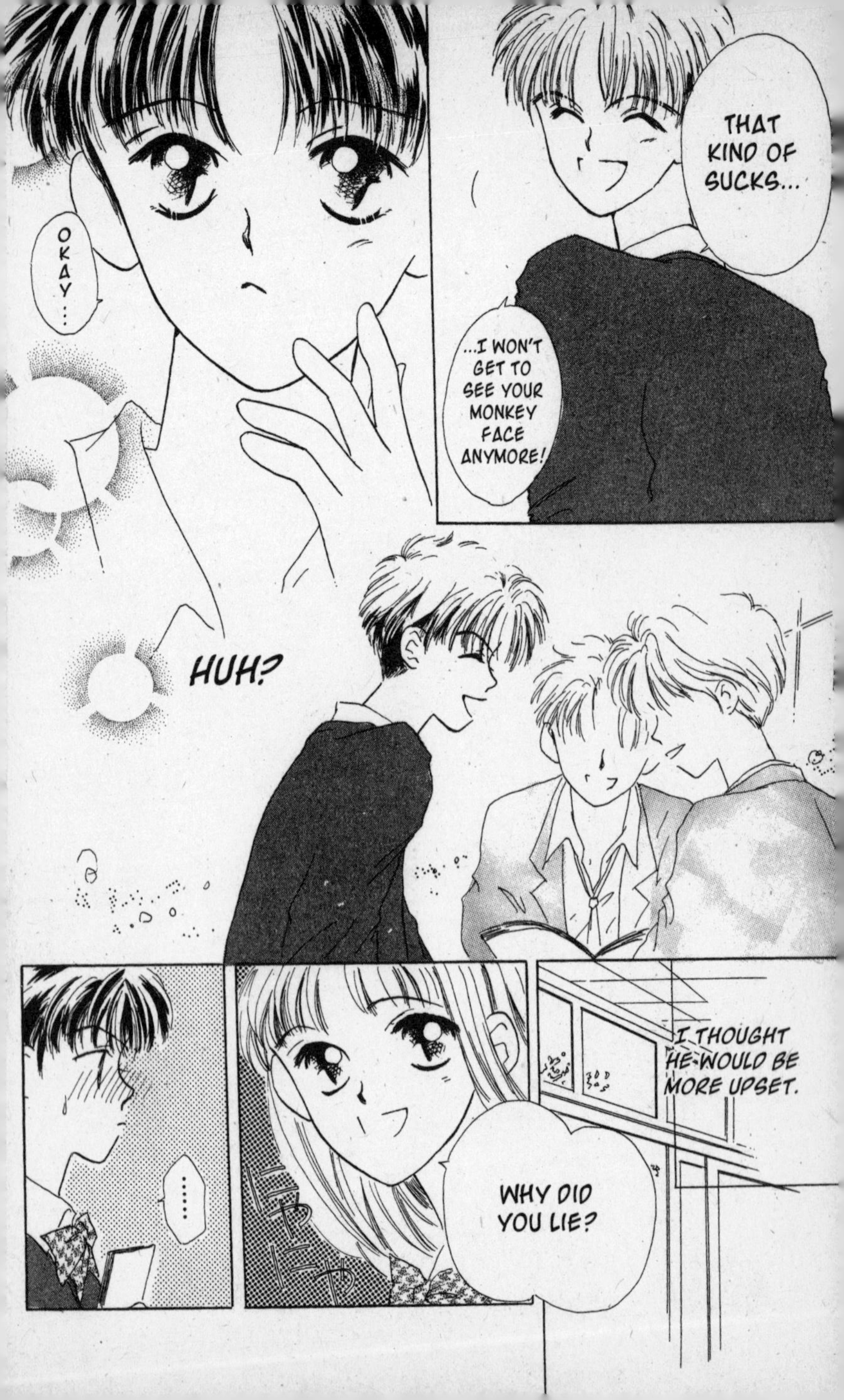
THAT KIND OF SUCKS...
...I WON'T GET TO SEE YOUR MONKEY FACE ANYMORE!
OKAY...
HUH?
I THOUGHT HE WOULD BE MORE UPSET.
WHY DID YOU LIE?
......

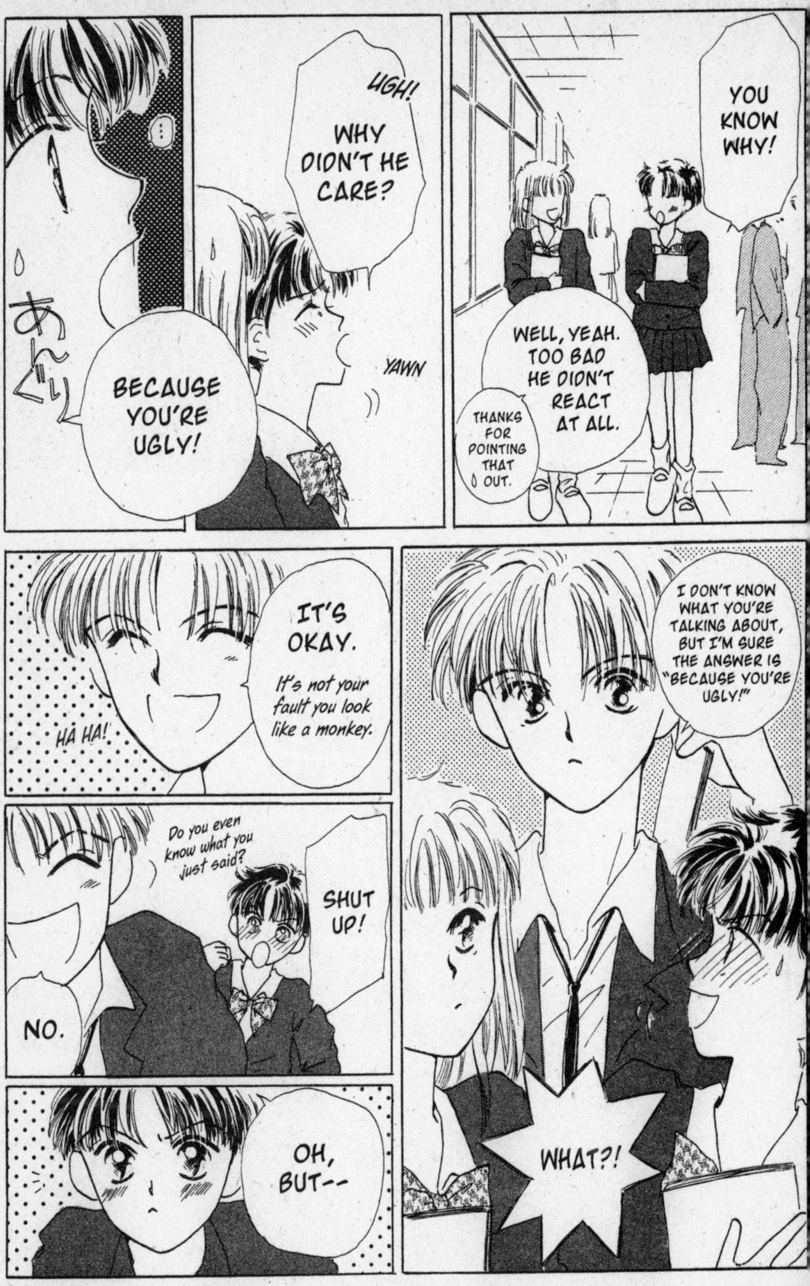
YOU KNOW WHY!
WELL, YEAH. TOO BAD HE DIDN'T REACT AT ALL.
THANKS FOR POINTING THAT OUT.
UGH!
WHY DIDN'T HE CARE?
YAWN
...
BECAUSE YOU'RE UGLY!
あんぐり
I DON'T KNOW WHAT YOU'RE TALKING ABOUT, BUT I'M SURE THE ANSWER IS "BECAUSE YOU'RE UGLY!"
WHAT?!
IT'S OKAY.
It's not your fault you look like a monkey.
HA HA!
SHUT UP!
Do you even know what you just said?
NO.
OH, BUT--

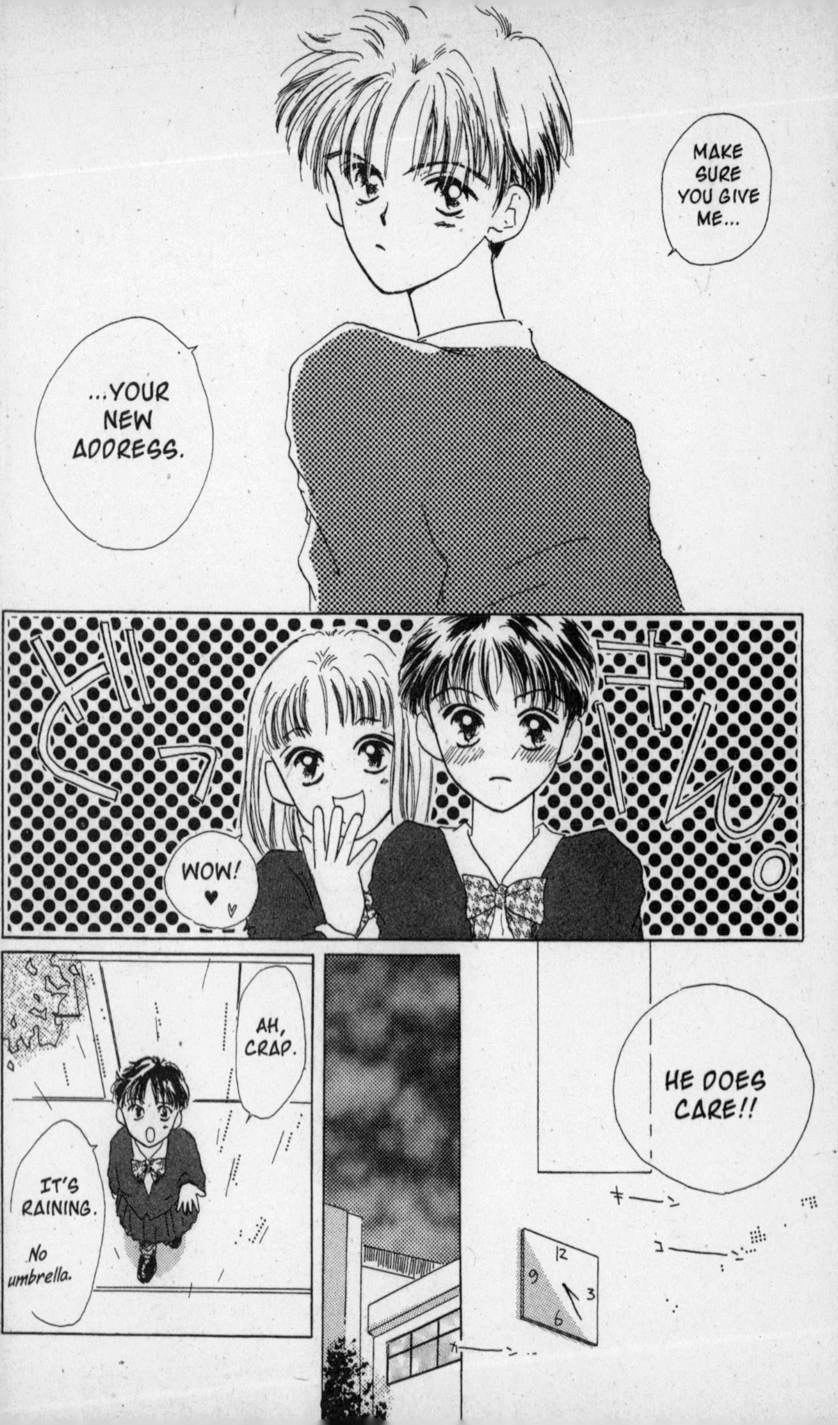
MAKE SURE YOU GIVE ME...
...YOUR NEW ADDRESS.
WOW! ♥
HE DOES CARE!!
キーン
コーン
カーン
AH, CRAP.
IT'S RAINING.
No umbrella.

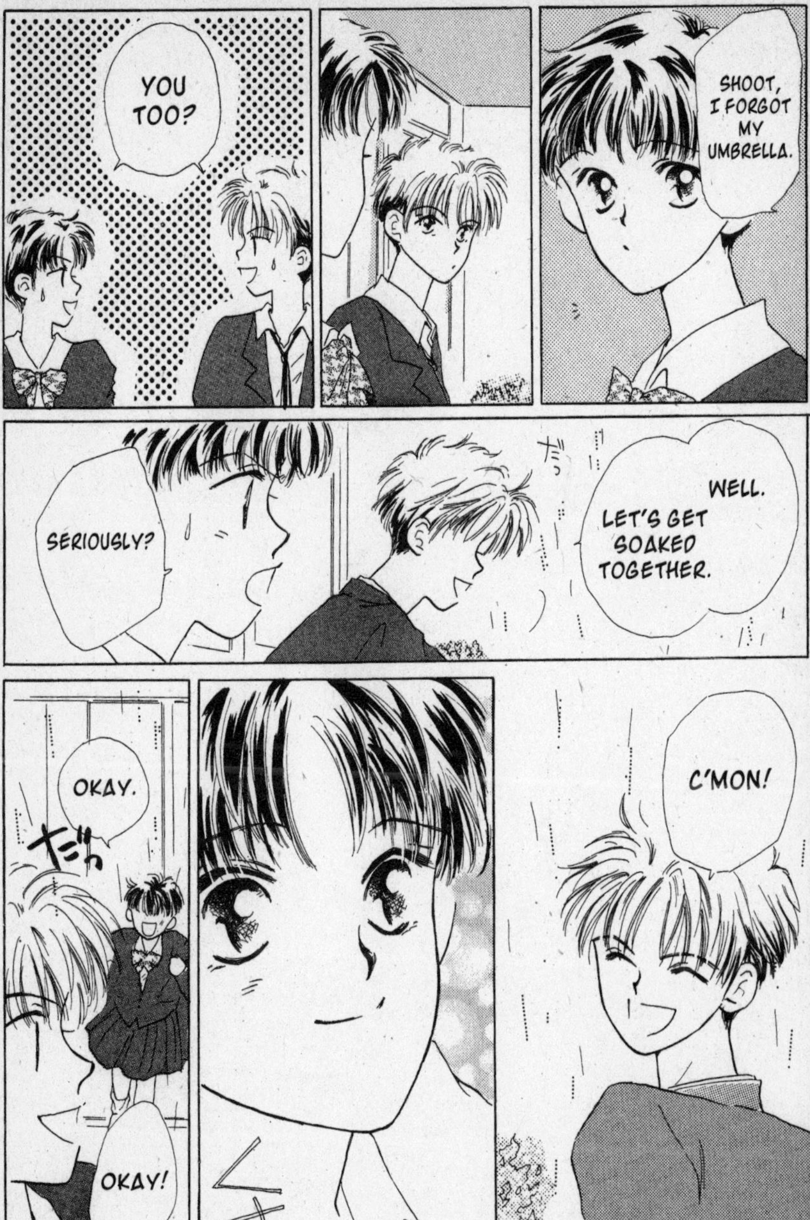
SHOOT, I FORGOT MY UMBRELLA.
YOU TOO?
だっ
WELL. LET'S GET SOAKED TOGETHER.
SERIOUSLY?
C'MON!
くす。
OKAY.
OKAY!

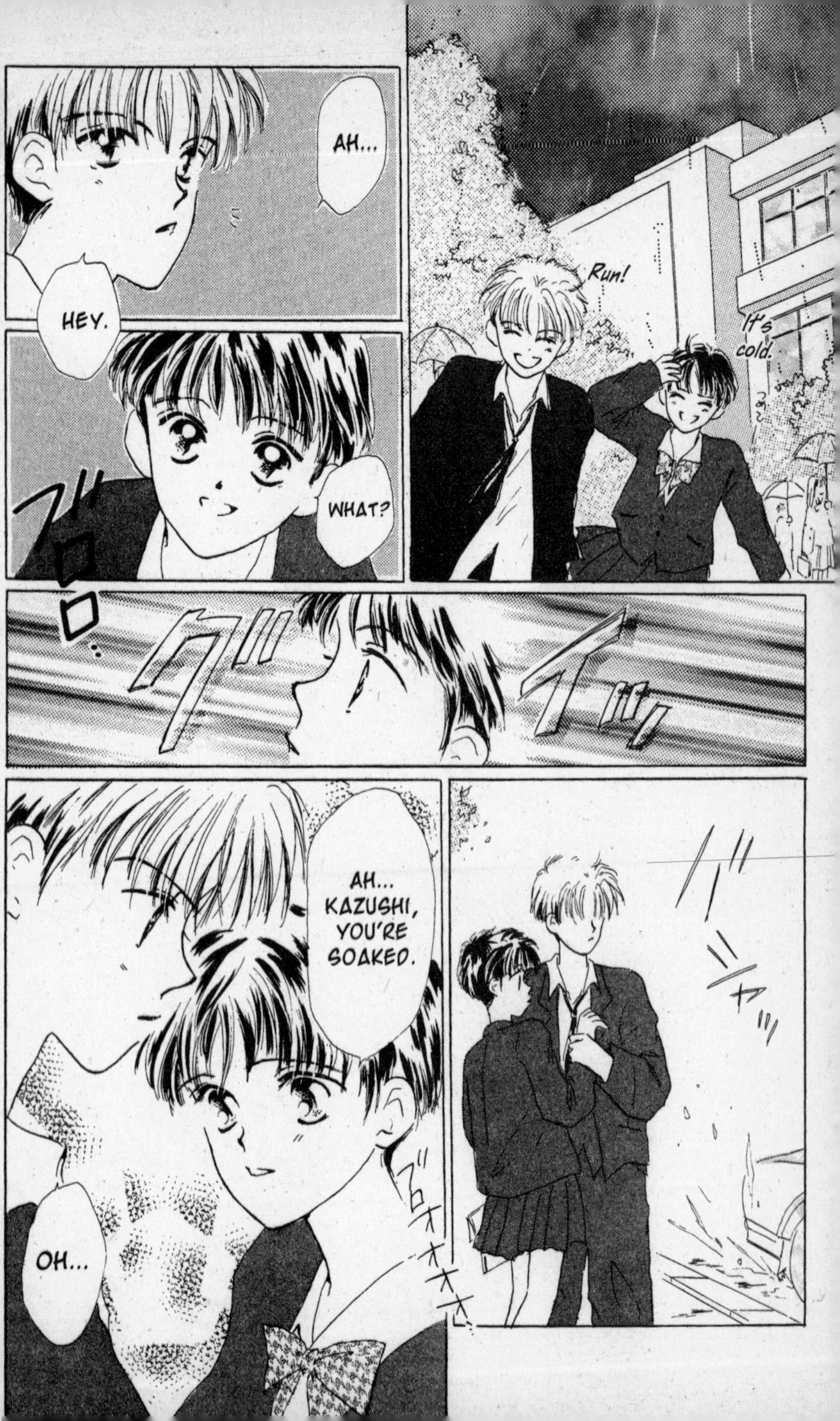
Run!
It's cold.
AH...
HEY.
WHAT?
AH... KAZUSHI, YOU'RE SOAKED.
OH...

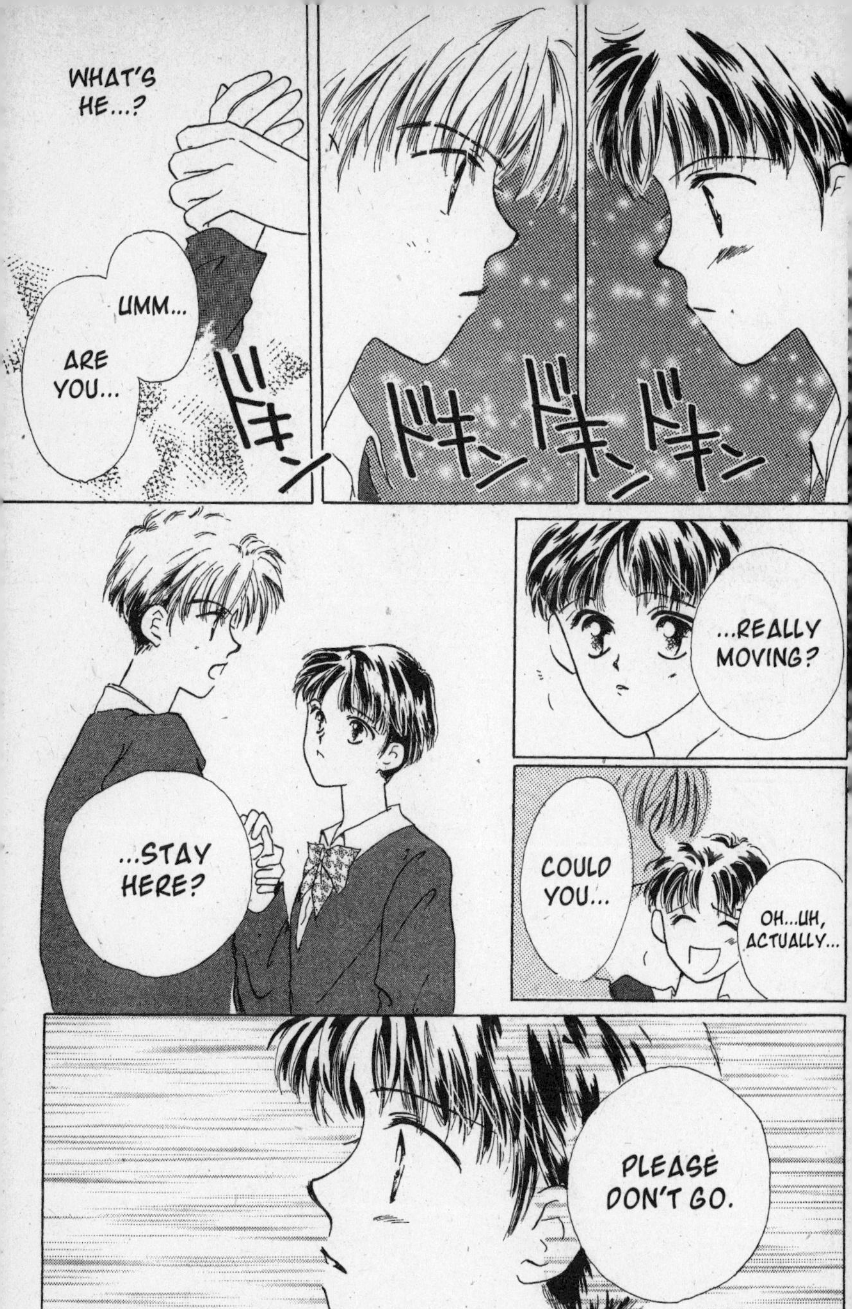
ドキン
ドキン
ドキン
WHAT'S HE...?
UMM... ARE YOU...
ドキン
...REALLY MOVING?
OH...UH, ACTUALLY...
COULD YOU...
...STAY HERE?
PLEASE DON'T GO.

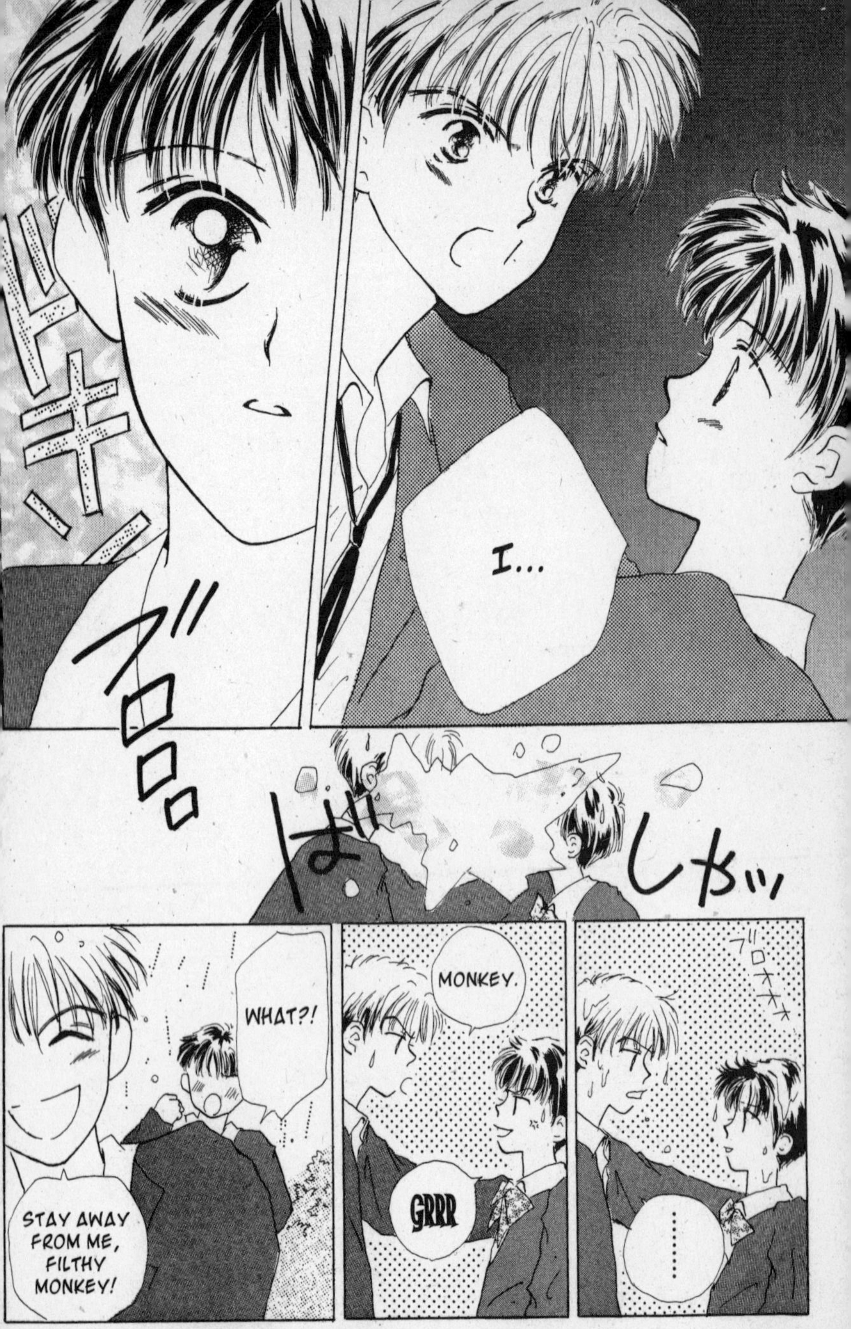

I...
ドキン
ブロロ
ばしゃッ
......
MONKEY.
GRRR
WHAT?!
STAY AWAY FROM ME, FILTHY MONKEY!

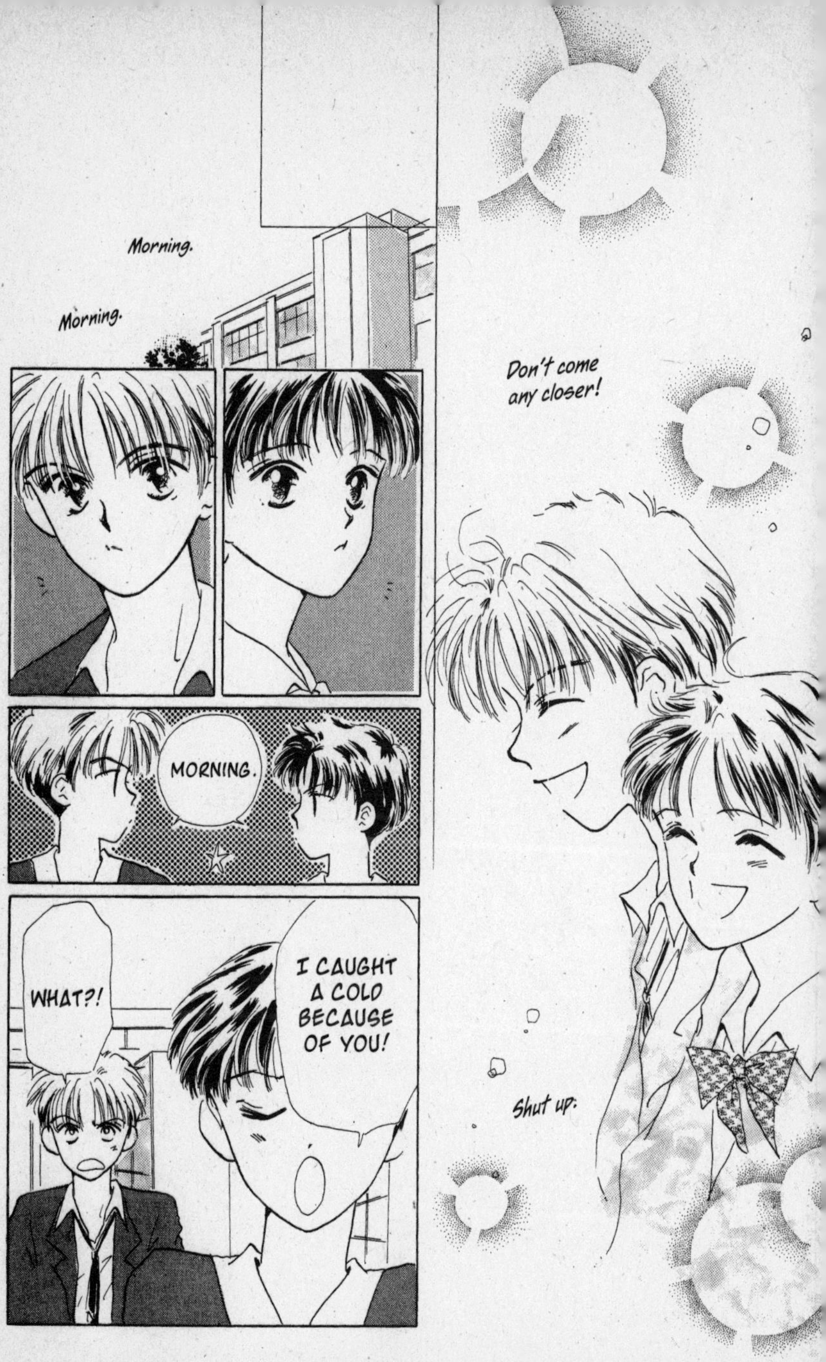
Don't come any closer!
Shut up.
Morning.
Morning.
MORNING.
I CAUGHT A COLD BECAUSE OF YOU!
WHAT?!

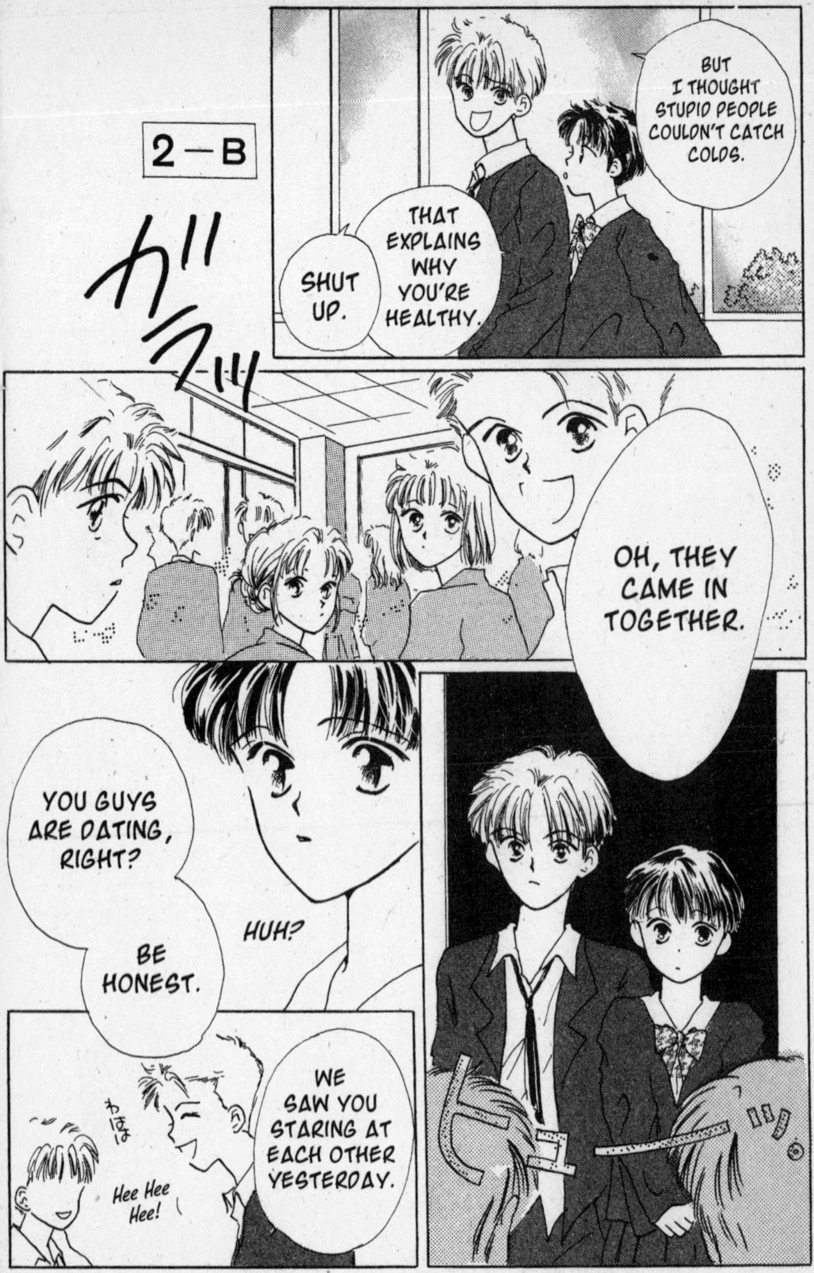
BUT I THOUGHT STUPID PEOPLE COULDN'T CATCH COLDS.
THAT EXPLAINS WHY YOU'RE HEALTHY.
SHUT UP.
2—B
ガラッ
OH, THEY CAME IN TOGETHER.
YOU GUYS ARE DATING, RIGHT?
HUH?
BE HONEST.
WE SAW YOU STARING AT EACH OTHER YESTERDAY.
わはは
Hee Hee Hee!

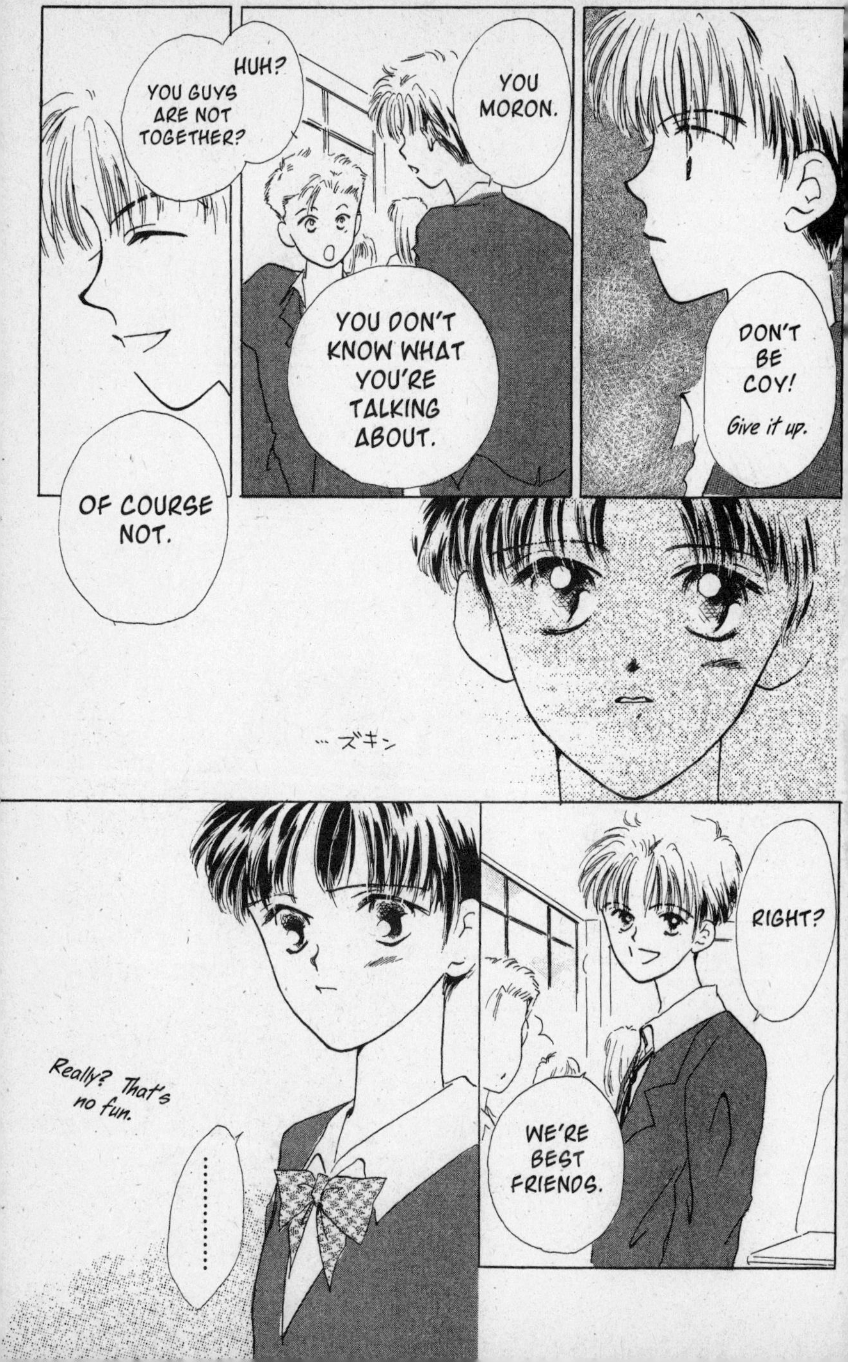
DON'T BE COY!
Give it up.
YOU MORON.
YOU DON'T KNOW WHAT YOU'RE TALKING ABOUT.
HUH? YOU GUYS ARE NOT TOGETHER?
OF COURSE NOT.
…ズキン
RIGHT?
WE'RE BEST FRIENDS.
Really? That's no fun.
……

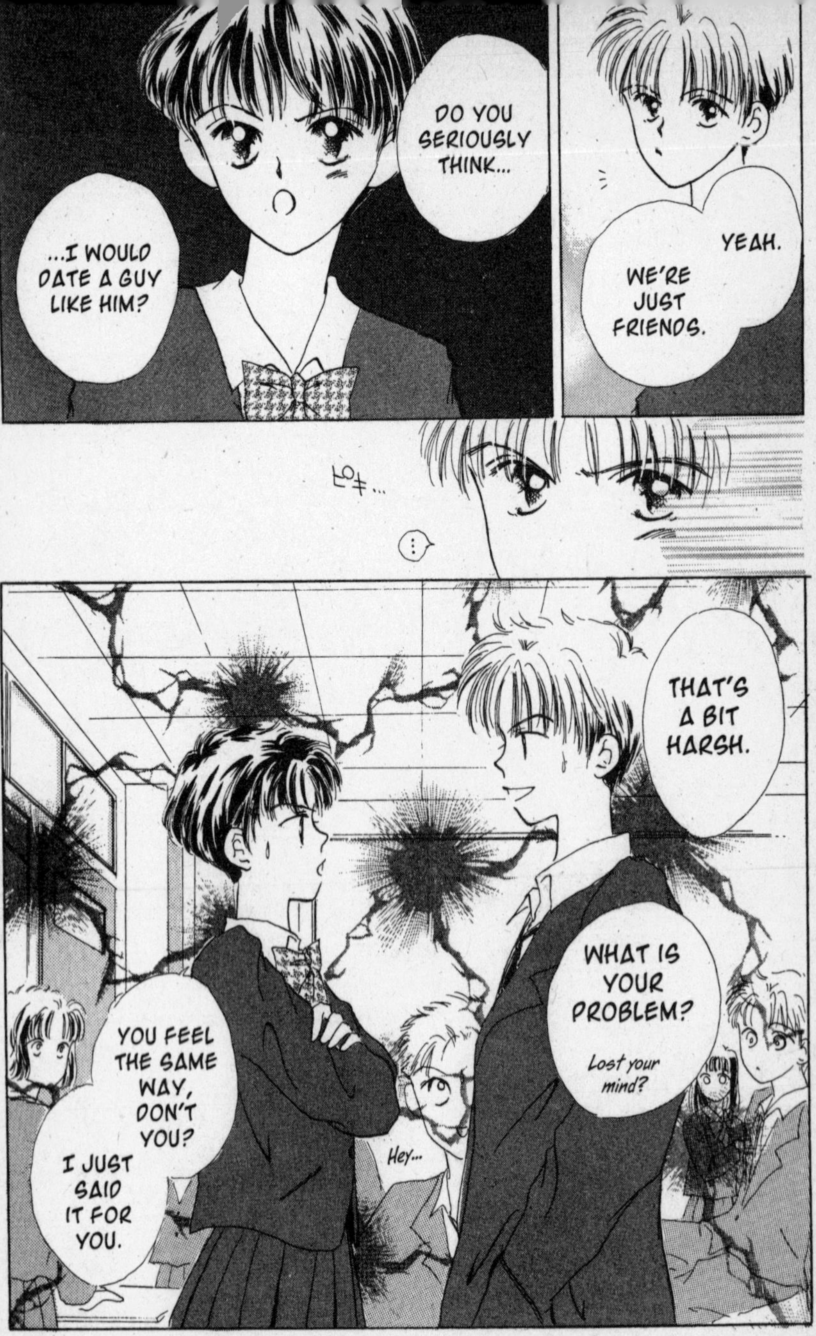
YEAH.
WE'RE JUST FRIENDS.
DO YOU SERIOUSLY THINK...
...I WOULD DATE A GUY LIKE HIM?
ピキ...
...
THAT'S A BIT HARSH.
WHAT IS YOUR PROBLEM?
Lost your mind?
Hey...
YOU FEEL THE SAME WAY, DON'T YOU?
I JUST SAID IT FOR YOU.

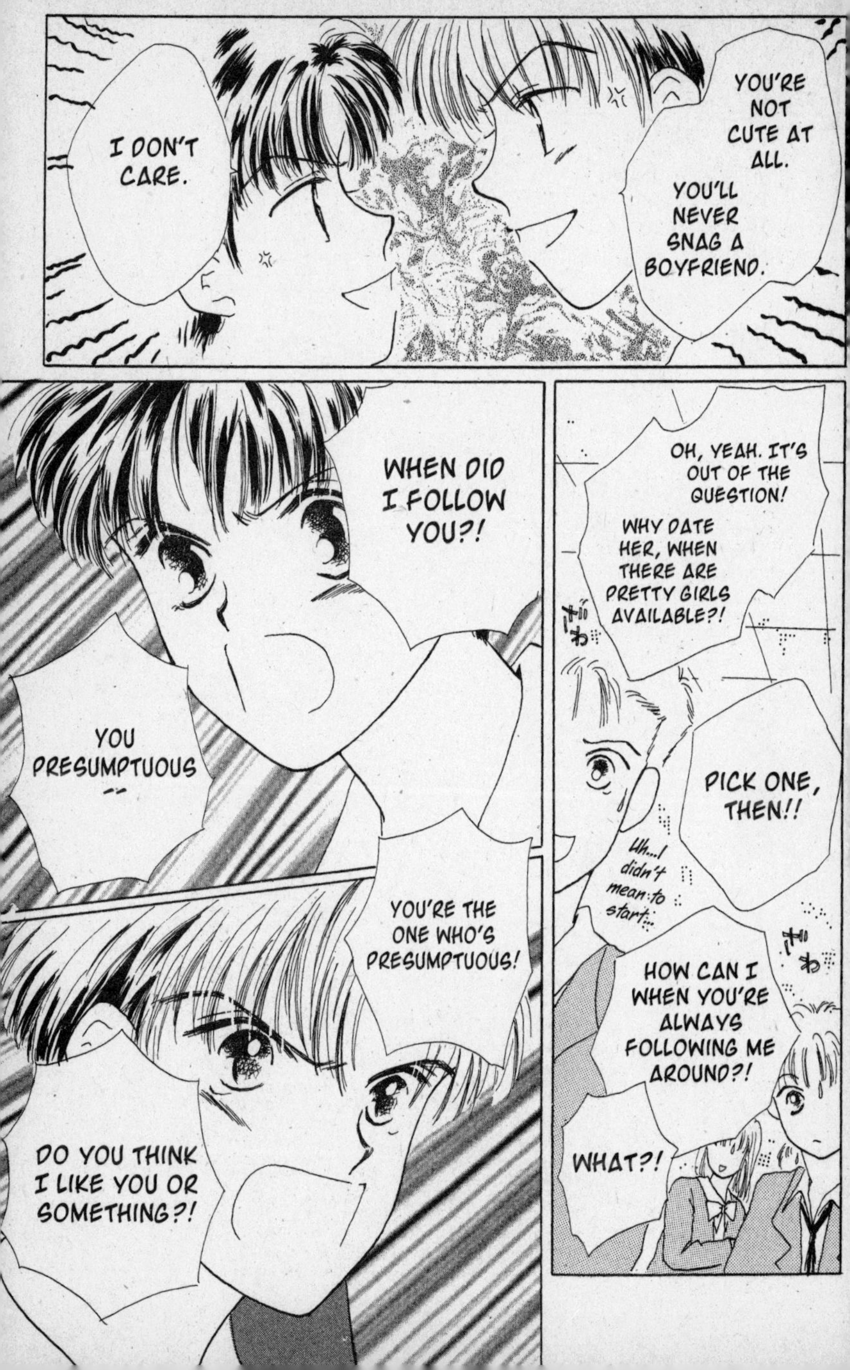

YOU'RE NOT CUTE AT ALL.
YOU'LL NEVER SNAG A BOYFRIEND.
I DON'T CARE.
OH, YEAH. IT'S OUT OF THE QUESTION!
WHY DATE HER, WHEN THERE ARE PRETTY GIRLS AVAILABLE?!
ざわ
PICK ONE, THEN!!
Uh...I didn't mean to start...
ざわ
HOW CAN I WHEN YOU'RE ALWAYS FOLLOWING ME AROUND?!
WHAT?!
WHEN DID I FOLLOW YOU?!
YOU PRESUMPTUOUS--
YOU'RE THE ONE WHO'S PRESUMPTUOUS!
DO YOU THINK I LIKE YOU OR SOMETHING?!

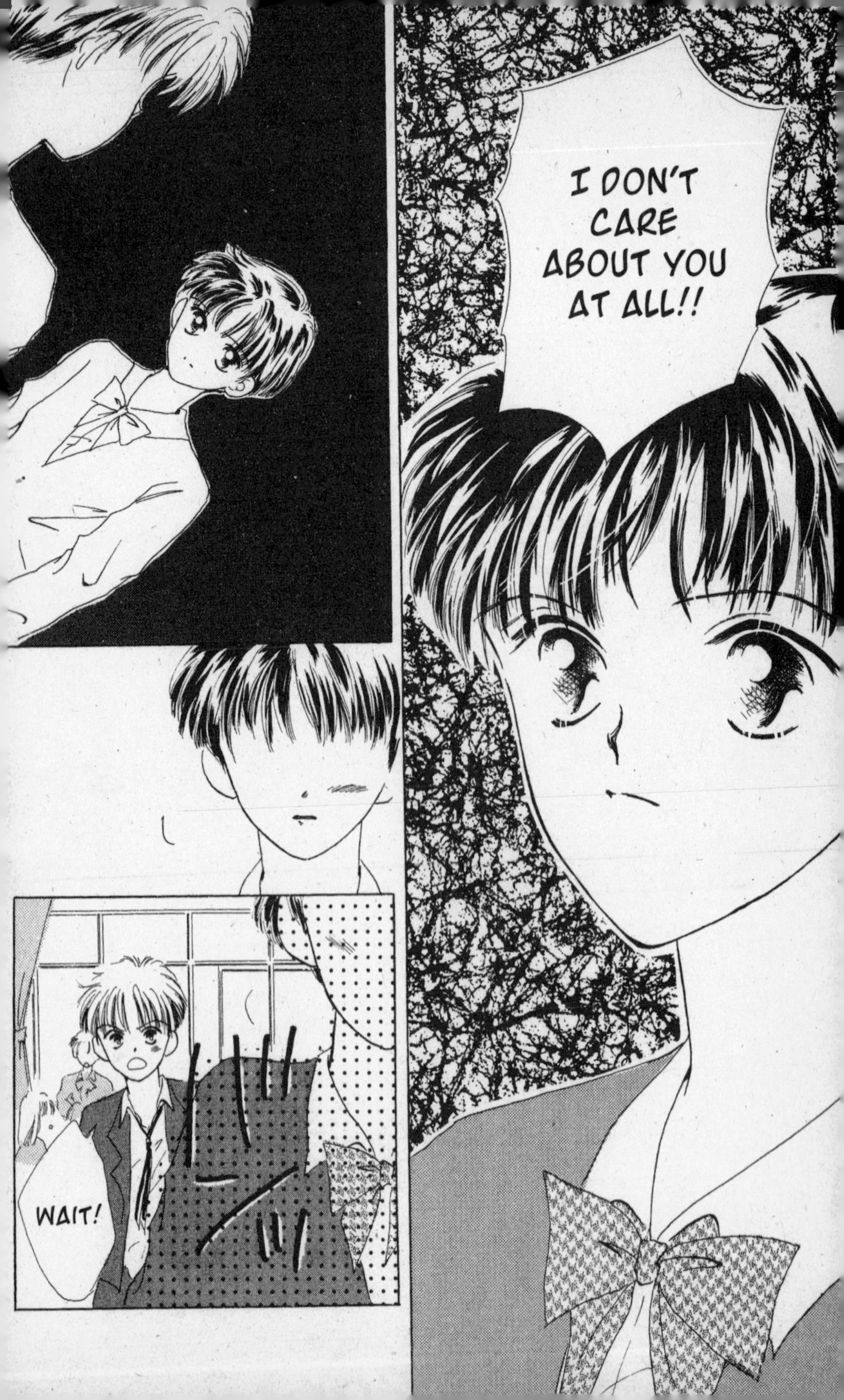
I DON'T CARE ABOUT YOU AT ALL!!
WAIT!

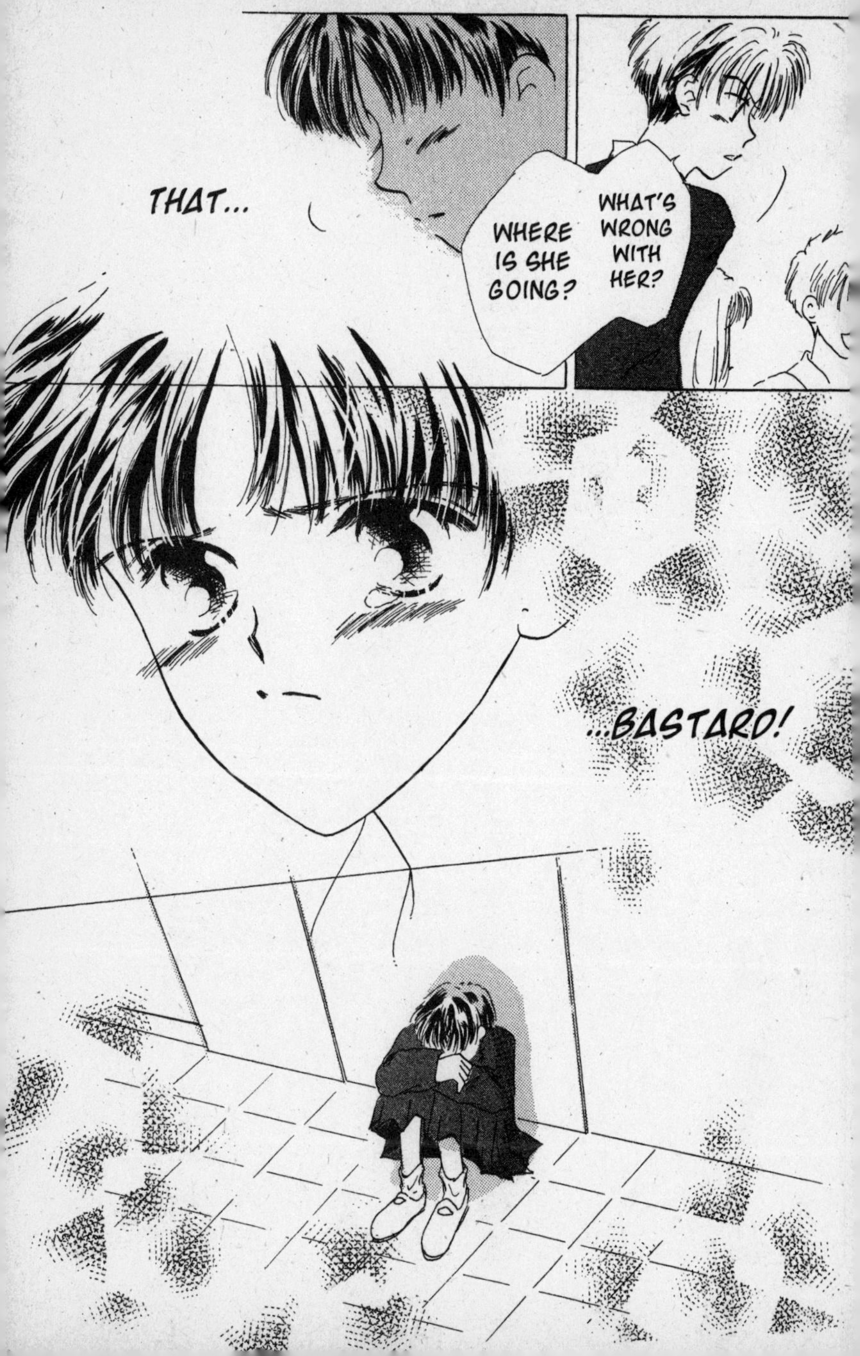
WHAT'S WRONG WITH HER?
WHERE IS SHE GOING?
THAT...
...BASTARD!

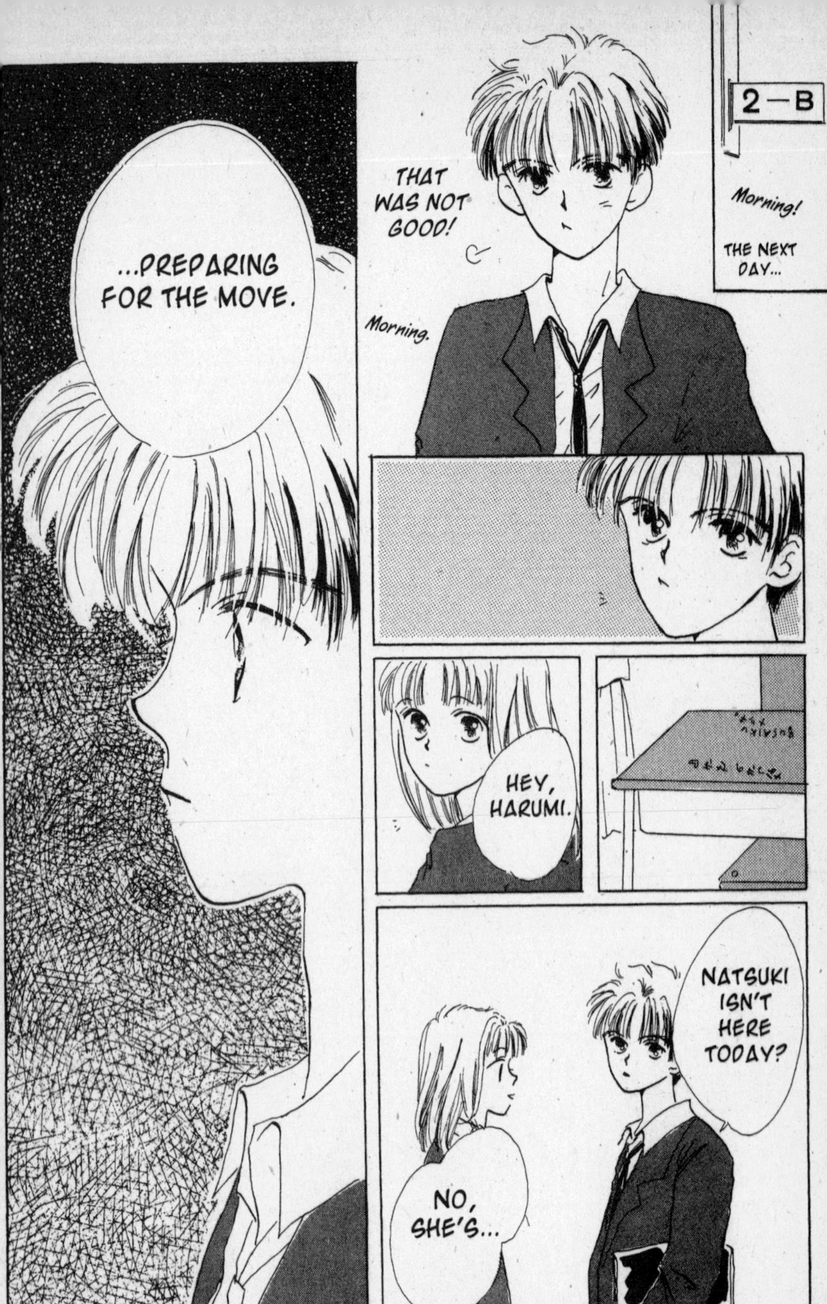
2—B
Morning!
THE NEXT DAY...
THAT WAS NOT GOOD!
Morning.
HEY, HARUMI.
NATSUKI ISN'T HERE TODAY?
NO, SHE'S...
...PREPARING FOR THE MOVE.

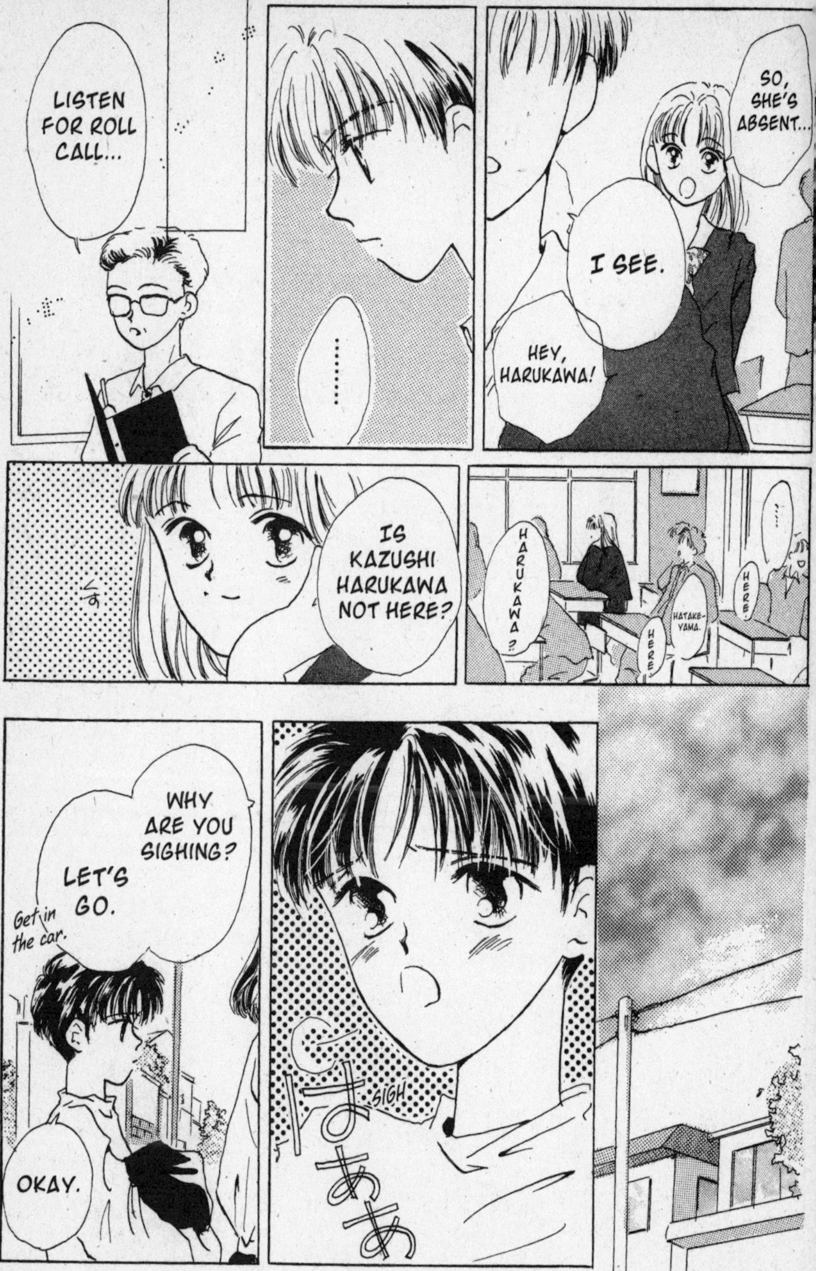
SO, SHE'S ABSENT...
I SEE.
HEY, HARUKAWA!
......
LISTEN FOR ROLL CALL...
......
HERE.
HATAKE-YAMA.
HERE.
HARUKAWA?
IS KAZUSHI HARUKAWA NOT HERE?
くす
はあぁ
SIGH
WHY ARE YOU SIGHING?
LET'S GO.
Get in the car.
OKAY.

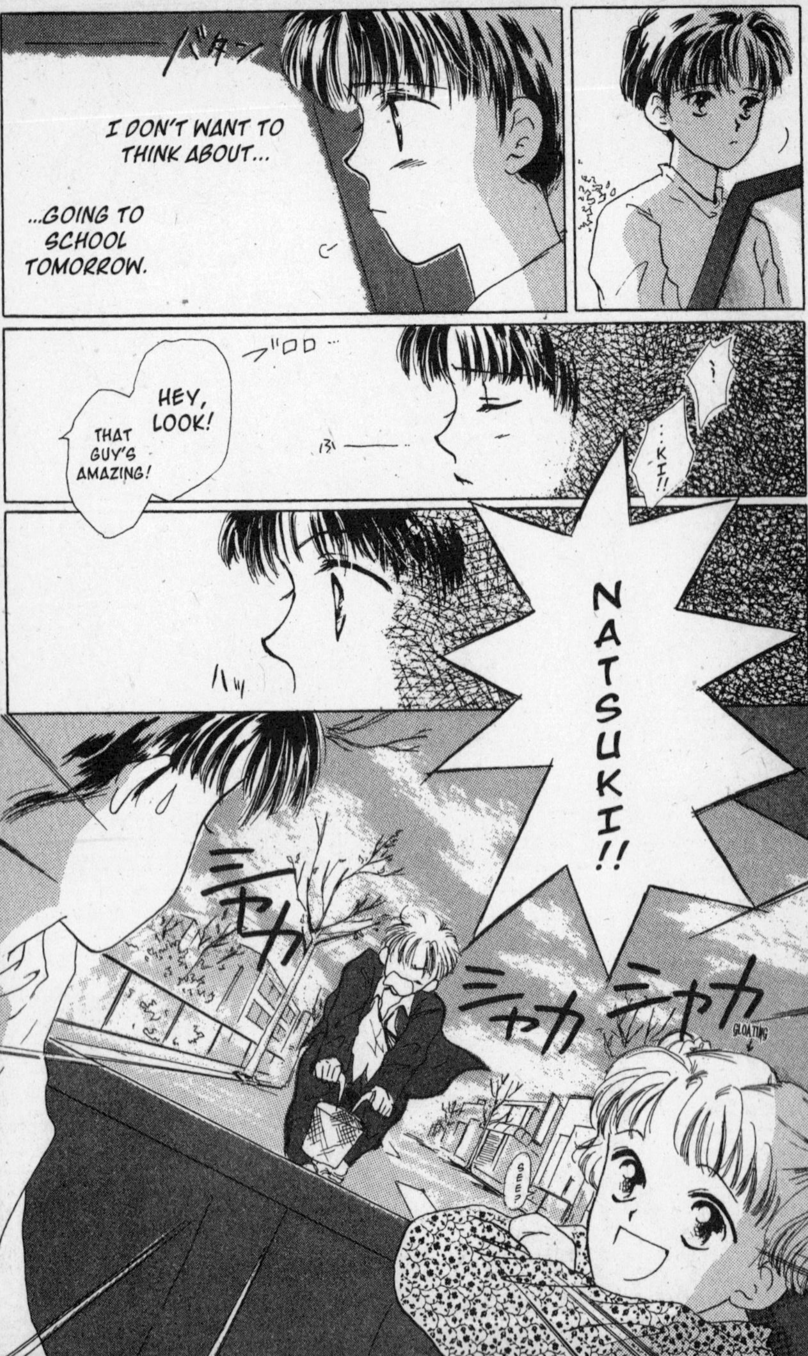
バタン
I DON'T WANT TO THINK ABOUT...
...GOING TO SCHOOL TOMORROW.
!
...KI!!
ふ―
ブロロ…
HEY, LOOK!
THAT GUY'S AMAZING!
ハッ
NATSUKI!!
シャカ
シャカ シャカ
GLOATING
SEE?

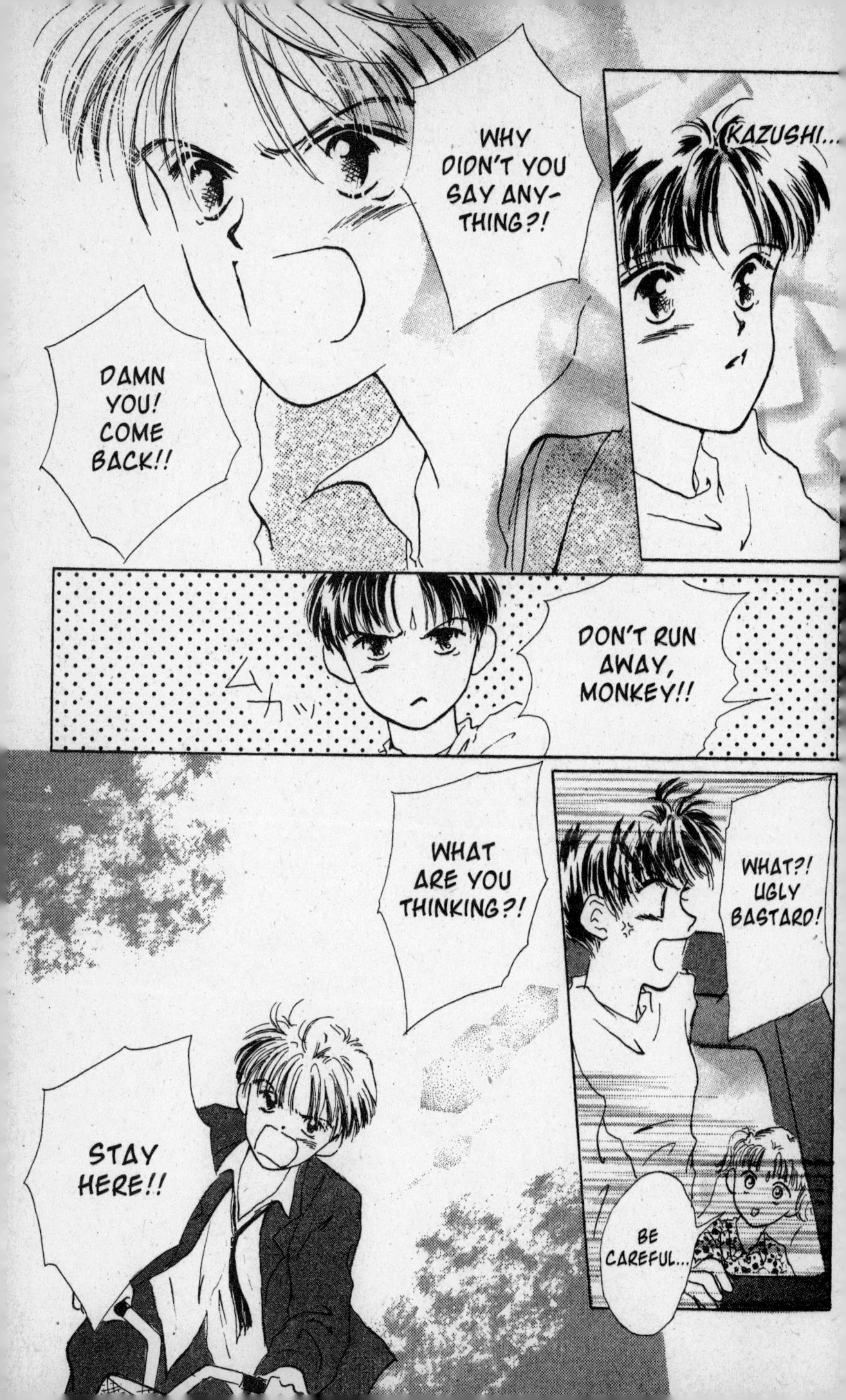
KAZUSHI...
WHY DIDN'T YOU SAY ANY-THING?!
DAMN YOU! COME BACK!!
DON'T RUN AWAY, MONKEY!!
WHAT?! UGLY BASTARD!
BE CAREFUL...
WHAT ARE YOU THINKING?!
STAY HERE!!

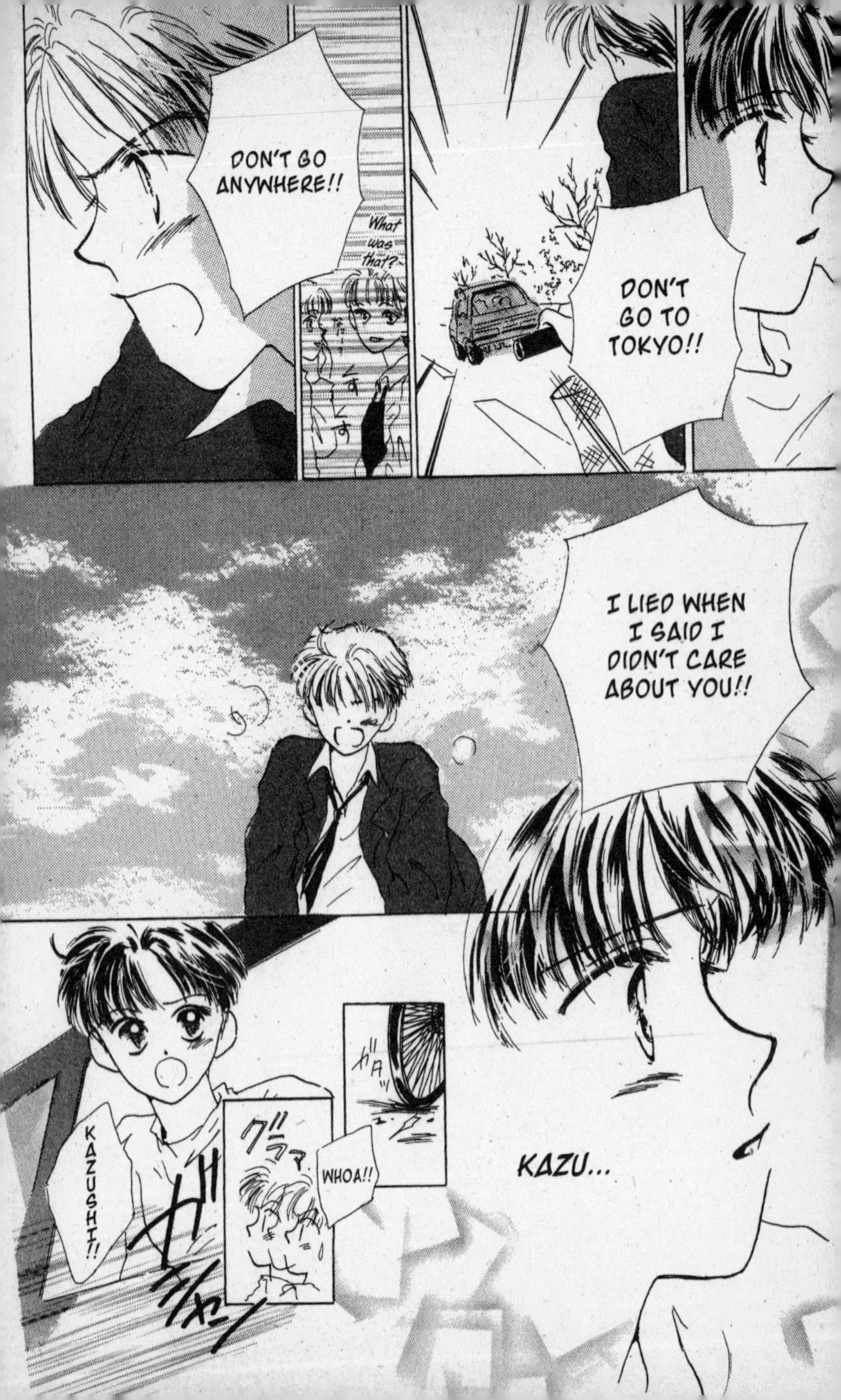
DON'T GO TO TOKYO!!
What was that?
DON'T GO ANYWHERE!!
I LIED WHEN I SAID I DIDN'T CARE ABOUT YOU!!
KAZU...
WHOA!!
KAZUSHI!!

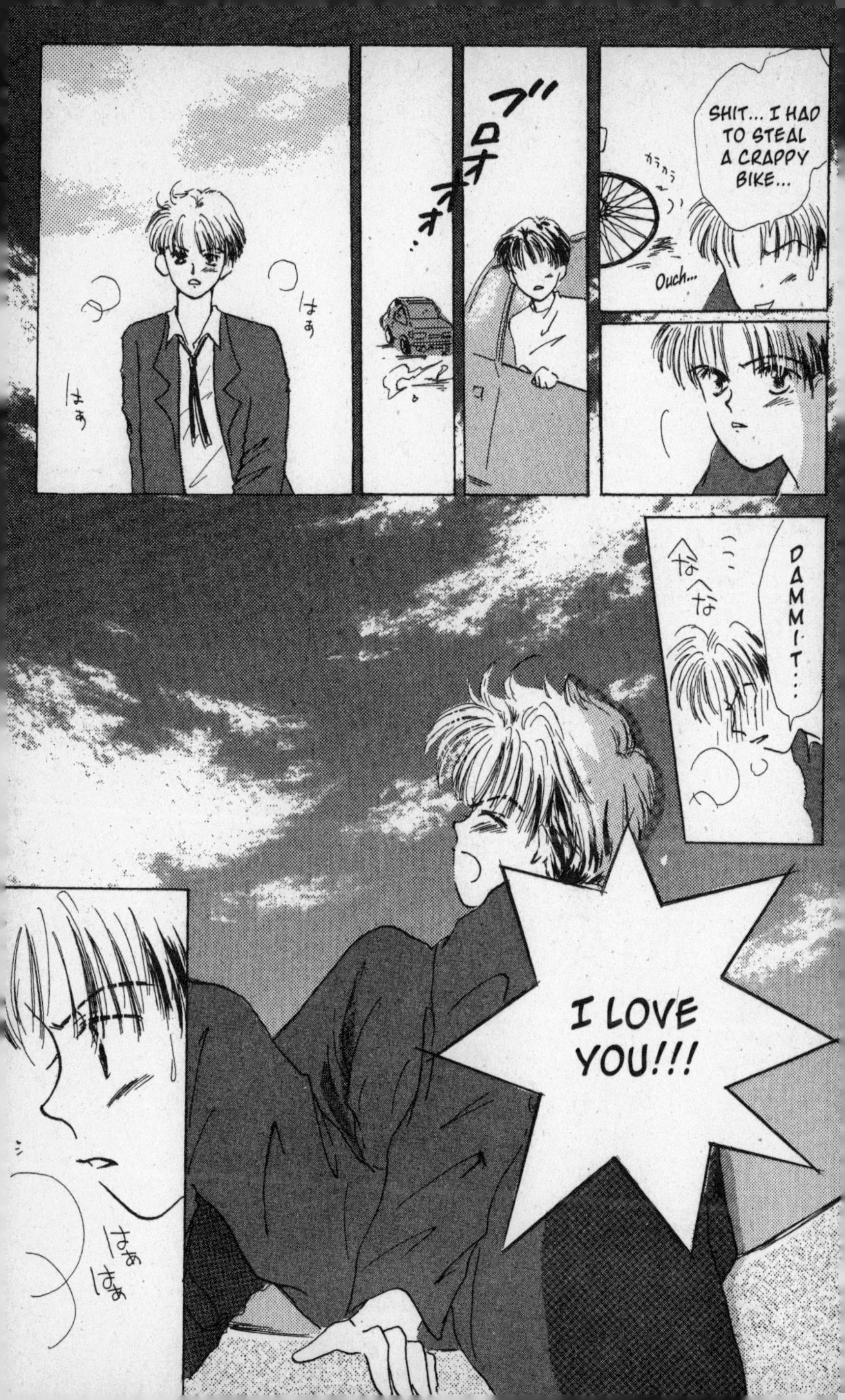
SHIT... I HAD TO STEAL A CRAPPY BIKE...
カラカラ
Ouch...
ブロオオオ…
はぁ
はぁ
へなへな
DAMMIT...
I LOVE YOU!!!
はぁはぁ

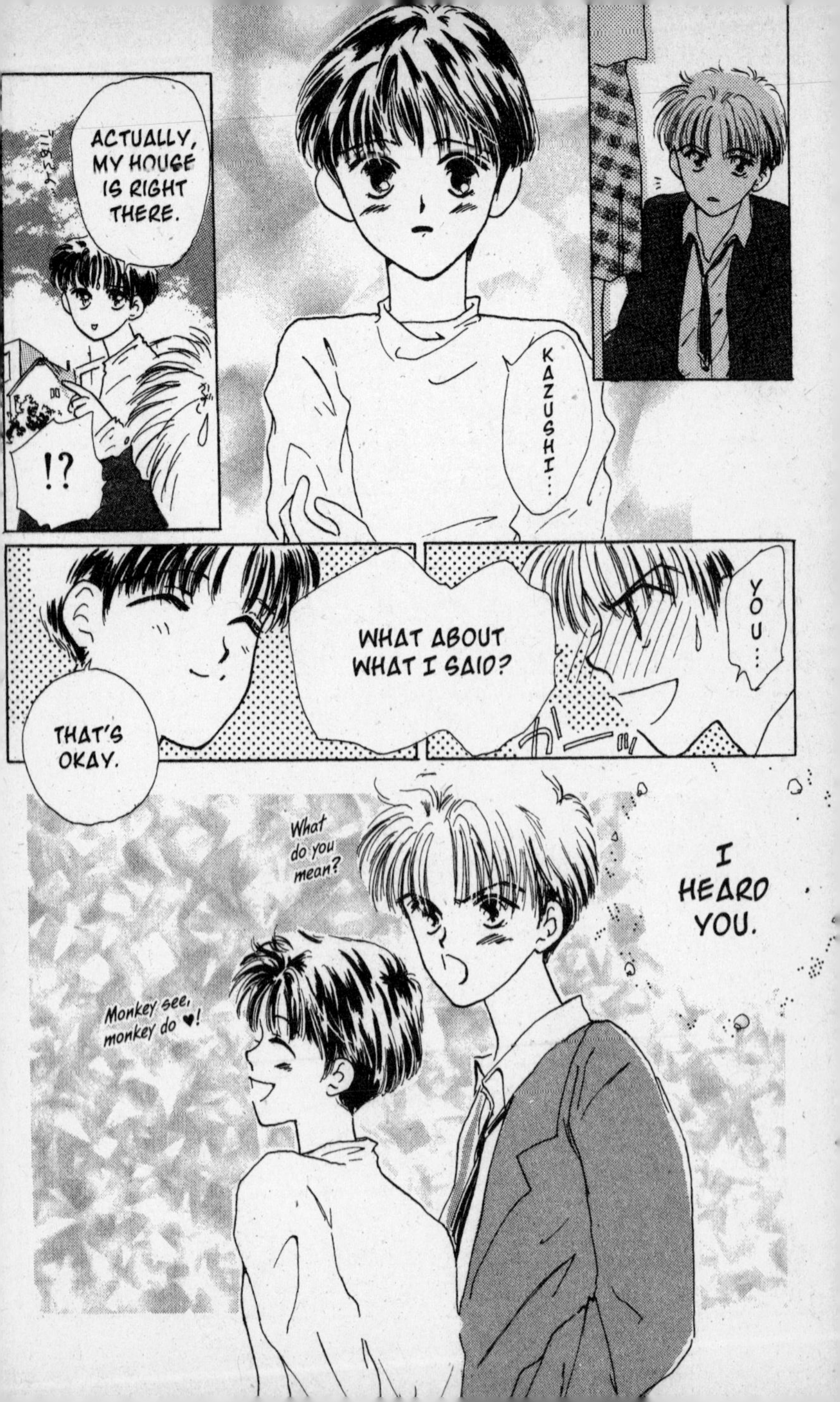
KAZUSHI...
ACTUALLY, MY HOUSE IS RIGHT THERE.
!?
YOU...
WHAT ABOUT WHAT I SAID?
THAT'S OKAY.
I HEARD YOU.
What do you mean?
Monkey see, monkey do ♥!

POST VOLUME SPECIAL BONUS MANGA

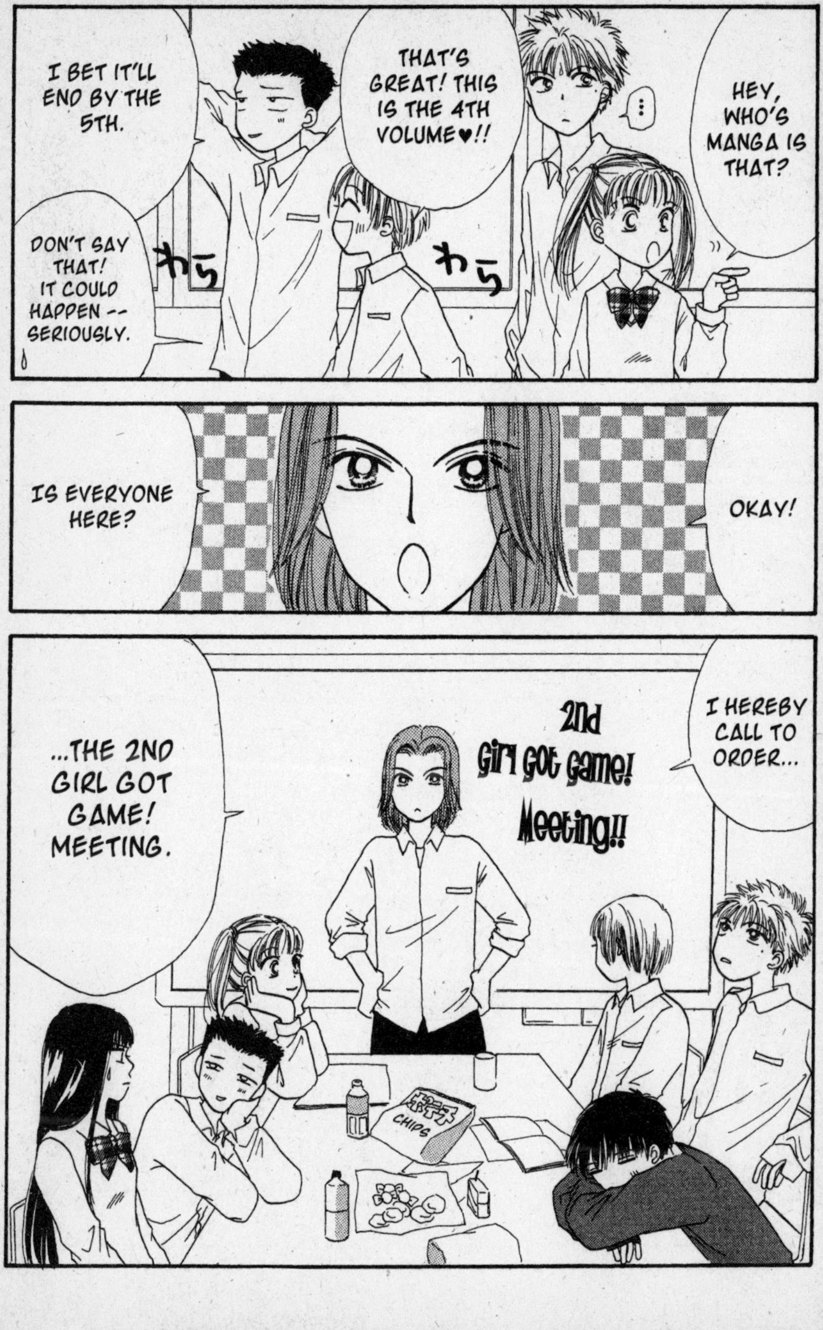
HEY, WHO'S MANGA IS THAT?
...
THAT'S GREAT! THIS IS THE 4TH VOLUME♥!!
わら
I BET IT'LL END BY THE 5TH.
わら
DON'T SAY THAT! IT COULD HAPPEN -- SERIOUSLY.
OKAY!
IS EVERYONE HERE?
I HEREBY CALL TO ORDER...
2nd Girl Got Game! Meeting!!
...THE 2ND GIRL GOT GAME! MEETING.
CHIPS

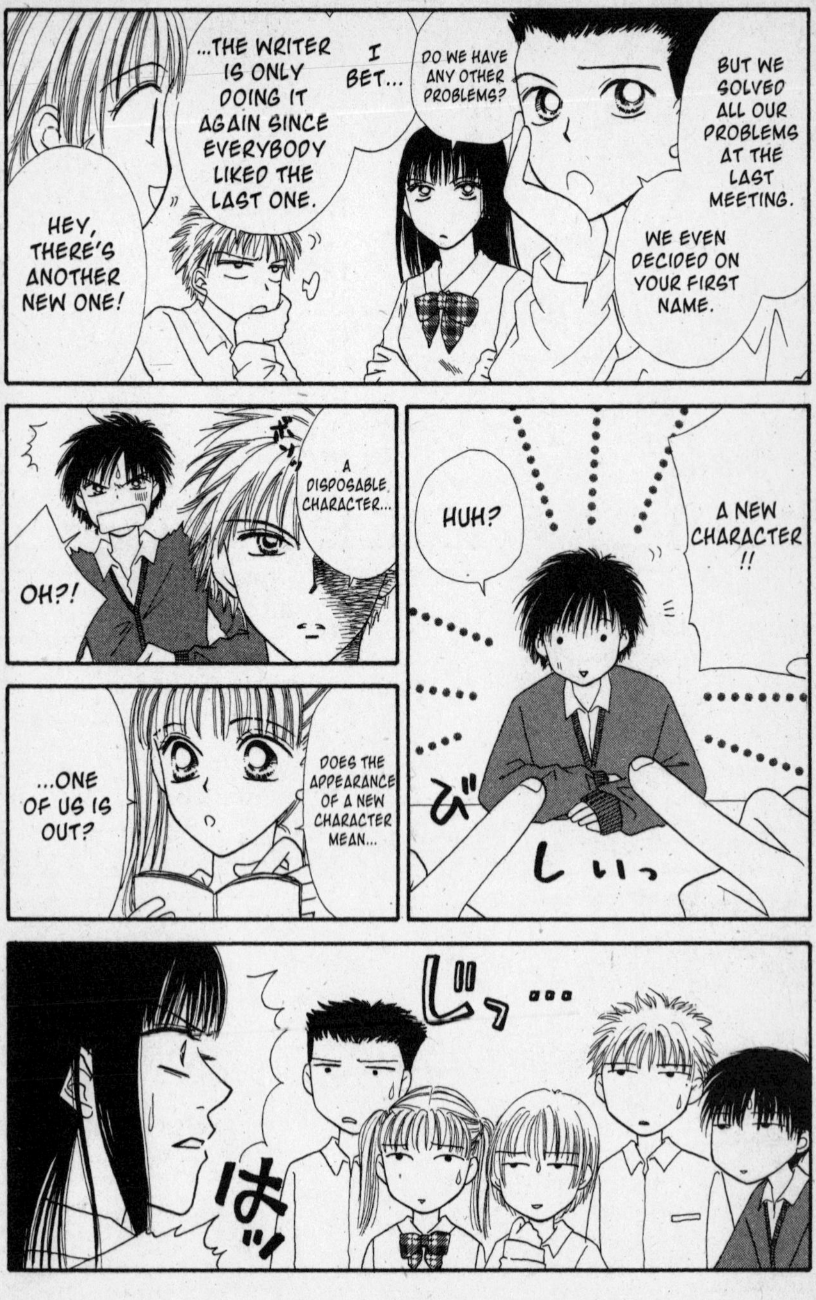
BUT WE SOLVED ALL OUR PROBLEMS AT THE LAST MEETING.
WE EVEN DECIDED ON YOUR FIRST NAME.
DO WE HAVE ANY OTHER PROBLEMS?
I BET...
...THE WRITER IS ONLY DOING IT AGAIN SINCE EVERYBODY LIKED THE LAST ONE.
HEY, THERE'S ANOTHER NEW ONE!
A NEW CHARACTER !!
HUH?
び
しいっ
A DISPOSABLE CHARACTER...
OH?!
DOES THE APPEARANCE OF A NEW CHARACTER MEAN...
...ONE OF US IS OUT?
じっ…
はッ!

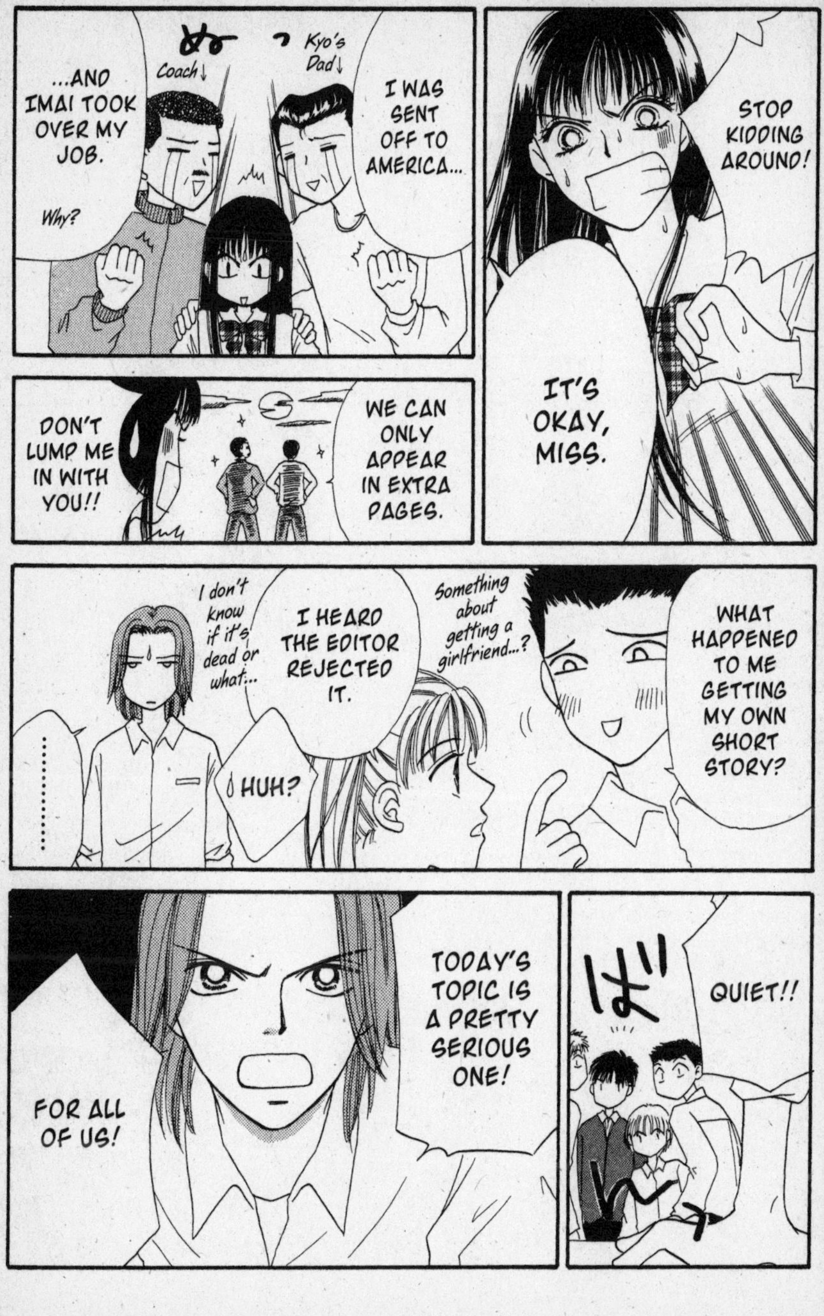
STOP KIDDING AROUND!
IT'S OKAY, MISS.
I WAS SENT OFF TO AMERICA...
Kyo's Dad↓
ぬっ
Coach↓
...AND IMAI TOOK OVER MY JOB.
Why?
WE CAN ONLY APPEAR IN EXTRA PAGES.
DON'T LUMP ME IN WITH YOU!!
WHAT HAPPENED TO ME GETTING MY OWN SHORT STORY?
Something about getting a girlfriend...?
I HEARD THE EDITOR REJECTED IT.
I don't know if it's dead or what...
HUH?
....
QUIET!!
ばっ
TODAY'S TOPIC IS A PRETTY SERIOUS ONE!
FOR ALL OF US!

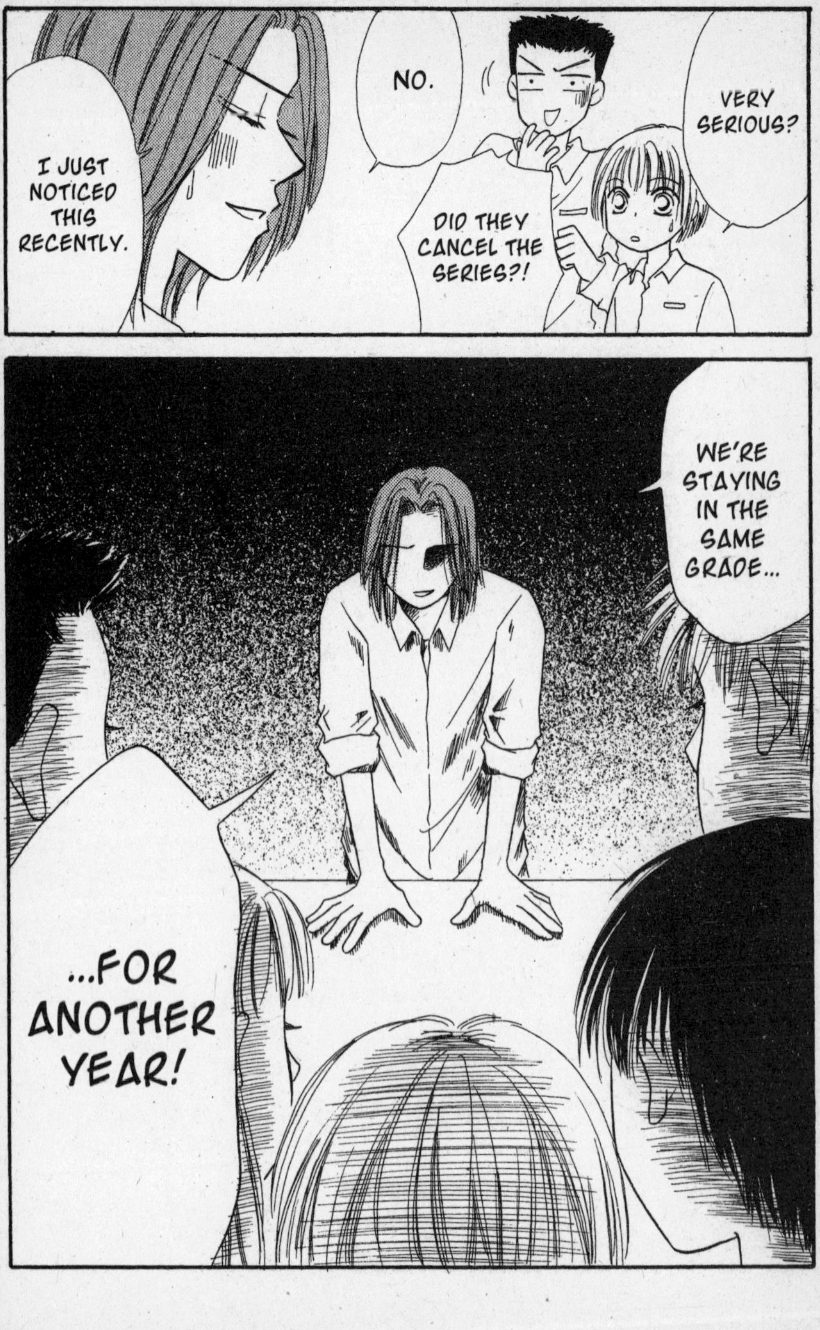
VERY SERIOUS?
DID THEY CANCEL THE SERIES?!
NO.
I JUST NOTICED THIS RECENTLY.
WE'RE STAYING IN THE SAME GRADE...
...FOR ANOTHER YEAR!

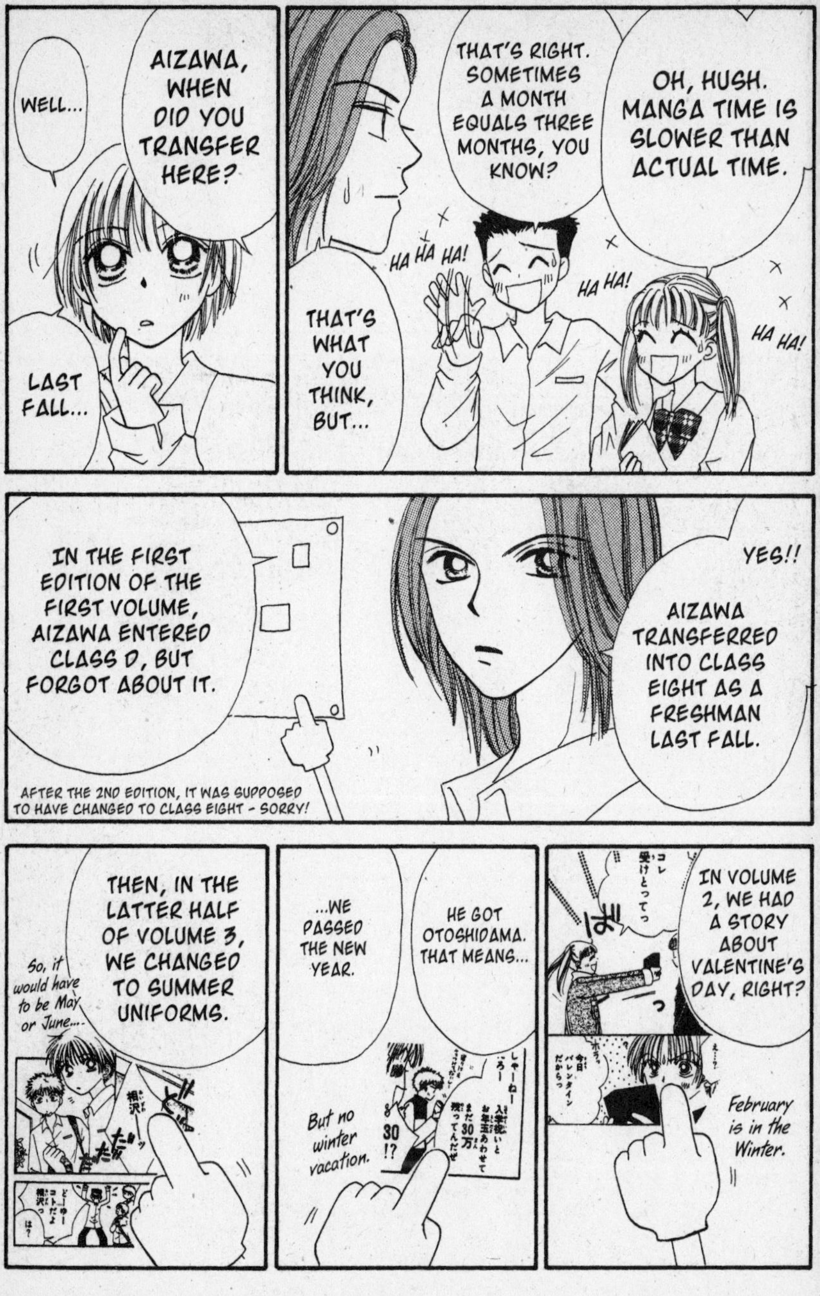
OH, HUSH. MANGA TIME IS SLOWER THAN ACTUAL TIME.
THAT'S RIGHT. SOMETIMES A MONTH EQUALS THREE MONTHS, YOU KNOW?
HA HA!
HA HA!
HA HA HA!
THAT'S WHAT YOU THINK, BUT...
AIZAWA, WHEN DID YOU TRANSFER HERE?
WELL...
LAST FALL...
YES!!
AIZAWA TRANSFERRED INTO CLASS EIGHT AS A FRESHMAN LAST FALL.
IN THE FIRST EDITION OF THE FIRST VOLUME, AIZAWA ENTERED CLASS D, BUT FORGOT ABOUT IT.
AFTER THE 2ND EDITION, IT WAS SUPPOSED TO HAVE CHANGED TO CLASS EIGHT - SORRY!
IN VOLUME 2, WE HAD A STORY ABOUT VALENTINE'S DAY, RIGHT?
コレ受けとってっ
ばっ
ホラっ今日バレンタインだからっ
え…?
February is in the Winter.
HE GOT OTOSHIDAMA. THAT MEANS...
...WE PASSED THE NEW YEAR.
しゃーねーなー
入学祝いとお年玉あわせてまだ30万残ってんだぜ
30!?
But no winter vacation.
THEN, IN THE LATTER HALF OF VOLUME 3, WE CHANGED TO SUMMER UNIFORMS.
So, it would have to be May or June...
相沢ーッ
どーゆーコトだよ相沢っ
は?

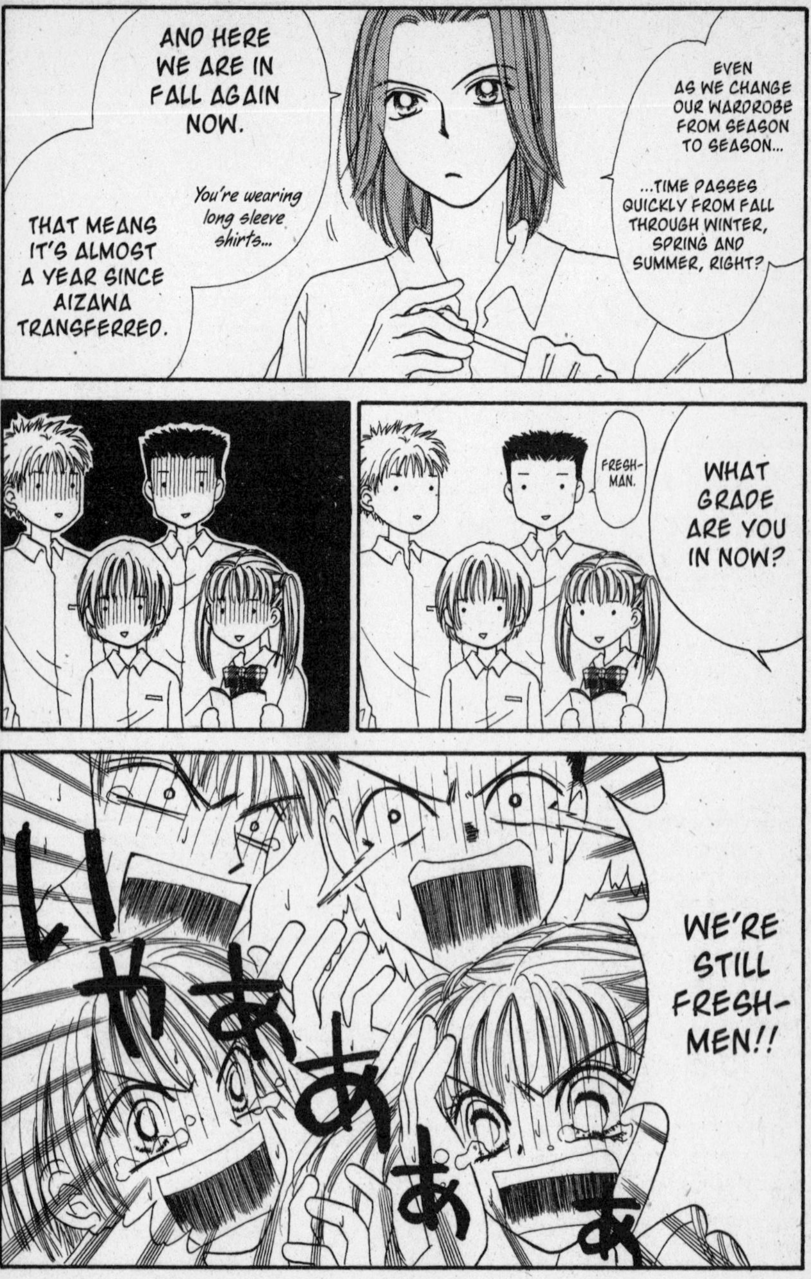
EVEN AS WE CHANGE OUR WARDROBE FROM SEASON TO SEASON...
...TIME PASSES QUICKLY FROM FALL THROUGH WINTER, SPRING AND SUMMER, RIGHT?
AND HERE WE ARE IN FALL AGAIN NOW.
You're wearing long sleeve shirts...
THAT MEANS IT'S ALMOST A YEAR SINCE AIZAWA TRANSFERRED.
WHAT GRADE ARE YOU IN NOW?
FRESH-MAN.
WE'RE STILL FRESH-MEN!!
いやああああ

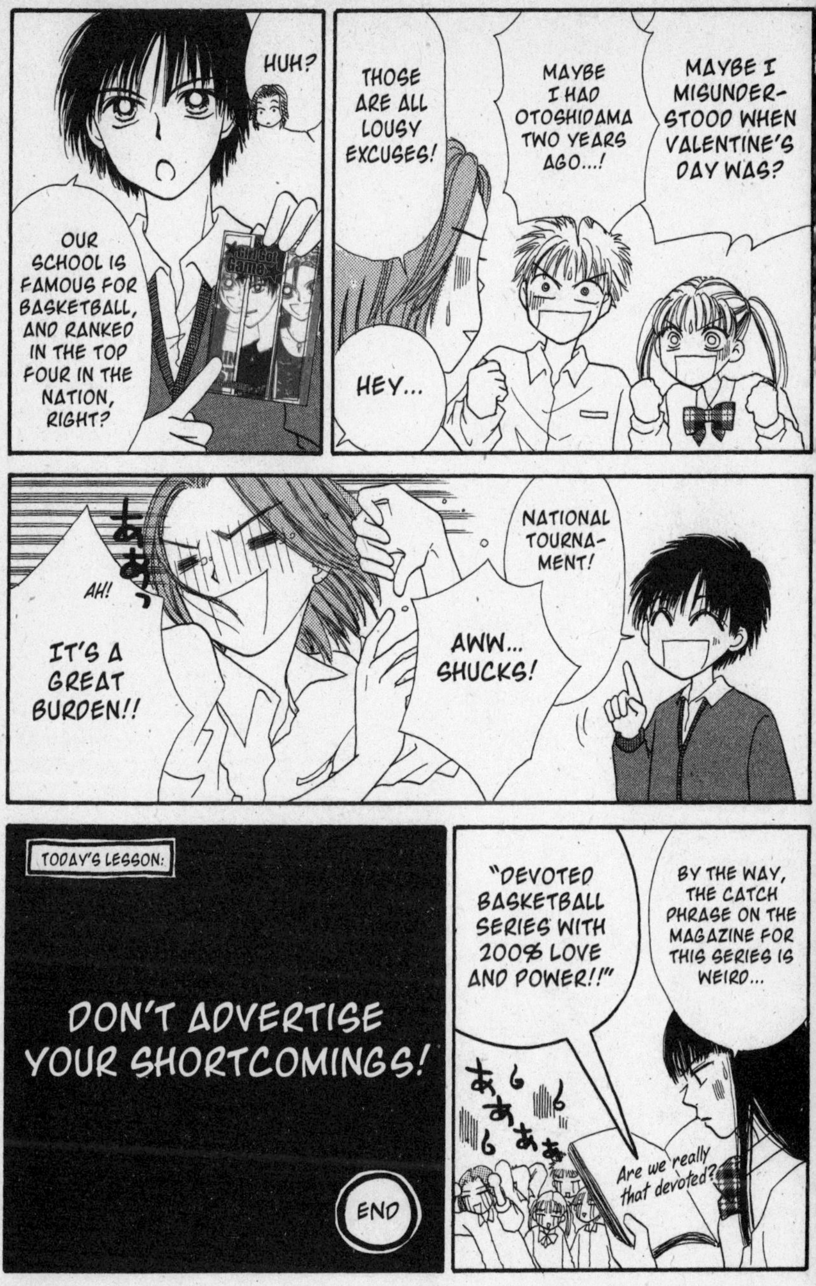
MAYBE I MISUNDERSTOOD WHEN VALENTINE'S DAY WAS?
MAYBE I HAD OTOSHIDAMA TWO YEARS AGO...!
THOSE ARE ALL LOUSY EXCUSES!
HEY...
HUH?
OUR SCHOOL IS FAMOUS FOR BASKETBALL, AND RANKED IN THE TOP FOUR IN THE NATION, RIGHT?
Girl Got Game
NATIONAL TOURNAMENT!
AWW... SHUCKS!
あぁっ
AH!
IT'S A GREAT BURDEN!!
BY THE WAY, THE CATCH PHRASE ON THE MAGAZINE FOR THIS SERIES IS WEIRD...
"DEVOTED BASKETBALL SERIES WITH 200% LOVE AND POWER!!"
Are we really that devoted?
TODAY'S LESSON:
DON'T ADVERTISE YOUR SHORTCOMINGS!
END

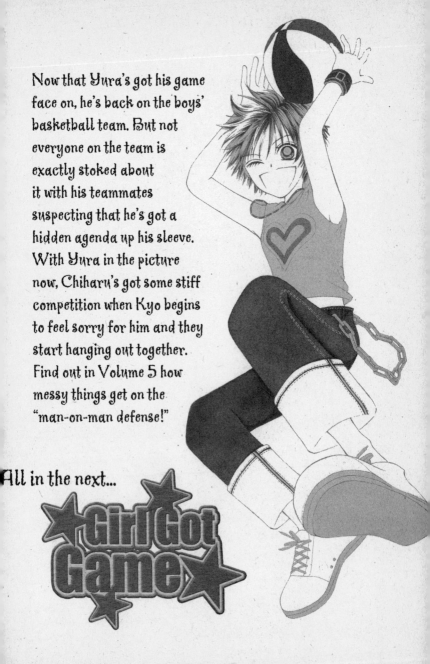

Now that Yura's got his game face on, he's back on the boys' basketball team. But not everyone on the team is exactly stoked about it with his teammates suspecting that he's got a hidden agenda up his sleeve. With Yura in the picture now, Chiharu's got some stiff competition when Kyo begins to feel sorry for him and they start hanging out together. Find out in Volume 5 how messy things get on the "man-on-man defense!"

All in the next...

★Girl Got Game★

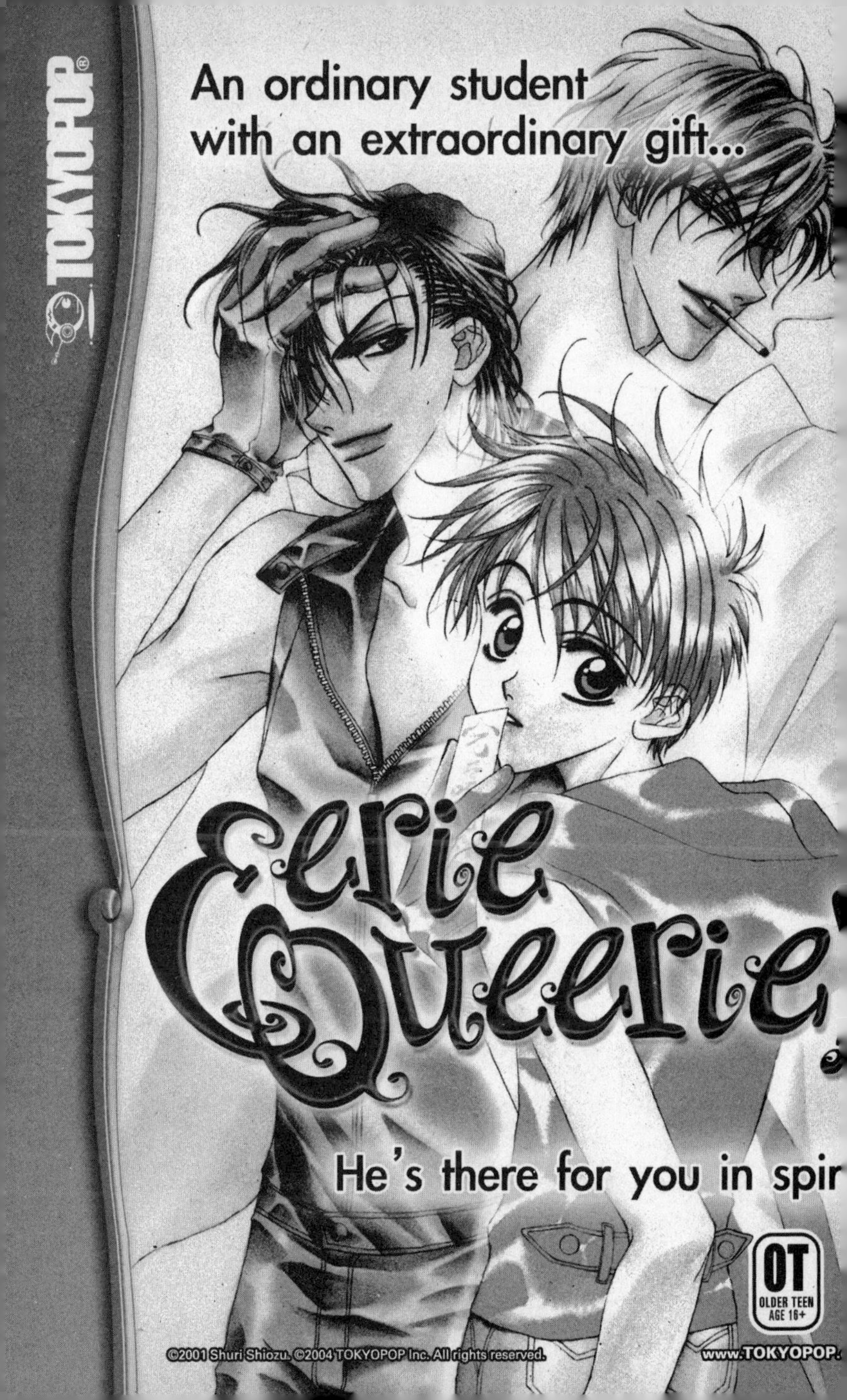
TOKYOPOP
An ordinary student
with an extraordinary gift...
Eerie Queerie!
He's there for you in spir
OT
OLDER TEEN
AGE 16+
©2001 Shuri Shiozu. ©2004 TOKYOPOP Inc. All rights reserved.
www.TOKYOPOP.

One
rocks to live.
One
lives to rock.
They've got nothing in common...except each other.
TOKYOPOP
One™
T
TEEN
AGE 13+
©2003 Lee Vin / DAIWON C.I. Inc. ©2004 TOKYOPOP Inc. All rights reserved.
www.TOKYOPOP.com

ALSO AVAILABLE FROM TOKYOPOP®

MANGA

.HACK//LEGEND OF THE TWILIGHT
@LARGE
ABENOBASHI: MAGICAL SHOPPING ARCADE
A.I. LOVE YOU
AI YORI AOSHI
ANGELIC LAYER
ARM OF KANNON
BABY BIRTH
BATTLE ROYALE
BATTLE VIXENS
BRAIN POWERED
BRIGADOON
B'TX
CANDIDATE FOR GODDESS, THE
CARDCAPTOR SAKURA
CARDCAPTOR SAKURA - MASTER OF THE CLOW
CHOBITS
CHRONICLES OF THE CURSED SWORD
CLAMP SCHOOL DETECTIVES
CLOVER
COMIC PARTY
CONFIDENTIAL CONFESSIONS
CORRECTOR YUI
COWBOY BEBOP
COWBOY BEBOP: SHOOTING STAR
CRAZY LOVE STORY
CRESCENT MOON
CROSS
CULDCEPT
CYBORG 009
D•N•ANGEL
DEMON DIARY
DEMON ORORON, THE
DEUS VITAE
DIABOLO
DIGIMON
DIGIMON TAMERS
DIGIMON ZERO TWO
DOLL
DRAGON HUNTER
DRAGON KNIGHTS
DRAGON VOICE
DREAM SAGA
DUKLYON: CLAMP SCHOOL DEFENDERS
EERIE QUEERIE!
ERICA SAKURAZAWA: COLLECTED WORKS
ET CETERA
ETERNITY
EVIL'S RETURN
FAERIES' LANDING
FAKE
FLCL
FLOWER OF THE DEEP SLEEP
FORBIDDEN DANCE
FRUITS BASKET
G GUNDAM

GATEKEEPERS
GETBACKERS
GIRL GOT GAME
GIRLS' EDUCATIONAL CHARTER
GRAVITATION
GTO
GUNDAM BLUE DESTINY
GUNDAM SEED ASTRAY
GUNDAM WING
GUNDAM WING: BATTLEFIELD OF PACIFISTS
GUNDAM WING: ENDLESS WALTZ
GUNDAM WING: THE LAST OUTPOST (G-UNIT)
GUYS' GUIDE TO GIRLS
HANDS OFF!
HAPPY MANIA
HARLEM BEAT
I.N.V.U.
IMMORTAL RAIN
INITIAL D
INSTANT TEEN: JUST ADD NUTS
ISLAND
JING: KING OF BANDITS
JING: KING OF BANDITS - TWILIGHT TALES
JULINE
KARE KANO
KILL ME, KISS ME
KINDAICHI CASE FILES, THE
KING OF HELL
KODOCHA: SANA'S STAGE
LAMENT OF THE LAMB
LEGAL DRUG
LEGEND OF CHUN HYANG, THE
LES BIJOUX
LOVE HINA
LUPIN III
LUPIN III: WORLD'S MOST WANTED
MAGIC KNIGHT RAYEARTH I
MAGIC KNIGHT RAYEARTH II
MAHOROMATIC: AUTOMATIC MAIDEN
MAN OF MANY FACES
MARMALADE BOY
MARS
MARS: HORSE WITH NO NAME
MINK
MIRACLE GIRLS
MIYUKI-CHAN IN WONDERLAND
MODEL
MY LOVE
NECK AND NECK
ONE
ONE I LOVE, THE
PARADISE KISS
PARASYTE
PASSION FRUIT
PEACH GIRL
PEACH GIRL: CHANGE OF HEART
PET SHOP OF HORRORS
PITA-TEN

04.23.04T

STOP!

This is the back of the book.
You wouldn't want to spoil a great ending!

This book is printed "manga-style," in the authentic Japanese right-to-left format. Since none of the artwork has been flipped or altered, readers get to experience the story just as the creator intended. You've been asking for it, so TOKYOPOP® delivered: authentic, hot-off-the-press, and far more fun!

DIRECTIONS

If this is your first time reading manga-style, here's a quick guide to help you understand how it works.

It's easy... just start in the top right panel and follow the numbers. Have fun, and look for more 100% authentic manga from TOKYOPOP®!